Blessings to

you Mrs. Gibson

" " "

Judy Greene

THE *Grandma* SYNDROME

JUDY GREENE

WESTBOW
PRESS®
A DIVISION OF THOMAS NELSON
& ZONDERVAN

Scripture quotations taken from the New American Standard Bible®,
Copyright © 1960, 1962, 1963, 1968, 1971, 1972, 1973, 1975, 1977, 1995 by
The Lockman Foundation. Used by permission." (www.Lockman.org)

WestBow Press books may be ordered through booksellers or by contacting:

WestBow Press
A Division of Thomas Nelson & Zondervan
1663 Liberty Drive
Bloomington, IN 47403
www.westbowpress.com
1 (866) 928-1240

Because of the dynamic nature of the Internet, any web addresses or links contained in
this book may have changed since publication and may no longer be valid. The views
expressed in this work are solely those of the author and do not necessarily reflect the
views of the publisher, and the publisher hereby disclaims any responsibility for them.

Cover illustrations by Paloma Swarthout.
Photography by Bethany Rigtrup.
Cover design by Janson Card and Westbow Press.

ISBN: 978-1-5127-4479-8 (sc)
ISBN: 978-1-5127-4480-4 (hc)
ISBN: 978-1-5127-4478-1 (e)

Library of Congress Control Number: 2016909237

Print information available on the last page.

WestBow Press rev. date: 08/23/2016

To Nana

*I like to think this will cause you to sing,
and the Lord will allow me to hear you.*

Acknowledgements

$\mathbf{M}$y darling Kelly Smith, beyond the shadow of a doubt you need to be at the top of this page. There I was, dwelling in an emotionally shaded valley, when you read one of my poems. Your exuberant reaction to my writing that one day was what propelled me into action regarding this story. Since I'd previously only written songs, scripts and grueling English Lit papers, I was a bit intimidated by the thought of actually doing this. But your enthusiasm filled me with the courage I needed to proceed. This story has been brewing inside me for so long. Thank you for being one of the hands that helped pull it out.

I have to thank you Mo and Papa for your strong support of this project. Sandy, your emotional support has been immeasurable as well as your spiritual support. Thank you for being so consistent in prayer. Thank you for taking time on the phone with me whenever I needed an uplift. And thank you for all your wise counsel, scripture verses and devotional slices. Bryan, I have to thank you for helping me with computer questions and needs. It's always good to have someone with computer savvy in the family.

Thank you to all of my wonderful readers. Carolyn Withrow, as the first person to read a portion of the unfinished manuscript, you provided the impetus for me to roll up my sleeves and continue after I shared the first few chapters with you. Your role in my completion of this project has been vital. Abbie Harkson Wentzel, your detailed feedback was so encouraging and such a blessing to my heart. Your warm words of fervent support touched so many deep places inside me. I was also happy to learn we both have a thing about names! Tina Veer, you've been right there beside me with every phone call and text, and I knew I could count on you for both editorial input and an honest assessment. I treasure you deeply and thank you profusely for being such a huge part of this project. Emily Veer, both you and your mom have been a strong force in making me feel this has been a worthwhile effort. Katie, April and Peggy, thank you all for taking time out of your busy lives to support this effort. CJ Van Green, thank you for your generous offer to do a final proofread.

Thank you, Bethany Rigtrup and Paloma Swarthout for your artistic contributions. Bethany, our day at the park was so blessed and fabulous despite the frigid temperatures! Thank you for all of your painstaking attention to detail. Paloma, you are such a gifted artist. Thank you for taking such great care to produce the most magnificent cover art. I hope the Lord blesses you with many more artistic endeavors.

+ Kyle

Nancy, where would I have been without all this travel literature you brought back from Chicago? Nowhere. Between all the maps, brochures and magazines, in addition to your verbal information, I was able to visit Chicago without actually going there.

Adria Goetz, thank you for jumping in to save my life in the eleventh hour. I'm happy to see you put your professional editing skills to good use.

Diane Mettler, I applaud you for acting as my grammar and punctuation nurse during the final revisions. You even went beyond the call of duty by soothing a few of my panic attacks. Your bedside manner is impeccable.

My dear Rachel, the Lord has used you mightily to mold and shape me into who I am today. You can never know the changes He's wrought in my heart through you. So thank you for the indirect role you've played in this story that's all about heart changes. You will always be my favorite girl!

Most importantly, I give thanks to my benevolent God for blessing me with this delightful playground. Thank You for planting all the people listed above in my life. Thank You for nurturing me through this process and for gently calling me back to the computer time and time again. And thank You for revealing greater and greater depths of Your love through this.

Chapter 1

Ann emerged from the shower prepared to enact her usual post-shower rituals. She wrapped one towel around her dripping wet body and one around her soggy head. Then she got out the hair dryer and cut through the steam on the mirror by blowing a large circle in the middle of it. Never mind that her niece and sister were sitting in her living room waiting for her to get ready. This was her Saturday and she wasn't going to break her leisurely routine for anyone or anything.

Though she thrived on her high-powered position at the magazine, she equally relished her time off. Landing huge accounts that kept *Top Rung* ever riding on top of the competition while delegating to inferiors from the throne of her executive office, easily gave way to her melting into the weekends with hours of endless self-indulgence. No one to report to. No phone calls to make. No stroking of executive egos. She would milk the moments of every Saturday and Sunday as though strolling through fields of endless flowers, pausing to take a whiff whenever she pleased.

But suddenly, the bliss was broken. She let out a shriek that launched her sister off the couch and into the bathroom in seconds flat.

"What in the world is going on? Don't tell me it's a spider because that would not be worth what you just put my heart through."

Keeping her distraught face focused into the mirror, Ann frantically pointed to some remote spot near the corner of her eye and howled, "Look at that! Do you see that?"

"See what?" Sara replied.

Ann turned away from the mirror and faced her sister squarely. "Right there—can't you see it? It's a wrinkle."

"You amped my heart with a load of sheer panic because of a *wrinkle?* Oh my goodness Ann, I can't believe you. You're thirty-two years old for crying out loud. It would be part of life's natural progression for you to start getting wrinkles here and there. And I can't even *see* it. You're being ridiculous."

"Well, what do *you* know about it? You've always quoted Mom over the years and sworn to 'grow old gracefully.' I flat out refuse to do that."

"So what are you going to do? Run out and start Botox treatments? You know—some of us have to commit to growing old gracefully because we can't afford Botox and professional foils and high-priced skin care. Some of us can't afford anything but generic brands from the grocery store. You forget why I'm even here in the first place."

"I know I know. You need my help while you go back home to Colorado to be interviewed for that new job and la-dee-da-dee-da. But if I were in your position, I'd max out every credit card on the face of the planet before I'd allow wrinkles to happen on my face and piles of gray on my head. You know how I am—just accept it."

"Well, I'll accept it a little more readily if you get a move on. We have to get to the airport in one and a half hours and I know how long it takes you to primp."

"You're in luck. I only half-primp on the weekends."

"Then half-primp quickly, if you would please. I can't miss this flight and I need to talk to you after you're dressed."

"Moving, moving," Ann sang as she kicked her sister out of the bathroom and proceeded to prepare herself for public viewing.

While Ann was getting ready, Valerie, her niece, scanned her aunt's condo with a critical eye. She was used to her mom's special brand of cozy: afghans slung carelessly across the furniture, plenty of artwork on the walls (some of which she'd created in her elementary school art classes), one table dedicated solely to framed pictures of family, a vase full of flowers that were nearing the end of their cut life—so many little touches that make a house a home. But as she looked at the walls of Auntie Ann's condominium, her eyes continually landed on … nothing. There wasn't a picture in the place. Not a single decoration. There was some sort of exercise machine in a corner, an end table or two, a couch, a loveseat, a TV, and nothing but a pair of lamps to adorn the tabletop surfaces. One tiny shelf above the couch held only three books. The titles either looked completely foreign or totally boring to her eleven-year-old brain: *How to Permanently Rid Yourself of Belly Fat*, *The Gluten-Free Life*, and *10 Key Components to Mastering Tae Kwon Do*. Not the most enticing literature. "Stark" was the only word that came to mind as Valerie completed her assessment of the place. So she decided to break the silence.

"So Mom—how long do I have to be here again?"

"Just a week, honey. I'll be back next Saturday."

"A week?" Ann burst from the bedroom like a torpedo. "Wait a minute—I thought this was just going to be a few days."

Sara cut her off while pushing her back into the bedroom, saying, "Let's come in here to discuss it." Once inside, she urgently instructed her sister, "Keep your voice down. You don't want to make Valerie feel like she's an inconvenience. She's uncomfortable enough as it is."

"She's uncomfortable? What about *me?* I don't know a thing about kids. I don't know what they like to do and I wouldn't have a clue as to how to talk to one of them. How am I supposed to entertain her the whole time? Are you kidding me, Sara? A whole week?

"I had to block out some extra time to become acquainted with things in case they hire me. They told me I'll need a few extra days to meet all the staff and that each of the candidates will have to create some sort of case scenario as a test so they can screen us more thoroughly. The interview process is just going to be way more involved than I first thought, and I want to scout out potential living arrangements."

"Yeah, but a week? My boss is only expecting me to arrive late and cut out early for two days at the most. And what about this driving thing? I'm supposed to drive all the way across town every day, twice a day, for a week?"

"First off—you may not have to be late to work. I have it arranged so you can drop Val off at seven and pick her up at 4:30. The school's really been working with me since Jim died."

"But why can't she just ride the bus like all the other kids do?"

"Because she'd have to be alone after school for an hour to an hour and a half, and I don't want her to be alone. At least not yet. So I'm covered in the morning because of band practice, and her teacher agreed to let her stay after school for an hour or so until I could get there. Look—she's had a really rough time of it and this week isn't going to be easy for her." She uncharacteristically raised her voice and asserted, "It's just a week." Remembering Valerie was in the next room, she softened her tone and added, "Come on. You can help me through one lousy week. You know what a difference this job will make for Valerie and I."

"But Sara."

"No 'but Sara,'" she said. "Just think of all the times I bailed you out when you were in college. You know—you don't have to serve her chocolate chip cookies straight from the oven like Mom used to do. And while we're on the topic, can you at least try to feed her something other than seaweed and rice?"

"Like what, for instance?"

"Like kid food. Mac and cheese, Froot Loops, Go-Gurt, bologna sandwiches …"

"Bologna? You actually want me to feed your kid bologna? Do you guys ever consume anything of nutritional value, or are you on a steady, fake food diet?"

"We can't all afford designer food, Ann. Besides—bologna has become a classic comfort food in our house." Her misty expression suggested she had momentarily left the room as she recalled, "Jim used to cut it up into shapes for Valerie's lunches. Every time it was bologna for lunch, she'd have to crack her sandwich before taking a bite, to see what was inside. Sometimes it was a flower, sometimes a dog or cat, sometimes it was her name." She laughed, "The short version anyway. Who could carve 'Valerie' into a slab of bologna? For Valentine's Day, the two of them cut it up into hearts for fried bologna sandwiches. We had it for dinner with a side of applesauce. Not a very uptown meal, but it beats raw fish and seaweed." With that, she tapped her sister on the shoulder and got up from the bed to announce it was time to go. They'd have to finish talking on the way to the airport.

Before opening the bedroom door, Ann warned her sister that she was going to make a convert out of Valerie. "By the time you get back, she'll be begging you for gluten-free pancakes and butternut squash soup."

"In your dreams, girl, in your dreams. Why do you think we're trying to move three states away? She's at an impressionable age and I need to keep her away from your seaweed-infested, sugar-starved, gluten-free ways. And P.S.—I brought you some authentic, unhealthy cow's milk, cereal, bologna and leftover spaghetti to give you a head start."

"Oh joy. Let's get out of here."

While riding the train to the airport, the topic of driving came up. Sara let her sister know that she preset the GPS in the car so Ann could find the school more easily; and between that, and Valerie's navigational skills, she ought to be just fine. But Ann was silent during this part of the conversation. "What's wrong?" Sara asked her. "Why does this driving thing seem to bother you so much?"

It took Ann a moment to respond. "Sara, one of the main reasons I live in downtown Chicago is so I don't have to drive. I got rid of my car so I could just walk everywhere or hop on the L if need be. I can't stand driving. In fact, I haven't driven a car for seven years. It's just so … uncomfortable."

"Ann. Are you afraid of driving? You couldn't be. You were always my fearless, rock-climbing, downhill racing, hang-gliding, daredevil sister who never shied away from a challenge. This cannot be true."

Ann's response was sharp and full of annoyance. "I don't want to talk about it anymore, okay?"

"Okay Tiger—backing off now. But I did want to revisit something that came up earlier." Bending closer to Ann so Valerie couldn't hear, Sara quietly assured her sister that kids are actually easier to relate to than most adults, so she need not worry about how to do the "kid thing." "And besides," she added, "Valerie will make it easy for you. You'll soon discover she's quite the talker."

They all fell silent for the rest of the ride. Valerie looked out the window and took in the sights. Sara mentally composed her to-do lists, and Ann focused all her energy on trying to tame the panic that threatened to overtake every nerve in her body. After all, what would probably be a walk in the park for most human beings was to her an ominously impossible task.

Hanging out with an eleven-year-old girl for an entire week.

As they pulled into the airport terminal, she was trying to figure out which was worse: the driving realities of the upcoming week, or the relational ones.

Never mind. This wild ride is about to begin no matter how I feel about it.

Since Valerie wanted to watch her mom's plane take off, she and Ann waited with Sara to check in and get ready to board. This extra time was perfect for Ann. The less time she had to be alone with Valerie, the better. Her conversational skills weren't even practiced with her peers outside of work, let alone with an eleven-year-old girl. What was it they said in that managerial communications class? "When you're faced with an uncomfortable social situation, just remember to ask a lot of questions. This will put both you and the person you're with at ease. They will feel like the focal point of the conversation, and you won't have to concoct a bunch of mindless small talk to fill the awkward air space."

Okay—I can give that a try. I'll practice it on the ride home.

Meanwhile, Valerie was entertaining her own thoughts. She wondered what life was going to be like with this complete stranger of a relative. The differences between her mom and her aunt were so vast, it was incomprehensible how they grew up in the same household. Auntie Ann was so cold and stiff. She was too perfect. And Valerie couldn't put her finger on what else it was that made her feel so uncomfortable around Auntie Ann. Maybe it would come to her later, after she'd been here a few days …

By now Sara was all checked in and it was time to go to the boarding gate. Sara and Valerie exchanged bear hugs and kisses, whereas the two sisters just did a quick half-hug, as if they were mere business associates. Valerie took all this in, and it only served to sink her further into insecurity regarding the coming week. *Good thing I'll have school and homework,* she thought, *I don't know what I'd do if this were spring break. It's bad enough that we have two days to go before Monday …*

Ann and her niece watched in silence as the airplane taxied around on the runway and finally took off. They gratefully stared at the distraction in the heavens until the plane became a tiny dot in the sky, leaving them no choice but to face the inevitable. They turned and walked toward the train with stomach knots churning and minds racing over how to survive the coming days.

Come on Ann, calm down, she told herself as they got on the train. *It can't be any worse than a business meeting or a power lunch.* After they settled in, Ann got down to business.

"So Valerie, what grade are you in again?"

"Fifth," was her monosyllabic reply.

"Well, how do you like it? Do you like your teachers? What's your favorite subject?"

Valerie recognized there was no genuine interest behind these questions. She knew her aunt was just trying to break the ice. But, although she didn't appreciate having to appease someone who really had no interest in her, she'd been raised to be polite at all times.

"I don't really like school all that much because the kids are mean to me. I like my teachers because they're really nice. And I have two favorite subjects. I like band and art the best."

"That's good," Ann replied. "School didn't used to be my favorite either. I thought it was a waste of time. I'd rather be out climbing rocks than sitting in a classroom."

Ann felt satisfied with this exchange. Although she completely missed the part about kids being mean to Valerie, she gave herself a pat on the back for having a complete volley in the conversation. *This was good,* she thought. *Valerie shared a bit of herself and I shared a bit of mine. Now, how much longer is this train ride?*

She looked across at her niece and faked a smile. Valerie faked one back and they spent the rest of the trip in silence.

Upon returning to the condo, Ann remembered that the first order of business should probably be a shopping trip. She truly had no kid-friendly food in her place and the little bit that Sara brought over was only good for a few meals. She had no mayo or mustard or even bread to complete the bologna sandwich requirement. She didn't even have butter for toast. All she had was organic coconut oil to act as a stand-in for all things buttery. No matter. She'd have to enlist the aid of her guest if they were to have a successful shopping trip. She called Valerie to the kitchen table and told her to dictate a list.

Ann tried to conceal her cringing as she wrote the list, which included: popcorn, Oreos, ice cream, mac and cheese, and a host of other non-nutritional items. This visit was going to be a task, to be sure.

As they prepared to go to the store, Valerie said she was hungry now and asked if there was anything for a snack.

"Let's see …" Ann said, while scanning the few items she had in her refrigerator. "How's about you just try some of this leftover sushi?"

"No way, Auntie Ann. I am not eating seaweed."

"You don't have to like it Valerie, just give it a try. Sometimes you don't know whether or not you really like something unless you try it. And the kind of sushi I have in the fridge isn't wrapped in seaweed. So make me a deal—try one bite. If you don't like it, you can spit it out. Then you can have a little of that leftover spaghetti your mom brought instead. Sometimes, when it comes to food, it's good to be adventurous and have an open mind."

As much as Valerie hated the idea of even trying sushi, she had to be polite. The experiment didn't go as Ann had hoped. Valerie tried one bite and ran to the sink as fast as her feet could carry her. "Ewww," was about all she could squeeze out of her pinched face as she rummaged around in the cupboards to find a glass. As she poured herself a milk chaser, she asked, "May we please add orange juice to that list?"

Ann noticed she was starting to get hungry too, so they settled down for a quick lunch of leftover sushi and spaghetti. Might as well not be starving for outing number one.

After lunch, Ann pulled out some shopping bags and they headed out.

Chapter 2

It was a bit windy outside, but clear, so they walked to the neighborhood grocery store. Ann always chose to walk when the weather allowed. Her fitness fanatic self could never get enough exercise and it always cleared her head. Valerie could barely keep pace with Ann's standard, rapid clip, but it got them to the store in just a few minutes.

Because Ann did most of her shopping at the health food store, the layout of this one was unfamiliar. Valerie, however, proved to be a great help as they navigated the aisles. In no time at all they were standing in the checkout line.

They were only two people back, but something was causing a holdup. Ann bent her head around the person ahead of her to see what was going on. It was a diminutive old woman apparently trying to dig money out from inside her gigantic handbag. It seemed to take forever for her to find her wallet. Ann was instantly agitated and began fidgeting with extreme impatience. She looked again, and the woman had not yet found her wallet. Finally, she let out a huge sigh of exasperation as she leaned forward to comment to the person ahead of her, "And that is why I never want to get old. This is just ridiculous. Why couldn't she just keep her money in one of those giant pockets on her handbag?" With a highly exaggerated roll of the eyes, she added, "Or send someone else to the store to do her shopping for her."

"Not so loud," Valerie whispered as she grabbed her aunt's jacket sleeve. "She might hear you."

"I'm beginning not to care if she hears me or not. Oh—bingo—I believe she's finally found it."

Visibly embarrassed by her aunt's behavior, Valerie once again tried to politely tell her to "shush."

Ann shook Valerie's pleading hand off of her jacket sleeve when she noticed the woman was now digging for exact change out of her coin purse.

"Enough is enough," she muttered as she briefly searched her own purse. She found a dollar bill, reached right past the person in front of her and threw it down in front of the cashier. "There. Does *that* take care of it?"

Even the person in front of her was made to feel uncomfortable by this impatient outburst. But it was worse for Valerie. She wanted to sink under the hood of her favorite hoodie and stay there until the end of the week.

Ann was oblivious to all this as the old woman looked her right in the eyes and graciously thanked her. Her warm and humble smile only earned her a forced and rigid smile in return. All Ann wanted was to check out and get back home. She didn't even notice the cashier's flushed attempt to avoid eye contact once they reached the register.

But Valerie did.

After they returned to the condo and put groceries away, Ann announced she had a yoga class at four. "So since I can't leave you alone, you'll have to come with me. If you want, you can do the class with me. If not, perhaps you should bring a book or something so you don't get too bored. The class is about forty-five minutes long. While you think about it, I'm going to go get changed."

When she came back out, Valerie hadn't moved from the kitchen table, so Ann assumed she wasn't going to participate in the class. Putting on her jacket, she said, "Okay let's go," but Valerie sheepishly looked at the kitchen table and didn't budge. "Well, come on," Ann repeated.

Valerie finally looked up. "I want to do the class."

"So what's the holdup?"

While Valerie's eyes quickly found the table again, she mumbled, "I don't know what I should wear."

"Well why didn't you just ask me?"

"I didn't want to interrupt you," Valerie said. "But if it will cause you to be late, I just won't do the class."

"No—you can do the class. Just go throw on a pair of sweats and something baggy on top. Wear a warm coat though. It's getting cold outside."

Once Valerie was ready, Ann applied her typical approach to time management as she rushed her niece out the door and ran a blitz to the L, then to the yoga studio. As they were taking their coats off, everyone swarmed around them to ask Ann who her little partner was.

"Oh, it's just my niece," she told them. "She's here for the week so I ..."

One of her yoga buddies interrupted. "Okay, 'just Ann's niece,' do you have a name? My name's Staci. Have you ever done a yoga class before?"

Staci's friendly demeanor swept through Valerie like a fresh summer breeze. She happily told Staci her name, adding that the only exercise class she'd ever done was P.E.

They both giggled and Staci put her arm around Valerie while saying, "Well come hang out with me. I'll show you the ropes. You don't mind, do you Ann?"

With a smile that lit up her entire face, Valerie responded with an enthusiastic, "Sure."

They walked away together and Ann felt relieved. A little unexpected backup never hurt. She watched the two as they unrolled their mats and chose a spot on the floor a little closer to the front. Ann couldn't help but notice how much Valerie seemed to open up with Staci. Until now, she'd begun to think her sister was spinning tall tales when referring to what a talker Valerie could be. But there she was, gabbing up a storm with a complete stranger. *Oh well—all the better,* she thought. *I'll be taking her to Tae Kwon Do with me on Monday, so it's good for her to be exposed to all the positives of these classes.*

By the time class was over, Staci and Valerie acted like best buddies. Staci had to give Ann the full report before asking, "Ann, why have you kept your niece such a secret? She's enchantingly delightful, and if I were you, I'd try to snatch her up for summer break." Then she threw her arm around Valerie and walked her to the coat rack before doing something that really took Ann by surprise. She gave Valerie a warm, lingering hug. Then she backed up and said, "Thanks for the fun Valerie, come back anytime."

On the ride home, Ann was reviewing a few of these things in her mind when she remembered to bring up the topic of Saturday night entertainment. "So, what do you and your Mom usually do on Saturday nights?"

"We usually have pizza for dinner, then we watch a movie and have popcorn or ice cream. Sometimes both."

"Both. Wow." Ann had a hard time swallowing that reality, but she kept the ball rolling by asking Valerie whether or not she brought any movies to watch.

"I did bring a few," Valerie told her, "but I've seen them all a million times and was hoping we could rent something."

"Well, there just happens to be a video store right by the condo. We'll swing by on the way home and you can pick out a few movies. I guess we could stop and get a pizza as well. But don't expect me to join you. I don't eat pizza. Or ice cream. In fact—don't expect to do a lot of food bonding with me while you're here. I'm on a pretty strict diet."

Valerie shrugged her shoulders and said, "Okay." It wasn't like she'd expected her aunt to go off the health food wagon anyway, but it was nice to hear they might be able to rent a movie.

By the time they returned to the condo, it was nearly seven o'clock. Ann was so relieved by this that she nearly felt happy while warming the oven for the pizza. It meant the day was almost over. And that meant all she had to do was get through Sunday. Then she'd have five school days with barely any interaction at all.

Easy peasy. I've got this.

While she was in the kitchen, Valerie was taking a shower and getting into her pajamas. She came out just in time. The pizza was all cut up and ready to go and all she had to do was pick out a movie. She chose *Tangled,* and they sat on the couch—Ann with her vegetarian soup and Valerie with her pizza. Ann had her laptop right beside her so she'd be able to do some work after finishing her soup.

While the previews were playing, Valerie asked Ann what the computer was for.

"Oh, I was thinking I might get some work done while you watch the movie."

Valerie aggressively aired her disappointment. "You're not even going to watch the movie with me?"

Ann was surprised by how strongly Valerie seemed opposed to this idea. She told her niece she wasn't really into kid movies.

"*Tangled* isn't just a kid movie," Valerie insisted. "My mom loves this movie and so do a lot of other grown-ups."

"Like who?"

"Like my teacher."

"Okay, that's two. I might not be part of the minority after all."

Valerie whined, "But my mom always watches with me. She won't even answer the phone when we watch a movie together."

Ann was unmoved. "Well, that's your mom. On the weekends I like to get some work done that's hard to get to during the week. I focus better without all the loud and crazy interruptions that derail me at the office."

"Then why don't you just take your computer into your bedroom?" Valerie asked. "Seems to me this movie might get a little distracting."

"I thought the least I could do is sit on the couch, since you and your mom usually watch together. Speaking of, isn't it time to start the movie?"

Valerie sighed, "I guess. I just wish you'd watch it too."

"I might watch a little. I probably won't be able to help it anyway, since I'm not in my bedroom. So go ahead and push play."

The movie began and Ann plunged into the computer like no one else was around. She looked up once in a while to see what was so great about this movie. She felt movies meant to entertain were a waste of time. Most of her TV viewing time was spent on Tae Kwon Do and workout videos. Occasionally she'd rent a cooking video. She couldn't even remember the last time she sat down to watch a movie.

Now that she thought about it, this seemed strange to her. Growing up, she and her family used to watch movies all the time. That is, when they weren't outside playing in the snow or going on hikes together. Ann recalled how in the winter, she, Sara, and her dad would come in from a day in the snow to an amazing crock pot meal. Mom frequently made her famous Irish soda bread to go along with it and sometimes she'd even make some of Dad's favorite Norwegian cookies to eat while watching the movie. They'd have dinner at the kitchen table and talk up a storm. About the day, about Dad's old days in Norway, about anything and everything that came up. They never lacked a topic, that's for sure. Oftentimes, they'd sit there so long that they'd decide to ditch the movie, break out the cards and play a few games. Sometimes they'd even 'break out the silly' and play a game of spoons. That's what Mom used to say. "Let's break out the silly." Dad used to be able to balance a spoon on the end of his nose. He was always good for a laugh.

Ann recalled how much she used to love hearing her mom laugh. It was downright musical. No wonder though. She played the violin like a maestro. Although her skill at playing classical pieces could rival any member of the New York Philharmonic, she preferred the happy lilt of Celtic music. Not surprising, since she was born and raised in Ireland. Once she started with the fiddle, it was all over. They'd all dance the rest of the night away right there in the kitchen. Sometimes Dad would lend his beautiful tenor voice to all the merriment. They couldn't have been happier. How lucky she was to have been born into such an amazing family …

Wow, she thought, *how did I get from movies to dancing in the kitchen?*

Valerie crashed through the reverie by pausing the movie. Ann had become so lost in all her reminiscing that the movie was halfway over and she had completely abandoned her computer.

Valerie announced it was "halftime."

"And what is 'halftime' when it comes to a movie?" Ann asked.

"It's when you pause the movie, then go get ice cream or popcorn or whatever you want to have while watching the rest of the movie."

"So, what are you going to have?"

"I'm thinking … popcorn."

As Valerie was in the kitchen popping popcorn in the microwave, Ann got hit with another wave of memories. Her mom used to make popcorn on top of the stove in an ancient kettle she brought over from Ireland. Sometimes she mixed it with seasoning salt and parmesan cheese. It was always magnificent. Ann wouldn't be able to pop popcorn on the stove if someone held a gun to her head. She always viewed it as some exotic art form that only her mother had mastered. Microwave popcorn was the only road for her. Or was, back when she used to eat it.

"Okay, ready," Valerie announced as she came out of the kitchen with a bag of popcorn and a napkin. "Are you sure you don't want any?"

Ann replied with her eyes stuck to the computer screen. "I'm absolutely sure." Then she thought she should at least try to sound enthusiastic, so she looked toward the TV screen and gestured with her fist in the air, "Roll 'em!"

Just then, the phone rang. It was Sara calling to check in.

"Sorry it took so long to get around to this phone call. There was a mix-up with the rooms, then they wanted to have a brief meeting before we had a chance to settle in. Then, they took us out to dinner. I wanted to call the minute I got here, but there was just no way. And, although I want to touch base with you, I'm really dying to talk to Valerie. Can you pass her the phone?"

"Yep, here she is." Ann handed Valerie the phone and said, "It's your mom."

Valerie beamed as she took the phone. "Hi Mommy, how are you? How was your airplane ride? Do the bosses like you?"

"Woah," Sara said, "slow down missy! I'm okay, the plane ride was fine and took no time at all, and I haven't had enough time with the bosses yet to know what they think of me. What I want to know is how are *you* doing? Is your Auntie Ann taking good care of you?"

"Well …" Valerie hesitated. She felt awkward answering this question with her aunt sitting right there. She even tried to avoid making eye contact with her aunt, for fear of revealing her true feelings. So she sat looking at the floor and came up with a diversion. "Um … we're watching a movie right now. At least I am. Auntie's doing some work on her computer. But it's halftime and I just made some popcorn."

"Oh. She's working on her computer is she? Well, I'll tell you what. I don't have long to talk tonight, so could you please put Auntie on the phone for a second? I'll say goodnight to you before I go."

"Okay," Valerie replied. She handed the phone to Ann and said, "My mom wants to talk to you."

Suspecting she might be in for a tongue lashing, Ann took the phone and walked into the bedroom. In an attempt to keep things light, she tried to sound upbeat. "Well hello there world traveler. How goes it over there in Colorado?"

Sara didn't waste any time cutting to the chase. "What's going on? Something's wrong with Valerie, I could tell by her voice. Help me out, Ann. This is going to be a long week and I won't present my best if I'm constantly worried about her."

"Nothing's wrong, what do you mean?"

"I know my girl. She sounds despondent. And why are you working instead of watching the movie with her? Watching movies together is something we do all the time. In fact, we call it our 'cozy time'. Can't you just watch it with her? It really doesn't require any effort on your part—all you have to do is sit there. Look—between losing both her grandparents and her father, you're the only family Val has left apart from a few cousins, aunts and uncles strewn across the world. Could you at least *try* to bond with her a little?"

Ann rolled her eyes and sighed, "Yeah, I guess."

Sara asked Ann to put Valerie back on the phone to say their goodnights, so Ann walked back to the living room and handed Valerie the phone.

While they finished their conversation, Ann plopped on the couch and waited. Valerie ended the call and Ann asked, "Are you ready?"

"Ready for what?"

"Ready to finish the movie."

Valerie figured her mom told Ann to watch the movie, so her reply was halfhearted. "Yeah, sure," she said while picking up the remote. She unpaused the movie and Ann kept her eyes on the screen until the end. Although she had shut her computer down, she was able to finish her work in her head while "watching" the movie. Valerie knew her aunt wasn't really tuned in because she didn't laugh, comment, or respond to the movie in any way. *Oh well,* Valerie reminded herself, *it's only a week.* By the time the movie ended, it was time to get ready for bed. They took turns in the bathroom. While Ann was brushing her teeth, Valerie was in the living room blowing up her air mattress. Since Ann didn't have a guest room, Valerie had to sleep on the floor. When Ann came out to say goodnight, Valerie asked her a very odd question: "Auntie Ann, do you pray?"

Ann's expression bordered on disgust as she asked, "Where in the world is *that* question coming from? Wow. Do I pray? No. No I don't pray. I used to a long time ago, but no. I don't. Not anymore."

"Why not?" Valerie asked.

"I don't know why not. I've never really thought about it. Why do you want to know anyway?"

"Because my mom and I always pray at bedtime. She comes in and we pray together, then she gives me a hug and a kiss. So I thought maybe you could pray with me."

Ann's response was stilted by the awkwardness she felt. "No, Valerie. I don't even remember how. Can't you just pray by yourself?"

Valerie sighed. "Yeah, I can … but I don't want to, 'cause Mom and I always pray together." She punctuated the significance of this by repeating, "Always."

"Sorry," Ann said. "Maybe another one of these nights. Maybe. You'd have to be the one to pray though. Like I said, I don't really remember how." Longing to escape the moment, she struggled with how to close the conversation and get to bed already. What flew into her mouth was, "So … um … goodnight. I'll leave the hall light on so you can find the bathroom."

"Goodnight Auntie Ann." Valerie just lay there with her eyes wide open for the longest time. She had to remind herself that being here with Auntie was a help to her mom. She began missing her mom immensely. Her mom was always so kind and full of hugs. She knew what to say and how to make Valerie feel better when the kids at school were mean. And she and her mom always had so much fun together. They frequently made crafts out of stuff that was laying around the house. Sometimes they'd crank up the music and dance in the living room. Then there were the times when they'd sit on the couch and read three books in a row. She'd barely been apart from her mom since her dad died.

She didn't even want to think about him right now. It was bad enough to miss her mom. Such an ache rose into her heart, that praying was more like breathing as she felt hot tears rolling down her cheeks.

"Dear Lord," she prayed. "I'm hoping You might give me a heart-hug. I miss my mom so badly. I'm sorry, but I don't like Auntie Ann very much. And I'm really sorry again, but I want to say I hate being here. But I know You don't want me to hate anything, so please help me. Help me with this hate I'm feeling. And please do something about Auntie Ann. She's not very nice. Thank you Lord. In Jesus' name, amen."

While Valerie was praying in the other room, Ann was lying in her bed with a few thoughts of her own. She was surprised by all the memories that had flooded her while the movie was playing. Now more were pouring in. Like how her and Sara's mother only let them eat their movie snack in front of the TV, but never a meal. Meals were only consumed at the kitchen table, with very few exceptions. She remembered times when she would help her mom bake in the kitchen. She pictured herself riding on her dad's shoulders when her hiking legs grew weary. She remembered pillow fights with Sara and real fights too.

They didn't fight often, but when they did, their mom and dad made them sit down with each other and make up. First they had to review the situation while their parents listened. Then they'd have to apologize for their part in the altercation. Then, they'd all join hands and … pray.

Now she remembered how often she and her family used to pray. They prayed together after ugly disagreements. They prayed before meals. And they prayed before bed. Wow. How did she forget all that?

Well, it's a good thing Sara is Valerie's mom, because I certainly wouldn't carry on the prayer tradition, she thought. As an adult, she really couldn't see the point. After all, natural disasters wiped out lives by the millions, others died of cancer or heart disease and some died in car accidents. So what good was all that God stuff anyway? If she had kids, she wouldn't want them exposed to any of that. She'd raise them to be realists just like she was. Not that she'd ever have kids anyway. She wasn't exactly the mom type.

"Oh enough," she spoke into the darkness of her bedroom. "Time to turn off this brain."

After closing her eyes, Ann drifted to an image of herself and her mother, dusted in flour and laughing in the kitchen. Wrapped comfortably within the arms of this vision, she slipped into a peaceful sleep.

Chapter 3

On the weekends, Ann typically woke up between 6:30 and 7:00 a.m. Today was no exception, but she woke in a bit of a fog. It took her a moment to remember her niece was sleeping on her living room floor and today was the day she dreaded most: Sunday. Spending one endless hour after another trying to figure out how to keep her niece entertained sprawled before her like a fully furnished torture chamber. It was bad enough her entire weekend day was being stolen from her, but she was at a complete loss as to how to spend it. *I guess we'll have to play it by ear,* was the only solution that played in her mind as she geared up to jump on the elliptical.

When she came out to the living room, Valerie was already up and dressed. With the bed made and air mattress put away, she was sitting on the couch. "Wow," Ann said. "I thought *I* was the early riser."

"I always wake up early when I sleep anywhere but in my own bed," Valerie replied.

"Well, have you had anything to eat or drink yet? I have all kinds of tea and I can make coffee after I get off the elliptical. Just help yourself to whatever you want. I'll be about thirty minutes."

"Auntie Ann, I'm only eleven. Mom won't let me drink coffee yet."

"Oh. I didn't think of that. Well, it doesn't matter. Just know that you don't have to wait for me. If you're hungry, eat something. If you want something to drink, you know where the cups and glasses are."

Valerie decided to search her bags for something to read. She didn't want to make it obvious that she was, in fact, waiting for Ann. Ever since she could remember, before and after her dad died, Sunday mornings were special. They always got up early, ate a light breakfast together and went to early service at church. After church they'd have a huge lunch. Oftentimes, they'd go to a restaurant. If not, they'd prepare an elaborate meal at home. Valerie always loved and looked forward to Sundays. But like her aunt, she'd been dreading this one since last night, for all the same reasons. What were two people who lived in two separate universes going to do with all these hours?

With a sigh in her heart, she picked up her Bible and decided to browse the Psalms. Her mom said the book of Psalms was the best place to go if ever you felt sad or lonely or even angry. David took every one of his emotions to God in the Psalms and always received comfort. She remembered that Psalm 23 was a good one. "The Lord is my shepherd, I shall not want. He makes me lie down in green pastures; He leads me beside quiet waters ... Even though

I walk through the valley of the shadow of death, I fear no evil; for Thou art with me …"

That's it, Valerie thought, *I'm in the valley of the shadow of death just like David was. And I don't have to be afraid of evil Auntie Ann because God is with me! Okay, I'll just think about that all day long instead of how much I miss my mom and wish I was home instead of here.*

Just as Valerie finished reading, Ann stepped off the elliptical and made herself a cup of coffee with her French press. Valerie went into the kitchen and poured herself a glass of orange juice, then sat at the kitchen table. She thought her aunt was going to sit down too, but this was not the case.

Ann announced that she was going to take a shower before coming out for breakfast. She added, "If you're not hungry yet, you can wait for me. I'm having a green smoothie, but I can also make some pancakes."

"Don't tell me—they're gluten-free, right?"

"Of course they are," Ann replied. "But they don't taste that much different."

"Okay, I'll try them," Valerie acquiesced. She'd forgotten to put frozen waffles on the grocery list. But at least the pancakes would be hot.

Once Ann came out and got busy in the kitchen, things began to feel a little like home. There was something cozy about activity in the kitchen. Valerie had never really thought about it before; but then, she rarely spent time away from home.

"Do you want some help?" she asked.

"Sure," her aunt replied. "You can mix the pancake batter. The directions are on the box."

Aside from Valerie asking where all the baking dishes and measuring cups were, they shared the rest of the breakfast preparations in silence. Ann worked on assembling her smoothie while Valerie painstakingly followed the pancake directions. Ann took out a frying pan and heated some oil, breaking the silence by asking if Valerie wanted to pour the batter.

"Yeah I can do that," Valerie said. "Do you have a ladle?"

"Yes I do. It's in the top drawer, right next to the stove."

Valerie found the ladle and poured three circles into the pan. Her dad taught her how to do this when she was seven years old. He showed her how to make Mickey Mouse by pouring one big circle in the middle of the pan and two smaller ones on top for the ears. She was worried about flipping it, so she asked her aunt for help. Since Ann had never attempted to flip a mouse in a pan before, one of the ears became detached and Valerie giggled. But Ann barely cracked a smile as she put the rest of Mickey on a plate. Valerie just couldn't figure her aunt out. Did she ever have fun? Did she ever laugh? Her musings were broken by Ann asking what she'd like on her pancakes.

"About all I have to put on pancakes is honey and peanut butter. And you might not like the kind of peanut butter I have. It's all-natural, with no added sugar or hydrogenated oils."

"What?" Valerie asked. "What in all of creation is that?"

"Let me put it to you this way—it doesn't taste like Jif."

"Well, okay, I'll try them with just some honey. But could we stop by the store again today and pick up some more breakfast stuff, like frozen waffles and syrup? Real peanut butter would be good too. I forgot to put those on the list yesterday."

With her back turned to Valerie, Ann became visibly rigid. She directed her grizzly response straight into the kitchen cabinet. "I didn't know this adventure would include going to the grocery store every single day."

"I'm sorry Auntie. I don't need syrup. I don't need waffles. And I'll eat your peanut butter. We don't have to go to the store every day. It's okay."

"No, it's all right," Ann sighed. Then the lights came on. "Come to think of it, another trip to the store might actually burn a little extra time. It's more than okay. Let's put a list together."

Aside from making a list, breakfast conversation was minimal, so Valerie decided to drum up some table talk. "So, what do you usually do on Sundays? My mom and I always go to church, then have brunch, then do fun stuff, then at night time after dinner we read, watch a movie or bake something. Then right before bed, we get ready for Mondays by making lunches for school and all that."

Ann's eyes widened. "School lunches? I hadn't thought of that. So do you and your mom do that together, or do you do it all by yourself?"

"We both do it. Sometimes we don't get to it, so Mom gets up early and makes my lunch."

"Great. So I'm also supposed to make lunches for school?"

Due to the generous load of irritation that accompanied this question, Valerie assured her aunt that she could make her own lunches.

"Well good. Okay then. If you need help, you can ask me. I'm just not used to all this extra stuff, especially on the weekends. And in response to your original question, on Sundays I usually get up early, exercise, run errands and do whatever I feel like doing at the moment. I might, for instance, go get my nails done or go for a swim or browse a bookstore or go to the park …"

Valerie cut her off with an animated string of dialogue that took Ann by surprise. "You go to the park? Do you mean the great big one? My mom and I caught the train and went to a big park a long time ago, but I don't remember the name of it. She says it's always pretty when the tulips come in and I think I saw some yesterday."

"Yes, you did see some yesterday. The tulips are always in full bloom in April and this year it's been warmer than usual. Sure—we can go to Millennium Park. We'll start with Lurie Garden, then visit the fountain."

"You mean the one that has faces in it?"

"That's the one. After that we can go see our reflections in The Bean."

"Is that the big shiny thing that people stand under and get their pictures taken?"

"Yes it is. A lot of tourists make it a top priority to snap pictures at The Bean."

"I think Mom has a picture of all three of us at The Bean from when Dad was alive. This will be so cool. I can't wait!"

With that, Valerie jumped up from the table and was about to run to the bathroom to brush her teeth and get ready to go, but Ann stopped her. "Not before you take care of your breakfast mess, please, thank you."

Valerie quickly cleared her dishes, wiped the table and finished getting ready to go. She was too excited to dwell on the fact that her aunt never said a single thing with a smile. And with the thought of tulips at Lurie Garden, she was able to brush away the feeling of being nothing but a nuisance to Auntie.

They couldn't have asked for a more perfect day. The sun was shining and it was quite warm for a spring day in the Windy City. They did wear light jackets, but even the wind seemed to comply with the desire of two individuals in need of a little outdoor entertainment. Chicago's trademark bluster tamed itself down to a brisk breeze as Ann and Valerie made their way to the park.

Lurie Garden opened its arms to Valerie's hungry heart as though the two had been lifelong friends. She wanted to enjoy every inch of it, so they lingered long over all the different flowers and shrubs. To Ann's surprise, Valerie could identify many of the flower and plant varieties. "Oh look—there's a patch of golden alexanders. And this is called glory of the snow. And these are Arkansas blue stars. Oh I love this place, Auntie. I wish we could come here every day."

Valerie was not surprised by her aunt's practical response. "Well too bad there are these little obstacles in life called work and school. How do you know so much about flowers and plants anyway?"

"My dad taught me. We used to spend hours in the garden and caring for the lawn. He got me a giant garden book for one of my birthdays and I look at it all the time. Every year he would help me plant my own little patch. I could plant whatever flowers I wanted. We also planted a whole bunch of tulip bulbs and he showed me how to take care of them so they'd come back the next year. We even had a small vegetable garden."

"Have you not been able to maintain the garden since he's been gone?"

"Yeah. I can keep up a little, but it's too much to do all by myself. My mom tries to help, but she's better at cutting the flowers than she is at growing them."

Ann sighed, "I guess it's in the gene pool. I'm not good with plants either."

Ann was feeling pretty good about this idea of going to the park. They'd already killed an hour and still had so much to see. She thought perhaps they should fit in a few more points of interest in order to stretch the clock even further. She suggested they stop by the Great Lawn and Pritzker Pavilion before heading to the fountain. Valerie was fine with the idea, so on they went.

As Ann had expected, the Lawn was packed. Everyone in Chicago seemed to be out grabbing a piece of this amazing weather. There were blankets and Frisbees and baseballs and mitts, and even a few guitar players filling the air with spring-inspired joy.

As they were taking in the sights, a big red ball came from out of nowhere and hit Valerie's leg. "Ow," she shouted, more from the surprise of it than the actual pain. It was just a cheap, plastic kid's ball, not really capable of inflicting much pain. She bent down to pick it up when she heard a very small voice calling, "I'm sorry. I'm really sorry." The voice sounded out of breath, but as she looked around, she couldn't figure out where it was coming from.

Just then, a little boy with a head full of blonde curls ran up to her and repeated one more out-of-breath time, "I'm sorry I hit you with my ball."

"Oh, that's okay," Valerie smiled. "I'm sure it was just an accident."

"Yeah," he vigorously nodded. "It was a assident."

Before the conversation continued, the three were joined by a young woman who had sprinted over to join in the apology. "Hi there. I'm Charles' mom. I'm really sorry about this. It's a little hard to keep control of the ball when he's such a good little kicker. Plus, it's feeling like the first day of spring so all the city is out today."

"You're telling me," Ann said. "I don't know if this weather was in the forecast, but we do have to grab it while we can."

"Yes we do," responded the young woman. "My name is Lisa, by the way. And this is Charles."

"Charles Latham the Third," the little boy proudly proclaimed. "My name is Charles Latham the Third." He turned to Valerie and asked, "Did I hurt your leg?"

"No, I'm fine," Valerie smiled. "How old are you Charles Latham the Third?"

"I'm five years old," he answered. "Do you come to this park all the time?"

"No I don't. I'm not from around here."

"Neither am I," he said. "I'm just here 'cause I have to go to the hospital to get a test."

"Oh. Are you scared?"

"No. I'm not scared. My mommy told me I don't have to be scared, so I'm not. And she gets to sleep at the hospital. And I get to have ice cream."

"You get to have ice cream?" Valerie asked. "What's your favorite flavor?"

"I like chocolate."

"Me too," Valerie giggled.

Ann silently marveled at this exchange. Communicating with children was completely foreign to her, but Valerie seemed to be a natural at it. Her contemplation was suddenly interrupted by Charles Latham the Third.

"Can you play ball with me?" he asked Valerie.

"Well ... I don't know ..." she looked to her aunt for a response to the question.

"Sure you can," Ann said. With a radiant, unauthentic smile, she added, "What are sunny Chicago days for anyway?"

So Valerie and Charles Latham the Third skipped off, providing another marvelous solution to the time game. Who knew how long they could entertain themselves out there on the grass kicking a ball around? But of course, this did not let Ann off the adult conversation hook.

Lisa was the one to open the exchange. "Your daughter seems very charming, but I didn't catch her name. Yours either for that matter. Charles does have a way of dominating social situations."

"Oh, she's not my daughter," Ann was quick to explain. "She's my niece. Her name is Valerie and my name is Ann."

"Oh, sorry. Apart from hair color, the two of you look quite a bit alike."

"No problem—although this is the first time I've been told we look alike. Then again, I rarely see my niece or my sister."

"Well it's too bad we couldn't all live in the same neighborhood. Your niece is such a little sweetheart. I'd borrow her to hang out with Charles if she lived nearby."

"Speaking of," Ann interjected, "why is Charles being tested?"

"About a month ago we discovered a few lumps above his collarbone. When I took him to our family doctor, he asked if anything else unusual had been happening with Charles. I told him there were a few things that I thought might or might not be out of the ordinary. Like his running out of breath so easily and his frequent stomach pain. Then he developed an eye twitch and started getting off balance once in a while. I was already thinking of getting him in just because of that, then we found the lumps. When I finally did get him in, our doctor recommended we get him to the hospital to be tested for neuroblastoma."

"What's that?" Ann asked.

"It's a form of cancer," Lisa replied.

At this, Ann was stumped. Not having a compassionate bone in her body truly put her at a disadvantage. Somehow, she needed to concoct a sensitive response. She dug deep and came up with the perfect reply. "That must be very difficult, since he's so young."

Lisa didn't appear to have noticed Ann's inner struggle when she responded to Ann's comment. "The doctor told us this form of cancer occurs most frequently in children."

"Oh." Ann tried to think of something more to say, but came up empty.

Just then Valerie and Charles returned from their short romp. Valerie explained that Charles had gotten too tired. "And his legs were a little wobbly so we decided to come back."

"Probably a good idea," his mother replied. "It's been so nice to meet the two of you. I wish we could spend more time, but testing starts first thing in the morning. We have one more normal evening to cherish before it all starts. I certainly hope to see you again sometime."

"Yeah," Valerie answered. "That would be really fun. Goodbye Charles Latham the Third."

"Goodbye," Charles replied.

It was obvious that Charles' mother was concerned, so they didn't linger over this departure.

Ann was drinking in the relief of being saved by the bell as they walked away. The intensity of the moment didn't even require her to offer the verbal courtesies that would normally follow such an encounter. No "have a nice day" or "so nice to meet you" or "I hope to see you again" was needed. Just a decision to move on to the next thing.

She turned to Valerie and asked, "Okay—you ready for The Bean or do you want to go see the fountain first?"

Valerie's voice was barely audible as she answered, "I don't know."

"What do you mean you don't know? Just a few hours ago, you were chomping at the bit to get here and see everything."

"I know, but I'm sad about Charles."

"It is sad but it doesn't have to ruin your whole day does it? We can still go see the other things in the park before going to the store."

"Yeah, but I don't feel like seeing everything else in the park right now. I'm sad about Charles. He's such a cute little boy and he can barely run and play. And he might have cancer. I don't feel like doing a whole bunch of things. Can we just go to the store and have lunch?"

"I guess. But I don't know what we'll do with the rest of this day."

"It doesn't matter, Auntie. Let's just go."

They went to the store and returned to the condo with very few words. Once there, Ann's first order of business was to call Sara. She was at such a loss as to how to spend all these hours with her despondent niece that she decided to call upon the expert for help. She made the call from her bedroom so Valerie wouldn't hear.

"Okay Ann, I only have a few minutes because we're actually working today. What's going on?"

Ann explained the situation to her sister, including the part about running into Charles Latham the Third and his mother. She told Sara about how their park trip was cut short and asked for ideas as to how to fill the remaining hours of the day.

"Well you know Jim died of cancer—I'm sure that had something to do with Valerie's sudden mood crash," Sara said. "Do you still have your violin?"

"Yeah, why?"

"Because I told Valerie about how well you played and she got pretty excited. She loves music and seemed very impressed by your musical abilities. Perhaps you could blow the dust off and play it for her."

"I don't think so, Sara. It's been forever and I don't really have the heart for it anymore."

Sara gave full vent to her exasperation. "Will you ever grow past thinking it's all about you? You have an eleven-year-old girl with you who's never been away from her mother for more than two days. Her dad died prematurely and she just got hit with a reminder bullet regarding that fact. You're the adult. Can't you put the heart needs of a child above your own?"

"Woah—back down will you? It's not like I've been raising Valerie from birth like you have. I've never exactly had to 'be the adult' with anyone but myself. I guess I better go figure this out. Besides—you have to get back to work and we have to figure out what to do for lunch."

"Well, I still think you should break out your violin. You're the one who got blessed with the music gene. God knows *I* didn't."

"Yeah, well, I wouldn't complain if I were you. You got Mom's strawberry blonde hair."

"I'd rather play the violin. But I do have to go. I just saw the top manager looking for me. I'll call later when it's about bedtime."

"Okay," Ann answered. "Talk to you later."

As Ann walked back into the living room, Valerie asked her who she'd been talking to.

"Oh, it was just your mom. I had to ask her a quick question. I would have put you on the phone, but she only had a few minutes to talk. She said she'd call later at bedtime."

"So what did you talk about?" Valerie asked.

"Not much. Your mom thinks I should pull out my violin and play it for you."

Valerie immediately perked up. "Really? Will you? I just love violin music. I wish I could learn how to play. My mom's always told me how good you are. She said Grandma used to play too and you're almost as good as she was."

"'Was' is the key word. I *used* to play well. I haven't played for so many years I doubt I'd be that great anymore."

"Well, could you at least try? It's probably like riding a bike. No matter how long it's been, you can just get on a bike and ride it once you've learned how. That's what my mom always says anyway."

Due to the fact that Valerie's enthusiasm seemed to return, Ann considered it. She figured if she could try to play a bit, perhaps Valerie's spirits would lift enough to go back to the park for a few hours. Then they could do dinner and a movie and ... *That's it. Decision made. Who cares how I play anyway? It's not like I have a real audience ...*

She told Valerie she'd try to play a little after all, but warned her not to expect much.

"Okay." Valerie sat down on the couch, stiffened her back with full anticipation and folded her hands in her lap. "You can just pretend I'm not here."

Ann dug her violin out of the closet and took it out of its case to tune it. She was surprised to discover it wasn't that far out of tune after all these years. It didn't take long for her to choose what used to be her favorite classical piece: Movement one of "La primavera" from Vivaldi's Four Seasons. Not only was this her favorite, but it seemed fitting since Chicago was experiencing such a beautiful spring day.

Valerie could not believe her ears. She sat motionless and awestruck throughout the entire piece. First of all, she was amazed by her aunt's ability. Secondly, she was so moved by certain sections of the music that she felt like crying. She wished the song could go on forever, it so soothed and lifted her aching heart. After Ann was finished, Valerie begged her to play another one.

"I could listen to you all day, Auntie. I can't believe how well you can play. And you haven't practiced for how long?"

"Truth be told, I've never been one to 'practice.'" Music used to feed me so much that I had to play. I used to get lost in it. It was a place to go when I felt sad or stressed out or even happy. But to answer your question, I haven't played for about seven years."

"Wow," Valerie exclaimed. "That's just about impossible! You played so well just now it sounded like you practiced two hours a day every day for a week straight! Wow!" she repeated. "My mom said she tried to learn, but she didn't like to practice so she never got very good."

"True," Ann answered. "She wasn't fond of practicing. But like I said, I wasn't either. The difference between your mom and I was that music was like breathing to me. It never felt like work like it did to her."

"That's why Mama says it was a gift given to you by God."

"Why does she say that?"

"'Because,' she says, 'you can tell when someone is given a gift from God when what they do comes naturally.' Like a really good artist can see a picture in their head and paint it. Or someone who's good at writing poems can just sit down and write one really fast. I had to write a poem for class once and it took me all day. But the girl sitting next to me said she wrote it in her head on the bus ride home after school and all she had to do was put it on paper once she got home. So you see? You have a gift from God."

"Yeah, well you know where I stand on the God thing. You can preach it all day long, but I'm not buying it. So don't even waste your breath."

Figuring a subject change might be in order, she asked Valerie if she wanted to have lunch, then go back to the park.

Valerie said she was getting hungry, and would like to go to the park, but she'd rather Ann play one more song first.

"Okay," Ann said. "What are you in the mood for?"

"I don't know the names of any songs, but my mom says you guys used to dance together in the kitchen when your mom played a certain kind of song."

"Oh," Ann said. "You must be thinking of the Irish tunes my mom used to play. That's called Celtic music. I don't know how well I'll do, but it's worth a try."

"Oh yeah—that's what you said about the last one."

Ann agreed to go for round two. This variety of music was her mom's specialty. Oh how she used to love those spontaneous dance moments they shared as a family. Although she wasn't fond of revisiting this closed chapter of her life, she'd do anything for a guaranteed trip back to the park.

She was shocked by Valerie's reaction to the song. Not even two measures in and Valerie was off the couch and dancing up a storm all over the living room floor. Ann admitted to herself that it always was impossible to sit still when in the presence of a lively, Celtic tune. She almost smiled as all the memories came rushing back with full intensity. But instead, she stopped short.

"Why'd you do that?" Valerie asked. "I was just getting started."

"Sorry," Ann answered. "I'm just getting really hungry and I want to be sure we get back to the park for a while today."

"Okay," Valerie sighed. "But we could have just skipped the park. I like the music."

"Me too," Ann fibbed. "But I'm getting pretty hungry."

They pulled lunch together fairly quickly and ate it without much conversation. They'd both strayed deep into the woods of their individual thoughts and didn't feel inclined to share. After lunch they cleaned up and returned to the park.

It was a bit anticlimactic compared to their earlier visit. The wind had picked up and a few clouds had rolled in to block the sun. They visited the fountain and The Bean, then decided to go back home because it started getting cold.

Just as they began to walk away from The Bean, a couple approached them with two kids in tow. The mother walked up to Ann and asked if she'd be so kind as to snap a family photo for them. Ann explained that she wasn't all that good with a camera, but Valerie quickly jumped in to save the day.

"I'll take your picture for you," she said. "I love taking pictures!"

She took about four of them and as both parents were thanking her, a lively conversation sprang up between them. Within minutes Valerie knew all of their names, what state they lived in, the ages and grades of both kids, and how long they'd be in Chicago. They continued chatting while Ann observed once again, with great fascination, how her niece could instantly bond with strangers as though they were long lost bosom buddies. Being one who preferred living a private life behind thick walls with no close relationships or social ties, she could barely comprehend this affable approach to life. She, herself, was always so guarded, even with those she worked with every day. She began wondering if this had always been the case, when the couple thanked her and Valerie once again and they all began saying their goodbyes.

As they parted, Ann just had to ask, "So Valerie, how is it that you came to be so good at becoming instant friends with total strangers?"

Valerie answered, "'If possible, so far as it depends on you, be at peace with all men. Romans 12:18.' I learned this verse in Awana. At first I liked it because it helped me with the kids at school when they were being mean. I decided to try and be nice to them anyway. Then I decided to be as friendly as I could with everyone, whether I knew them or not. I just think it makes everything feel better when people are friendly with each other."

"Oh I see. What's Awana?"

"It's a church group for kids who get together on Wednesday nights to play games and learn Bible verses. I've been going for about two years. My mom thought it would help me make church friends since I didn't have any friends at school."

"Why are the kids at school so mean to you?" Ann asked.

Valerie lowered her eyes and answered, "I don't know why. I'm kind of quiet at school. Not like the popular girls."

"Well you sure aren't quiet around me and everyone else I've seen you meet."

"That's because grown-ups are usually nicer than kids my own age. Kids who are younger than me are always nicer too. And it's easy to talk to you because you're part of my family."

"Hmm. Well let's get home, shall we? It's getting cold."

Valerie shivered, "Yeah, it sure is."

Ann wanted to call her sister again the minute they walked through the door. She forced herself to resist, however, since her sister was obviously busy and already planning to call later. She just couldn't fathom how Valerie, a person everyone seemed to love, couldn't mix with the kids at school. She could tell Valerie didn't feel like talking about it. Not that it mattered to Ann all that much, but she couldn't help but wonder.

While she'd been rattling all this around in her head, Valerie had planted herself on the couch with a book she'd found in her backpack. Ann seized the opportunity to call her boss. She wanted to warn him that Valerie's stay would be extended, so her schedule was going to be somewhat crazy all week.

"Bad timing Ann," he responded. "You know we have to tie up the Green Jeans account by the end of next week at the latest."

"I know Marvin, but there's nothing I can do about it. There was no one else who could watch Valerie while my sister's out of town."

"Okay Ann. But you better work your magic with Green Jeans. This account is too big to lose and out of anyone else on the team, I know you're the one to get the job done."

"I appreciate your confidence Marv. I've been in tight situations before. You don't have to worry about Green Jeans."

"I have two words for you Finlayson: prove it."

"Okay Marv, don't worry. See you tomorrow."

"Yeah. See ya."

After Ann hung up, Valerie asked, "So having me for the week is going to cause problems at your job?"

"No. Not really. Wait—I thought you were reading a book. Do I have to make all my calls in the bedroom?"

"No," Valerie answered. "But when my name comes up I can't help but feel curious."

"I guess I can give you that one. I'm always curious about everything myself. My secretary tells me that's half the reason I have this position at the magazine. I have to research everything and understand all facets of every company I work with so I know who I'm dealing with right up front. Before I even get them on the phone, I know the names of several department heads, what their job functions are and where they all like to go for lunch. I learn all their idiosyncrasies and even what their kids do for extracurricular activities. Really puts me in the driver's seat when it comes to a power lunch. I can chat about all their kids' awards and what their spouses do for a living while winning them over and perfectly positioning them for the take."

Valerie's eleven-year-old brain could only follow portions of that dialogue so she was left with only one question. "What's 'the take?'"

"Oh—that's the part where you move in for the kill. You let them know that not only are you buddies now, and could probably attend all the same cocktail parties from here on out, but you're also the one who can put their company on the map like no other. You let them know that there is no one else like you and if they want to get anywhere with their business, they need *you* to help them get there."

"Hmmm. 'No one else like you.' There's a verse in the book of Isaiah that says the same thing about God. Let me try to remember …"

"Valerie, I'm sorry, but I really don't want to hear any more about what the Bible says. I don't read it. I don't want to read it. And I don't really care what it has to say about God or anything else. I hope you can get this through your skull. I know you and your mom do the church and Bible thing, but I don't. So please stop bringing it up every five minutes."

"Sorry Auntie Ann." As she said this, her eyes were once again focused on the floor. She didn't realize she'd been bringing it up "every five minutes." It honestly didn't feel that way to her. She couldn't help but share all the beautiful treasures that had been planted so deeply in her heart. Her relationship with God was all she had apart from what she shared with her mom. He was the only One who fully understood her. He was the only One who truly cared about her. He was the only One who was never too busy for her and never pushed her away when she needed someone. And, since she didn't have a dad on earth anymore, He was the only One who could fill that space.

How could her aunt be so against Him? How could she be so against His Word? Had she ever read it? Did she know the comforting words and wisdom that lay within its pages? Wasn't she the least bit curious about the amazing, sovereign God about whom it was written? How could anyone reject the absolute, unshakable security that existed in God alone? What she had learned in the last four years since her dad died was that this world can be a painful place, full of cruelty and bullying. So how could anyone in their right mind deny the tender, unwavering kindness of God?

She realized just then that her auntie wasn't evil after all. She was someone in desperate need of prayer. So Valerie resolved to get right on it and make Auntie Ann her top prayer project.

Ann, of course, was oblivious to the stir she'd caused in Valerie's heart. All she knew and cared about was that this dreaded Sunday was drawing closer to its end and they were fast approaching dinner, movie, shower and get-ready-for-school time. In addition to all that, there would also be a time-consuming phone call from Sara, so things were looking pretty good. So good in fact, she decided to pop in one of her workout videos to kill a little more time.

"You sure exercise a lot," Valerie commented.

"Yes I do," Ann said. "It gives me energy and keeps my head clear for all the work I have to do at the magazine. And—I've never wanted to be a flabby mess. I do everything I can to hang onto my size two."

Valerie rose to her feet. "It sounds like fun. Can I try?"

"Sure," Ann replied. "This particular video is kind of dancy and fun. You might like it."

Valerie seemed to take right to it. She kept right up with all the moves as though she'd practiced a hundred times. When the video was over, Ann had to ask, "Do you and your mom have some videos like this at home or something?"

"No, I've never done this before. It sure was fun though. I'm going to ask Mama if we can get one. I think she'd like it too."

"Wow," Ann replied. "You have some dance in you. You should take lessons."

"I would love to do something like that. But we don't have a lot of money for extras. It's enough that we have to rent a tuba for band."

"Do you like playing the tuba?"

"Well … not really all that much," Valerie answered. "But I had to pick something at the beginning of the year. We have to take band in fifth grade."

"Well, if your mom gets this new job she might be able to finance some lessons that have more to do with where your true interests lie."

"Maybe," Valerie agreed. "But even if she can't, it's okay with me. We have all sorts of fun even if we can't spend money on extras."

"That's a very good attitude. Meanwhile, it's almost four—we should figure out what to do for dinner. And, I'm thinking there might be time for a movie, as long as we first take care of showers and getting ready for tomorrow."

"Yeah, I guess," Valerie responded. "I usually have to go to bed at 8:30 on school nights."

Ann was unable to mask her enthusiasm as she asked Valerie what she might like for dinner. They were finally coming down homestretch of the longest day of her life and 8:30 could not come soon enough. Dinner choices were made and Valerie was first in the shower. Of course, this was the precise moment Sara chose to call.

The phone rang just as Valerie was stepping into the shower.

"Hey Sara, bad timing."

"How'd you know it was me?" Sara asked.

"Because I already talked to my boss and no one else ever calls me unless I ask them to."

"Wow sister, we need to fix *that*!"

"What do you mean? Do you still think I need a boyfriend?"

"Yeah, maybe. It might not be such a bad idea. I mean, you haven't been serious with anyone since Doug and that was how many years ago?"

"Sara," Ann replied. "How many times do I have to tell you I don't want or need a man in my life? I'm perfectly fine with the way things are. I love my job and I can do whatever I want in my spare time. Some women would kill to have my life."

"I don't think that's true," Sara said, "because most women are relational. They like hanging out with other people. Especially members of the opposite sex. But you, my clamshell sister, seem to be missing an element or five in that closed heart of yours. But I'll stop torturing you with my 'you need a boyfriend' lecture. Is Val handy?"

"No. That's what I meant when I said your timing is bad. Valerie just stepped into the shower."

"Oh rats. How's she doing? Were you guys able to figure out what to do after I got off the phone from you earlier? Did you break out your violin?"

"Actually, I did. And Valerie really enjoyed it. Did you know she's always wanted to learn how to play?"

"Of course I know that—she talks about it all the time. Just another reason for why it would be so great to land this job. I'd actually be able to afford a few extras. I wish you weren't so down on God. I'd like to be able to ask you to pray for me."

"Yep, well, I'm not going there. But I do want to ask a question while Valerie's still in the shower. She keeps bringing up how mean the kids are at school. Why are they so mean to her?"

Sara's voice grew grave. "After Jim died, Valerie shut down. She didn't want to play at school during recess. She stopped raising her hand to answer questions in class. She stopped talking to the kids at school and they started making fun of her for being so 'weird.' It got worse when the only kid who'd have anything to do with her was already tagged as the geekiest kid in first grade. It's consistently gone from bad to worse and I can't stand the thought of her being in that school for one more day. I would so love a fresh start. For both of us. See—there I go again—verging on the precipice of asking you to pray for me. Will I ever learn?"

"I guess not," Ann answered.

Just then, Valerie came into the living room with her pajamas on and her head wrapped in a towel. "Well looky here—saved by the kid in the towel." Ann turned to Valerie and said, "It's your mom."

While Valerie and her mom talked, Ann got busy in the kitchen. She decided to make herself gluten-free eggrolls from the freezer, and mac and cheese for Valerie. While she was getting things assembled for a quick prep, she began to recall what happened with Doug.

He was the one she knew she'd spend the rest of her life with. Until she discovered she was nothing but a fling to him. Although they were together through most of high school, she didn't have what it took to beat the top yearbook coordinator and drama queen of the school. This was the knockout, bleached blonde who got the lead in every high school play. And play she did. It only took one for her to steal Doug's heart away. *Oh well*, she inaudibly reminded herself, *if it was so easily stolen, it was never really mine to begin with*. Then she chastised herself right out loud in the kitchen, "Oh please—a little more syrup on those pancakes? Goodness—could you get any more cliché?" She rolled her eyes at herself one more time as Valerie entered the kitchen.

"My mom wants to talk to you again," she informed Ann while handing her the phone.

"Hey," was all Ann had to say. She knew her sister would take the conversational lead.

"Hey Ann, I just wanted to thank you one more time. Valerie told me all about your day. And although I know hanging out with kids isn't your thing, she really had fun today. She told me about that Charles kid and I love her heart. She asked me to pray for both Charles and his mom. She also told me about you playing the violin and your little dance session. So come on Ann, don't tell me you didn't have a little bit of fun today."

"Sorry Sara, I guess I'm a good actress. Of course, not so good that I could compete with Alicia in high school, but good enough to suit my own needs."

"Oh yeah," Sara remembered. "Her name was Alicia."

"Yes, and thanks for bringing it up by the way. Here I was, living in my blissful little fog, and then you have to go and bring up Doug. Oh well—I can push him out of my head just as fast as you walked him back in."

"Sorry, hon. I'd like to see you get together with someone again someday. They're not all creeps like Doug was and I wish you could become acquainted with a more positive side of the dating game. I mean, just having had the short time I had with Jim has convinced me that there's such a thing as a positive relationship. So my heart isn't closed. I just wish yours wasn't either."

"Well, I hate to change the subject dear sister, but it's dinnertime. How's about we touch base tomorrow?"

"Okay," Sara said. "Talk to you tomorrow."

As Sara ended the call, she was overwhelmed with concern for her sister. After their parents died, Ann withdrew into some sort of cocoon. She began to isolate and bury herself in all things solitary. Whether it was schoolwork, exercise, or this prestigious magazine job, Ann kept herself shut off from the rest of the world. But worse than all that was her insensitivity. Although she'd never been the emotional type, she seemed to have become an unfeeling hull of a human that repelled anyone who came anywhere near.

Had they not been raised in the same home, Sara would have left Ann in the dust years ago. She certainly wasn't the type of person Sara would keep around as a friend, or even an acquaintance. This dispassionate coldness is why Sara was so uncomfortable about leaving Valerie with Ann, but she had no choice. There just wasn't anyone else who could help out. Then there was Ann's enormous ego. Sara had never seen the likes. According to Ann, there was only one person on the planet who deserved undivided attention at all times. And she could be so condescending. And disgustingly vain. "Okay—enough," Sara said to herself.

She had so worked herself up over her sister's depraved character that she decided she'd better do something about it. So she dove right in: "Lord, I'm sorry I'm so worked up over my sister's terrible character flaws. It isn't like I don't have any of my own. But Lord, at least I'm aware of mine. Ann doesn't even *see* the sorry state of her heart. She's completely blind to who she is and how she treats people. Lord I just beg You to step in and do something. I don't even have a specific request for what You might do. You're the One with all the good ideas. All I know is that my sister is in a very bad place. Her heart is completely shut down and she's totally isolated. She hurts others from her imagined seat of superiority and she doesn't even know she's doing it. But Lord, how could she be expected to behave otherwise when she doesn't know You? Until we come to know the Author of love, none of us can reach outside ourselves to love others. And Ann's so locked up inside herself that she doesn't even know she needs You. So please unlock her Lord. Please introduce Yourself to her and reveal to her how deeply she needs You. In Jesus' name, amen."

While Sara prayed in her hotel room, Ann and Valerie sat down to dinner. After dinner, Valerie was put on cleanup duty while Ann showered. When Ann came out of the shower, she suggested Valerie get ready for the morning before pulling out a movie. So Valerie laid out her clothes and made her lunch. She picked out a movie without even asking for her aunt's input. In fact, she figured she'd probably end up watching the movie by herself. But this time it didn't bother her. She was on a mission. The minute the lights went out and it was time to go to sleep, she was going to pray for Auntie Ann. And she knew if she stuck to this mission every single day, God would do something. She didn't know exactly what He'd do, but she knew it would be big ...

Chapter 4

4:45 a.m. came early as Ann struggled to get out from under the covers. She'd set the alarm early to ensure she had enough time to get ready for work, fight the foreign concept of rush hour traffic, and possibly get lost on the way to school. Seven o'clock was just around the corner and she didn't want to make Valerie late for school.

Valerie, on the other hand, had set her phone alarm to six o'clock. Since she was unaware of her aunt's master plan, she was a bit rattled when the elliptical shook her from her slumber at five. She shot up from her bed and rubbed her burning eyes before getting up to put her bed away.

She was so sleepy that everything seemed to take twice as long as it normally would. She got dressed in a daze and took forever deciding what to have for breakfast. Settling on waffles and syrup, she'd finally sat down at the kitchen table when Ann informed her she didn't have much time left to get ready. So she ate breakfast as quickly as possible, swallowed a gulp of milk and sped to the bathroom to brush her teeth and hair.

As she looked in the mirror to finish with her hair, she remembered her mission. Last night she had vowed to pray fervently for her aunt to change. Then she remembered something her mom had mentioned many times over the years. She always spoke of how God's Word is so full of wisdom, that sometimes you could quote it to people in need of such wisdom and they wouldn't even know it was from the Bible. She decided to try this on her aunt, on top of all the prayers, figuring it might help things along. Right then, she resolved to look for as many opportunities as possible to speak the Word of God to her aunt for the rest of her visit.

After getting off the elliptical, Ann rushed to get ready. She'd laid her clothes out the night before and as she had her makeup routine down to a fine science, that didn't take too long. Hair went up, coffee was assembled for the road and breakfast was a banana she threw in her bag for later. At 6:05 she asked Valerie if she was ready to go. On their way to the garage, Ann expressed her dismay over leaving later than she'd planned.

Valerie added another piece of woe to her pot. "I'm sorry to tell you this Auntie, but Mom's car has to warm up awhile before driving it anywhere. It's really old and doesn't run very well if you don't warm it up first."

"Great," Ann grimaced.

Valerie showed Ann how to work the GPS and it wasn't until about 6:15 that they pulled out of the garage. Because Ann's frustration was so visible, Valerie tried not to talk much.

Fighting through the heart of the city to get onto the freeway was a living nightmare. Ann's steady stream of impatience made Valerie cringe to the depths of her soul. She was accustomed to people at church who strove to rein in such strong emotions. Even the mean kids at school were like docile bunny rabbits compared to her aunt.

"Where'd you get your license Bozo? You know—they're not legal when you dig them out of a Cracker Jack box … Gas is on the right, you moron … Hello—green means go …" And on it went until they got to the freeway.

By the time they reached the on-ramp, Valerie could no longer contain herself.

"You know Auntie Ann—you really shouldn't talk like that to people."

"Why not? They can't hear me."

"Yeah but, 'the mouth speaks out of that which fills the heart.' So if this meanness toward people is in your heart and you speak it in places where they can't hear you, one of these days you're going to slip and say horrible things to someone's face because you're so used to speaking your hate."

"I suppose that's another Bible thing?" Ann groused.

"Sure is Auntie Ann. Um—I think we just passed the exit to get to my school."

"Errrg," Ann growled as she positioned herself to take the next exit and backtrack. Then she plastered on a smile and jeered, "All this scintillating conversation so enthralled me that I was completely distracted."

At that moment, Valerie was feeling thankful for the fact that at least her aunt didn't ever seem to swear. The kids at school did all the time. And although Auntie had the personality for it, she hadn't uttered a single swear word since Valerie arrived. While she continued to ponder this, they turned onto the street where her school was located.

When they arrived at the front entrance Ann asked, "Do you need me to walk you in or anything?"

"No thank you Auntie, I'm fine."

Ann popped the trunk and watched as Valerie struggled to get to the front door with her huge backpack, lunch bag, and tuba case. It barely registered with her, however, as she prepared to battle traffic again to get herself to work. She hadn't driven and parked in downtown Chicago for so long, she barely knew which street to try and park on. *Oh well, point and shoot,* was what she told herself as she pulled back out onto the street and headed toward the freeway.

Trying to get to the office from Valerie's school was just as frustrating as it was driving to the school. Possibly even more so. Traffic had thickened and people seemed to be weaving in and out more than before. One driver cut her off and she barely missed rear-ending him. Of course, she had plenty to say about all this, but since she didn't have the voice of conscience sitting next to her, her comments grew even more colorful.

As she neared The Loop, she braced herself for trying to find street parking near the Sears Tower. She decided it would be best to take the first spot she found, so she ended up on Franklin. She openly snarled at the meter for robbing her at the rate of $6.50 per hour. By the time she reached the office, she did not possess a single nerve fiber that was capable of handling stress.

She was barely through the door when the department secretary, Cassie, told her she had a call holding on line four.

"Can I at least hang up my coat?" Ann snapped. "Who is it anyway?"

"Murphy Lawman with Green Jeans."

"Oh goody. Thanks Cassie."

She tried to gain some composure as she picked up the phone. "Hello Murphy," she spoke with as much brightness as she could muster. "Thanks for getting back to me so soon. I'm a little pressed for time at the moment, so I'm hoping to fire a few questions at you and get some short version answers. And I do mean short."

Her secretary's ears perked up. Ann was already worked up about something. She figured it wouldn't be long into the conversation before Ann's trademark rudeness would rise to the surface. Of course, this wasn't the president of Green Jeans. Ann would tend more closely to her manners if it was. But Murphy was just an assistant. So Cassie tuned in.

"Like I said Murphy, do you think your team will be able to manage a four-page spread in time for the May issue? I need to know whether or not to push it aside until June … Murph … Murph … Murphy," she barked, "I asked for the short version please. I don't care if your boss is out of town and hasn't checked the numbers yet …" Cutting herself off, she said, "Look—I'll email you all of my questions and you can give me all your short and simple answers once you have them. But if I don't hear from you by Friday, I'll assume you don't wish to be in the May issue. And I have to tell you Murphy, shorts season is coming, so you may want to act fast if you hope to catch the summer shoppers … Murphy … Murph … No, I do not want to hear about why you might not make it. A simple yes or no is all I need." With a final breath of exasperation she added, "Just look for the email," before abruptly hanging up the phone.

As she hung up, she caught Cassie glaring at her. "What?" she sneered.

"Do you have to be so short with absolutely everyone you encounter? I'm amazed that you lure, capture and keep any of your clients."

"Yeah, well in business it's necessary to be direct and to the point. If other people can't grasp the importance of verbal economy, I can't help but educate them. It's a hard-edged, competitive world out there and the course of business might take a turn for the better if I educate one moron at a time. And you can't get to the top …"

"I know," Cassie sighed, "unless you have what it takes to climb the ladder. Well, get down from your soapbox, here comes a delivery."

A courier approached Ann's cubicle and stood looking at her.

"Well?" she asked. She interrupted the pregnant pause that followed by asking, "Do you speak?"

Obviously flustered, the courier fumbled with the words, "Are you Ann Finlayson?"

"Yes I am, so what next?"

"Sign here please," the courier responded as his shaking hands handed her the delivery register.

She grabbed it out of his hand, impatiently scribbled her name and practically knocked him over with it while handing it back. Then he just stood there.

"Well?" she asked.

"Just wondering where you'd like me to put the package, ma'am."

"You can drop it in the garbage can for all I care. It's nothing but some small, hometown clothing line sending a sample … Just put it over there against the wall." With her classic fake smile, she added, "Is there any other guidance you'll be needing today?"

"No ma'am," he replied as he sullenly slinked away.

Bradley Newman, one of the assistant editors, caught this entire exchange as he stood waiting to ask Ann a question. As the courier left, Bradley tapped him on the shoulder and asked, "How's it going Bud?"

"First day on the job," the courier answered, "I'm kind of nervous."

"Oh—you're doing great," Bradley beamed. His encouragement sent the courier away with a smile of relief as he went on to face the rest of his day. Once he was out of earshot, Bradley turned to Ann and asked, "A little hard on him weren't you?"

"No … maybe." She grunted a note of exasperation and continued, "People like that just irritate me."

Cassie chimed in. "Who doesn't irritate you?"

"Good question," Ann replied. "But you know, I came here today with every one of my nerves already frayed by having to drive in and park. And I can't believe parking is $6.50 an hour. That's outlandish!"

Bradley said, "It's cheaper once you get outside The Loop. And did you know you can only park on the street for two hours?"

Ann was mortified. "Are you kidding me? You mean if I want to park on the street for the day, I'll have to keep moving my car?"

"Pretty much," Bradley said. "But the parking garage is only $15.00 a day. Still pricey, but if you do the math, an eight hour day on the street could add up to about $52.00."

Ann put her hands on her head and raised her voice to a high-pitched lament. "This is outrageous. And totally frustrating. I'm already behind on everything today." Then she lowered her voice and asked, "Bradley, do you think you could move my car into the garage?"

"I certainly can and I certainly will. What are you driving, where are you parked and where are the keys?"

As Ann answered all of Bradley's questions and gave him the keys, he told her she'd have to tell him why she's driving and parking in the first place. He knew she lived downtown and normally took the L or walked to work.

Once the coast was clear, Cassie openly called Ann to the carpet regarding her most recent advertising decisions.

"Are you still going to use that jeans ad even though almost everyone in this office is opposed to it? There is nothing decent about their ads. Their models are all scantily clad and overly suggestive. And let's not forget the smoky eyes and pouty lips. There's even a small coalition of women who have come against Green Jeans because of it. But you must know that. It's headline news."

"Cassie," Ann responded. "One of the reasons *Top Rung Magazine* has skyrocketed to the top over the last few years has been because of the smart, savvy ads I brought on board. Now I intend to keep *Top Rung* on the cutting edge of the media industry. We will surely lose our present position if we must bow to the whims and wants of the National Knitting League. Leave all that soft, cushy, sugary stuff to the *Home and Garden* people." She punctuated her vexation by sharply snapping her hand in the air.

"Wow. You are a piece of work."

"She certainly is," came a voice from the next cubicle over.

It was Sean Mobley, the newest member of the advertising team. He came around the corner and said, "You know Cassie—I did catch this entire conversation and I have to agree with Ann. With today's technology and the constantly evolving innovations of the new generation, we've catapulted into a new era. Move over Grandma. Hello Amazon, Facebook and Twitter."

Ann raised her eyebrows and gloated victoriously at Cassie, while Cassie simmered silently at her desk.

Just as Bradley returned from moving the car, Ann began throwing everything from her desk onto the floor. Without looking up she asked, "Have you seen my pen?" Before he could answer she yelled loudly enough for the entire office to hear, "Does anyone have my pen?"

Bradley asked, "Is it gold with black lettering?"

Ann said, "Yes," and he told her he'd be back in a second.

"Do you mean this pen?" he asked while holding a gold pen up in the air.

"Yeah, that's the one. Where did you find it?"

"I thought it looked familiar this morning as I passed by someone's desk on the way in. I won't tell you who the 'someone' is though. I'm a great respecter of human life. I will, however, inform this fairly new individual that this pen is not available for use by anyone but you."

"Thank you," Ann replied. "My dad got it for me when I graduated from college. It's a Mont Blanc and he had it specially engraved for me. He said I would do great things with this pen."

Bradley was surprised by Ann's candor. The Ice Queen rarely displayed moments of vulnerability.

Ann broke his thoughts by asking, "So Bradley, what's your take on the Green Jeans ad campaign?"

"Well, since you asked, all I can tell you is this: When my brother died, I got very tight with my niece. I wanted to be a sort of father figure for her since she'd lost the man who would normally play such an integral role in her life. He was an incredible dad. And my niece, Amy, was terrific too. She was bright, she was fun and she was the light of everyone's life. She was also innocent and pure. Not the mall-hanging, boy-chasing, boldly made-up type like so many girls her age. My brother and sister-in-law took great pains to ensure Amy would steer clear of that peer group and those choices. All that said, had she ever been approached to model for one of those Green Jeans ads, I would have protested with every fiber of my being. And if my sister-in-law ever underwent a radical character change and said yes to such a thing, I would have shown up at the photo shoot with a very large coat, thrown it over my niece, tossed her over my shoulder and carried her kicking and screaming right out the door, never to return. Does that answer your question?"

"Why yes, it most certainly does," Ann said.

After that, Bradley handed Ann her keys and said he had to go have a quick meeting with the boss.

This time, it was Cassie's turn to gloat. Rather than verbalize her sense of triumph, however, she decided to change the subject. "Hey, we're having a potluck for Nancy next Monday, what can you bring?"

"I don't know," Ann replied. "Put me down for some cookies."

"Okay, what kind are you making?"

Ann declared with a false grin, sarcastically batting eyelashes and her best mock-Southern accent, "Why, I'll just whip up a batch or two of my ever-so-delectable chocolate chip cookies."

"Yum! Those will be a hit!" Cassie smiled.

"Well, sorry to burst your bubble but I don't really bake. I barely even cook. So—I have a ten in my purse—why don't you just pick me up whatever sounds good next time you go to the store between now and then?"

"You know," Cassie prodded. "If it weren't for Nancy, you wouldn't even have a job. She's been with the company for thirty years. Don't you think you could put in a little effort here?"

"Yes, she hired me. But my ingenuity and hard work is what has raised this department to its present level. And you work for me, remember?"

"Oh thank you so much for the unpleasant reminder."

Before Cassie could speak another word, Ann fanned the ten dollar bill in the air, singing the word, "cookies," before placing it on Cassie's desk and turning to walk away.

Cassie caught her mid-stride, however, saying she had two more questions to ask. "Before I forget, Nancy wants to know if you want any of her plants. She's moving out of the office this Friday."

"No, I'm no good with plants. I just kill them. What's your second question?"

"I'm just wondering why you're suddenly driving to work."

Ann told Cassie all about having to take her eleven-year-old niece in while her sister was in Colorado. She told her about having to drive Valerie to and from school and basically let Cassie know how much of an inconvenience it was to have to do all this.

Cassie asked, "What's all this 'have to' jazz? Why can't you just enjoy your niece? Eleven is a great age."

"Kids fall into the same category as plants," Ann answered. "I'm no good with either of them."

"Well you should send her my way. My daughter's near the same age and while Craig's in the hospital it might be a pleasant distraction."

"Craig's in the hospital again?"

"Yeah—they're going to put him through some pretty heavy chemo so they thought it would be best to keep him at the hospital. Things haven't been looking so good."

As tears threatened to invade Cassie's eyes, Ann looked for a way of escape.

Thankfully, Bradley chose that moment to re-enter the scene. He said, "Hey Ann, Marvin wants you to assemble the advertising troops ASAP. He says he knows about the dissension in the ranks regarding Green Jeans and he wants you to quell all the interoffice mumbling and grumbling. He's tired of hearing it and hearing about it. And since you and he are on the same page, he'd like you to preside over the meeting."

Ann happily complied. Before moving down the hallway she shot a "so there" look over her shoulder to Cassie, but Cassie ignored it. She did, however, get up from her desk and follow Ann in order to take notes if need be. Once Ann got everyone together, she began the impromptu meeting.

"Look," she began. "I know a lot of you are opposed to this four-page spread we're aggressively pursuing with Green Jeans, but I want you all to know we're going forth with the ad and Marvin is all for it."

A few protesting voices piped in with, "But it isn't family-friendly," and "How would you feel if it was your own daughter?" But Ann put her hand up and drove the meeting to its inevitable end.

"I'd like to remind all of you that you still have jobs because we've been doing everything we can to keep *Top Rung* on the cutting edge. We are a magazine that stays on top of the competition through up-to-the-minute advertising, snappy articles, timely fashion and innovative health pieces. We aren't here to be family-friendly. We're here to appeal to the mainstream masses who want to look good and feel good, and who have the dollars to support those desires. We exist to help the rich get richer and to supply them with solutions to all their travel needs, gadget needs, home décor needs, fitness needs and fashion needs. We serve the upper class masses who can afford luxury condos, facelifts, designer dogs and sixty-foot yachts. Our job is not to be warm and fuzzy, but to maintain a clientele that will keep our financial boat afloat. Have I made myself clear?"

"Perfectly," Sean answered. "And I like what I hear. I believe your priorities are quite in order and you *are* head of this department for a reason. You follow your instincts and you haven't gone wrong yet." At this, he gave her a private wink, causing her face to flush with a deep shade of crimson. Cassie was the only one to catch it. "And, might I add, anyone who can't handle the goals and objectives of this department may do well to consider the alternative. After all, the chief editor of this magazine is full throttle on the Green Jeans ad. So take it from one who knows—life in the unemployment line can be a bit dismal."

Ann was so grateful for this support. Until now, she'd felt like an absolute loner in all this. Even Bradley, who seemed to be a potential ally, proved to be in full opposition to this ad campaign.

As they broke up and moved back to their cubicles, Cassie whispered, "You actually like that jerk?"

"What jerk?"

"You know very well I'm referring to Sean."

"What do you mean, 'like him'?" Ann asked.

"I mean, he made you blush."

Ann was embarrassed that Cassie noticed. She made the excuse, "I'm just not used to public attention."

"Yeah, sure, okay," was all Cassie had to say about that.

Valerie spent most of recess in her favorite bathroom stall. She wasn't in the mood to do this day, let alone the playground. She desperately wanted to talk to her mom, but knew this wouldn't be a good idea. Her mom was still in the middle of the interviewing process and couldn't be interrupted. And, she didn't want to make her mom worry. She just wished she had someone to talk to about how mean the kids had been getting lately. Last Friday, one of them said they'd like to take her long blonde hair, wrap it around her pretty little neck and choke her with it. Although she felt safe with the band teacher, she didn't want to tell her because she was afraid of word getting out that she'd tattled. Then the kids would really pound her. If she knew her mom was getting this job for sure, it wouldn't matter if she told or not. They'd be packing up and moving over spring break, never to be heard from again. But when they spoke on the phone last night, her mom made it sound like they'd need a few more days to decide.

Ever since that one girl threatened Valerie the way she did last Friday, Valerie felt afraid to be anywhere near those kids. All she had to do was make it to Thursday. Friday was a teacher in-service day and the following week was spring break.

A part of her wished she would have told her mom about what happened, but her mom was so preoccupied with packing and making sure to include everything for the trip. While doing laundry and cleaning out the fridge, she also fretted over whether or not Valerie had all her school clothes and everything else she'd need for the week. Again—Valerie didn't want to be a bother to her mom and worse, make her worry.

She couldn't tell Auntie Ann because Auntie didn't seem like the type of person who would care very much. All she seemed to care about was herself. In fact, she'd probably get annoyed if Valerie mentioned any details to her. Valerie just didn't understand her aunt at all.

Mostly, Valerie longed from here to high heaven to tell on these kids so they could get what they deserved. Provided, of course, that her mom got the new job. Then they could just leave the state and the school forever. But without knowing what was happening in Colorado, it was too risky to tell anyone.

So Valerie decided to have a chat with the only One she knew it was completely safe to talk to.

She prayed her mom would get the job in Colorado. She prayed someone could get the message about these mean kids and make something happen so they wouldn't be able to hurt anyone, ever again. She prayed she could do a better job in this situation. She asked God to help her forgive these kids. She asked Him if He could please change their hearts so they wouldn't be so mean. She prayed her aunt would come to know Him and that she would change. And just as she was about to utter another prayer, the bell rang. Recess was over.

Ann wrapped things up and prepared to cross town to pick Valerie up from school. She knew this drive wouldn't be as bad as the morning commute due to the fact that the time crunch was minimized. She didn't have to get Valerie to school by such and such and get herself to work on time as well. She did, however, have the band teacher to consider. Because this teacher gave of her own time to accommodate Valerie, Ann wanted to respect that sacrifice by being on time. She cut her day short by nearly half an hour.

The trip to school wasn't half bad. She navigated through traffic quite well and found the exit for the school the first time, instead of passing it and having to backtrack. When she got to the school, she texted Valerie to let her know she was outside the building. Valerie came to the car fully loaded and Ann popped the trunk so she could put her things in the car.

On the way home, Ann told Valerie they would be attending a Tae Kwon Do class at seven. That meant Valerie would have to do her homework, eat dinner and do whatever it would take to get ready for the morning, before they left for class.

Valerie didn't have much to say to this information beyond a one-word response. All she could think about was her mom's nightly phone call and getting to Thursday in one piece. All she could see was Felicity's face right up against hers, threatening to choke her with her hair. She couldn't understand what made those kids hate her so much. She tried to be nice to them, but nothing worked. She wished she could catch a magic carpet to Colorado right now and be done with this nightmare.

She was happy she didn't have much homework. By the time they got home, there wouldn't be much time to fit everything in before Auntie Ann's class. The minute they got to the condo, she jumped in the shower, made her bed and did everything else to prepare for the morning. She told her aunt she wasn't hungry for dinner and spent the rest of the time before Tae Kwon Do doing homework.

The class was across town so it took twenty minutes to get there. On the way, Valerie asked what Tae Kwon Do was and Ann provided her with a detailed description. Valerie asked how long Ann had been practicing Tae Kwon Do and Ann told her it had been about seven years. Valerie asked if there were belt colors in Tae Kwon Do like there were in some of the other martial arts and Ann told her there were.

"So what color are you on?" Valerie asked.

"I actually have my black belt," Ann replied.

"No way!" Valerie exclaimed. "Wow—so you're really good at it! What do you do once you have a black belt?"

"Well … my instructor wants me to teach, but I don't want to."

"Why not?" Valerie asked.

"Because," Ann said. "I wouldn't want to lose my love of this art form. I feel if I were to teach it, it would no longer be my number one oasis. I don't think I'd be a very good teacher if what served me best as a haven from stress became a duty to perform. So I just pop in every Monday and Thursday for what has become my favorite workout."

"My friend Jeffrey used to take Karate. Then he moved away. What made you want to learn Tae Kwon Do?"

"I wanted to be able to protect myself. It only took one time for a stranger to approach me inappropriately to convince me to seek out some sort of self-defense class. And since my plan was to live and work in downtown Chicago, relying only on my feet and public transportation to get from place to place, I figured the sooner the better. So I found the place we're going to now."

"A stranger tried to get you? Were you scared?"

"I was terrified. I was on my way to the train station when someone tried to grab me. Fortunately, another man came along and intervened. That's another thing that convinced me to take classes. I didn't want to be some damsel in distress who needed a man to come along and save me. What if that man hadn't shown up that night? I might not be talking to you right now. And, I've always believed that guys shouldn't be the only tough ones in the world. We girls can be tough too. And we need to be."

"Wow," Valerie marveled. "You're just like Katniss Everdeen."

"Who is that?" Ann asked.

"She's a character in one of the movies we rented."

"I guess I'll have to find out later. We're at our stop. And just to let you know—this class is intense—so no more talking until it's over."

The class rented space from a dance studio, so the room they entered was lined with mirrors and ballet bars all around. Valerie was instantly intrigued. She pictured herself coming to this room with a boombox full of music, and endless hours of dancing. She would dance to her heart's content, stop long enough to catch her breath, and start all over again. She was in love with this room.

Meanwhile, Ann was being greeted by all her fellow students. They didn't seem quite as interested in Valerie as the yoga girls had been, so Valerie just stood back, listened and observed.

One slender, short, red-headed woman put her arm around Valerie's aunt and said, "Hey Ann—so good to touch base with you. Dave and I are leaving in the morning to go to Florida for a week. He won the trip as a bonus for winning so many cases last month. In fact, they're making him a partner. So I won't be in the office all week. Not like you ever need me or anything, but I wanted you to know. He just found out about all this last Friday. It's kind of exciting."

As the two of them continued to talk, Valerie was able to surmise that this lady was Ann's doctor and her husband was an attorney. That's about all she could understand.

As she was piecing this together, a very lean, muscular, gray-haired Asian man took the floor with a great air of confidence. Valerie figured he must be the teacher. As he stood in the front of the room, the students began lining up in rows. Ann and the doctor were in the front row with two others. Valerie noticed they were all wearing black belts. In fact, as the lineup continued, she noticed all the rows were comprised of students wearing the same color belts. As soon as they were all in place, they bowed twice. Next, they sat on the floor and there was silence for about two minutes. After that they stretched, then finally got to the good stuff.

Valerie was fascinated by all the rapid movements and high kicks her aunt was able to perform. Some of the movements reminded her of a complex dance routine. It didn't matter that she was unable to speak or participate. Watching this was just as entertaining as any of her favorite movies. And she couldn't believe her aunt. She really did seem like a character straight out of *Hunger Games*. One would never guess by looking at Auntie Ann that she had this ferocious warrior living inside her. She could be mean, but her physical abilities appeared far more threatening than anything she could do verbally.

Valerie was so mesmerized that the ninety minutes of class flew right by. Before she knew it, class was over and everyone was saying their goodbyes. She heard the doctor asking her aunt whether or not she had her cell number. Auntie Ann told her she did, then they hugged and parted ways.

As they left the building, Valerie was loaded with questions.

"Why did you bow twice at the beginning of class?" she asked.

"We bow first to the flags, then to the Master. Did you see the two flags in front of the ..."

Valerie cut her off with another question. "Why were there some people in the back who didn't have the same uniforms as the rest of you?"

"Because the beginners start at the back and ..."

Valerie interrupted again, and this time Ann bit her head off.

"If you want me to answer a question that *you* ask, please don't interrupt while I'm answering *your* question.

"Sorry Auntie," Valerie murmured with her head lowered and her enthusiasm fully deflated. She was quiet for the rest of the ride home, which might not have been the best thing. Being thrust into silence enabled her to retract into her own thoughts which caused everything that had been happening at school lately to flood back into her mind. Having just witnessed her aunt acting like some warrior woman from a movie didn't help. It only served to remind her of how small and mousy she was by comparison.

By the time they got home, Valerie had herself convinced that she was totally worthless and probably deserved everything those kids were doing to her. After all, she didn't have her aunt's great confidence or the ability to fight anyone off physically *or* verbally.

Ann noticed the radical silence and knew her statement had everything to do with it. But she never could understand why a person would ask a question, then talk all over the top of the answer. Once again, she found herself at completely irritated odds with all of humanity. But she knew Sara's phone call was coming and she wanted to redeem her present "bad aunt" score before Valerie got a chance to tattle on her. However, they were so close to the condo that she decided to wait and talk to Valerie once they got inside and could sit down.

Once they got there, Ann immediately defended herself to Valerie.

"Look—I know I shut you down by saying what I did, but you have to understand that if you ask a question, you should wait for the full answer before firing another question. Otherwise, why ask a question in the first place?"

With her eyes full of tears and a face stained red with emotion, Valerie blurted, "I'm just not good at anything."

"What do you mean you're not good at anything?"

"Well … I'm good at something," Valerie sniffed. "Mama says I have a green thumb. I told you my dad and I did a lot of gardening. Once I planted irises for Mama that grew to be four feet tall."

Ann was puzzled by this sudden shift from raw emotion to garden chit chat. "Well, that's pretty amazing. I kill every plant I get. People at the office even stopped buying me flowers for my birthday. Now they just buy me things like pine nuts and gift certificates for the health food store. But back to you. What's so bad about having a green thumb?"

"It's okay, but it's nothing great like what you can do. You really are like Katniss Everdeen. You could be a superhero in a movie. You could be a special agent for the FBI or a bodyguard for someone famous. You could whip anyone on the street who tried to attack you. All I can do is grow plants."

"You can also dance. Not everyone can do that."

"I know, but dance classes cost so much money and even if I were a great dancer, it still wouldn't be as cool as what you can do."

"What's so cool about being able to fight? Why is this so much better than having a green thumb or being able to dance?"

"Because being able to fight like you can is the sort of thing people really admire. If I could fight like you, I'd probably be more popular at school. And if any of the kids ever tried to …"

The phone rang. Sara's perfect timing again. Valerie's face lit up instantly.

"Why don't you go ahead and answer it?" Ann said.

While Sara's phone call continued to lift Valerie's countenance, Ann went and made sure everything was ready for the morning. They were already off schedule by about half an hour and she was hoping this phone call wouldn't take too long. She didn't have much to report to her sister, so when it was her turn to talk, she intended to keep it short.

Sara asked how things were going and Ann said, "Fine." She asked how the drive to school was this morning and Ann said the same thing.

"Okay then. Since you don't have a lot to say, I'll just drop this little news bomb on you. They want the final three candidates to stay through next Monday. So if I make it that far, I'll either catch a late flight Monday evening, or first thing Tuesday morning."

"Oh my heavenly days," Ann said. "I guess I don't have to tell you what an inconvenience this is because you already know. Oh well, Cassie at work said she'd like to have Valerie over sometime to hang out with her daughter—that could buy me some sanity time. I've never heard of an interview process that took this long, but I guess it is what it is."

"I do wish you could just enjoy Valerie. She's really a ball of fun to have around. But I haven't seen any evidence of your former self showing up anytime soon, the one who *used* to be a ball of fun. I'll just have to keep praying for you."

"Yeah—you do that. Watch me resist. Funny you said that though. Cassie said the same thing …"

"What 'same thing'? I said about five things."

"The 'thing' about just enjoying Valerie. You and Cassie seem to be on the same page about a lot of things."

"I think I like this Cassie girl," Sara smiled, then yawned. "Well, we all need to get to bed, so I'll check back in tomorrow. Can you pass me back to Val?"

"Okay, here she comes," Ann replied.

After they all got off the phone, Ann announced it was time to go to bed.

"Aw," Valerie complained. "I was hoping for some ice cream."

"Sorry—you'll have to wait till tomorrow. It's almost 9:30 and we have an early getup."

They quickly finished getting ready for bed. Valerie didn't know how exhausted she was until her head hit the pillow. She struggled to stay awake long enough to squeeze out a prayer. As always, she prayed for her mom to get this job and for Auntie Ann to become a nicer human being. And as usual, she told God she'd leave the details up to Him as to how to make that happen. But she prayed the hardest about the kids at school and what to do about it.

"The kids are getting meaner, Lord, and I'm feeling really scared. I almost told Auntie about it, but then the phone rang. I don't know who else I can tell. I'm still afraid to tell the band teacher and I can't tell my mom. It seems like Auntie Ann is the only one I have to talk to. But who knows what she'd do even if I did tell her? Please do something to help me, Lord. I'm really scared and I don't know what to do. But I know You do. So I'll go to sleep trusting You to do something, because I know that Your ear is not so dull that it cannot hear, nor is Your hand so short that it cannot save." Drifting off into a dreamy sleep, she tried to continue, "And thank You for giving me just three more days of school and ..."

And off she went.

Chapter 5

Ann's alarm broke her slumber far too early. It had been quite some time since she'd hit the snooze button, but this morning she couldn't help herself. She was unaccustomed to her routine being affected by anyone or anything and last night's pre-bedtime dialogue kept her up later than usual. Consequently, she just had to take that "five more minutes" so generously offered by the snooze button. Then ten. Then fifteen.

It was 5:05 a.m. before her feet finally hit the floor. She groggily began slashing minutes in her mind. Fifteen minutes on the elliptical, quick shower, hair up. Again. *Oh I can't wait for my life to get back to normal.*

Valerie was out. Not even the elliptical was able to rouse her from her bed this morning. Ann tapped her on the shoulder at about 5:20 and told her she had forty minutes to get ready.

Both of them were off kilter and out of sorts as they danced around each other, trying to rush. Valerie kept dropping things. Her air mattress was taking forever to deflate, so she abandoned the bed project and opted for kitchen duty. She dribbled jam and butter on the counter and had to clean that up just when she dropped the butter knife on the floor and caused another time-consuming mess. They seemed to make little progress as the clock kept ticking, but somehow managed to make it to the garage by 6:15.

Ann cut the token car-warming ritual in half and they pulled out at 6:17. Still not enough time to fight traffic and get to school by seven.

As a result of all this, Ann's temper was far shorter than it was yesterday. All sorts of name-calling and degrading comments flew from her lips as she tried to get on the freeway.

Valerie had a short wick herself, so she also let a few words fly. "Auntie," she sharply chided, "what is desirable in a man is his kindness!"

"Listen up you pint-sized pocket prophet," Ann spat. "I do not want or need your preaching. I'm doing all this as a favor to your mother. If you so much as give me two more words of your God stuff, I will ship you off to my secretary's house all the way to next Tuesday and that will be that. Have I made myself clear or do I need to put in it writing for you?"

"No, you don't have to write it," Valerie mumbled.

In this brief moment, her heart shut down completely. She knew she wouldn't be able to talk to her aunt about anything, let alone about the kids at school. She couldn't have been more disappointed. She couldn't have felt more alone. She decided right then that she would no longer pray for her aunt to become a nice person. She knew this was impossible. So instead, she released her aunt completely into God's hands. She quietly told Him, from inside her head, that He could have her aunt and do with her whatever He saw fit to do. She was out of words.

When they finally got to school, it was ten after seven. Ann asked if she should come in to talk to the band teacher and Valerie told her no, she could talk to Mrs. Campion after practice. Valerie grabbed her things from the trunk and sprinted toward the double school doors while Ann pulled out of the parking lot with a major handicap. Not only was she running late, but that layer of stress had become generously overlaid with agitation the moment she spoke those vile words to Valerie. She had no idea how she was going to rectify this situation. Her sister would kill her if she caught wind of this. She was sitting on a powder keg of emotional explosives and she didn't even know it.

By the time she got downtown, she'd worked her mind into a raging mess. How was she going to fix this? Should she tell Sara before Valerie got a chance to talk to her? Should she ask Cassie for help? Surely she'd know what to do.

A perfect storm brewed as Ann's emotional stress collided with her gross intolerance of driving in downtown Chicago. As she approached the stop light that put her just one block away from the saving grace of the parking garage, she didn't see the small figure on her right. An elderly woman, cloaked in black, began entering the crosswalk just as the light turned green. Ann spotted her just as she began moving the car forward. She barely missed hitting the woman as she slammed on her brakes.

Laying on the horn and letting off inaudible expletives served only to stop the woman in her tracks. With a dazed expression, she looked straight into the car and into Ann's eyes. Upon making eye contact, the dazed expression was replaced by an all-knowing, piercing gaze. Ann felt as though the woman was seeing straight into her soul. At the same time, everyone behind Ann was honking now, and yelling out their windows.

Pushed to the brink, Ann rolled her window down and yelled, "Come on old woman—get out of the crosswalk already—the light's about to turn red again. Do you need to get your walking license renewed? Do we need to open a geriatric lane just for you? Can you even comprehend what I'm saying to you?"

Then the strangest thing happened. Rather than move a single inch toward the curb, the woman remained standing in front of Ann's car and raised her hands straight up into the air. She turned her head to the sky and began shouting something in a foreign language.

At the end of her apparent rant, she lowered her hands and head and once again levelled her piercing gaze at Ann. Then, just as the light turned red again, she locked her eyes on Ann's and smiled. Not only did this smile seem unusual considering the circumstances, but it held something that took Ann completely by surprise: a sense of great accomplishment. The woman even accented the expression with a nod of the head as if to say, "so there," before finally ambling to the other side of the street.

By the time Ann made it to the office, she was frazzled to the point of no return. She wasn't in the mood to talk to anyone and felt as though she could use a small, padded, soundproof room to scream in. She was met, nonetheless, by Cassie who gave her a briefing on the morning's agenda before she could even get to her desk.

Right after that, the courier from the day before approached Ann's desk with another delivery.

"Oh. You again," Ann grumbled.

Due to the abuse this courier suffered the day before, Cassie played protective ally by offering consolation and advice. "Don't be offended by how she speaks to you. The truth is, rudeness has taken up permanent residence here and we now have to charge it rent. It was here long before you got this job and try as we might, we can't seem to be able to evict it."

The young man smiled at Cassie and mouthed the words "thank you" as he handed the delivery register to Ann so she could sign it.

She grabbed it from him and moved it farther from her eyes so she could see the screen. After he left, she picked up the package and noticed she couldn't read the return address to see who it was from. She pulled it an entire arm's length away and still couldn't make it out. It was an absolute blur. She'd never had vision problems before. She wondered how impaired vision could come on so abruptly. She reasoned it must have something to do with her lack of sleep, and proceeded to get to work.

Only she couldn't find her pen. Again. As she began ransacking her desk, Bradley walked up and stopped her.

"Looking for this?" he asked. He held her pen in the air.

"Is this some sort of joke?" she snapped. "Because if it is, I'm not laughing. Just give me my pen and get on with your day."

"Oh I'll get on with my day all right. But first I have something to show you. Behold the custom pen holder."

He walked around her cubicle and showed her a few hooks on the wall that he had installed before she got to the office. He set the pen inside the makeshift penholder and told her he'd be right back. He went to his own cubicle and returned with a large coffee mug stuffed with cheap ink pens that she could leave on the corner of her desk in order to appease "potential thieves."

In the midst of her frenetic morning, this was more than medicine. She gave him a rare, genuinely heartfelt smile and thanked him.

He asked her if everything was all right because she seemed a little off.

"I've just had a crazy morning. I had an explosive conversation with my niece on the way to school, then almost ran into a woman in a crosswalk. She just refused to cross the street. It was so strange."

Ann retreated back to the moment as she related the story, but it was impossible to transport Bradley into the scene. She wished she could because it was so unsettling. But since she couldn't, she moved on.

She told him about how stressful it was for her to do all this driving since she hates to drive, let alone in downtown Chicago. She told him about how difficult it was for her to have Valerie at all since she had no experience with kids and swore she would never have any.

Before she could continue, however, Bradley interrupted her with a proposal. "Why don't I take over niece-driving duty for you?"

"What? Did you really just say that?"

"Yes I did. My position here is not quite as high profile as yours, so it wouldn't be as costly to Marvin for me to be a little late for the next few days if traffic were to rear its angry head. Besides, I miss my niece. It would be fun for me to hang out with yours. I love kids."

"Wow! You're on!"

Ann couldn't believe the sense of relief she felt as a result of Bradley's offer. Ten thousand bowling balls fell from her shoulders as she drank in the reality. No more fighting morning traffic. No more crazy old ladies making her stop at intersections with green lights and arresting her heart with threats of near-deadly collisions. No more having to rush to get to the parking garage by eight. No more ripping her niece's head off while trying to play a role she was never meant to play. Without this added stress factor, she felt she could really sink her teeth into the Green Jeans ad and tie up all the other loose ends in time for the May issue.

"You could even go pick her up today. She usually gets picked up around four. Wait. That wouldn't work. Your car's in the parking garage too. How can we make this work?"

"It probably wouldn't be a good idea for a total stranger to show up at Valerie's school and offer her a ride home 'because Aunt Ann said I could.' She doesn't even know me. And schools usually have a list of friends and relatives who are authorized to pick up students. I'm thinking I should meet Valerie before just showing up on the school's doorstep."

Ann scrunched her forehead. "Oh. I guess you're right. I hadn't thought of all that. Well, would it work for you to follow me to the school and she could ride to the condo with you? No—that would be awkward."

Bradley offered an alternate plan. "Why don't you pick Valerie up as usual and I can come over and make dinner tonight? My ex was a culinary student. I can make a mean orange Peking chicken with jasmine rice and cabbage salad.

I'm sure your niece would love it and it would satisfy all your low fat, gluten-free needs. That way I could meet your niece on her turf and it wouldn't be so awkward for her to be taxied around by someone she barely knows."

Ann had to give it some thought. It would be quite strange to have Bradley Newman in her own private surroundings, but he seemed to know more about this kid thing than she did.

"Yeah, I guess that would be a good idea. It might also be a good little ice-breaker. As I said, Valerie and I had a bit of a fallout this morning."

"One taste of my famous Peking chicken and all of life's stresses will simply melt away. Should I also plan some sort of dessert?"

"No, I don't think so. Valerie stocked up with some of her favorite forms of sugar, so we can probably come up with something. That is, the two of you can. I'm not all that big on dessert. Or sugar. Or processed food of any sort."

"I'm sure Valerie and I can manage dessert quite nicely without you. You just don't know what you're missing Miss Finlayson."

"Probably not. But for now, I'm feeling the clock. Let's get on with the work day, shall we?"

"But of course." Bradley bowed as he said this, and as he left, he gave Cassie a little wink.

"I think he has a crush on you," Cassie noted.

Ann squawked incredulously, "A crush? On me? No—I don't think so. Besides, there's no way I would ever have anything to do with a guy like Bradley."

"Why on earth not?"

"He's just too nice. I mean—driving all the way across town twice a day to help someone he's never even met before? Who *does* that? It just seems a little … doormat-ish."

"Doormat-ish? You think that's the behavior of a doormat? You need to widen your scope. Why not view it as the behavior of someone who actually looks beyond himself and his own needs? Then again—I guess you wouldn't know anything about *that*, would you?"

Ann flew into defensive mode. "What's *that* supposed to mean? And why do you care anyway? I'm perfectly happy with my life just the way it is and frankly, I can't even see where any guy would fit into the grand scheme of things."

"I care because I think everyone should have a chance at true intimacy and the deep joy that comes with it. Because you know what Ann Kathleen Finlayson? Life is fleeting and can evaporate in a heartbeat. And true love comes along so rarely." She fought back tears. "I guess I'm just steeped in what's going on with Craig."

Ann ignored Cassie's sudden display of emotion.

"Well, Cassie. If I were ever to fall for someone, he wouldn't be the Mr. Nice, doormat type. He would have to be someone with an innovative, progressive sort of mentality. Someone with a transcendent form of intelligence, who could think outside the box." With a dreamy expression and a bit of a sigh, she continued. "Someone like … Sean."

This instantly dislodged Cassie from the valley of deep reflection.

"I can't believe you find that bullish, arrogant, superficial man attractive in any way, shape or form. And I can't believe you're calling Bradley a doormat. You've probably never heard this before, but 'What is desirable in a man is his kindness.'"

"You did not just say that," Ann caustically blurted. Anger had sprung into her mouth with such vehemence that even Cassie, who was used to Ann's venomous ways, cringed at its potency.

"Woah. Back off missy. Just offering a little third party opinion."

"Well don't. I don't want or need to hear anything you have to say on the subject and I especially don't want or need any more Bible quotes. Not today. And not ever. And P.S.—I don't need a personal relationship trainer either. It's bad enough having my sister in that corner. I don't want to hear it at work. Speaking of, I'm stepping back into that mode now. I suggest you do the same."

"Yes ma'am," Cassie sighed.

As Ann began shuffling through papers, she noticed once again that she couldn't read anything unless she held it an arm's length away. She was too proud and too vain to ask Cassie if she had a pair of reading glasses lying around. She'd have to make an eye appointment as soon as possible. But for now, it was really interfering. Perhaps she could sneak down to the drugstore at lunchtime and pick up a magnifying glass. That would be easier to hide than a pair of glasses.

This morning Valerie had a spelling test and a math quiz. She could barely focus on either one. Her mind kept drifting to what life might be like if her mom got the job in Colorado. And she kept going over the horrible words her aunt spoke to her in the car. She felt like she never wanted to be alone with Auntie again. How could she be so mean? Valerie was so tired of people being mean to her that she could barely finish the math quiz she was working on. In fact, the teacher was telling the class to turn in their work when Valerie noticed she'd only completed half of it.

One of the students walked around collecting the papers while Valerie debated. She didn't know if she should turn in her quiz half done or hold onto it and ask the teacher for more time.

She decided to hand it in. Who cared if she got a bad grade? What difference would it make? Especially if she moved to a different school. She'd have to prove herself all over again anyway, and chances were, she'd return to her straight "A" self as soon as she got away from these mean kids.

She'd arranged to escape them by spending lunchtime and recess in the band room, then all she had to do was get to the end of the day. After that, it was only two more days to freedom.

The math teacher told the kids to pull out something to read or to do other homework while she looked over the quizzes. If she noticed a lot of people getting the same problems wrong, they'd go over the concept again before the end of class. When she got to Valerie's quiz, she noticed it was incomplete. She knew this wasn't typical Valerie. She looked up and caught Valerie's eyes and signaled for her to come up. When Valerie got to her desk, she asked if there was a problem.

"No," Valerie said. "I'm just a little tired today and couldn't concentrate very well.

"Well, why don't you go ahead and take this back to your desk? It's okay if you finish it now. This quiz wasn't about speed, but about comprehension. I don't want to move on until I know most of the class understands this current concept."

"Yes, Miss Moberg."

Miss Moberg couldn't help but notice Valerie seemed off. But Valerie did say she was tired. Miss Moberg then dismissed the observation and continued to grade the rest of the quizzes.

After completing the quiz, all Valerie could do was sit and wait for lunchtime. Then it was merely a matter of getting to her locker and to the band room. The kids were never as threatening in the busy hallway as they were on the playground. They'd make comments and gestures, but no threats. It seemed to take forever, but the bell finally rang.

"Oh—so did perfect little Valerie get in trouble today?" someone hissed as she walked to her locker.

"Yeah, what happened in math class Miss Perfect? Did you forget how to do long division?

"Yeah, did you get smacked upside the head with a dumb rock? Too bad I wasn't the one holding the rock. I would've knocked you out with it."

One of the office staff came down the hall at that moment, so the kids had to stop. But one of them did the choking signal again as they all walked away, laughing.

Valerie made it to the band room safely. The next hour was such a relief, she just wanted to go to sleep.

She laid her head down on a desk and did just that.

As challenging as it was, Ann decided to work through lunch with her faulty eyesight rather than go to the drugstore. She felt it would be better to stay planted and get as much done as she could before going to get Valerie than it would be to lose an hour. She did her best and left the office earlier than yesterday.

She was nervous about how to make things better with Valerie before Sara's phone call that night. This was definitely not her area of expertise. If the words "I'm sorry" were a part of her everyday vocabulary, it might not seem as difficult.

She tried to compose some potential ice-breakers as she left the office and made her way to the parking garage. Everything she thought of sounded phony to her. Things didn't get any better as she fought her way onto the freeway. Traffic was backed up just enough to put her on edge again as she struggled to get to the exit, then to the school. At least this time she was aware of her impatience, so she decided to keep her words to a minimum when Valerie came out to the car.

Once Valerie got everything loaded into the trunk, she let out a giant sigh while plopping into her seat like a ton of bricks.

"Bad day at the office?" Ann asked.

"No. Just a bad day."

Superficial conversation felt like the safest route to take.

"What did you study?"

"Not much. Same ol' stuff."

"How much homework do you have?"

Valerie shrugged her shoulders and mumbled, "Not much," then sank further into her seat with giant sigh number two.

Ann felt her impatience rising again. "Look—if you don't want me to talk to you, just tell me. I'll gladly back off."

Valerie shot straight up in her seat. "You know what Auntie? I don't want you to talk to me. I don't. You don't really care about how I'm doing. You just ask me questions because you feel like you have to. I was so excited to come see you and stay with you while Mama was out of town. My dad's gone. My grandma and grandpa are gone. You're all I have left besides Mama, and you're mean. I wish the week was already over."

Ann didn't have a response for this outburst. They were almost to the condo and not only had she failed to make things better, but she hadn't told Valerie about Bradley yet. She decided to wait until they got inside before saying anything.

Once inside, they hung up their coats and put their lunch things away. Valerie dug into her backpack and was about to start homework when Ann interrupted.

"Valerie, I know I haven't been very good at this. I've never really been around kids before and I'm used to living by myself. And you know how much driving stresses me out. So there's a very nice gentleman who works at my office named Bradley and he's offered to drive you to and from school every day."

Valerie was appalled. "You're having someone I don't even know drive me back and forth to school? Starting when?"

"Starting tomorrow. But he won't be a complete stranger. He's coming over for dinner tonight so you can meet him. In fact, he's going to cook it too."

"Really?" Valerie brightened immediately at the thought of an authentic meal being prepared for her in Auntie's kitchen. Auntie wasn't much of a cook.

Just then the doorbell rang.

Valerie liked the idea of a good dinner, but felt shy about meeting her new chauffeur. She hung back from the door while Bradley walked in.

But it turned out there was no need for Valerie to lurk in the shadows. Nor did she have to battle her shyness with strained politeness. Bradley made it easy. He greeted her warmly with a full smile and friendly eyes.

"So you must be Valerie?"

"Yes," Valerie answered.

"Well I'm Bradley, but you can call me Brad. Just don't use the word 'mister' around me because I'm nowhere near old enough for *that*. Have you ever done any cooking, Valerie?"

"Just a little," Valerie said. "My dad and I used to do a little bit of cooking."

"Well that will be just fine. I'll make you my sous chef."

"What's a sous chef?" Valerie asked.

"A sous chef is the top assistant to the chef in the kitchen. Generally, it means I get to boss you around. But I'll try to be civil, Mademoiselle Valerie." At this, he took a bow.

Valerie giggled so hard her shoulders shook.

Ann was so relieved by how things were going, she excused herself to go take a shower.

After she left the room, Bradley cupped his hand around his mouth and lowered his voice. "*Someone* around here has to be civil, right?" With an all-knowing smile and a wink he added, "I *know* your aunt."

Valerie laughed so hard and so loud, she thought Auntie would hear her through the bathroom wall with the fan blowing and the water running. She almost stopped herself in case Auntie might run out and ask what they were laughing about. It felt so good though, she decided to keep going and laugh even harder. By now, Bradley was laughing too.

While the two cooks were busy in the kitchen, Ann relaxed in the shower. She had no idea Bradley's presence in her condo would relieve so much of the pressure she'd felt since Valerie got here. It was so great to have someone else on entertainment duty. Not only that, but Bradley had such an easy-going personality that Valerie instantly felt comfortable with him.

This idea of his to come over and meet Valerie over dinner was brilliant. She wondered how he'd obtained all this wisdom. He didn't have any kids of his own. Ann didn't even think he had a girlfriend. But the one thing she found most surprising was how comfortable *she* felt having him here. Something about his mannerisms and natural charm reminded her of someone, but she couldn't think of who. She shook the feeling and cut the shower short. She was getting hungry.

She threw on yoga pants and a sweatshirt and wrapped a towel around her wet head. Just as she stepped out of her bedroom, the phone rang.

"That's going to be my mom," Ann heard Valerie say to Bradley.

This is great—I don't even have to be on phone duty.

"Hi Mommy. Guess what? Auntie Ann found someone at her work who's going to drive me to and from school and he's over here fixing dinner and I'm helping him make it. We're having orange Peking chicken and rice. He showed me how to make perfect rice so now I can make it for you when you get home ..."

Ann walked into the kitchen while Bradley was adding some final touches. "Well, you certainly made my day."

"How so? What's a little bit of dinner? That's not enough to make an entire day."

"No, but Valerie and I got off to a rough start this morning and nothing improved when I picked her up from school. In fact, it got worse. I was just trying to figure out how to make things better when you came to the door. Then in you waltz with a handful of magic dust and voila! I've never seen Valerie so happy. I'm thinking we should trade places for the duration. You can hang out here with Valerie and I'll take over your place. You certainly have a way with her that I do not."

"Oh, it isn't any kind of magic. I told you I love kids. And who wouldn't fall in love with Valerie? She's a beautiful young lady and a sharp little cookie. This is going to be fun."

Just then Valerie announced, "Auntie, my mom wants to talk to you."

"Excuse me, *Mister* Bradley, duty calls."

"Hey you—none of that 'mister' stuff," he smiled as he grabbed a hand towel and wound it up to swat her arm.

He just missed her as she took the phone into the bedroom. She knew what was coming.

"So … Bradley huh? He sounds pretty amazing. Cooks fancy chicken and everything. And he volunteered to drive Val to and from school, or was this your idea?"

"He volunteered. I was telling him about how stressful all the driving's been and he offered to drive for the next few days."

"And what about the romantic implications of this little dinner party? Valerie is totally smitten. How 'bout you?"

"No way. I could never fall for a guy like him. He's too nice."

"There is such a thing?"

"You really are exactly like my secretary. The two of you need to hook up and do lunch sometime."

"All right, I'll get off your case about the Bradley thing. But how are things otherwise? Valerie had nothing else to talk about."

With great relief, Ann uttered the words, "Things have been just fine."

"You're always going to say that."

"Probably."

"Well then, chatterbox, give me back to my daughter so I can say goodnight."

Valerie and Sara ended the phone call and everyone sat down at the kitchen table.

Dinner was quite enjoyable. Ann kept being astounded by how all this was feeling. It acutely reminded her of how things used to feel in the home she grew up in. She half expected someone to jump up and start dancing right there in the kitchen. But instead of getting up to dance, she rose from her chair to announce it was time to call it a night.

Valerie adamantly protested. "But we haven't had dessert."

"True that," Bradley piped in. "We cannot end such a marvelous meal without a little ice cream. Or brownies. Or both."

"Mmmm—ice cream. We don't have brownies, but we do have chocolate sauce."

"Good enough. Let's clean up this dinner mess and dish up."

As Bradley and Valerie tended to kitchen business, Ann continued to try and figure out who Bradley reminded her of. She didn't have long to ponder, however. The two of them had the kitchen cleaned in no time and were trying to figure out bowl sizes.

"How much do you want?" Bradley asked Ann.

"Oh—I don't eat ice cream. I'm completely off dairy and who needs all that extra fat anyway?"

"We do." Bradley smiled straight into Valerie's eyes as she responded with wide eyes and an exaggerated head nod.

They took their bowls into the living room and Valerie lamented that it was probably too late to watch a movie.

"Yes it is," Ann said as she eyeballed the two heaping bowls of ice cream. She couldn't take her eyes off those bowls. For some reason, that ice cream was looking like the greatest creation on earth. It had been so long ... and all that chocolate sauce ... she used to love hot fudge *and* butterscotch on her ice cream. Suddenly, she couldn't stand it anymore. "I guess I could have a little."

"Sure," Bradley said. "Grab a bowl."

So she did. She tried to keep her portion small, but she wanted it so badly she figured it would be better to fill up with a generous serving to begin with than it would be to go back for seconds. After all, she had an image to maintain.

They all sat on the couch with their ice cream as though this were an everyday occurrence. Bradley and Valerie chatted and giggled while Ann just listened to the two of them. Oddly enough, it felt good to be here. She hadn't experienced such a slice of life since childhood and she found herself enjoying it.

She even felt reluctant about reminding everyone that they had an early morning to get up for. But, remind she did, and Valerie and Bradley moaned as they got up from the couch.

When it came time for goodbyes at the door, Bradley said, "Goodnight Pumpkin" to Valerie and she said, "Goodnight Mister Bradley," to him. They both had a giggle over this.

While closing the door, Ann felt a little sad to see him go. She refused, however, to entertain this thought. *I'm just tired,* she told herself. And she was. She felt like she'd eaten lead for dinner. Getting ready for bed seemed like an uphill climb that was almost beyond her. She'd never felt like this before.

Valerie, on the other hand, felt rejuvenated. She tucked herself in with a song in her heart and thanksgiving to God for the miracle of Bradley Newman. She couldn't wait to see him in the morning. She prayed her prayers about her mom's job and Auntie Ann's bad temper and the kids at school. And again, she thanked God for this magnificent turn of events. Somehow, it felt like He hand-picked Bradley to help her heart withstand the remainder of this visit. She bubbled over with gratitude for nearly half an hour.

Ann was out as soon as she laid down.

Chapter 6

Ann woke up sharply at 2:15 in the morning. She was drenched in sweat and so were all the sheets. She got up and changed her clothes, then the bedding. Once she climbed back into bed it was nearly three. Normally, she could fall right back to sleep. But not this morning. She tossed and turned continually, feeling wide awake all the way to 4:30. Finally, she fell back into a choppy sleep and woke to the alarm going off at six. She heard Valerie leaving shortly thereafter. She felt so groggy and disoriented, it took a moment for her to shake it off and remember she didn't have to take Valerie to school.

She got dressed for the elliptical and had to cut it short at twenty minutes because her hips were starting to hurt. *Strange. That's never happened before.*

After getting off the elliptical, she languished with her coffee and the delicious feeling of being alone and relaxed. No having to rush to get Valerie to school. No playing mother hen while keeping her niece on task. No awkward conversational moments on the drive to school. Bradley could go ahead and live the "I love kids" dream. This was the life for her.

Although she could have spent two more hours right there at the kitchen table, duty called her to go get dressed and ready for work. She pried herself from the table and went to her bedroom. As always, she'd assembled her office attire the night before. But it didn't seem to match this elated sense of emancipation. This was a day for a pencil skirt and heels. Her bright, floral blouse would do nicely, as would her brand new blazer. She was even in the mood for a splash of light perfume.

As she proceeded to put all this on, she was thanking Bradley Newman all over again for setting her free. But there was a slight problem. She couldn't zip her skirt.

"What?" she spoke into the bedroom air. "I've only worn this skirt once before and it fit like a charm."

In a flurry of code red exasperation, she practically tore the skirt in order to get it off in a hurry. Then she had a good long look in the mirror. A conversation between herself and her reflection immediately ensued.

"What in the world? What is *this* all about? I know I had ice cream last night, but how often do I do *that*? It certainly couldn't have done this to me overnight. Or could it?" Turning to catch a side view, she repeated, "Could it?"

What Ann saw in the mirror was a little extra padding around her hips and waist. No one on the planet was more disciplined than Ann Finlayson in the department of diet and exercise. No one. There was no reasonable explanation for this. She might have to interrupt her doctor's vacation after all. Or, perhaps any medical clinic would be able to tell her if it was possible to blow up like this just by eating a bowl of ice cream. But she couldn't call now—she had to figure out what to wear to work. She did have one pair of slacks with an elastic waistband that she reserved for those days when she wasn't in the mood to go to work. She called them her daytime pajamas.

Even those were a little snug, but the morning was marching forward and she still had hair and makeup to do. She moved to the bathroom where the light was a little brighter.

The headshot that met her in the bathroom mirror sent shock waves to her heart—her gorgeous mane of brunette hair was streaked with gray.

She gasped so hard she almost ran out of breath. How in the world could this happen? Is there a disease a person could catch that could do this? Could she be sleep-walking? No. That was real coffee she had in her cup at the kitchen table. She couldn't go to work like this. What was she going to do?

She had no choice. She had to call Peggy. Now. But what was the time difference between Chicago and Florida?

That's right. They're a few hours ahead.

"Dr. Peggy Jantzen," said the voice that answered the phone. "Please feel free to leave a message as I am unavailable at this time. If this is an emergency, please call 9-1-1."

Well this was most certainly an emergency, but Ann doubted the 9-1-1 operator would see it that way. Some people at the office might view it as such, but she couldn't let them see her like this in order to offer their opinions. She had to fix this before stepping one foot inside the office door.

She put her gears into motion and drew up a battle plan: She could swing by the drugstore and pick up some hair color on her way to work. Perhaps they'd even let her use their bathroom … That was that. She was out the door and down the street before she remembered she hadn't eaten breakfast or put on any makeup.

Great. Anything else?

In addition to some sort of hair dye, she decided she could also buy a little makeup, just to get her through today. And while she was at it, she may as well get a magnifying glass too.

The woman who greeted Ann as she entered the drugstore was a bit too jolly for this hour of the morning. Especially given Ann's present state of mind. She seemed over-accommodating, as if no one had stepped into her store for a month. But Ann was on a mission with a time crunch, so she set her annoyance aside and asked where the hair color was. The woman showed her the aisle and Ann scanned the shelves for a product she could just brush through as a touch-up, like something one of her clients had advertised in the magazine. She found something she thought would work, as well as emergency makeup and a magnifying glass. At the register, she asked Miss Over-the-Top if she could use her bathroom to put some of this on before work.

"Big meeting at the office?" the woman asked.

"Yes that's it," Ann replied. "And I'm running very late."

"Say no more. Just go right through that door in the back. There's an employee rest room off to the left of the storage area. Disregard the mess." Then the woman smiled and added, "I'm Charlotte. Nice to meet you."

Ann just nodded politely and ran to the bathroom.

She couldn't believe how haggard she looked. Was her night that ragged or was it because she was standing in fluorescent lighting? Never mind—she had enough of a makeover to perform. She'd have to come by later and get some sort of serum, or retinol cream, or whatever it was people used for this sort of thing. As if "this sort of thing" was the norm for her …

She was in such a hurry that it was a struggle to open all the packaging. She was excited to try the hair stuff—it looked like it could really work. In fact, it worked just fine. She was able to get rid of every gray streak she could see. A little makeup and she'd be good to go. Problem was, she still couldn't see close up. Another puzzle she needed time to dig into. She did the best she could, but time had run out. She still looked exhausted, but it was nowhere near as glaring as it was when she first looked in the mirror.

On the way out the door, she thanked Charlotte and ran to the office as fast as she could. Oddly, she was out of breath by the time she reached the elevator. Normally, such a jaunt wouldn't phase her. *Another anomaly,* she thought, while trying to recover on the way up.

"Wow, what happened to you?" Cassie asked as Ann went to the coat rack.

"I know. How late am I?"

"Almost a full forty-five minutes and Marvin's been asking about you."

"Great. Does he want me to check in first thing?"

"Yep. And he wants Sean to join you."

As if on cue, Sean stepped around the corner and grinned. "Are you ready, beautiful?"

"As I'll ever be," Ann replied.

She just couldn't get on top of all this. She hoped to gain some composure while walking down the hall to Marvin's office, but it wasn't happening. She had to do one more mirror check before meeting with Marvin, so she told Sean she needed to use the bathroom.

At least the lighting in the office bathroom was softer than the drugstore's harsh fluorescent lighting. She wasn't fully satisfied, but it was better than before.

At least the hair was. Her eyes looked horrible. Seemingly worse than they did at the drugstore. Could her restless night have caused that much sagging in her eyelids? And as she leaned forward she noticed deep grooves extending from the corners of her eyes. She'd heard the term "crow's feet" before, but had only ever seen it on old people. Extremely old. This had to be related to the gray hair thing. How was she going to get through this meeting, let alone this day? She needed to go back to the drugstore. Pronto. But Sean was waiting in the hall.

When she came out, Sean asked what happened to the back of her head.

"What do you mean?" Ann asked.

"You have all these gray streaks in your hair."

Ann tried to act casual. "Oh, that. My niece thought it would be fun to try and play with my hair color last night. She used some peroxide on it to see what would happen and I guess it gave me gray streaks. I haven't had time to fix it yet, does it look very bad?"

"Well, put it this way, you'll want to fix it as soon as you get home. That's a fine example of why I never want to have kids. You just can't live a normal life with them around. They always need something or they're asking a million questions or they're breaking things or in your case, messing with your hair. On top of all that, they're nothing but an anchor. Or even a noose. Forget your freedom once kids come along. Goodbye life. Hello whiny, time-consuming, money-draining little leeches. Sure you're up to this? You look a little tired."

"Yeah, I'll be fine."

It turned out Marvin just wanted to let Ann know he wanted Sean to be her new right-hand man. Not just for the Green Jeans campaign, but for all future advertising ventures.

"He's a shark with great instincts, just like you Ann. Sometimes Newman's a little too soft. So from now on, I want you and Sean to work as a team. You need someone in your corner who's just like you, Fin."

"Yes sir, I'm sure it will be a worthwhile partnership." She couldn't really care less about a thing Marvin had just said, but she had to say something. He seemed satisfied enough with her response. He dismissed them with a couple of pats on the back and something about having a great feeling regarding all this. Of course, he had to comment on Ann's hair the moment he noticed it and once again she had to repeat the peroxide story.

While returning to her desk, Ann wrestled with the task of how to wrap her distracted mind around work for the next few hours.

As usual, Cassie had to know every detail of Ann's life, both private and professional. "So what was that all about?"

"Gratefully, it wasn't about my being late. Marv just wants Sean and I to work as a team from here on out."

"Figures. Ever since Marvin decided to go so hard after Green Jeans, I've doubted his character *and* his personality assessment skills. In the past, he's always relied most heavily on Bradley's input. But ever since this opportunity with Green Jeans came up, he and Bradley have been at odds."

"Let's change the subject, shall we? I don't think I can stand to hear the words verde denim one more time today."

"'Verde denim.' Cute. How'd your date go?"

"What date?"

"You know—Bradley coming over and fixing dinner so he could meet Valerie—that date."

"It was fine. And it wasn't a date. Speaking of, is he here yet?"

"Yeah, he came in around 7:40. He's helping Noel proofread an article before it goes to typesetting."

"Okay. I'm anxious to hear the report about the drive to school this morning. I don't know why, I guess I just want to check in. Valerie fell head over heels in love with him last night."

"So the girl has the gift of discernment. You should take notes."

Just then, Ann's cell phone buzzed. It was a text from Peggy. Because this conversation could not be accomplished via text, Ann quickly got up to make her way toward the bathroom. This was when Cassie noticed the back of her head.

"What on earth happened to your hair?"

"I'll tell you later, I have to go make this call."

Ann was so relieved to hear Peggy's voice once she reached the bathroom, she felt she could cry. Yet another anomaly. She was not the crying type.

"Peggy—I'm so glad to hear from you. How's the vacation going?"

Peggy filled in a few details, then drove to the meat of the matter. "So what's up? I know you wouldn't have interrupted my vacation unless it was something important."

"It's beyond important Peggy. It's so unbelievable, I don't know where to begin."

She thought it best to start with yesterday, when she first noticed her vision was impaired. She told Peggy about waking up in a sweat and being wide awake at three in the morning. She told her about gaining a skirt size overnight, and the gray hair that so copiously covered her head that she had to buy hair color on the way to work. She told her about having to use the bathroom in the drugstore to apply the color and missing some in the back, and how everyone had been pointing it out since she got here. Of course, she had to ask whether or not one small bowl of ice cream could cause enough weight gain for her to outgrow one of her favorite skirts.

Peggy was silent for quite some time. Finally, she asked, "Did you really wake up with gray hair? I've never heard of such a thing. As for everything else you're describing, it sounds like menopause. But you're only thirty-two and menopause doesn't usually come on this suddenly, or at your age. As for the impaired vision, have you started taking any new medications?"

"No, but I have been using a new protein powder in my smoothies."

"No—there isn't anything in a protein powder that could cause impaired vision. The only thing that seems likely for all these symptoms coming on at once is menopause. You could have a thyroid condition, but that wouldn't explain the hair and faulty eyesight. We just need to run a few tests when I get back in town. For that matter, you could even go to a doc-in-the-box if you don't want to wait for me to get back. I'm so sorry Ann. This just sounds so strange. Whatever you decide to do, keep me posted okay?"

"Okay. Thanks a lot Peggy. And thanks for making yourself available to me on your vacation. Now go get back to it!"

"I most certainly will. Dave's waiting for me by the pool with a couple of mimosas on ice."

"Sounds wonderful Peggy. Thanks again, and have fun. Talk to you later."

Ann ended the call and stood like a dead weight in the middle of the bathroom. She couldn't move. Menopause? How? That would be impossible. But it sounded like the best explanation. Nancy used to talk about all she was going through. The night sweats, the hot flashes, the instant eight-pound weight gain. But Nancy's hair turned gray gradually and her vision started failing in her late forties. It didn't all happen at once.

Then, something slowly dawned on Ann. Nancy didn't have a spontaneous run-in with an elderly voodoo woman in a crosswalk while trying to be on time for work.

Ann recollected the picture of that woman standing in the crosswalk, blocking traffic at a green light while shouting a slew of unintelligible words toward the sky that she alone could translate. Could it be possible? Could this woman have put some sort of curse on her? If that was the case, she could also remove it. Ann didn't have to go to a doc-in-the-box or get tested by Dr. Peggy Jantzen. She already knew the answer. And she was going to do everything possible to take matters into her own hands. Unfortunately for now, she had to get back to work.

She wished she could swing by Nancy's office and grill her on the realities of menopause before going back to her desk. But she was already behind and distracted, and how could she explain her curiosity to Nancy anyway? She could probably come up with a good lie, but it would feel too awkward. She'd have to weather this alone for now.

When she returned to her desk, Bradley was there to greet her. "I came by earlier, but you were detained. I just wanted to let you know the drive to school was great. Your niece is a real treat—we had tons of fun on the way to school. I didn't get a chance to meet the band teacher, but I did walk Valerie into the school with all her gear. I got to carry the tuba. Since when did elementary school grow to be so small? When I was a kid, those hallways were endless and the lockers were enormous. Oh well, glad to have escaped. I'd ask 'how 'bout you,' but I can see how busy you are. And tired. Did you sleep okay?"

"Not really," Ann answered. "But if you don't mind, I do have to get back to work. Thanks for the report."

"No problem. I'll check back in before I go pick her up."

"Sure. Okay."

Ann was never good at social graces, so it wasn't a shock that all this dialogue was void of smiles, or even a whole lot of eye contact. Bradley did, however, notice something was off, but knew better than to ask. Besides, he too had a full day ahead, especially since he had to leave the office early to get Valerie from school.

Ann muddled slowly through her pile of paperwork. It would have been so much easier if she could actually read. But progress was slow with the magnifying glass—she could only read bits at a time. At least it was serving its purpose though—not even Cassie was able to catch her in the act.

But Sean almost did. He popped around the corner to check in on his newly appointed sidekick. Ann nearly jumped out of her skin when he materialized from out of nowhere.

"So what do you think, partner? We're going to make quite the team, aren't we? We've seen eye to eye on everything since day one and I think this Green Jeans ad is in the bag. Did I hear you say there would be a conference call with them on Friday? Perhaps I could join in."

"Sorry Sean, I'd rather you didn't. I've been working with them for some time, so I know all their angles and idiosyncrasies. And quite frankly, I'd rather do a dry run with you on a smaller account since I've never worked in tandem with you before. Green Jeans is just too valuable a client for me to feel comfortable jumping right into those team waters with you."

"See, that's what I like about you Finlayson. You know what you're about and you aren't afraid to show it. In fact, I find this so alluring that I'm hoping we can go for a drive in my new car one of these Saturdays. This coming Saturday is supposed to be stunning. We could drive out into the country with the top down and go to my favorite little inn for lunch. Just you and me. No kids. No phones. No office interruptions. We could get better acquainted and perhaps quell some of your misgivings about working with me."

"I don't have misgivings, Sean. I've just been working solo for years and the thought of having to partner with someone else is a tough one for me to accept."

"All the more reason for you to say yes. Come on Ann, let's go have some fun together."

Ann gave him half a smile. "I'll give it some thought and get back to you. I have my niece to consider, so I'm not all that free at the moment."

"Well you just say the word," Sean said over his shoulder as he returned to his desk.

Ann checked the time. Just a half hour more and she could break away for lunch. She thought she might squeeze in a quick trip to the park after the drugstore. Surely her sweat equity in this company had earned her a long lunch after all these years.

While she was pondering this, Cassie added her two bits toward the exchange Ann just shared with Sean. "If you really must spend time with Mr. Wonderful, I told you I'd love to have your niece over sometime. She could even spend the night. It could be a pleasant break for both you and her."

"I'll give that some consideration," Ann responded as the minutes ticked toward lunchtime.

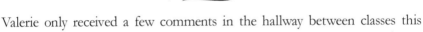

Valerie only received a few comments in the hallway between classes this morning. "Hey, we noticed the new bodyguard today. Don't think he's going to scare us away. Unless you were able to stuff him in your locker."

Hate-filled laughter followed as Valerie sunk her head and proceeded to her next class.

With only one and a half days left before spring break, she found it hard to focus. As the math teacher wrote things on the board and talked about current concepts, Valerie thought about Bradley. She wondered if she might be able to tell *him* about what's been going on at school lately. He seemed to be the nicest guy in the world, nice like her dad was. He was patient and funny and liked to spend time in the kitchen. She wished he could meet her mom and move to Colorado with them.

The math teacher broke her musings by calling on her. Valerie had no idea what Miss Moberg had just been talking about, so she struggled to find a response. Then, in front of the entire class, Miss Moberg told her she wanted to speak with her after class was over.

Once class ended and everyone was filing out of the classroom, Miss Moberg reminded Valerie to stop by her desk on the way out.

"Valerie, is everything all right with you? You haven't been yourself lately and although I know math isn't your top subject, you're one of my star students."

"How can that be? I'm terrible at math."

"Yes, but you try so hard. And whenever you don't understand, you ask questions. You know Valerie, that kind of determination is what separates the good students from the great ones."

"Thank you Miss Moberg. I guess it's that my mom's out of town and I'm staying with my aunt, so everything's different right now."

"Okay Valerie, I'll accept that. But I will be keeping an eye on you. Please know that you can talk to me about anything, anytime."

"Okay Miss Moberg. Thank you."

Following this exchange, Valerie practically ran to the band room. She'd packed her lunch in her backpack today so she wouldn't have to go to her locker between math and lunchtime.

It probably helped to stay after in math—the hallway was fairly clear as she made it to the band room. If she could make it safely through today, she'd only have one day left ...

Ann checked the clock again. 11:53. "Good enough," she spoke out loud as she began gathering things together to step out for lunch.

First stop was the drugstore. Although the saleslady she met this morning could be a little much for her private nature, Ann appreciated her helpfulness and felt confident in her expertise. She entered the drugstore knowing she'd probably end up needing Charlotte's input.

"Back already?" Charlotte asked as Ann walked through the door.

"Yeah, I ran out of time this morning. I just have to pick up a few extra things."

"Hey—I didn't catch your name this morning. Did you get mine?"

"Yes Charlotte, I got your name. My name's Ann."

"Well Ann, again, if you need any help you just let me know."

"Thank you, I will."

Ann found the cosmetic aisle and was instantly overwhelmed with all the anti-aging products lining the shelves. One manufacturer had four different lines of product, all offering to aid in the battle against aging. There was eye serum, eye eraser, daily repair serum, one for crow's feet and dark circles and one to erase the appearance of fine lines and wrinkles, and wasn't that just about the same thing? She decided to try reading the labels more closely to better determine what the differences were. As she did, she noticed she couldn't move the product labels far enough from her eyes to be able to read them.

As she sighed out loud, Charlotte came around the corner with a pair of reading glasses. Ann thanked her and explained that she didn't usually need glasses, she thought something must be wrong and really needed to get in for an eye appointment.

"I know honey—it happens to all of us once we reach a certain age."

Ann rolled her eyes and resisted the urge to argue the fact that she wasn't really a *certain* age. She did, after all, appear to be. How could she possibly explain anyway? Who would believe her? *In fact,* she thought, *I wish there was someone I could talk to about all this.*

As she shook herself back to the business at hand and set her mind to deciphering the differences between Moroccan oil and argan oil, she noticed Charlotte was hovering just inches away. As if on cue, Charlotte asked, "So you're gonna fight it are ya?"

"What do you mean?"

"I mean, are you going to fight the aging process?"

Ann responded with her entire face twisted in shock that Charlotte would even ask such an absurd question. "You bet I am!"

"Yeah—I used to do it too. Hair dye, concealer, age spot remover. But then I got tired of the fight. I began telling myself that age spots created texture and the dazzling sparkle in my hair looked like tinsel at Christmastime. She jabbed Ann with her elbow as she chuckled, "How blessed am I to have my head lit up like Christmas all year long?"

Ann was horrified. "How could you possibly laugh about it?"

"Well sweetie—there I was looking in the mirror one morning before beginning the daily rituals. Standing there, face to face with the inevitable, I decided to start laughing about it." With another twinkly-eyed giggle she added, "But I haven't given up completely. I still keep up with some of the facial stuff. And don't I just look like Liz Taylor in her glory days?" More light-hearted laughter.

"Well, there's no way I can laugh about it. And what is the difference between eye serum, seven day rejuvenating eye cream, and daily retinol treatment? Do I really need to buy five different products just for my eyes? I just don't know where to start."

"Here. Let me help you." Charlotte loaded Ann's arms with all of her best, and least time-consuming options, and walked her to the cash register.

Along the way, Ann asked Charlotte what it really takes to win the battle.

"It all depends on how hard you want to work at it and how much time and money you want to spend. Some of my friends are retired and they have all day to go to the gym and get regular spa treatments. They color their hair regularly and frequently foot bills for eyelifts, tummy tucks and Botox treatments. They pay top dollar for department store cosmetics and they look beautiful. I don't have time or money. I'm not complaining, but before and after work here, I'm primary caregiver to my mother. By the end of the day I don't have time or energy left over for exercise. And I buy all my cosmetics right here."

She gave another hearty laugh as they reached the register. Before ringing Ann up, Charlotte touched Ann gently on the arm and looked intensely into her eyes. "We all have our own story, honey." Then she added, "You'll find your way," with such a soft, encouraging smile, that Ann automatically smiled back.

She was astonished by a wave of emotion that suddenly emerged from some deep corner of her heart. Somehow, this woman's tenderness, her authentic care and concern, managed to touch a long-forgotten piece of Ann that vibrated within her and begged for a chance to respond. How could this be? It certainly wasn't the first time someone had shown Ann kindness.

Just as she remembered to return the reading glasses, and before she paid for her bag of cosmetics, she saw something out the corner of her eye.

She looked out the store window and caught the tail end of a figure passing by who appeared to be wearing a black cloak. Without time to explain, Ann picked up her bag, threw the glasses on the counter and bolted for the door. She told Charlotte she'd come back and pay for all this after work as she ran out the door.

Sure enough, it was the old woman from the morning before that was moving down the sidewalk toward the crosswalk. She seemed a little faster today. By the time Ann reached the corner, the woman had already crossed the street and disappeared into the crowd.

Ann could not believe her bad luck. She had come so close. She couldn't help but believe this woman was responsible for all her current woes and would surely be able to reverse the process if only Ann could catch her. But she was encouraged by the fact that she'd seen the old lady. In a city the size of Chicago, it was highly unusual that Ann saw the woman at all, let alone one day after the incident. This told Ann that her newly acquired life's ambition was somewhere within reach: she might just be able to hook up with this woman after all.

She felt so jubilant she decided to go back and pay Charlotte now, rather than wait until the end of the day. Then she'd swing by the health food store for lunch on her way to the park. Life felt good when one had hope. The sun on her face smiled in agreement.

Ann was able to keep conversation to a minimum when she returned to the drugstore to pay Charlotte. For one as talkative as Charlotte was, she also seemed to possess that brand of sensitivity that told her when a person needed space or happened to be in a huge hurry. After stopping at the drugstore, Ann picked up her favorite gluten-free wrap sandwich from the health food store and was off to the park.

Once she got there, she decided to sit by the fountain. This crazy warm weather had given half the city the same idea and she barely found a place to sit. As she looked into the fountain pool where a bunch of people were wading, she thought she saw two familiar forms—a little boy with a head full of blonde curls and a petite woman with the same hair color. She didn't think it possible that twice within the space of an hour she could run into people she'd only seen or met once before in the most crowded section of downtown Chicago. But it was. Just as she noticed them, the pair turned around and began walking out of the pool.

The little boy spotted her first. She saw him point in her direction. After picking up their shoes, the two walked directly toward her. As they drew nearer, Ann strove to remember their names. The little boy was easy enough. He kept insisting they call him Charles Latham the Third. Such a mouthful was not so quickly forgotten. But the mother's name completely escaped her.

"Hello again," the mother said as they approached Ann. "I'm so sorry. I know it was just a few days ago, but I can't remember your name. I do remember your niece's name though. Charles talks about Valerie all the time. He keeps hoping we'll run into her again."

"Is Valerie here too?" Charles asked.

"No, she's at school," Ann replied.

Then she turned to Charles' mother and confessed she didn't remember her name either. But she could "hardly forget a name like Charles Latham the Third." As she said this, she looked toward Charles and he beamed.

"True, his name is tough to forget. But thanks for forgetting mine, now I don't feel so bad. My name's Lisa."

"Mine's Ann."

"Well it's nice to see you again Ann."

"You too. Charles was about to undergo some tests last time Valerie and I saw you. Did you already go through the testing process?"

At this question, Lisa's countenance fell considerably. "Yes, he was tested. It turns out he does have neuroblastoma. They're about to begin treatments. First, they'll try to shrink the tumors with chemotherapy, then a surgeon will have to go in to remove what's left."

Charles exuberantly cut into the conversation. "Yeah, and I've been getting lots of ice cream! Mommy tells me I don't have to be scared 'cause of all these doctors, 'cause sometimes I get scared. I can't help it though. I wish Valerie could be here. I like her. Why do you look so different? You look like my grandma used to look."

"Charles. That's not polite," Lisa said while apologizing to Ann with her eyes. "We need to be getting back to the hospital."

She shifted her embarrassed attention toward Ann. She too had noticed a significant change in Ann's appearance, but of course, she knew better than to say anything. "I'm so sorry," was all she could think of to say as she prepared to leave. "I do hope to see you again sometime soon."

"Could just happen," Ann responded. "I come here a lot on my lunch hour once the weather starts getting nice."

"Well, hopefully we'll meet again."

"Yes, that would be lovely."

That would be lovely? Who is this stranger living inside me? Not only had she spoken these words, but she actually felt them. She was genuinely concerned about Charles' health. She truly wanted updates on his progress and she found his mother to be a refreshing human being who was easy to talk to. Again—who was this person? Two days ago she wouldn't have cared a lick about Charles Latham the Third or his mother. Nor would she have found herself inextricably bonding with some stranger of a saleslady at the local drugstore. Could it be that this curse, or whatever it was, was changing her on the inside as well as on the outside? It sure felt that way. Oh well—one thing she knew for sure—she had to get to a mirror, and quick. After what Charles Latham the Third said, she wondered if anything new had developed in her appearance. The very thought settled inside her like a ball of lead.

There was only one safe place she could think of to do a mirror check: Charlotte's drugstore.

She made her way back with a sinking feeling in her gut. She thought back to Saturday, just five days ago, when she shrieked in her bathroom over one small wrinkle. There could be no shrieking over this. Whatever was happening to her was supernatural and unless she could capture that elderly woman, there wasn't a thing she could do to stop it. Her only response was involuntary—her insides caved into a fetal position while a feeling of hopelessness threatened to lay hold of her heart's helm. She was a vulnerable sail with no wind. In this state of despairing doldrums, she reached the drugstore.

As the bells on the drugstore door jingled to announce her arrival, Charlotte was with another customer at the counter. She greeted Ann with her smiling eyes and when Ann pointed to the bathroom, Charlotte gave her a nod.

Ann took her time. She didn't want to face the mirror, but the clock was running out on her lunch hour. When she finally rallied the courage to look, she could not believe her eyes. The gray streaks she'd covered this morning were back with a vengeance. The skin above her eyelids was drooping so severely it was practically touching her eyelashes. The grooves fanning out from the corners of her eyes had deepened, and patches of finely webbed lines underscored her eyes above her cheekbones. She was a mess. It was so bad, she resolved to buy a pair of dark glasses on the way out.

But first she'd try to work some magic with the hair color and cosmetics.

She started with the hair. This time, she remembered the back. Although the touch-up color seemed to do the job, she was going through it in a hurry. She'd have to buy more, along with the dark glasses. The eye goop Charlotte recommended seemed to work well on all the lines, but it appeared only surgery could relieve the sagging skin over her eyelids. Perhaps she could blame that on too much sodium or something. She only wanted to wear glasses as a last resort. After all, how could she explain *those*?

When she finished and came out of the bathroom, there were no other customers in the store. She found a pair of glasses and more hair color while Charlotte joked that they'd have to become Facebook friends. Since Ann was in serious mode, she informed Charlotte that she didn't do Facebook.

"I was just joking," Charlotte laughed. "But I'm not when I say I'm willing to be a friend to you. It looks like you're having a rough time with all this. I'm here anytime you need someone to talk to."

Ann was genuinely warmed by this and she thanked Charlotte as she approached the register. While Charlotte rang her up, she mentioned she might just take her up on her offer. "After all, there's no one else I can talk to about all this. So thanks again Charlotte." Then she looked Charlotte right in the eyes and said, "I'm really grateful for all your help."

They said their goodbyes and Ann tried to beat feet back to the office. But her hips were hurting again and it felt like she could only move so fast. As she walked, she thought again about all these emotions that kept knocking on her heart. It was so not her. *Maybe it has something to do with the hormone thing …*

Once she arrived at her desk, Ann could barely focus on all that sat before her. She kept being interrupted by extreme hot flashes that made her want to take her blazer off, yet she knew she'd have to put it right back on once the moment passed. How could she keep running through that routine without being noticed? Everyone in the office knew when Nancy was having a hot flash. She'd announce it by complaining of the heat, then she'd lose a layer or two, and five minutes later she'd be freezing to death and piling the layers back on again. Ann needed to be more discreet. She forced herself to quietly endure the heat and hoped Miss Doesn't-Miss-a-Thing wouldn't notice the beads of sweat on her forehead.

Cassie did mention it once when Ann finally had to wipe her brow with a Kleenex.

"What's the matter, are you hot or something? You're usually freezing."

"I know. I guess it's all the running around I did during lunch."

"Well why don't you take your jacket off?"

"I would, but this blouse fits a little funny in the sleeves."

"Oh you're probably just being picky. Who cares anyway? It's not like the cameras are rolling here in the office."

"I care, that's who. And I apologize for interrupting this pleasant conversation, but I'm facing a pile of work and would like to get out of here in time for dinner."

She wondered how long she could keep up with these off the cuff explanations for her looks and behavior.

Bradley stopped by about an hour later and told Ann he was leaving to get Valerie.

"We already have dinner planned. Valerie was full of ideas this morning on the way to school. She's so funny. She was sure to tell me what you can and can't eat, so we settled on something that would fit within your dietary parameters."

"And what would that be?" Ann asked.

"That would be a surprise," was all she could get out of him. Then he left.

Ann braced herself for Cassie's matchmaking comments, but Cassie only mentioned it must be nice having a new set of chefs in the house.

Feeling grateful for the short commentary, Ann tied up as many loose ends as she could before calling it a day. She was dreadfully uncomfortable from sitting. Her back hurt, her hips hurt and she was tired of having to do her work with a magnifying glass. She also felt bloated to the point where it felt like she was popping out of her pants. She couldn't wait to get into her yoga pants, and maybe even a robe when she got home. So she left about fifteen minutes early and took her time getting home. It was so good not to have to drive, and walking seemed to relieve her soreness.

When she entered the condo, she was instantly mesmerized by the smells that wafted from the kitchen. She was starving and couldn't wait to see what her team of chefs had concocted for dinner. But they wouldn't let her in the kitchen.

"Sorry my lady," Bradley said. "The kitchen is presently off bounds to you. Mademoiselle Valerie will serve you tea in your bedroom so you can enjoy some refreshment while you wait for dinner. Might I suggest a long, relaxing shower while you wait?"

Despite Ann's serious nature, smiles erupted like a geyser from deep within her heart as she readily complied with this newly presented to-do list. Obediently, she made her way to the bedroom and patiently awaited the maître-d's arrival with the tea. A giggle even rolled from her chest as Valerie walked in with a serving tray and a towel draped over her forearm. How could she remain in her state of doom and gloom in the face of all this fun? It was such a tonic to her soul that she readily left her dark cavern to fully embrace the moment.

"Thank you, Madame Valerie, for your four-star service."

"Hmm-hmmm," Valerie grunted. "That would be 'Mademoiselle,' Miss Auntie. 'Madame' is used for married ladies."

"Pardon me, Miss. My French is a little rusty."

"All is forgiven, Miss Auntie. Now if you'll excuse me, I must return to the dinner preparations."

"Very well then, you're excused."

Right after Valerie left, Ann broke into another impromptu fit of giggles.

Here she was, sitting in her bedroom and laughing like she did when she was a child growing up in her Colorado home. It had been so long since she'd last felt this way, yet a distant familiarity subtly promised to move into sharper focus as the evening progressed. She decided not to fight it. After the day she'd just had, with all the mirror checks, touch-ups, trips to the drugstore and having to perform at the office, it was a relief to drop the professional façade in the safety of her own home.

She couldn't exactly confide in Valerie and Bradley about what was going on, but from the way they were acting, it felt to Ann as though a slice of Charlotte had joined them for the evening. She warmed herself with these thoughts as she sat on the edge of her bed, sipping her entire cup of tea before getting in the shower.

Just after she stepped in, she heard the phone ring. She figured it must be Sara and decided to call her back after dinner. She luxuriated in the warm water as she rehearsed how she might broach this topic to Sara. "Some lady zapped me in a downtown crosswalk and I became an old lady overnight." *No.* "Can you believe it? I woke up with gray hair this morning and my skirt wouldn't fit. I'm thinking I may have been visited by a bacterial infection." *No.*

How was she going to bring this up to Sara? Of all the people in the world, her sister was one of the few she could really trust. But this would be difficult to take in, even for a person she'd known and trusted since birth. As she was talking herself into a morbid state of discouragement, Valerie shouted through the door.

"Hurry up Auntie. Dinner's ready."

"I'm coming," Ann shouted back. She hadn't called those words out from the shower since high school. This really was feeling like family week.

Once out of the shower, she threw on her loungy clothes and decided to join the dinner party with her towel wrapped around her head. She didn't know how well this touch-up stuff held when it came to shampooing, and was afraid of grays showing through as her hair dried. She tightened the towel and quickly dabbed on more eye goop before exiting the bedroom to sit down for dinner.

She walked into the kitchen and a few more of the crusty edges that lined her heart crumbled with what her eyes beheld. Valerie and Bradley had placed a tablecloth on the kitchen table and there was a vase of fresh flowers sitting in the middle of it. The table was set with place settings and cloth napkins. It looked for all the world as though they were dining in a quaint Italian restaurant.

Again, Ann smiled in spite of herself. She was so deeply moved by this scene that she placed one hand on her chest and said, "I don't have any words you guys. This is ... really nice." She found Bradley's eyes and repeated, "Really nice."

Bradley responded, "Well my dear, are you going to dine with that towel wrapped around your head? We can wait five more minutes you know. If you need to go blow it dry or something, we can most certainly wait."

"No. I like to keep it on sometimes after a shower. It does a wave job on my hair that cuts time in the morning, so the towel thing really works for me."

"Alrighty then. Shall I have the maître-d describe tonight's menu for you?"

"That would be delightful," Ann replied, playing along with the restaurant game while silently enjoying every minute of it.

Knowing her cue, Valerie recited the menu. "This evening we will be serving an organic ground turkey with fresh marinara served on a bed of gluten-free quinoa pasta. On the side you can have your choice of spring greens salad and balsamic vinaigrette or delicious focaccia garlic bread. Or both, if you really want to."

At this, Valerie broke into a huge giggle and Bradley joined her. He praised her for doing such a good job, then joked about not being able to find good help these days. He told her she was such an exception to today's norm that he would soon put her in charge of all the staff. As they started laughing again, Ann not only caught the easy rapport between the two of them, but she noticed how animated Valerie was with Bradley. She also noticed how deliriously happy Valerie seemed, as if she was in the presence of her very favorite uncle. At the same time, she felt shame.

Since Valerie had been left in her care, the two of them had barely spoken. And frequently when they had shared words, Valerie had closed her petals like a flower tucked in for the night. Only she wasn't settling in for a peaceful night's sleep. Ann had shut her down.

In an instant, the times when Valerie was happy and animated flashed before her. Like when they walked through Lurie Garden and when Valerie got so excited about Ann's violin playing.

Then the other moments cropped up. The times when Ann was downright mean to Valerie. Like when she made Valerie feel bad for having to go back to the grocery store or the other day when she went so far as to call her a name in the car on the way to school. 'Pint-sized prophet,' was it?

In light of this family-friendly atmosphere, Ann was appalled by her own behavior. She couldn't put her finger on how, but the pre-crosswalk incident Ann seemed to be slipping away.

Somehow, she would have to make an apology. But that urge would have to be on hold while she figured out a few more things. Like how to break through the thick wall of pride she'd constructed over the years, and how to transfer the utter humility she was feeling from the inside to the outside. Expressing emotions had never been her strong suit. Even growing up, she never talked about serious emotions. Instead, she played them out, alone on her violin.

But enough with the introspection. It was time to dish up.

All through dinner, Bradley and Valerie continued their light-hearted banter while Ann just drank it in. They didn't seem to mind her silence as she ventured back to years gone by, dissolving in the comfort of family memories and how they lined up with sitting right here at her kitchen table. In fact, they let her wander in her own little world until it came to the end of the meal.

"Last call for my ever-so-delectable focaccia garlic bread," Bradley announced.

Up until this official announcement, Ann had been eyeballing that bread and noticing how incredible it smelled. Long before she went gluten-free, garlic bread had been one of her favorite comfort foods. There was a part of her that said, *"Come on now Miss Discipline, you can overcome this."* But it was quickly overruled by the voice of ultimate reason that suggested, *"Nonsense. You're already popping out of your pants due to some chance meeting with a crazed old lady in a crosswalk. What difference will it really make?"* The voice of reason won and she plunged headlong into garlic bread nirvana while Valerie and Bradley cleared the dishes.

After she finished, she remembered she needed to make a call to Sara, and asked her host and hostess if they'd mind her escaping into the bedroom with a phone call.

"No problem here," Bradley replied. "We have cleanup and dessert to manage. You go ahead, we'll be just fine."

Ann took the phone to the bedroom and dialed her sister. She actually felt nervous. She had no idea how to tell her sister about what was happening. Before she could think anymore, Sara answered the phone.

"Hey hon, how's it going? I hear Mr. Bradley is there again tonight. I can't even tell you how borderline obsessed Valerie is with him. But I *can* tell you—I think it's a God thing for him to be there at all. Valerie was feeling so uncomfortable at the beginning of the week. And now, it's as if Dad and Jim had rolled themselves together to reappear in Valerie's life. I won't press you about snatching up this Brad guy, but he sounds so wonderful. I'm tempted, but I promise you I won't. Anyway, how's life?"

"Funny you should ask. I don't exactly know where to start."

"Start at the beginning. That always helps."

"Well that's the problem—I don't know where the beginning would be. How's about the part where I woke up with gray streaks in my previously brown hair and my favorite skirt wouldn't fit? Then there's the part about my eyelids sagging like an eighty-year-old's and crow's feet appearing from out of nowhere. Remember when I shrieked you into the bathroom last Saturday over a wrinkle? Well, what's happening around my eyes now is like some sort of private Armageddon. It's like the aging Nazis are tromping all over my face saying, "You think that was bad? Take a look at this.""

"Ann. Back up. I don't get this. You woke up with gray hair? Can we just start from there?"

"Okay. In a nutshell, I started having all these 'symptoms' following a run-in with an elderly woman in a crosswalk yesterday. I yelled at her because she wouldn't move and I think she put a curse on me."

"Sorry hon, I have a hard time believing in curses. Why don't you send me some pictures so I can get a better feel for what you're talking about? Have you been able to get to the doctor at all?"

"I called my Tae Kwon Do buddy about it. She's a family practitioner. She said it sounds like I'm going through menopause."

"But you're way too young for menopause. Just shoot me some pictures and I'll be praying about all this. I can't even imagine …"

"Neither can I. The worst part is having to hide it from everyone. And what really has me convinced this must be some sort of curse is, I cover all the gray with touch-up color and it returns four hours later. The same thing with all the wrinkles. Who knows what I'll see in the mirror tomorrow morning? And at the rate things are going, I might just grow out of my closet too."

At this point, Sara was feeling acutely for her sister. But she was also beyond skeptical. How could it be that a person could age overnight? Yet her sister was distraught and in need of support, so she answered as honestly as she could.

"Sorry Anna. I can barely wrap my mind around all this. I'll just have to see it."

"Sara, I know I'm in a vulnerable state, but I'm still going by 'Ann' rather than 'Anna.'"

"Excuse me for slipping. My big sister heart wants to wrap its arms around you, so your little girl name just flew into my mouth."

"You're excused. I think I better get back out there. Any word on who they're hiring yet?"

"Not yet. They're hoping to know by Saturday. It turns out they might want to hire two of us."

"Oh good. Well, keep me posted and I'll send you pictures in the morning. I'm giving you back to Valerie."

"Okay, hon. Have a good night."

"You too."

Ann walked the phone out to Valerie and noticed the kitchen staff had prepared brownies to go with the ice cream. "Will you be joining us for a bowl of sugar?" Bradley asked.

"I'm not sure. It looks great, but I just ate garlic bread and that may have to serve as my dessert." But the brownies were looking so good, she was tempted beyond reason. Whether it was a need for comfort in the midst of her circumstances or hormonal imbalances upsetting her internal apple cart, Ann seemed to be losing her battle with discipline. She decided to give in, but only to a very small portion.

By now, Valerie was off the phone so they all sat in the living room. Valerie chose this moment to tell Ann about Friday. It turned out there was a teacher in-service day and all the students got to have the day off.

"It's really cool because next week is spring break, so we get a lot of time off."

Bradley added, "Yeah, so Val and I were talking on the way home from school and I could probably take the day and show her the town. I was telling her we could go to the Pier, then up to the Skydeck. We could wrap it up at Giordano's and if we time it just right, you could meet us there for dinner. Marv actually owes me a day off, so it would work out perfectly."

"Hmm …" Ann deliberated. "I guess that would be all right. I'm sure Sara wouldn't mind either. She hasn't even met you and you've been given her solid stamp of approval. Friday is my conference call with Green Jeans and finishing touches on the May issue. I'm sure the office could spare you."

"Sounds like a good day to miss," Bradley commented.

Valerie asked, "Is that a yes, Auntie? I've never been to the top of the Sears Tower. It would be so fun!"

"Sure. I don't see why not."

Valerie shot up, ran over to where Ann was sitting, and hugged her so hard Ann thought her neck might snap. "Thank you Auntie. Thank you so much!"

Until now, Ann was unaware of how exhausted she was truly feeling. Perhaps it was the large meal she just consumed, but she could barely keep her eyes open. Reluctantly, she made the announcement, "Hey guys, I think it's coming up on time to call it a night."

They all took their dishes into the kitchen. Bradley offered to wash them quickly, but Ann kicked him out. "I'm falling asleep on my feet right now. I can't tell you how much I appreciate everything you've been doing, but those dishes can sit in that sink all the way to the next election for all I care. I have to go to bed."

Bradley pinched the top of the towel that was on her head and said, "Okay, boss. See you tomorrow."

Valerie gave him a giant hug at the door and told him she couldn't wait for Friday to come. He said "likewise," and she told him she wished he didn't have to go. He tapped the top of her head and said something about her being a silly girl and just where would he sleep?

Ann felt like a foreign exchange student as she observed this warm interaction. It caused her to consider her own lack of close-knit relationships. But she didn't ponder it for long—she felt like she couldn't stand up anymore.

After Bradley left, Ann was first in the bathroom while Valerie inflated her bed. When she took her towel off, she noticed that her hair was almost a solid silver, so she put it back on. She wanted to say goodnight to Valerie and wasn't about to do it with a head full of silver hair.

When it was time to say goodnight, Ann grappled with what she might say. She knew she'd been wrong all this time, but couldn't bring herself to admit it and make things right. So she decided to be ultra-nice instead.

"I'm glad you get to have so much fun on Friday. And I have to thank you again for being such a good maître-d tonight. I'm sure Bradley would have been lost without you."

"Yeah, probably. But I better go brush my teeth before I get too tired."

"Okay," Ann replied. "I guess I'll see you tomorrow after school."

"Okay Auntie. Goodnight."

Ann said goodnight in return, but part of her didn't want to end the evening there—she felt her interlude with Valerie was incomplete. She wanted to share more, but had no idea of how to make this connection happen. So she went into her bedroom and crawled under the covers.

While feeling the weight and warmth of the blankets on top of her, she felt the urge to do something she hadn't done since her parents were alive.

Pray.

She struggled with this for a few reasons. For one, she stopped believing in God forever ago and had a tendency to slam anyone who tried to convince her of His great attributes. For another, she'd have to admit to wrongdoing and why was this so hard for her anyway?

Regardless, she felt like it was either 'fess up, or rot inside like a butternut squash gone all wrong. She had to do something about this heavy feeling. And one little prayer wasn't the same thing as a lifelong commitment. So she offered up a single prayer.

"Dear God. This is Ann. You know I stopped believing in You a long time ago, but please don't hold that against me. I know I made Valerie feel bad. Please help me make it up to her. Amen."

In the other room, Valerie had some prayers of her own.

She only had one day left at school before spring break. Things worked out today, but she still worried about tomorrow. She almost told Bradley about the mean kids on the way home, but they got to talking about Friday and her heart had become so light that the former topic flew out the window. So she poured her concerns out to the One she knew she could always talk to.

"Dear Lord, I know one of Your names is El Roi, the God who sees. I know You see everything that's happening at school. Please watch over me tomorrow and protect me. And please give Mama this job so I won't ever have to go back to this school again. And thank You for Bradley. He's so nice and since he's been taking me to school, I've barely had to be alone with Auntie. I'm sorry to feel this way, but You know how mean she can be. And I gave up a little on praying for her after she yelled at me, but I know I shouldn't give up like that. So please change her heart and help her be a nice person. In Jesus' name, amen."

Alone in her hotel room, Sara was praying too. She poured out her usual prayers regarding this job and she asked the Lord to comfort Valerie while they were apart. But she barely knew how to pray for this recent newsflash from her sister. She confessed this as she began to pray for Ann.

"Lord, I just don't get it. How could something like this even happen? I mean sure—in Your world all sorts of unbelievable things can happen. Like how you caused large bodies of water to part not just once, but four times in the Old

Testament. You made Balaam's donkey talk. You turned Nebuchadnezzar into a beast who ate grass for seven years. You made Moses' hand get leprosy, then turned right around and healed it. You made the sun stand still so Joshua could win a battle. I could go on and on, but You're the One who wrote the book—I don't have to tell You about all the incredible things You've done. The point is, You made all that stuff happen way back when. Do You perform miraculous works like this in today's world? I've heard stories of how sometimes You do things for missionaries in third world countries, but this is twenty-first century, USA. And even if You did use some old woman to put a 'curse' on Ann, why would You do that? I'm guessing You'd have to be the One behind such an act. I don't believe in magic and I know what You have to say about it in Your Word. But enough about how and why and all that. Could You please surround my sister with extra, heaping doses of love and care? If she really is aging prematurely due to whatever reason, I can't imagine how she'd be feeling right now. Especially since she's always been so vain to begin with. Please be with her in a mighty way and bless us all with a good night's sleep. In Jesus' name, amen."

So Sara, Valerie and Ann placed their hearts in the hands of the Almighty and drifted off to sleep.

Chapter 7

Ann jolted from a sound sleep at three. She was drowning in sweat again. As she changed her clothes and put towels on the sheets and across the pillow case, she vowed to have Peggy put her on some sort of hormones the minute she got back from Florida. In fact, she bet Peggy could even call in a prescription. Her mind was racing with all these to-dos and she couldn't turn it off.

She decided she may as well change the bedding after all. Her quick fix with the towels probably wouldn't get her to sleep any sooner. She was feeling so awake she felt tempted to jump on the elliptical. But knowing her hours before work were short-lived, she crawled back under the covers.

From there on it was covers on, covers off. She tossed and turned like crazy, and there were times when her stomach hurt so badly she had to curl up in a ball and rock to try and make the pain go away.

She was so exhausted by the time the alarm went off that she repeatedly pushed the snooze button all the way to 6:30. A week ago she would have brutally chastised herself for performing such an act. Not only did her regimented world disallow sleeping past six o'clock on weekdays, she never skipped her morning workout and now she wouldn't have time.

Despite the extra half hour of sleep, she could still barely force herself out of bed. When her feet finally did hit the bedroom floor, she discovered her hips were already hurting. They hurt so badly, she had to sit on the bed for a good long time before getting up. With this amount of pain and stiffness, she probably wouldn't have gotten on the elliptical even if she hadn't slept in. She also decided Tae Kwon Do would not be happening tonight.

When she looked in the bedroom mirror she realized she'd have to call Cassie to say she'd be late. Her hair was pure silver, almost white. There was no way her wimpy touch-up color could raise a fist to this challenge—she needed to swing by Charlotte's shop and saturate her head with some serious chemicals. She called Cassie at home to give her a heads up before getting dressed.

Things quickly went from bad to earth-shattering. She went to put on her stretchy dress slacks and they were so tight it felt like she needed to wear something in the next size up. It was so uncomfortable she knew she wouldn't be able to get through the day wearing them. Then it dawned on her she might not own a single article of clothing that would accommodate this new body. Her closet and drawers were solely stocked with size two pants, skirts and dresses.

Devastation drove her to sit back down on the bed. This was where her world almost stopped. She'd been a size two since high school and had worked ever so hard to maintain it. It was almost more than she could bear. Then, just as despair closed in to fully possess her, the picture of that old woman smirking at her through the car window flashed in her mind again. She recalled the final "so there," self-satisfied nod of the head the woman offered before finally crossing the street.

This image propelled her to her feet with all the fight she was born with. She stood back up and declared, "Oh no you don't, old woman. I will not let you knock me down and reduce me to a pile of spineless Jell-O. You are not going to defeat me because I'm going to put up a fight. I'm going to find you and we're going to have it out or my name isn't Ann Kathleen Finlayson. I'll find something in my closet that will work for today, and hole-in-the-wall clothing shops are a dime a dozen in downtown Chicago. Don't start your victory dance yet."

Then a text message buzzed her phone. It was her sister. All it said was, "pics?"

"That's right. I was supposed to send her pictures." As Ann was speaking this into the mirror, she realized now would be the perfect time to snap some shots. *After all, I look way worse than yesterday. She'll have to believe me now.*

As she prepared to take some pictures, she calculated the time difference between here and Denver. She thought, *Sara must've texted right after she woke up. It's 5:50 in the morning there. Maybe she didn't sleep well either …*

She cut off that thought trail by deciding she'd better get moving if she was going to make it to the office at all. She took and sent three pictures and finished getting ready to go out the door.

She found a dress with a flouncy bottom that might work for hiding her hips. She didn't own a springy, lightweight scarf that would serve to cover her sagging neck, so she'd have to stop at a clothing store after dyeing her hair. She found a sweater that would work to hide the loosening, puckered skin on her arms. At least she could blame the AC for her need to wear long sleeves in the office.

She zoomed through the rest of the morning routine. Before heading out, she made sure to check her bag for all her new essentials: dark glasses, touch-up hair color, eye goop and magnifying glass.

All she had to do now was figure out which hooded coat would work best to hide her hair on the way to the drugstore. She settled on a light raincoat and made her way to the drugstore as fast as her sore hips would allow.

When she got there, she pushed the door open with a force that threatened to crash the jingle bells to the floor. She called Charlotte's name while searching the store aisles.

At first, Charlotte didn't recognize the voice coming from underneath the hood of the vanilla-colored raincoat.

"Ann is that you? Why are you wearing a raincoat on this beautiful spring day? It's supposed to get up to seventy-one degrees today."

"I'm wearing the raincoat because you won't believe what's under the hood. Are we the only two people in the store?"

"Yes, for now."

"Okay Charlotte, take a look at this."

Ann pulled the hood off to expose her silver head and even Charlotte was shocked by the sight. "Well I've never seen anything like this before. How could it turn completely silver overnight?"

"You tell me," Ann grumbled, feeling agitated even though the question was legitimate. "I woke up this morning and this is what it looked like."

"Well like I said, I've never seen anything like this before. What do you want to do?"

"I want to dye it. I want to cover all of this completely. Can you recommend a really good hair dye? Then I still have some touch-up for later."

"Honey—I have some dye that will cover you for three months. You won't even need to use the touch-up."

Knowing Charlotte might not believe the crosswalk, old lady curse thing, Ann decided to skirt that topic for now. "All right Charlotte, could you help me apply it too? I'm running late, and on top of everything else, I need to shop for some clothes before work."

"Sure, I can help you. As long as nobody else comes in."

She told Ann to go wait in the bathroom while she shopped the shelves for the right color. Then she showed up with a towel and told Ann how to distribute the hair color for the best results. "I don't really need to stand here and help you," she explained. "It's mostly just a waiting game. Oops. There's someone now."

She left to respond to the bells on the drugstore door and returned moments later. "It was just someone asking for directions. How ya doin'?"

"I think I'm doing fine." With her head upside down over the sink she asked, "How much longer do you think I should leave it in?"

"About ten more minutes. Now what's this about going shopping before work?"

"Well, you wouldn't believe it, but I seem to have outgrown my closet overnight. So I need more clothes for work and some scarves to cover my neck."

"What do you mean you outgrew your closet overnight? Did you eat too much pizza for dinner or something? Maybe you just need to take a laxative."

"No Charlotte, it's not that simple. I've sprouted hips. I've never had hips before. I've been a size two since high school and suddenly, I might be a size four."

"Size two?" Charlotte laughed. "I've never seen a size two in my life. And what's this about hips? We're women. We're supposed to have hips. You know—once I went through the change I began to thank God for my bountiful booty. Made me more womanly. I never was a stick figure, but I decided to make peace with my hips. Besides girl—I don't see anything in your basement that needs fixin'. Looks to me like you might be a whoppin' two and a half." Then she laughed her Charlotte laugh and became a bit more reflective.

"You know, there can be a brittleness to perfection, Ann. If overdone, it repels more than it attracts. So if your pursuit of the perfect size two makes you brittle, wouldn't you rather be a softer size four?"

Although Ann refused to swallow the "grow old gracefully" pill Charlotte was tossing at her, she felt a freedom with Charlotte that she had nowhere else at this time. At work, she was killing herself to maintain her shark persona. At home, she was doing everything she could to appear normal to Valerie, and now Bradley. She'd just told Sara about her predicament, but Sara didn't believe her. It was such a comfort to be with Charlotte right now, not having to pretend. For the first time in her adult life she was experiencing true friendship. And it felt good.

"Time's up," Charlotte announced. "There's a hair dryer over there in the corner. Can't wait to see the ravishing new beauty."

She giggled her way out the door and Ann finished up in the bathroom. Charlotte certainly knew her stuff. The hair color worked perfectly. There wasn't a single strand of silver left in her head. *But I'm still keeping the touch-up with me at all times. This might be gone before lunchtime.*

When she walked out of the bathroom, Charlotte greeted her with a light, springy scarf that matched her dress beautifully. "How's this?" she asked as she walked up to meet Ann.

"I don't know—do you have a mirror?"

"Right over there," Charlotte pointed. "I just got these out of their boxes last night. The hair color looks good."

"Sure does. I can't thank you enough."

"No big deal," Charlotte said. "I used to be a beautician. Quit 'cause my arms were aching so much. Hey, if you ever get tired of fighting the gray, I have a card here for a friend who owns a wig shop down the street."

"Thanks, but I don't know that I'd want to go *that* far."

"I don't know. You seem to be fighting it pretty hard. I, for one, think you should just roll with it. Just think," she said with a smile, "the older you get, the more people might regard you as cute or adorable." Another sparkly-eyed giggle rolled out of Charlotte's heart.

"But I don't want to be 'cute' or 'adorable.' I just want to be regular old me. That is, the younger version."

"I know, sweetie. We're all still twenty-two inside and the world wants to treat us like we're some sort of relics or dusty old wall hangings. But we all know we're still twenty-two and wouldn't they all be shocked if they just took a closer look? You know—when it comes to pursuing that youthful appeal, people can fight so hard they lose sight of what really matters."

"What do you think matters, Charlotte?"

Charlotte stopped fidgeting with the scarves she'd been sorting and looked Ann straight in the eye. "People, Ann. People matter."

Food for thought popped into Ann's head as they approached the register so she could pay for the hair color and scarf. A million people in her past had probably preached the same principals, but for some reason, she was able to receive them from Charlotte.

As she said goodbye and left the store, she got to thinking about Sara. And this morning's text. And how Sara was already trying to touch base with her at 5:50 Denver time. Her sister wasn't contacting her because she'd had a restless night. She sent the early text because she cared. Hadn't she always?

Ever since Ann graduated from college and got this job, Sara had looked out for her. After their parents died, Sara began fussing over her as though she were a child rather than a grown sister. And what had she shown in return? A selfish cold shoulder. She was barely there for Sara when Jim died. When had she become so unfeeling? What had caused her to become so hard and calloused? And cynical?

Her thoughts were broken by a familiar cloaked figure across the street. Ann called out, "Hey," and the woman looked up and made eye contact. Then she shook her head and ran around the corner. Ann knew she wouldn't be able to catch the woman because the traffic lights weren't in her favor. But she was quite puzzled by one thing: the woman knew she was trying to make contact and appeared to be eluding her on purpose.

Hadn't she had enough fun at Ann's expense?

"Oh well," Ann concluded for the time being. "I've seen her twice in the past twenty-four hours. Surely I'll be able to connect with her soon."

Then she looked at her watch and realized that thanks to Charlotte, she could skip shopping for now and get to the office by nine. Not bad for a morning she'd called in late for. She made it to the Tower by 9:05 and was stepping off the elevator moments later. As usual, Cassie was the first face she saw when she finally made it to the office.

"Nice dress," were Cassie's first words when Ann came through the door. "A pleasant departure from all that tailored, power-playing executive stuff you always wear."

"Thanks. I had a bit of a time finding something to ... match my mood today."

"Mood? And what mood would that be?"

Ann dug deep. "I'm feeling relieved that this conference call is coming tomorrow and the Green Jeans campaign is almost in the bag."

"Oh. I would have chosen black for that. Before I forget, I told Marvin you were running late, but he still wants you to check in."

"Okay, thanks."

Ann made it to Marvin's office just as he was stepping out for more coffee. "Oh, Ann, so good to see you. Cassie must've told you to stop by. If you don't mind my taking a bite out of your busy schedule, can we step into my office for a moment?"

So much sarcasm. She tried to play it down with the casual approach. "Sure Marv, whatcha got?"

They entered his office and he shut the door behind them. "Finlayson. I don't know what's going on with you, but if you blow this Green Jeans deal I may have to make some radical moves in this office."

"What do you mean Marvin? The conference call is on for tomorrow and I'm pretty sure Mr. Fleming is going to commit to the four-page spread."

"Well, I just noticed you've been having trouble getting to the office on time and your lunches seem to be getting longer."

"Understood. I think things will get back to normal for me the minute my sister comes home and my niece isn't living with me anymore. I've been a bit distracted lately."

"Just see to it that nothing comes between you and that conference call tomorrow."

"Done deal, Marv. You have nothing to worry about."

"You know my favorite words."

"Yeah. 'Prove it.'"

"There's my girl. Now get back to work."

Ann got back to her desk just as the new courier was about to have Cassie sign for a package.

"Is that for me?"

"Yes ma'am, it is."

"I can sign for it."

As she took the delivery register, she looked for something to say that would make up for her prior harsh treatment of this young man. She gave him a smile and asked how his fourth day on the job was going. "Any better?" she asked while trying to make eye contact.

She became acutely aware of the damage she'd caused by his apparent reluctance to make eye contact. He looked at his shoes and responded with a near whisper. "Yes ma'am. I'm getting to know my way around a lot better."

"Good. And from now on, don't call me 'ma'am'. Makes me feel old."

"Okay ma'am … I mean … what should I call you?"

"Miss Finlayson. And what shall we call you?"

At this point he looked up. Ann still had a smile on her face and he appeared to relax. "Tim. My name is Tim."

"Alrighty then, Tim. We'll see you soon."

"Okay, Miss Finlayson. Thank you."

"Thank *you.*"

"Who are you and what have you done with my boss?" Cassie had to ask.

"Funny. And original. I've just been doing some thinking lately, that's all."

"Well think away, girl! I don't know where it's coming from, but I do hope to see more."

"Maybe you will." As if she'd never opened her eyes to her office surroundings until now, she noticed a sign on the wall by Cassie's desk that she'd never seen before. "What's that sign on your desk?"

"Which one? This one? It says, 'All is Vanity.'"

"What on earth does that mean?"

"King Solomon repeats it several times in the book of Ecclesiastes. It means everything we deem important in this life is temporary and fleeting. All the things we chase after—ultimate beauty, prestige, financial success, flaming popularity, the perfectly chiseled body—are fleeting. In the end, they don't matter at all. The only two things that do matter are our relationships with God and with those He's planted in our lives. All the rest is nothing but vanity. I have it on my desk as a constant reminder of how precious life is. I saw it in a thrift shop the first time Craig went through treatment. Every time I look at it, I pray for him. Losing him would be like losing my whole world."

People, Ann. People Matter.

"I'm sorry you have to go through this, Cassie."

This being the first time Ann had ever acknowledged what Cassie might be going through, Cassie fielded several emotions at once. Surprise, shock, validation, and a warmth that overruled it all. She fought back tears as she expressed her heartfelt gratitude. "Thank you Ann. That really means a lot to me."

She had to turn her head because she couldn't hold back the tears any longer.

She didn't need to hide—Ann was already in her own head and on her own track. She couldn't help but analyze the fact that for the second time in the past few days, she was met with a recurring theme. And both involved Cassie. The first one was that Bible verse that had angered her so much. What was it? "What is desirable in a man is his kindness" or something like that? Valerie said it in the car, then Cassie repeated it once Ann got to the office. Then this morning, Charlotte referred to the exact same concept Cassie just addressed with that sign on her desk. About placing people at top of the priority list rather than putting them in second, third or even tenth place like she usually did. Ann wasn't ready or willing to consider the God thing, but she certainly felt introspective about how she'd been treating people for the last chunk of years. She wished she could take the rest of the day off.

Bradley, with his consistently impeccable timing, chose now to swing by Ann's desk.

"So everything went well with today's drop-off. We need to hash out the logistics regarding tomorrow. Marv said yes to my day off, since he did owe it to me after all. Valerie is stoked about this 'hang out in Chicago' day. All we need is a green light from you. So what do you say, boss?"

As always, Bradley brought smiles to Ann's face she didn't even know were there. "I already told you last night it would be fine. All we need to do is figure out times. I usually leave at around 7:15 or so, but I can't leave Valerie alone. Could you come hang out until she wakes up while I sneak off to work?"

"Of course I can!" Bradley's bubbling enthusiasm ushered Cassie right into the conversation.

"So Bradley. Why don't you bring Valerie by the office so I can meet her? I have an interest in bringing her home for a play date and possible overnighter. Think you could manage that?"

"Yeah, that would be fun." He turned to Ann. "Has she ever been to the office before?"

"No. There hasn't really been any reason until now. Who knew she'd be in such high demand?"

"Of course she's in demand. How could anyone resist such a terrific kid?"

Another pang stabbed Ann's heart. Since Valerie's arrival, she'd only thought of her niece as an inconvenience. Yet everywhere Valerie went, a fan club followed in her wake. How could she miss what shone like a beacon in everyone else's mind?

She tossed up another prayer to a God she didn't believe in. "Please God, help me improve this tense relationship I have with Valerie. She deserves more from me, but I still don't feel up to the task. Amen."

Her musing and silent prayer had blocked all surrounding dialogue. Bradley broke through her momentary cloud of self-examination by asking, "So what do you think Ann?"

"What do I think?"

"Yeah. Should I bring Val by the office tomorrow so she can meet Cassie and possibly schedule a play date and sleepover?"

"Oh … yeah … that would be good."

"Okay, fine then. I guess we should all get back to work."

"Probably a good idea," Ann muttered.

The last thing on her mind was work. She felt the need for a three-month sabbatical. She was normally such a workaholic that she never took time off apart from all the designated holidays. She cherished the unstructured time the weekends offered, but the rapid pace of office life was what really made her feel like she had a heartbeat.

She'd often suspected that if she were left alone for too long in the solitude of her private life, her existence might not matter at all; she might just disappear altogether. So normally, she thrived on the daily grind. But today, she wasn't in the mood. She muddled through until it was almost noon, then decided to cut out early. She had some shopping to do.

Valerie kept watching the clock during math. Only a little more than three hours and she'd be free. No more worrying about being knocked out in the hallway or on the playground. No more threats between classes. She couldn't wait for class to end.

When it finally did, she realized she couldn't get to the band room without making a pit stop first. She gathered up all her things and headed toward the bathroom. Once they filed out of the classroom, three of the mean kids rushed ahead of her and commanded her to go into the bathroom. They didn't need to since she was on her way there anyway, but everything felt all wrong.

Two of the regular five tormentors stayed outside the bathroom. Once she entered behind the other three of the group, they seemed to want to hang around for a while. She was able to ignore them as she went into a stall. But as soon as she came out, one of them grabbed her by the shoulder.

"No one's here to protect you now, golden girl. Remember when I said I'd wrap your pretty hair around your throat and choke you with it? Well today's the day. And your bodyguard isn't here to protect you, so I recommend you don't start screaming like a baby or else we'll do some *real* damage."

Valerie was so scared she felt paralyzed. Tears streamed down her face despite her efforts to appear undaunted by this attack. She didn't know what to do. She knew time was short, and all that came to mind were two words.

"Jesus, help."

No sooner had she spoken these words than the company was joined by Miss Moberg, her math teacher.

"Is everything all right in here?" she asked everyone present.

The three bullies left the bathroom in a hurry and laid into the two outside who were supposed to stand guard.

"Are you okay, Valerie? You look a little pale. I told you that you could always talk to me. Is there anything I can do for you?"

"Yes. I don't feel very good. I'd like to go to the nurse's office please."

"Okay Valerie, I'll walk you there."

Once they got to the nurse's office, all the nurse did was have Valerie lay down for the entire lunch hour. They were trying to determine whether or not she needed to go home for the rest of the day.

Ann made her way to one of her favorite consignment shops while munching a sandwich she'd thrown together this morning. She was almost there, so rather than finding a place to sit and finish her lunch, she threw the rest of her sandwich away before stepping inside the shop. After her meeting with Marvin, the last thing she wanted to do was turn this into another extended lunch hour.

This shop had a reputation for carrying upscale clothing from Chicago's finest. It took no time at all to find a handful of ensembles that would carry her through the next few work days. Feeling fully confident that she'd soon be running into her curse lady, she didn't see the need to restock her entire wardrobe.

After the consignment shop, she decided it might be a good idea to visit the wig shop Charlotte recommended. She'd locked on to the fact that Bradley would be showing up at her place in the morning as she was running out the door, and she wanted to cover her bases. What if she woke up tomorrow morning and her hair was pure white? All she had was touch-up. She hadn't had the foresight to purchase an extra box of full strength color this morning, and frankly, she was tired of the fight. Charlotte was right—perhaps a wig would be a more simple solution.

She raced to the shop on the business card Charlotte had given her this morning.

The first thing she saw when she entered the store was a red and orange wig with spikes on top, perched upon a mannequin's head. The mannequin was dressed in a leopard print coat, tight black pants and spike heels. Ann questioned Charlotte's opinion of this shop owner as her eyes landed on one colorful wig after another. She was about to leave when a woman called out from behind the sales counter.

"Can I help you find anything?" The woman was older. She didn't appear to be much younger than Charlotte.

"Yes. Charlotte from the drugstore referred me."

The woman cut Ann off with enthusiasm. "Oh, you must be Ann. Charlotte called me this morning and said you might be stopping by. Let's take a look over here."

Charlotte was right on target with this recommendation. The woman who helped her could have been Charlotte's clone for all her sweetness and tenderness toward Ann. She went beyond the professional civility that those in customer service must adopt. Like Charlotte, she truly cared. And together they found a match and a style that would suit Ann beautifully.

Due to Charlotte's phone call, the shop owner felt as though she and Ann were already dear friends, so she offered Ann a discount when they got to the register.

The wig shop owner's name was Lydia, Ann wanted to remember that. While she was at it, she decided to occupy her mind by practicing some other names on her way back to the office. There was Tim the courier. Charlotte was now a piece of her heart, so her name was a no-brainer. Lisa was the mother of Charles Latham the Third and who could forget *his* name? Having never been good with names, Ann felt determined to work on retaining the names of all the key players in her new life.

This engaging challenge made her trip back to the office breeze by quickly. It was a good thing too.

Once she got there, Cassie told her to call the school immediately.

Ann called the school office right there at her desk, leaving herself wide open to all of Cassie's attacks, opinions and criticisms. But all Cassie did was express concern over what might be going on, and offer to help in any way she could. *God bless Cassie,* Ann thought, in spite of herself.

According to the school nurse it seemed the best thing to do for Valerie would be to pick her up from school and take her home. Ann cleared it through Marvin first, emphasizing the fact that the Green Jeans conference call wasn't until ten o'clock the next day, and wasn't that more important than what was happening in the office right now anyway?

Marv fell for it and Ann scrambled to find Bradley for a ride.

She stumbled across him downstairs in some specialized editing room where common footsteps rarely trod. She didn't even have to go into the full story. All she had to say was Valerie was in some sort of physical distress at school and needed to be picked up, and Bradley was right on top of it.

They left immediately and Bradley sped as quickly as he could to get to the school. On the way there, Ann was acutely struck by Bradley's behavior. He was acting like a concerned father over his own daughter's crisis at school. The concern all over his face, and his focused navigation to get to the school as quickly as possible, made his love for Valerie crystal clear. Ann wished she contained half as much of that fondness toward her niece.

On the way, they discussed very little. Bradley mentioned what they might have for dinner while Ann waded into a sea of emotions she could barely sort out.

She never really got back to Valerie after their blowout two days ago. Bradley had stepped in and made everything so rosy that a few things got shoved under the carpet. Not that Ann minded. A part of her so enjoyed the relief Bradley provided that she was willing to ignore the carpet bulge and bide her time until Sara got back. For some reason, this recent turn of events reminded her of that unfinished business. Between the call from school and how popular Valerie seemed to be with everyone else, she felt she should try to get the relationship on better footing. It might also earn her some bonus points before Sara's return.

She spoke her mind to Bradley. "Why don't you just give us a ride home, then Valerie and I can have leftovers and watch a movie or something? I can't tell you how much your appreciation of Valerie means to me, but I think this might be the perfect invitation to a bond-with-the-niece night. Would you feel terribly offended if Valerie and I just have a girl night tonight?"

Bradley gave it some thought before giving an answer. "I think this sounds like most favorable piece of news. Besides, we don't know what's going on with her yet and it might be better for the two of you to be alone."

"Okay then. I don't think I've told you how grateful I am that you happen to be in this small piece of my life. I was feeling so lost about what to do with a young, pre-teen girl, then you just swooped in and made everything so easy. I feel I owe you a solid year of savings."

"Watch out Fin. I might just hold you to it!"

They both chuckled over this as they landed on the school's doorstep. Valerie wasn't there waiting for them, so Ann got out and sought the nurse's office on her own.

Once she found the office, her heart was chilled by Valerie's reception. "Hello Auntie," Valerie said as her eyes scanned the hallway with a look of discouragement. "Are you here by yourself or is Bradley here too?"

"Bradley is outside waiting in the car."

This was obviously *not* okay with Valerie. Her stilted response made it clear she didn't want much to do with Ann at all. "Um...thanks for coming."

Valerie's discomfort with Ann was so obvious that even the school nurse seemed to notice.

They met Bradley in the parking lot. Once they got in the car and started talking, it came out that Bradley would not be spending the evening with them.

"But I don't get it," Valerie protested. As she continued, her voice escalated with frantic anger. "Why can't Bradley come over for dinner again tonight?" Her unspoken words were, "I don't want to be alone with you Auntie."

Despite the knife blade Valerie's reaction was plunging into Ann's heart, she remained resolved. "I just thought it might be good for you and me to spend some time together. We haven't seen much of each other lately and you're about to step into the social zone. You guys are having your fun day tomorrow and my secretary wants to have you over for a play date and overnighter this weekend. So I thought we could watch one of those movies you brought over. I'll even eat some popcorn with you."

She tried saying this with a smile in her voice, but Valerie seemed disinterested. She withdrew into the backseat of Bradley's car and didn't say another word.

When they pulled into the parking garage at the condo, Bradley seemed at a loss for words. He was concerned for Valerie and wanted to treat the situation with as much sensitivity as possible. So he got out of the car and tenderly touched her shoulder before she and Ann entered the building.

"I'll call later to check in, okay?"

"Okay," Valerie smiled weakly.

"Are we still on for tomorrow for our big day on the town?"

Valerie's nearly inaudible response was delivered with her eyes glued to the concrete floor. "Yes, we are. I just wanted you to come over tonight."

"Well, your aunt has something special in mind, so you just have to believe something good is coming your way as a result of this evening."

Bradley's words penetrated Valerie's heart with such consolation that she wrapped her arms around his waist and wouldn't let go. She remained in that position for so long, Ann had to play the heavy and snap her back into reality.

"Come on Valerie. You heard Bradley. He'll call tonight and the two of you will have the entire day tomorrow."

Valerie sighed a begrudging sigh while continuing to hang onto Bradley. "Okay Auntie."

Bradley noticed that something unspoken seemed to be bothering Valerie. Her hug was like a death grip as he peeled her off so she could go inside.

Finally, she let go and he stepped into his car to leave. As he did, Ann mouthed the words, "thank you," to him as she turned to escort Valerie into the condo.

Since Ann was on a mission, she didn't register the distance of Bradley's preoccupied state. His concern for Valerie was deeper than hers, pulling him out of the moment and into his own thoughts. He was troubled that he couldn't stay to comfort Valerie in her distress. So troubled, that he just nodded and waved her off before pulling out of the garage.

Without taking notice, Ann and Valerie made their way to the condo. Once there, Ann began interrogating.

"So what's going on with you Valerie? Something tells me you don't visit the nurse's office all that often and you don't exactly seem sick. Care to explain what's going on?"

"No I don't. I just want to know why today couldn't be a regular day with Bradley coming over for dinner and all of us having brownies and ice cream and me learning how to cook while you just go take a shower."

Due to Valerie's anger and defensiveness, Ann knew there was more going on than Valerie cared to admit. And since extracting the truth from those who chose not to be forthcoming was one of her greatest talents, she remained undaunted by Valerie's unwillingness to speak.

"So you're not sick. And yet, you went to the nurse's office today. And, it was serious enough for them to call me at work. And here I am with the rest of the day off, but you're not really sick. So what's going on Valerie?"

Valerie looked at the floor.

Ann played the blackmail card. "Look Valerie. If you don't want to talk to me, I'll be forced to call your mother and tell her what's going on."

"No Auntie—please don't call Mama. If you do, she'll come home and ruin her chance to get this job and we'll never get to move away and I'll never get to go to a different school."

At this point, Valerie broke into tears.

Although Ann had experienced some changes following her crosswalk encounter, she still wasn't good with the tears thing. So she just sat on the couch next to Valerie, allowing her time to cry it out until she slowed down and began breathing steadily again.

Ann picked up the conversation there.

"So it sounds to me like the biggest reason you want your mom to get this job is that it will enable you to move away."

Valerie wiped her face with her hands while sniffing profusely. While she assembled herself, Ann ran and grabbed some tissue for her. By the time she came back, Valerie was ready to talk.

"Okay Auntie, I'll tell you what happened. But you have to promise not to tell Mama."

"All right Valerie, I promise."

Valerie told her all about everything that had been happening to her at school since last week. She told her about the five kids who kept threatening her on the playground and how their threats kept getting more and more serious. She told Ann what they'd said about choking her with her hair, and how they kept gesturing about it in the hallway between classes. Then she told her what had happened earlier in the bathroom. She explained that she really did feel sick to her stomach after that and she knew she'd be safe in the nurse's office. She felt it would be okay to just go home since there were only a few hours left of school anyway, then she'd be on break.

While Valerie shared, a red hot rage brewed within Ann that threatened to fly straight out of her mouth and sizzle every ounce of trust that Valerie had just so reluctantly offered. She was angry that Valerie had kept all this a secret for so long. She was fuming with thoughts of violent vengeance toward the horrid children who had caused her niece so much agony. She was mad at the school for not noticing. And she was mad at herself for not fostering an environment where her niece felt safe to share such atrocities. It was all so jumbled that she decided to remain silent for a while as she tried to compose herself.

As the angry emotions subsided, a wave of guilt rolled in to take their place. Poor Valerie had been suffering from fear and terror all week and Ann had been treating her like a piece of useless furniture. No wonder Valerie had wanted Bradley there so badly. No wonder her attitude toward Ann was so sour that the school nurse had noticed. She could hardly blame Valerie for her feelings toward her.

But for now, she couldn't take time to examine all that. She had to provide support for Valerie rather than sink inside herself and pronounce a self-inflicted beating.

She struggled with what to say next. After a long pause she said, "I'm going to have to call the school."

Valerie grew desperate again. "Please don't call the school Auntie. They should know about it, but what if my mom doesn't get this job? Then the kids would find out I tattled and they might try to get me anyway. Can you at least wait to find out about this job?

"I guess I could," Ann lied. "Your mom thinks she might hear by Saturday, so that's only two days away. But they will have to know soon. Because if these kids aren't reprimanded, they'll hurt someone else. They need to be stopped."

"I know Auntie. Thanks for not telling my mom."

"No problem. Hey—it's almost three and I have to check in with the office before everyone leaves for the day. Why don't you get in the shower while I make my call, then I'll take mine after you finish. We should get all that knocked out so we can get on with our evening. We might even be able to fit in a double feature."

"What's a double feature?" Valerie asked.

"It's where you watch two movies in a row."

"Oh. My mom and I do that a lot. I never knew what it was called."

"Well, the best part about it will be eating dinner on the couch while watching the first one."

"That will be fun. My mom said you guys were hardly ever allowed to do that when you were little."

"That's true. It was a no-no unless something special was going on."

"Well what's so special about today?"

"Let's just call it the kickoff to your nice, long school break."

Valerie smiled for the first time since Ann picked her up from school. "That's special all right!"

Valerie got into the shower and Ann seized the opportunity to call the school. Although she could hear the water running, she still felt safer going into the bedroom to make the call.

Ann knew the band teacher would still be there because Valerie usually stayed in the band room with her until four or 4:30. She'd managed to get Valerie out of earshot for this conversation, but time was still of the essence. She began to worry when no one picked up after five rings. Finally, someone answered.

"Hello. My name is Ann Finlayson. May I please speak to the band teacher?"

"Sure—I'll go get her."

Ann sat on the bed facing the mirror while she waited. The day had moved so swiftly after lunch that she hadn't taken time for a mirror check. Her hair was already streaked with gray and her eyes looked horrible. She wondered why no one had said anything. She ran out and got her bag with all her essentials and decided to touch up her hair during the phone call. Just as she sat back down, a woman's voice came to the phone.

"Mrs. Campion here."

"Hello, Mrs. Campion? This is Ann Finlayson, Valerie's aunt. I'm calling because I was hoping to swing by the school to talk to you tomorrow around lunchtime. That is, if you're going to be there."

"Yes, Miss Finlayson, I'll be here until around two o'clock. So any time before then would be fine. Is everything all right?" She sounded like a concerned grandmother as she continued. "I heard Valerie had to go home early today."

Ann had to lie again. She wanted to discuss all this in person, so she kept it light. "Oh yeah—everything's fine. I was just hoping to catch you before next week when everyone's off."

"Okay then Miss Finlayson, just stop by the school office to tell them you're here. I'll let them know to expect you."

"Okay. Thanks Mrs. Campion." After hanging up, Ann felt glad Valerie had someone so warmhearted in her corner. Mrs. Campion sounded like a gem.

Now, back to her hair. By the look of things, there was no doubt it would be pure white by morning. She was sure she'd have to wear the wig and was happy she'd made the purchase. But for now, she couldn't sit through another night with a towel on her head, and she wasn't about to don that wig unless absolutely necessary. So she quickly ran the touch-up through all the gray. She finished as the water in the shower shut off.

She and Valerie traded places in the bathroom. Once in the shower, Ann took her time.

This was going to be a long evening. She didn't know exactly what she'd say to Valerie. Her main goal wasn't necessarily to apologize, but to get on better footing before Sara got back from Colorado.

Suddenly, she felt anxious about the evening and wished she hadn't kicked Bradley out of it. He'd served as such a great buffer the last few evenings. Everything was so easy with him around. His even-keeled personality and good nature actually made her feel at home in her own place. And he was so much fun. She hadn't felt so comfortable since her dad was alive. Like Bradley, he could diffuse any tense situation with his warm smile and quick wit. Aside from the fact that Bradley didn't seem to have any musical talent, he and her father were very much alike.

So that's who Bradley reminded me of the other night.

His absence was felt even more keenly after Ann got out of the shower and into her comfy clothes. There were no delicious smells wafting from the kitchen and no giggles meeting her ears as she walked out of the bedroom. The dining room table was bare except for last night's flowers. She had to admit she missed him.

Valerie was the one to verbalize the thoughts Ann wouldn't dare speak.

"I miss Bradley. I like having him here. It's like when my dad was alive. He makes everything fun."

Although Ann wrestled with her emotions regarding Bradley, she had to agree. But all she said was, "Me too." Then she changed the subject. "Let's clean out the leftovers and move into the living room for movie time."

"Okay," Valerie answered, "which one do you want to start with?"

"I want to see the one with that warrior woman you keep comparing me to. What's her name? I think it starts with a 'K.'"

"Oh yeah. Katniss Everdeen. Yeah, we can watch *Hunger Games*. After that we can watch *Catching Fire* if we have time."

"Okay, good idea."

It took them a while to get through the movie because Valerie had to keep pausing it to explain what was going on. The movies could be a bit tricky to follow unless one had first read the books. Valerie had read all three, so she was able to clear the fog for Ann every time Ann got lost.

At the end of it, Valerie said, "See? You're just like Katniss Everdeen." Then she slumped into the back of the couch and sighed, "And I'm nothing but a whisper. People either ignore me or act mean toward me. Except at church. But people at church have to be nice."

"I wasn't always like Katniss Everdeen, you know. At school, I was one of the quiet ones. I never hung out with the popular kids. In fact, everyone called me the violin geek. I wore thick glasses from second grade all the way through seventh. I had to wear a giant mouthpiece for a year before getting braces in fifth grade. I was alone most of the time and only had one friend. She moved away when I went to junior high. In high school I had a boyfriend for a little while, but he dumped me for one of the more popular girls. So you see? You're not the only one."

"Thank you Auntie. Hey, do you think it's too early to call Mom?"

"No, I think it's okay to call. Now would be a good time, in fact. I can clear the dishes and get the popcorn going while you're on the phone."

As Ann got busy in the kitchen, she took a trek back to those buried years from her past. She'd forgotten so much. As she pictured that tiny girl with the thick glasses, so many memories poured in all at once. She remembered being alone most of the time. She had one friend, but she didn't live very close so they couldn't get together very often. She began hiding away in her bedroom and playing her violin whenever she felt lonely.

She remembered how her dad used to stand in the hallway during those times. He'd wait outside her bedroom door until the music stopped. When it did, he'd knock on the door and offer to take her out for a walk in the woods or down to the river. Or, he'd offer to take her into town for ice cream. In the winter they'd slap on the snowshoes and wash away the sadness in the crisp mountain air. He never asked any questions. He just offered his compassionate nature and sunny disposition as a bright, open door leading out of a dark cave. As with Bradley, there wasn't a dark cave that could contain anyone with him around.

As she got older, her violin continued playing the role of best friend, but she also developed an interest in some of the more daring outdoor sports like rock climbing and hang-gliding. She'd always been an avid hiker, but loved to challenge herself with some of the more unique outdoor adventures. Apart from the fact that it was wise to have spotters around in case of mishaps, these were all solitary activities.

She thought, *At least Valerie's good at making friends outside of school. Everyone adores her. She's better off than I was at that age in some ways. Socially that is …*

Then she giggled right out loud as she recalled another facet of her childhood. She couldn't stand to see other kids being tormented by those who were bigger, stronger and meaner. When she saw kids being picked on during recess or after school, her tiny, bespectacled form would stand up to the perpetrators with such confident conviction that they'd back down every time. She may have been a geek, but she was a force to be reckoned with when it came to bullying. This, she would not share with Valerie. She had to laugh again as she pictured her younger self. Then she spoke right out loud, "Hello, little Ann. How did I manage to lose you?"

As Ann waited for the popcorn to pop, she wondered how she'd managed to forget so much of her childhood. It was as if she'd slid into a never-ending fog bank after her parents died. Her thoughts were broken by Valerie calling her to the phone.

Ann passed popcorn duty to Valerie, took the phone and walked into the bedroom. "Hey Sara, any word yet?"

"Nope. For sure they're going to let us know on Saturday. But look sis. This job is no longer on the top of my priority list. You are. I saw those pictures. It looks like you've been working on a movie and just spent two hours in hair and makeup. I can't even believe it's you. My heart is breaking over how you must be feeling."

"Oh Sara—you know me. I don't feel, I just deal."

"And that's part of your problem. If you need me to, I'll bag this job and help you through this. I still can't believe it. Some lady really zapped you in a crosswalk? Have you seen her since?"

"Yeah—I've seen her a few times, but I can never seem to catch her—and no, you can't bag this job. Valerie would especially benefit by this move."

"Why do you say that? Has she been talking to you? Have the kids at school been mistreating her again?"

"No, nothing like that. She just thinks it would be fun to go back and live where we grew up." *Man I'm good.*

"Well I'm praying like crazy for you. I'm so sorry you're going through this."

"Thank you. I know I've said this before, but the worst part is having to hide it from everyone. I even bought a wig today."

"A wig? Really?"

"I had no choice. By the way things have been going, my hair will be pure white in the morning. And, I'm going to have to wear dark glasses all day to hide my aging eyes. I don't know how much longer I'll be able to keep hiding this. I just need to capture that woman and have her undo this curse."

"Okay then, that's what I'll pray for. Meanwhile, can you give me back to Val so I can say goodnight?"

"All right, I'll talk to you tomorrow."

Valerie and Ann barely hit the couch with their huge bowl of popcorn before the phone rang again. Bradley was making his check-in call a little on the early side.

"Hello Ann. I hope I didn't catch you in the middle of a movie. I just couldn't wait to check in on Valerie. She seemed so distraught and I wanted to make sure she was truly up for tomorrow."

"Oh yeah, she's up for it. And things are much better now than they were when you left. We've been dining on leftovers and popcorn and we're hoping to complete a *Hunger Games* marathon. We were just about to start movie number two."

"Then make no delay. Pass the phone to my girl and I promise to keep the conversation short."

When Valerie was this excited, there was no such thing as a brief conversation. She was loaded with questions and apparently, Bradley was offering up potential points of interest. She was on cloud nine as she paced the living room floor throughout the duration of the call. She broke out in giggles numerous times and seemed reluctant to pass the phone back to her aunt.

"Okay," she sighed, "here's Auntie."

"So," Ann said, "everything's a go? Shall I look for you around seven?"

Bradley's voice brimmed with enthusiasm. "Absolutely. And be sure to have the coffee ready. I'm bringing over a newspaper and biscotti to enjoy while I wait for Sleeping Beauty to arise from her slumber."

"Well, alrighty then. I'll see you in the morning."

Somehow, time had flown by since they got home and it appeared as though they might not have time to watch the second movie after all. At least not the whole thing. So they decided to watch it until the bowl of popcorn was empty, then get ready for bed. Ann knew she was in for a rough night and early getup, so she couldn't indulge in a late night with Valerie.

Valerie seemed fine with that. All she wanted to do was hurry up and get to tomorrow, so going to bed early was not a problem. While she made her bed and got ready, Ann went into her bedroom and decided to prepare her early bird arsenal now, instead of waiting for her eyes to fly open at three in the morning.

She armed herself with fresh towels and bedding to cut time when she woke up in a sweat again. She laid out her clothes, wig and glasses on top of the dresser. And she contemplated how she might get around questions regarding her dark glasses; not only from Bradley in the morning, but from everyone at the office too. She thought perhaps she could just slather on the eye goop and avoid eye contact with Bradley in the morning. It would be tough to explain dark glasses inside the condo at seven in the morning. Then she could come up with some lame excuse to see her through the rest of the day. But she couldn't think of it now. Between the emotions of the day, and the sleep she'd been missing the past few nights, fatigue overwhelmed her.

She left the bedroom to say goodnight to Valerie, who also appeared to be overwhelmed by exhaustion. All the lights were out and she was fast asleep.

Of course she's out, Ann thought, *relief alone probably hit her like a sleeping pill the minute her head hit the pillow.* Ann thought of how much Valerie had been through this week and how she must have suffered with keeping everything a secret. She felt thankful for Bradley all over again as she considered what weight he'd truly been lifting from Valerie's heart these past few days. Again, she wished she could be better at this kid thing. Or was it this human thing?

Enough already. Go to bed.

Chapter 8

The clock was merciful this morning. Instead of her eyes flying open at three, Ann woke up at 2:15 a.m. At least this would allow more time to sleep between changing the sheets, going back to bed, and the 5:45 alarm. She didn't even give a thought to hormone replacement this time around. She had both Bradley and the conference call to contend with in the morning. Hormones would have to wait.

When the alarm did go off, Ann wished she had set it for 5:30. She would've hit snooze at least twice before forcing herself out of bed. As she maneuvered herself out from under the covers and onto the side of the bed, she noticed every muscle was aching. She thought it would be nice to squeeze in a massage after the conference call, but remembered she had a date with the band teacher today. *Well, maybe after that,* she thought while getting to her feet and stretching her shoulders.

Although the mirror was right in front of her, she avoided looking into it. She already knew what she might see and was afraid of how bad reality might be. She turned away from it while climbing into her size four skirt, and waited to see what the bathroom mirror would say.

When she finally looked, she found her suspicions were true. Her hair was pure white. But it was still as thick, long and healthy as it had been before all this started. In fact, she gave herself a compliment. "Not bad for a young, old lady. If you were seventy-five years old, you'd be quite the babe!"

She thought of Charlotte and laughed out loud. It came out so unexpectedly she had to peek into the living room to see if she woke Valerie. She remembered Charlotte describing the moment when she looked in the mirror and decided to accept the inevitable. If it weren't for the fact that Ann was only thirty-two years old, she might find herself in that same mindset right now. Her white mane was downright dazzling. But it was time to move on.

There wasn't much time before Bradley got there, so she ran to the kitchen, put the coffee on, finished getting dressed and took extra care with her makeup. She didn't know how she was going to hide her eyes from Bradley, but she was determined to save the glasses for the office. Last of all, the wig. It truly was the perfect selection. The style and color were exactly the same as her real hair, except the wig had a few more layers. She looked at the clock and realized she only had about ten minutes before Bradley showed up. She packed her bag and sat down with a cup of coffee.

Bradley came to the door shortly after Ann sat down. She'd kept all the lights off but the one above the stove, so it was fairly dark in the condo.

When she opened the door, Bradley was all smiles and early morning salutations, but Ann was on a mission to get away from him as quickly as possible. She barely looked at him as she tried to squeeze through the door with her head turned away. She mumbled something to the tune of, "Sorry— woke up with a headache and the light is hurting my eyes and I have to go get ready for the conference call. Bye."

Bradley watched her go. Although he was puzzled by her behavior, he didn't dwell on it. After all, he had a date with a cup of coffee and biscotti, the newspaper, and a most enchanting eleven-year-old girl.

As Ann hurried out of the building and onto the street, her mind was racing with everything but the conference call. Panic arose as she began to consider the possibilities of her immediate future. How could she keep up with this masquerade? She couldn't go on wearing dark glasses forever. Even if she could afford an eyelift, it probably wouldn't last more than a day. What if she never ran into that old lady again? She'd have to quit work. Then what would she do? She wished she had time to run by Charlotte's store. Charlotte was the only person in her world who was there to fully embrace her in this new life. She didn't know Ann's true age. All she knew was a person in need for whom she had a natural affinity. Ann didn't know why. For so many years she hadn't been close to anyone but her sister. She just didn't possess the sort of personality that attracted intimate friendships. Not until Charlotte came along …

Her screaming mental wheels screeched to a halt with the realization that she was supposed to drive Sara's car to work today. Her original plan was to wrap up the conference call, meet with Marvin, then drive to the school. Time was of the essence, so her debate couldn't last long. She could come back and get the car after the call, but she didn't know how long the call and meeting with Marvin would take. She didn't want to delay Mrs. Campion's lunch hour, so her hope was to get there a little before noon. It just wouldn't work to go back and get the car later. She'd have to turn around and get it right now. But that might throw her into an encounter with Bradley and Valerie on their way out for their adventure. Oh well, she could put the glasses on now. She already told Bradley she had a headache, so she could easily play that card if need be. She decided to head back to the condo.

Fortunately, the garage was empty when she got there. Bradley and Valerie were nowhere in sight.

By the time she reached the parking garage at work, parked the car, walked to the building and hit the elevator, it was nearly 8:15. Of course, Cassie had to toss tardiness in Ann's face the minute she walked through the office door.

But Ann stopped her short. "Not today, Cassie. I'm not in the mood."

"Okay fine, but what's up with the dark glasses?"

"I have a headache and my eyes are super sensitive to light right now—can you just let me get through the door in peace?"

No sooner than she got behind her desk and started shuffling paper around did she notice a plant seemingly suspended in midair, just two inches away from her face. Then she remembered it was moving day for Nancy.

"Hello Nancy. I almost didn't recognize you behind that plant."

The plant moved away from Ann's face and onto the floor. "Well, I almost didn't recognize you behind those glasses. New look for the office?"

"No. I have a really bad headache and my eyes are sensitive to light."

"Sounds like a migraine. Have you ever had one before? You should get yourself to the doctor and have that checked out."

"Well I can do no such thing this morning, to be sure. The conference call is at ten and I still have to review my notes."

"Oh. The conference call. You must mean with Green Jeans. It feels so good to be moving out of my office and ending my days with this company, especially in light of this phone call."

"What do you mean Nancy? I've never heard a word from you on the Green Jeans campaign. Why haven't you said anything?"

"Because I've been hiding in my office and quietly planning my life beyond *Top Rung Magazine*. When I first came to this magazine, it operated under very high moral and ethical standards. It didn't look anything like it does today. Then it began disintegrating little by little. A bit of compromise here, a little business favor over there—somehow corruption has seeped into this company and this Green Jeans alliance is the last straw—I want no part of it."

"You mean that's why you're leaving?"

"Yep."

"I thought it was so you could enjoy an early retirement with your husband and explore other options. I had no idea."

"Well I am exploring other options, but I'd already been considering this before Green Jeans came along. As I said, Marvin's decision to pursue Green Jeans was the last straw for me. And frankly Ann, I'm shocked over your support of this. I've held you under wing for so long and taught you all the tricks for success in this industry, and you decide to hurl headlong into this campaign ..." She stopped mid-sentence and collected herself.

Ann couldn't have been more devastated. She couldn't have been splayed open more deeply had a machete been thrust through her gut. She wanted to sit down, but Nancy wasn't finished.

"But—I still love you. And since you don't want any of my plants, I'd like to offer you a chance to take some of my artwork. Come down to my office and see what I have. Whatever you pick is yours and I'll take the rest. Since the office will be yours now, you can either leave the artwork in there, or you can take it home. Whatever I have is yours." She picked up her plant and moved toward the door. "See you in a few."

This made Ann feel a little better. At least Nancy didn't hate her to the point of writing her off completely. She had to sit down for a minute. When she first stepped into this position, she was green. She had college smarts, but no life application. Nancy was right there to bridge the gap. For some reason, she'd taken a liking toward Ann right away and had adopted herself as Ann's number one mentor.

She taught Ann how to navigate difficult business calls and gain the upper hand during a power lunch. She even helped Ann learn to dress for success. She was always there as Ann's mentor, but sometimes her influence was more like what Ann would call an office mom. She had all the sharp-shooting smarts of a high-power executive, but she also possessed something even stronger:

Grace.

She frequently reminded Ann that she could be the biggest shark in the pond, but she needed to guard her heart. She consistently warned Ann of the dangers of becoming brutal and unfeeling in her pursuit of success.

Nancy was who Ann aspired to be. She respected Nancy more than any other, yet Nancy just chewed her to a pulp. She thought this would be the perfect time to go look at artwork.

As she stood to walk down the hallway to Nancy's office, Cassie began to speak. Since Ann didn't trust herself to appropriately handle any of Cassie's input right now, she put up her hand and walked away. Fortunately, Cassie honored the hand.

As Ann walked to Nancy's office, she reflected on the fact that she'd never even *seen* a Green Jeans ad. All she did was feed off of Marvin and Sean; she fully trusted their belief in the campaign and agreed that it might take *Top Rung* to the next level. As she approached the office door, she vowed to keep this information to herself.

Once inside Nancy's office, Ann was instantly transported to another world. First, her ears were greeted by the soft sounds of water flowing over rocks in a small, tabletop fountain. Then her eyes were met with a variety of nature scenes, all artfully shot by a gifted photographer. There were mountain scenes full of pine trees with filtered sunlight streaming through the branches. One of the pictures was shot from a cliff overlooking a rocky ravine with a river shining down below. Another was a river scene that looked as though it could have been shot right by the house she grew up in. She could almost smell the pine trees. She could hear the sounds of the river stampeding over the rocks. She closed her eyes and remembered the thrill of finding the next handhold on one of her climbing excursions. These were all places she'd rather be right now. It made her wish she could be Sara, moving back to their home state.

It also caused her to realize that over the course of all these years, she'd never truly known Nancy. She'd only relied upon Nancy to help her become the success she was today.

She moved across the room to study the last photo in the collection. It was simply a close-up of earth-toned river rocks with water cascading over them. There was a caption at the bottom, handwritten by a talented calligrapher. It read, "How blessed are the people who know the joyful sound."

Just then, Nancy came into the office. She walked over and stood shoulder to shoulder with Ann as they looked at the picture. "Oh, so you like my favorite one. Bird sounds, water sounds, silent sounds broken by sudden breezes through pine branches … it all takes you right up to the shoreline of heaven."

Ann, lost in her reverie, answered as though in a trance with no one else in the room. "Yes, it does take you right up to the shoreline of heaven."

Nancy bubbled with delight over Ann's reply. "I didn't know you were acquainted with the One who created all this beauty."

Ann's heart froze with sudden coldness. "Look Nancy, if you're referring to God, you can stop right there. My parents were Christians, my niece and sister are Christians, but I don't do the God thing. I only agreed that the sounds of nature are beautiful and magical."

"Then I know what to pray for. I'll pray you get to the second part of the verse. That you might come to know Him so you can 'walk in the light of His countenance.'"

Now Ann was irritated. She snapped, "I don't even know what that means."

"It means that as you enter into a relationship with the Almighty, you become filled with a joy that rises above every circumstance—it causes you to experience life through a sharper, more powerful lens. All of His creation comes to life exponentially compared to how you've known it before. You experience His presence at all times, and the intimacy that results causes His light to shine in and around you, and you feel His peace. And, as His countenance shines from within you, people are drawn to that light."

With great aggravation, Ann cut Nancy off. "The last thing *I* need is for people to be drawn to me. I'm not really all that fond of people."

Ann had begun to feel tense because of the time. And she never could tolerate any form of preaching, not even if it came from her beloved Nancy.

"Well then, I'll leave you to your thoughts. I have another trip to make to the car."

Ann took the picture they'd been discussing off the wall and selected three more to take home with her. In the back of her mind she was thinking of how perfect it was that she drove today. This framed artwork would have been impossible to get home on foot.

Sean came through the door and reminded Ann of the time.

"I know what time it is, Sean."

"Well, you're cutting it a bit close aren't you? Only fifty minutes to showtime. But before you go, did you remember our date? Are we still on?"

Ann recalled the conversation where they'd discussed future possibilities, but nothing had been set in stone. "You mean the drive in the car with the top down to your favorite lunch spot, 'date?'"

"The very same. Are we still on?"

"I don't know what you mean by 'still'. We never made concrete plans."

"Well let's make them now. I can pick you up tomorrow at eleven o'clock. It will be our way of celebrating our victory over Green Jeans."

Ann couldn't help but feel flattered. If he only knew what was under this wig, these glasses, these clothes. "Sure, why not? But for now, as you know, I have to get to my desk and dive into my notes. Do you think you could grab a couple of these pictures?"

She was grateful for the help. Multiple trips might have cost her a full ten minutes. But now she could focus on her notes and prepare for the phone call with a good five minutes to spare.

For some reason, she was nervous about this call. She hadn't felt like this since her first year with the magazine. Perhaps it was lack of sleep. Or was it the hormonal imbalance? Or, could it be she was feeling deflated after being torn up by Nancy? Regardless of the reason, the tiger in her tank had been replaced by a mewing kitten. By the time the phone rang, she wasn't ready.

Murphy Lawman opened the conversation. He was the numbers guy, so he entered through that door. "Hey Ann, Patrick and I were able to run all the final numbers just yesterday. Before Patrick went out of town, he'd been leaning in a certain direction that I tried to give you a heads up about the other day, but ..."

"But I kept cutting you off."

"Yes you did. So all I can do now is deliver the final answer. We decided that for the spring issue, quantity mattered most. So rather than target a handful of high-profile magazines with four-pagers, we opted to go for a greater number of two-page spreads, with only a couple of four-pagers."

"So what are you telling me Murphy? What does this mean for *Top Rung?*"

Now Patrick Fleming entered the conversation. "It means, Miss Finlayson, that we're only going to require two pages of *Top Rung* space for this promotion. Had you more time to discuss this with Murphy last Monday, the answer could have been different. But we're too close to the wire now. You know. Deadlines."

"But Mr. Fleming, I'm sure we can make you an offer that would change your mind."

"No, Ann. Our decision is firm."

Murphy came back on. "Sorry Ann. I tried to talk to you."

"I know you did Murph. I'm sorry too."

With that, they said their goodbyes.

Ann didn't want to wait for the axe to come to her. She marched herself straight down to Marvin's office and prepared to lay her head on the chopping block.

The results of the conversation were written all over Ann's face, but Marvin still had to ask. "So, how'd it go?"

"They settled on a two-page spread and wouldn't budge from their decision."

Marvin's face reddened. "I told you not to blow this, Finlayson. I told you. And Sean tells me you brushed him off when he asked to take part in the conference call. I thought I made it clear I wanted the two of you to act as a team."

"I know you did Marvin, but I'd been solo on this for so long. I thought it would be better to fully incorporate Sean on the next big project."

"Well Fin, I'm thoroughly disappointed in you, to say the least."

"I'm sorry Marv. I don't know what to say. So I guess now's as good a time as any to ask if I could take a long lunch to go talk to one of Valerie's teachers."

Marvin's response was acrid. "You know what Ann? You can take the whole day off. And come Monday, I'm not really sure *who* will be taking over Nancy's office. It was going to be you Ann. But now … let's just say some major changes are coming down the pike." His eyes narrowed, shooting arrows into hers. "So, yes. Take the day and do with it whatever you please."

Ann responded uncharacteristically to the boss with whom she'd always had such an easy rapport. She nearly whispered, "Yes sir," and walked out the door.

Valerie woke not long after Ann left. She was so excited to get out the door that she enlisted Bradley to deflate her air mattress, then fold and put her bedding away while she got dressed and ready to go.

On the way to Bradley's favorite bagel shop, Valerie told him about the day she and Auntie had at Millennium Park recently. Then she told him about the time she went there with her parents when her dad was still alive, and asked if they could go there first, after breakfast. She said she wanted to take some scrapbook pictures in front of The Bean. He said it was no problem, the Navy Pier could wait.

Valerie couldn't believe all the selections at the bagel shop. There were at least five different kinds of breakfast bagels and they were all huge. Her eyes grew wide when Bradley placed her bagel in front of her. She declared she wouldn't be able to eat the whole thing, even if it did look so much better than Auntie Ann's health food. Bradley assured her he'd help.

As they left the bagel shop, Valerie provided more detail about the day she and Auntie spent at the park. She told Bradley how much she loved Lurie Garden and asked if they could go there too. She told him about Charles Latham the Third and how sad it was that he had cancer. She also expressed her longing to see him again. As she continued to stream her happy fountain of chatter, he listened intently, adding few words of his own. This adventure seemed to have popped the cork off of Valerie's energy bottle, and Bradley was happy to indulge her need to talk.

When they reached the park, the first order of Valerie's business was to get some shots of them at The Bean. They took pictures of each other, then a stranger clicked one of the two of them. They swung by the fountain to see the faces. Valerie tried to get a picture of that, but it turned out a little blurry. "Oh well," she said. "The pictures at The Bean and the ones we get from Lurie Garden are the ones I wanted most."

While walking to the garden, Valerie told Bradley about her love of flowers and shared with him all the things she and her dad used to do. This is what told him how they would wrap up their trip at the Navy Pier.

Once they got to the Pier, the rides became priority number one. They started with the carousel, then went on the wave swinger. Valerie loved how high the swings went and how they sailed "right out over the water too!" She wanted to save the Ferris wheel for last, because that was the best of the three in her opinion. She explained to Bradley that her mom was afraid of heights, but she loved them. Then she proudly announced she must take after Auntie who used to do all sorts of fun things like hang-gliding and rock-climbing, something Bradley never would have guessed.

Bradley told Valerie what a shame it was that it was a Friday in April. He said he would have taken her on a boat ride, but during March and April the boats only ran on the weekends. And he couldn't take her to the Sears Tower via water taxi, because those didn't start running again until May. So if she was game, the only "boatish" thing they'd be able to do today would be the remote control version. She said she was game, and they had a grand time racing their boats in the brilliant spring sunshine.

After that they walked all around the Pier. Valerie loved the views of the city and the lake. She exclaimed, "Our day on the town just couldn't have been any better!"

Bradley assured her the day wasn't even half over yet. He mentioned the fact that she was probably too old for the Children's Museum and asked if she might want to check out the Funhouse Maze. When she asked what that was and he described it to her, she said a boat ride sounded like more fun. So he decided to unveil his surprise.

As they approached their final destination, Bradley made Valerie close her eyes. They made their way slowly so she wouldn't trip. When they arrived and Bradley told Valerie to open her eyes, she let out a gasp. They had just entered the Crystal Gardens. The six-story glass atrium with its fifty-foot arched ceiling was breathtaking, especially when the sun was shining. Valerie was beside herself and asked Bradley if she could just run around and look at everything.

He cut her loose and she bounded away. Intermittently she'd come back with flushed cheeks to report on the beauty of the hanging twinkle lights or how cute the frog fountains were. She said she wanted to get married here and he told her people did that all the time. Five minutes later she came back again to let him know she was going to own a flower shop someday and make bridal bouquets for people's weddings. She continued to flit about for ten minutes more before running up to him again. But this time, it was only to throw her arms around him and thank him over and over for the best day ever.

He could not get over this child. Her attitude was so refreshing. So many kids her age already had a sense of entitlement, where they had to have every gadget and gizmo, the best tennis shoes, and the endless list of worldly possessions that Valerie seemed to eschew. They had to be at the mall or constantly gluing themselves to all forms of social media, and the more expensive the vehicle for that media, the better. Be it smartphone or notebook, they always seemed to long for the next best thing.

Then there was Valerie. With a heart that swelled so easily with gratitude, that took delight in the simplest of things, she outshone the sunlight pouring through the glass walls and fifty-foot ceiling of the atrium. He smiled to himself as he thought this is what Cinderella must have been like when she was eleven.

After Valerie had her fill of the atrium, Bradley decided it was a good time to grab some lunch. But since Valerie was still full from breakfast, they decided to go to the Food Court where she could have ice cream and he could enjoy a great hot dog. While they dined, Bradley promised to take Valerie to Garrett's Popcorn Shop before going to the Sears Tower. He said she could pick whatever flavor she wanted. So they made that stop and headed for the Tower.

When Ann made her presence known to the receptionist in the school's administration office, she was told Mrs. Campion was in a meeting. She couldn't help but think that was strange since she called before leaving, but she embraced the opportunity to have a sit and gather her thoughts. She didn't know what had rattled her most—the failed conference call, Marvin's reaction, or Nancy's stance on Green Jeans. When did she stop seeking Nancy's input for all her biggest decisions?

She'd already lost her stomach on this emotional roller coaster ride, so she decided to flip through one of the magazines in the waiting area rather than strain her brain any further. She even took her dark glasses off. No one but the school nurse had ever seen her before, so she felt relieved of the need to hide.

She didn't want to take out her magnifying glass to read, so she contented herself by looking at the pictures. But only seven pages in and she was dealt another devastating blow: a Green Jeans ad. She had landed on page one of a four-page spread. What she saw verified the validity of what everyone at the office had been trying to tell her. She didn't even have to look at the next three pages.

Once again she felt nauseous. A thousand questions vied for space in her head as she tried to hide her inner turmoil. Why hadn't she ever looked at an ad before? Why didn't she get Nancy's opinion in the first place? All her big talk about the National Knitting League or whatever she'd called them. Why hadn't Cassie gone the extra mile and just shown her an example? Had she become that unapproachable? And what about Sean? Did he know the truth about this company? She may have been a shark, but this material was unacceptable. How could any magazine endorse a company that would manufacture such questionable advertising?

Of course, this was when Mrs. Campion decided to enter the waiting area. And someone else was standing with her. One of Valerie's other teachers perhaps?

Just a week ago, Ann was a master at compartmentalizing her emotions. But today she found herself wondering how she would make it through this meeting. She'd barely had time to recover from the events of the morning and now, the Green Jeans bomb. Oh well, at least the talk wouldn't have to take that long. How much time could it take to say you have bullies in your school and they need to be dealt with?

The three made pleasant introductions while walking down the hall to the band room. The need to perform such mundane courtesies served to calm Ann's nerves to some extent. She observed that Mrs. Campion and Miss Moberg appeared to have been comparing notes, and felt encouraged by the thought that they might have already been onto something.

They reached the band room, found chairs to sit in, and Ann dove right in.

"I want to thank the two of you for meeting with me today. As you know, my niece has been staying with me all week. For a few years now, she's been tormented by some of the kids in your school. It wasn't until yesterday that she provided detail as to just how serious this situation has become."

She told them everything Valerie had experienced since last week, starting with the comment one of the kids had made about choking her with her own hair. She told them about the gestures in the hallway between classes and all the other events leading up to yesterday. When she got to the part about the kids swarming Valerie in the bathroom, Miss Moberg spoke up.

"We would like to thank you, Miss Finlayson, for coming forward with this. We've both had our suspicions for quite some time. Yesterday, I walked into the bathroom and unwittingly sabotaged the plan those kids had staged to hurt Valerie. I know exactly who they are. They've always been troublemakers. I'd been asking Valerie all week if anything was bothering her. She just hasn't been herself lately."

"No, she hasn't," Mrs. Campion interjected. "Valerie has always been such a precious girl. Her sweetness is positively disarming, even rare in this day and age. You must feel blessed to have such a lovely niece."

Fake smile. Fake nod. Ann couldn't exactly tell them there were times this past week when she'd practically treated Valerie worse than the bullies had. She deflected the comment by stating she had to be somewhere else soon.

They assured her the bullies would be reprimanded, and exchanged contact information with her so they could keep her posted. They thanked her again and commended her for being such an outstanding advocate for her niece. In closing, Mrs. Campion stung her one more time by mentioning how fortunate Valerie was to have such a supportive relative in her corner.

When all was said and done, she couldn't get out of the building fast enough.

More than ever, Ann was feeling the need for a shot of Charlotte. She decided to make the drugstore her next stop after ditching the car back at the condo.

Valerie was so excited about going to Auntie's office. She'd always wanted to visit her aunt in the Sears Tower, but between school, work schedules and the distance factor, they could never seem to coordinate a time. So when she and Bradley got to the office and Cassie told them Ann was gone for the day, Valerie was visibly disappointed.

But Cassie wasn't going to allow that to spoil the moment. She told Valerie how much she'd like to have her over, but didn't know how Valerie might feel about hanging out with all her kids. "Well really," she said, "I only have three of them, but my youngest makes it feel like an entire tribe."

Valerie explained that she gets along with all kids.

Cassie let out a deep chuckle. "Yeah—well you've never met my six-year-old, Simon. He loves to pester his two older sisters."

Valerie responded with great confidence. "Oh, I know all about six-year-old boys. Sometimes I help in kid's church on Sundays."

"So, would you like to come over tomorrow? If you feel comfortable enough, you can even spend the night."

"Oh yes—I'd love to come over tomorrow. Auntie doesn't like to have me around on the weekends anyway."

Bradley and Cassie exchanged questioning looks.

Cassie went on to tell Valerie all about her three kids. She told her how old the girls were and what their favorite movies were, what some of their hobbies were and a little bit about their church. She told Valerie she could go to church with them on Sunday morning and Valerie said that would be great, especially since she didn't get to go last Sunday. She explained that her aunt didn't do the "God thing," so she had to skip.

As the two continued talking, Bradley sent Ann a text.

When Ann stepped into the drugstore, she didn't see Charlotte. There was an older woman putting things on a shelf near the back of the store, but no Charlotte. Ann called to the stranger from the front of the store.

"Hello. Do you work here?"

The woman looked up and walked toward Ann while answering, "Yes I work here. What can I help you with?"

"I came to see Charlotte. Do you know when she'll be coming in today?"

"I'm sorry, no, I don't know when she'll be in today. She had to take her mother to the hospital this morning. She's going to call as soon as she finds out what's going on."

For some reason, this news hit Ann like one more brick and she felt the need to get out of the store immediately. She told the woman she'd be back later to check for further information. She was in such a hurry to leave, it sounded as if the jingle bells on the door were close to crashing to the floor when she slammed it shut.

Once she got outside, a deluge of tears threatened to spring from her heart, out through her eyes, and down her face. But she wouldn't let them. Instead, she tried to analyze why she was feeling this way. She wondered if it was because Charlotte was unavailable when she needed her. Or, was it the news about Charlotte's mother? She knew, after all, what it was like to lose a parent. By the time she completed the analysis, the moment of imminent tears had passed. She decided to head for the park.

After finding her favorite seat by the fountain, the sunny day sounds of the park acted as a monotone tonic to her troubled soul. Kids splashing in the water, someone playing guitar in the distance, laughter and pleasant conversations, all blended into a solid drone of soothing sound. Coupled with the warmth of the sun, there was no fighting her fatigue. She began to doze.

But, no sooner had she drifted off than she heard a voice calling her back to consciousness. "Ann—is that you?"

As she came to, it took a moment for her to realize the voice that called her out of her slumber was Lisa, Charles Latham the Third's mother. She was thankful she'd put her dark glasses back on.

"Hello, Lisa. Sorry—I'm a bit groggy at the moment. I fell asleep."

"Oh, I'm sorry if I woke you, you probably needed it. I couldn't see that you were asleep because of your glasses. If you'd like, I can let you finish your nap. I was just on my way back to the hospital."

"It's all right. I probably couldn't go back to sleep anyway. Where's Charles?"

"He's at the hospital. He wanted to come, but he's feeling nauseous and tired from the chemo."

"So, they've already begun treatment. How long is this going to take?"

"There's no telling. It depends on a lot of factors, like how long it takes for the tumors to respond to the chemo. Since he's so young, they don't want to be too aggressive ..."

As Lisa continued providing Ann with the details, she noticed how weary-worn Lisa appeared to be. She thought about how Lisa's face was a mirror image of how she, herself, was feeling on the inside. Consequently, she became overwhelmed with compassion and understanding. But since she was unaccustomed to feeling such emotions, she felt clumsy about how to respond. She paused, then thought of Valerie.

"You know, Valerie still talks about Charles all the time. She wonders about how he's doing and wishes she could see him again."

"Funny you should mention that. Ever since we met you two last Sunday, Charles hasn't stopped talking about Valerie. In fact, that was the hardest part about his not being able to come today. He thought perhaps we might run into the two of you again."

"Well today, Valerie's exploring the city with a co-worker so Charles didn't have to miss out on anything. But I'm thinking I might be able to get her to the hospital for a visit one day next week."

Lisa's face lightened at this. She said his hope button might work a little more effectively if he had more than just her and the hospital staff to encourage him. Not that the staff wasn't great, she mentioned, but they weren't family and Dad's text messages from Afghanistan could only go so far.

"Wait—your husband's deployed? They won't allow him to come home to see his son while he's in the hospital?"

Now Lisa looked as though she might cry. "Things would be simpler if Stanley were an enlisted man. But he's an officer and his role over there is pretty important. They're trying to work something out, but there's so much red tape."

"Oh I know all about red tape, believe me. What about other relatives? Don't you have anyone who lives nearby?"

She wanted to kick herself for asking such a foolish question. Of course there weren't any relatives nearby. If there were, Charles would already have more support than Lisa, the staff and a load of text messages from Dad.

Lisa didn't seem to mind the question. "No. His grandma, my mom, passed away last year and Grandpa hasn't been in the picture for years. He was my stepdad and he never really paid that much attention to me growing up either. So I haven't even tried to contact him. I just don't have the heart for it."

The two heavily-burdened women sat in silence awhile, lost in their own thoughts. Ann was the first to speak.

"I do have to get going. I have some things to take care of before meeting my niece and co-worker for dinner tonight."

She was really just anxious to see if there was any news of Charlotte's mother yet.

"I should be getting back to the hospital too. Charles will be anxious to hear about my trip to the park. Do you really think you could get Valerie to the hospital next week? If you're serious, I'd like to tell Charles about it. He'll be so thrilled."

"Absolutely. You can count on it. Just let me put your number in my phone."

She searched every pocket in her purse and couldn't find her phone anywhere. Perhaps she left it in the car.

"That's okay," Lisa said. "Just let me put yours in my phone and we'll hook up later. I'll send you a message right away."

As Ann rose to her feet, she answered, "Good plan."

She couldn't believe how stiff and sore she felt after sitting for so long. It probably didn't help that she'd fallen asleep either. As they departed, Ann felt compelled to give Lisa a hug. It was so overpowering that she went ahead and put her arms around Lisa, telling her she'd be looking forward to their next visit.

As they let go of each other, Ann could see some tears had streamed down Lisa's cheeks during their embrace. Inside, she felt the same way. This brief break from such a taxing stretch of pain and isolation was a great relief to both of them.

As she made the trek back to the drugstore, the mixed bag of emotions she carried wreaked havoc on her thoughts. She began to bash herself all over again as she considered the events of the day. The encounter she had with Lisa made her think of how dreadful she'd been to Cassie. Not once had she offered a word of encouragement when Craig was in the hospital. She berated herself again for her mistreatment of Valerie. She blew the call with Green Jeans, a failure which marked the first time in seven years that she didn't get her way with a client. Then again, would she have wanted to win them over? A no-page spread would have been better …

Her heart darkened as an emotional bird of prey clamped its talons deep into her soul and refused to fly away. Between struggling with the weight of this ominous presence and her physical soreness, it was difficult to walk to the drugstore.

When she finally got there, the jingle bells lightened her mood.

Charlotte's replacement looked up from behind the counter and recognized Ann right away.

"They found out it's pneumonia," she announced. "They're going to keep her in the hospital overnight. She might be able to come home tomorrow."

"Oh that's great," Ann smiled. "Do you mind if I sit down in that chair for a minute?"

"Sure, that's why Charlotte put it there. She noticed a lot of her customers just wanted to stay and talk, so she put that chair near the register so she could visit in between customers."

With a wave of fondness, Ann said, "That sounds like something Charlotte would do."

Then the woman asked Ann a strange question. "Are your hips hurting?"

"As a matter of fact they are. How did you know?"

"Been there, done that. Just a minute—I'm going to go get you something."

She disappeared behind a stack of shelves and returned with something that made Ann's skin crawl. *Oh no,* she thought, *I am not going there. The dark glasses are bad enough, but I am not going to use a cane.*

She told the woman she wouldn't be needing a cane just yet. She said her doctor just informed her she needs some physical therapy and that she'd be starting next week, so thanks but no thanks.

"So you're just going to be in pain all the way to next week? Okay—suit yourself."

As she disappeared around the corner again, Ann thought to herself that she seemed a bit quirky. Then she let out an inward laugh and softly said, "Oh yeah Miss Gluten-Free, Automobile-Phobic, Fitness Freak? I guess we're all a bit quirky in our own way."

When the woman returned, she decided introductions were in order. "My name's Cecile, by the way. You can come by and visit any time. And be sure to keep me posted about how physical therapy is going. I still think you could use a cane though."

Despite Cecile's quirkiness, there was something about her that substantially lifted Ann's spirits. What a social butterfly she was becoming. All these new alliances. She giggled as she considered what it would be like to form a knitting club with the likes of Charlotte, Lydia and now Cecile. To be true to herself though, it would have to be a yoga club.

After leaving the store, her hips hurt so badly and she felt so exhausted, she decided to hop on the L.

It had been years since she'd used public transportation on a sunny day. The rhythm of the L was lulling her to sleep for the second time today. Her head kept drooping and jerking back to awareness. At one point, she thought she'd caught a glimpse of the old woman. But the train was moving so fast, she couldn't be sure. Anyway, with her hips in this condition, she doubted she could catch the woman even if she were close enough to catch.

She thought ahead to what she needed to do once she got home. She should probably shoot Sara a message. Sean too, if he hadn't already tried to contact her. Why would she want to follow through with this date anyway, in light of what she now knew about Green Jeans? Oh yeah, there was the flattery factor. And she was raised to stick to her commitments. Just because people had flung flakiness at her over the years, didn't mean she needed to practice such behavior. What she really wanted to do was something else she hadn't done in years.

Take a nap.

The minute she reached her stop, she remembered she might have left her phone in Sara's car, so she decided to swing by the garage first thing. Sure enough, it was right there on the seat. Good thing this was a secure building. Anywhere else and she probably would have come home to a smashed windshield.

She checked messages as she walked to the condo. There was a message from Sean, one from Lisa and one from Bradley. She opened Bradley's first.

All it said was, "Are you okay?"

She wondered why he would ask such a question, and looked at the time the message was sent. 12:35 p.m. She was somewhere between the meeting at the school and walking to the park at that time. Then she remembered he and Valerie were going to swing by the office today. Cassie must have told him the news.

She started to text him back, then decided it would be better to call.

He answered right away and it was difficult to hear him. She asked where he was and he said, "We're still in line, waiting to get up to the Skydeck."

"Wow. It must be busy today."

"Yeah. I think a lot of kids took advantage of the in-service day today and the rest are probably tourists. So is everything all right? Cassie told me things didn't look so good."

"Let me just say it was a bad day at the office. I'll share more details with you later. I can barely hear you."

"Okay. I'll call you just before we leave the Skydeck to go to Giordano's."

Her response was framed with a grin. "I don't know why you keep pushing this Giordano's thing. You know I don't do pizza."

"This from a girl who just gorged herself on garlic bread two nights ago? They do offer alternatives, but I don't think you'll be able to resist Chicago's finest pizza."

She heard him smile into the phone and it comforted her. She would have kept the conversation going, but it was too difficult to hear him above the din of the Skydeck line. "I'm going to go now Bradley. I can barely hear you. Call me before you leave."

By now she was inside the condo and turning on lights. She sat down on the couch to check Sean's message.

"What's your address? Eleven o'clock tomorrow?"

She sent him the address, said they were still on, and questioned herself once again right after she sent the message. Why was she going through with this? She wasn't the same person she was at the beginning of the week. So much had transpired. Not only had she aged physically overnight, but she was changing on the inside as well. For the first time in years, she felt a kinship with a handful of people other than her sister. She found herself actually caring about these people. She'd even begun to feel bothered by her harsh treatment of others. It usually didn't faze her to take a bite out of someone else's self-esteem. But now she wondered how she'd ever come to be such a beast.

Worst of all, she'd hurt Valerie. Not just a family member, but her only friend's daughter. How could she ever apologize to this tenderhearted child?

All this pondering served to knock her out again. The couch cushions were soft and inviting and she couldn't spin her wheels anymore. She was weary of puzzling over everything, all the time. She gave in to those cushions, stretched out and instantly fell asleep.

Two hours later, the phone rang.

In her rummy state, Ann couldn't locate the phone. Somehow, it had fallen behind the cushions. Once she got to it, Bradley's voice hit her like a foghorn.

"Hey Miss Ann, we're heading over to Giordano's. How soon will you be able to get there?"

"It might be a minute since I just woke up, so go ahead and order if you're hungry."

"Okay, don't take too long though. Valerie wants to saturate your ears with the day's events."

"Okay. Just give me some time to put myself back together."

The events of her own day had preoccupied her to the point where she'd barely given her appearance a thought since morning. She had her wig, glasses and scarf, so all the bases were covered. But when she looked in the bathroom mirror, her reflection told a different story.

The dark glasses weren't going to help what was happening below her eyes. What she'd feared the most had finally taken place. Her cheeks were beginning to droop and fine lines had formed around her mouth. She remembered one of the jars of product Charlotte had recommended for this sort of thing and decided now would be the time to try it.

Either that or a face mask, she thought as she rummaged through her cosmetic bag.

She found the jar and applied it liberally. It helped somewhat. She thought if the lighting inside the restaurant was dark enough, it might not be as obvious. Then the phone rang. It was Sara.

121

"Ann, I'm glad I caught you. Are you in the middle of something? Do you have a minute?"

"Yeah. I'm actually home now. Marvin gave me half the day off."

Sara didn't know the implications of this.

"Oh how nice. You can start your weekend early."

"Yeah I guess that's true. So what's up?"

"We're in the middle of a break while the managers have yet another meeting. But before he went into the meeting, the man who will be my immediate supervisor should I get the job, gave me a very positive piece of news. He said they've pretty much settled on me and I'm not supposed to tell any of the other candidates. He said they don't yet know who number two will be. So that made it sound like I'm definitely in. Don't spill the beans to Valerie yet. I just had to call because I'm beside myself. Like I said before, tomorrow's the day they make the official announcement. What's up with you? Why did Marvin give you half a day off?"

"Sorry Sara. I don't have time to talk about it right now. I'm getting ready to join Bradley and Valerie for dinner at Giordano's."

"The pizza place? Are you going to eat something there or just sip a glass of water?"

"Well, you know they have items on the menu that are gluten-free."

"Like what? Lettuce? Okay sis—go get ready. I don't want to hold you up. But call me later, okay?"

"Okay. I'll talk to you soon."

Ann finished getting ready by putting on the wig and scarf, but saved the glasses for when she got to the restaurant. For some reason, this gave her a momentary sense of freedom from the aging nightmare.

When she got to the restaurant, she put the glasses on and found Bradley and Valerie. She knew the first lines of dialogue would be about the glasses and she was prepared.

Valerie beat Bradley to the punch. "Why are you wearing those glasses Auntie? We're inside a restaurant."

"I knew both of you would be wondering. Bradley, do you remember this morning when I told you I woke up with a headache and my eyes were a little light-sensitive? Well that hasn't gone away. I've had to wear these all day."

"Wow. Are you going to get in and see a doctor about that? No wonder you were acting so strange this morning."

"Well that, and I was preoccupied with getting ready for the conference call."

"That's right. Black Friday. Well, we have a host of stories to regale you with. You'll soon forget all about that wretched phone call."

How much did Cassie tell him? she wondered.

Valerie exploded with details of the day. While barely pausing to breathe between sentences, she told Ann, "We went to a really cool bagel shop for breakfast, then we went to the park and took pictures at The Bean, then went to the fountain. I tried to get a picture of one of the faces, but it didn't turn out very well. Then we went to Lurie Garden, then to the Navy Pier. I got to go on that giant Ferris wheel! And we got to race boats. We wanted to go on a real boat but couldn't. And this great big swing swung us out over the water. And we went to this place called the Crystal Gardens. Have you ever been there Auntie? It's like a dream! I told Bradley I want to get married there."

"Wow," Ann replied, "that sounds like a very full day."

"That was only the first part Auntie. After that we went to your office and I got to talk to Cassie. She's really nice. I'm going there tomorrow and I'm even going to spend the night. She said if I felt comfortable, I could stay Sunday too. We're all on spring break at the same time and her oldest daughter can watch us on Monday. Would that be okay, Auntie?"

"It's fine with me as long as it's okay with your mom. So you liked Cassie, hmm?"

"Oh yes. I liked her a lot. She reminded me of one of the ladies at my church. I get to go to their church on Sunday too!"

Ann couldn't remember a moment when Valerie was quite this full of words. And apparently, she was just getting started.

"Then we got to go to the Skydeck. It was packed, so we had to wait forever. Then we finally got to go stand on the Ledge. It's all glass and you can see everything from up there! I thought of you, Auntie, and how you used to go rock-climbing and hang-gliding all the time. I wasn't afraid at all. Just like you!"

Ann had to laugh at this. "You mean the old me. I'm not so fond of heights anymore. Maybe it's from living in the city for so long now."

Valerie asked if Ann had ever been to the Skydeck before and Ann told her no, she hadn't.

"Well maybe if you went up there, you'd find out you still love heights, just like I do!"

"Maybe. But I'm in no hurry to get up to the Skydeck any time soon."

Bradley had to join the exchange. "Are you kidding me? You've been in Chicago how many years now and you've never been to the Skydeck? This is pathetic. We have to fix this."

Ann was happy to be wearing dark glasses as she looked down at the table in embarrassment. "No, no, we don't have to fix this Bradley. I'll be fine if I never go to the Skydeck."

"All right, subject change. Let's take a look at this menu. I'm starved. But don't think I'm finished with this topic, Finlayson."

Bradley and Valerie settled on a pizza and Ann ordered a salad. Sara was almost correct. She was eating lettuce. And chicken. And other veggies. She smiled as she thought Sara lost that one.

But when the pizza arrived, Ann suffered from the same battle she'd experienced with the garlic bread the other night. She tried not to focus on how good it looked when Bradley interrupted her thoughts.

"So with this pizza, we have now covered the four basic food groups: hot dogs, ice cream, pizza and ..."

Valerie blurted, "Bagels and cream cheese!"

"Nope. I was thinking of the popcorn we got you at Garrett's."

"Oh yeah," Valerie remembered. "I'm going to share it with Cassie's kids tomorrow when we watch a movie."

Bradley couldn't help but notice the way Ann was looking at the pizza.

"Go ahead and have a piece. Make it one of the really big ones. Then your craving will be satisfied and you can get on with life. Come on now, Ann. Have some pizza and celebrate the fact that your bad day at the office has officially come to an end."

Ann finally did give in and while Bradley was reaching for his second piece, he recalled another slice of their time at the Pier.

"Your niece here is quite the dancer. There was a band playing near the Atrium before we went in. Valerie broke into a dance and had everyone around her watching and smiling. They all clapped at the end of the song and Valerie laughed and took a bow. Quite the natural little performer. Too bad you had to miss it."

"But Bradley, Auntie's seen me dance before. She played her violin for me the day we went to the park and I danced all over her living room."

"Violin? First, you're a hang-gliding rock climber and now you're a violinist? What other secrets have you been hiding under your hat, Miss Finlayson?"

Ann felt flushed by this attention. She wasn't fond of the spotlight and pursuing it was never her motive when it came to indulging her life's passions.

"It's no big deal," she said. "My mom was an accomplished violinist and I just followed in her footsteps. I've never played with an orchestra or anything."

"But she could," Valerie added adamantly.

"Then it's settled," Bradley declared. "We're going to your place after dinner and you're going to give us a concert."

"Bradley, I'm tired."

"Don't think you're getting out of this one, Annie. I will not take no for an answer."

Ann sat still with her dark glasses hiding all the emotions that clamored for attention in her heart. *He called me Annie. Only one person has ever called me that.*

But before she could finish musing, Bradley was paying the bill and rising everyone to their feet.

"Come along now kids. We have a concert to catch."

Valerie and Bradley chatted all the way to the condo while Ann remained silent. How was it that Bradley was so adept at touching some of her deepest nerves? As usual, he and Valerie left her to her thoughts and didn't force her to join their happy conversation.

Once inside the condo, Ann began to feel a little nervous about the prospect of pulling out her violin. She didn't know why. It was just Bradley. And she didn't really have to play. She knew Bradley wouldn't push her if she flat out refused.

It was Valerie who wouldn't take no for an answer. "Okay, Auntie. Go get your violin. Would you like me to get it for you? I saw where you keep it in the back of the closet."

Then she turned to Bradley. "You won't believe how good she is."

Back to Ann. "Will you play the same two you did last Sunday? The pretty one and the dancy one?"

And back to Bradley. "Do you know how to dance, Bradley? Because if you do, you're going to love the dancy one."

With all this prompting from Valerie, Bradley had to add his two bits. "Now Ann—I know you can say no right to my face. But can you so easily deny your ever-so-insistent niece? I don't think so. So let's have it."

Now, Ann had to smile. Surprisingly, it was the fun factor that won her over. Down the hall and to the closet she went. While she was in there, it flashed through her mind that she should dig out some other treasures from the back of the closet one of these days.

Her audience waited patiently on the couch while she tuned. Then, as Valerie had requested, she began with the Vivaldi piece.

Bradley was floored. He felt as though he should have paid admission for this. How was it that this extraordinary talent had lain dormant for so long?

She ended the first piece and Bradley chided her again for keeping this a secret. "How dare you hide this from me! You could quit the magazine today and join the Chicago Symphony Orchestra. They would take you. They would take you right now. I don't know if you should move to the second song after all. I may faint from sheer shock." He put his hand on his forehead, leaned back and said to Valerie, "You'll be sure to catch me, won't you?"

Both Ann and Valerie laughed at that. Then Valerie got up and told Ann to start the second song.

Ann had every intention of playing the lively Celtic tune Valerie had requested, but this time she included the airy introduction her mom used to play. Valerie started to protest, but Bradley put his finger to his lips, shook his head and put his hand to his ear, telling her to listen.

The music was haunting and wispy, like columns of smoke rising from the chimney of an ancient cottage in Ireland. Bradley heard an imaginary pennywhistle and a drum in the background, while smelling the fog-soaked sod in a place he'd only seen in pictures before. But Ann took him there now. Again, he was awestruck by her gift.

Then he was jolted from the scene as immediately as he had climbed in.

Ann got to the lively part. Valerie, who had sat down for the quiet introduction, sprang instantly to her feet when the music picked up. She tore up the living room with sheer bliss while Bradley kept time with his hands and feet.

When Valerie caught sight of this, she grabbed Bradley's hands and made him dance with her.

Now it was Ann's turn to be amazed. She had to take back what she thought of Bradley a few days ago. When she realized he was so much like her father, except for the musical part. Bradley could dance. This fed her all the more and she kept the song going far beyond its end.

After she ended the song, Valerie begged for just one more.

Ann gladly complied. She played an old-fashioned country fiddle tune while Bradley and Valerie consumed the living room floor with their feet. She couldn't believe how much fun she was having. Her smiles were just as wide as theirs. She didn't even analyze when the last time might have been that she enjoyed a musical moment like this. She just savored the here and now. When she ended the song, all three of them collapsed on the couch and laughed their heads off.

Once they caught their breath, Bradley turned to Ann. "Miss Finlayson, you have positively won me over. There's no turning back."

Ann beamed at this, but behind the dark glasses, concern had furrowed her brow. Thankfully, though her feelings were all-consuming, no one could tell how she was struggling behind those glasses. She decided this would be the perfect time to call it a night.

"You guys, I'm beat from this day. I need to call it quits."

"That's right. I forgot about your bad day at the office. When do I get to hear about that?"

Ann was flabbergasted. How could Cassie have resisted the urge to provide him with details? She was sitting right there while the conference call was taking place. It wouldn't be like her to keep her mouth shut if she was privy to any amount of gossip.

"When you sent me that text earlier about how I was doing, I figured Cassie must have told you. So she didn't say anything?"

"No. All she told me was that Marvin gave you the rest of the day off and you left without saying goodbye."

"That's right. I did. I'll have to apologize to Cassie for leaving like that."

"Well, perhaps we could hook up sometime over the weekend. I'd like to hear the details. How about after I drop Valerie off? I'm picking her up at nine and could probably come back around ten or eleven."

Ann remembered her Sean date. She told Bradley she had plans for the first half of the day, but perhaps they could get together later. She told him she'd call.

After they all said their goodbyes, Valerie picked up the phone to call Sara.

Once again, she recounted every detail of the day. She covered the same ground she did at the restaurant, but then had to add the part about dinner and the music party that followed. She grew particularly animated during this segment of the report. She had to tell her mom all about how she and Bradley danced while Auntie played the violin. And just when Ann thought Valerie would end the call, she heard, "Oh and I almost forgot ..."

Ann couldn't do much but wait for the phone while Valerie continued. Who was she to interrupt an eleven-year-old girl who had just swallowed the best pain reliever ever offered to man? There couldn't have been a better piece of timing than that which this day on the town provided. Following yesterday's trauma, she would have believed God Himself custom-made this day for Valerie, had she believed.

Finally, it was her turn to get on the phone. "Hey Sara, long time no talk."

"Ha-ha, girlie. So you were going to tell me why Marvin gave you half the day off. What happened?"

As she walked into the bedroom, she answered, "I'll give you the short version. I blew a conference call with a major account today. I'm still so sick about it I don't have the heart to supply details. In a nutshell, some positional shifting might be happening at the office as a result, and I might end up on the bottom of the heap."

"Oh no, Ann. I'm so sorry."

"You know, that's not even the worst of it. My entire face is aging now. Until tonight, it was mostly around my eyes, throat and arms. But I'm this close to looking like a seventy-five-year-old woman. This close. And I'm not going to be able to keep hiding it." For the first time since all this started, every ounce of vulnerability regarding this aging issue rose to the surface and tears threatened to escape her eyes. "I don't know what I'm going to do, Sara."

Sara could hear the emotion in her sister's voice and she didn't know what to say. Were there any words in the entire English language that could possibly be strung together to comfort or encourage her sister? She couldn't think of a single one. So she told Ann how sorry she was that she was going through this, and the only thing she knew to do in such a dire situation was pray.

Ann breathed a heavy sigh. "I figured you might say that." But she wasn't annoyed this time, just deflated with hopelessness.

She told Sara she had to go. When she hung up, she remembered she hadn't mentioned tomorrow's date with Sean.

Doesn't that tell you anything?

She ignored that internal voice for now and went out to say goodnight to Valerie. Once again, the power of exhaustion robbed her of that opportunity.

Valerie was out.

Chapter 9

Ann woke to the sounds of hubbub in the kitchen and the smell of bacon. Metal was clinking, drawers and cupboards were opening and closing, and the jovial voices of Bradley and Valerie rose above it all.

She looked at the clock. 8:15 a.m. She couldn't remember the last time she'd slept in so late. It felt so good not to wake up feeling exhausted that she lay on her back for a full five minutes while soaking in the sounds and smells coming from the kitchen.

Bacon.

When was the last time she tasted that? Her dad used to make at least one big breakfast every weekend and bacon was her favorite. He used to let her snatch one piece before everyone sat down. She'd always go for the crispiest one she could find. She wondered if Bradley made it crispy too. Or perhaps he favored the flabby, fatty version that she couldn't stand. She bet on the former.

Although she didn't want to face the mirror, the smell inarguably called her out from under the covers. She skipped the mirror for now and went straight to the closet to dig out her robe and slippers.

When she did catch a glimpse of her reflection, she wasn't surprised. Everything on her face was drooping. How was she going to hide this? She couldn't wear a scarf across her face to the breakfast table. Then she remembered Charlotte had given her some sort of facial mask while loading her up with skin care a few days ago. She recommended Ann use it twice a week for now, then she could taper off to once a week.

The problem was, all the facial products Ann hadn't used yet were in the bathroom cabinet. She'd have to scoot in there without being seen. So she cracked the bedroom door and yelled, "Hey you guys—don't you know a girl needs her beauty sleep? What's all the ruckus about?"

Bradley spoke first. "Come out here and find out, Beauty Queen. We have Saturday morning essentials waiting for you in the kitchen."

Valerie added, "Yeah, you better hurry before we eat it all!"

Ann shouted her alibi before attempting to get to the bathroom. "Well don't peek. My hair's a mess and I have bags under my eyes. Stay in the kitchen, got it?"

Bradley deepened his voice and tried to sound like a private taking orders. "Got it, Chief."

Ann put her wig on and made it safely to the bathroom.

She rummaged around for what she thought must be the mask. She didn't have her magnifying glass, so it was hard to tell. She found a container of something she hadn't used yet and was able to get it far enough away from her eyes to make out what she thought was an "m" and a "k." Charlotte had told her it was some sort of Egyptian mud, and when she slathered it on, it worked like a charm. It was thick and gray, mixed with brown granules.

When she stepped into the kitchen, she explained herself. "This is part of my Saturday morning regimen. If it scares you too much, just look the other way."

"But Auntie. You didn't put that goop on your face last Saturday."

"Yes I did. I washed it off right before you and your mom got here." Oh how she longed to be released from the need to keep manufacturing these lies.

Bradley adopted a British accent. "Well I, for one, think it becomes you quite nicely my lady. After all—didn't you say you had bags under your eyes? Thank you for sparing us."

As usual, Bradley had everyone laughing and feeling lighter than they'd been before he showed up.

Ann recalled something that had flashed through her mind when she was in the bathroom. "I thought you were going to pick Valerie up at nine."

"I was, but I decided to risk knocking on the door early on the off chance that Valerie might already be up. And she was." The two of them grinned at each other. "So let's dig in, shall we?"

Ann took three pieces of bacon and a biscotti for her coffee.

"Beware Miss. That biscotti is not gluten-free."

Ann pointed her pinky in the air and struck an aristocratic pose. "Thank you Sir, but I'm in the mood not to care."

And she wasn't. Sean was coming over at eleven o'clock. She was so tired of the fight that she hadn't given a thought as to how she might manage her appearance for this "date." She just enjoyed the moment and asked Valerie what day one with Cassie and the family was going to look like.

Valerie said the girls had an extra bike, so they might go for a bike ride, then have a picnic in the backyard.

"That sounds like fun. A bike ride sounds a lot better than my … thing."

Bradley remembered she had plans for the first part of the day and curiosity got the better of him. "What's your 'thing'?"

"Nothing much to speak of. I have somewhere to go at eleven, that's all."

"Well let me know when your 'thing' is over. Remember. I'm still waiting for details of your bad day at the office."

"I know. I just have to play it by ear. I'll let you know as soon as I can."

"I'll hold you to it, Fin. Why don't we clean up this mess and get ready for our … things?"

Ann smiled and rolled her eyes at him while grabbing dishes from the table.

"Thank you for your contribution, but you are officially released from cleanup duty. Valerie and I can take care of the rest. I mean, really—have you looked at yourself in the mirror? Who knows how long it will take you to get ready for your 'thing'?"

If only he knew.

As she excused herself from the kitchen and made her way back to the bedroom, she realized she didn't want this moment to end. She sighed and said goodbye to them over her shoulder. "I'll see you guys later. Have fun at Cassie's, Valerie."

"Okay, I will Auntie." She giggled, "Have fun at your thing."

Once Ann returned to her bedroom, she realized she probably would need extra time to get ready for this date. Her heart wasn't in it and she'd have to be ultra-creative with her face looking like this. Although she was relieved by not having to hide the truth from Valerie and Bradley as they called out their goodbyes, she could barely muster any energy for performing this great transformation. So she sat on the bed and pondered her wardrobe.

The phone forced her to get up. She figured it must be Sara and hurried to get to it before it stopped ringing. Because her face was still slathered with Egyptian mud, she had to be careful not to touch the phone with it.

"Hey Sara."

Sara's voice was filled with excitement and nervousness. "Oh Ann, I just can't stand this waiting period. They're taking us all out to brunch in about an hour, then they're going to let us know."

Ann didn't want to cut Sara off, but she felt she couldn't do this call justice while contending with all the face goo. "I'm sorry, Sara. Can I call you right back? My face is covered with Egyptian mud and I can't concentrate very well as I try to keep it from touching the phone. Let me go wash it off and call you back."

Sara sounded disappointed. "Okay, but please make it quick. I'm dying here."

They hung up and Ann removed the mask as quickly as she could. She looked in the mirror and felt encouraged because the mask seemed to have helped. She didn't want to keep Sara waiting, but Charlotte told her it was important to moisturize while the skin was still damp. So she quickly threw on some heavy facial cream and ran back to call Sara.

By the time she got Sara back on the phone, her sister acted as though it had taken months to call back. "What took you so long? Have you no mercy? My moment of truth is about to arrive and you just take your time while I sit twitching with impatience? I'm about to go crazy here."

"Sorry. I have something to get ready for too. Bradley and Valerie just left and like I said, I couldn't hold an important conversation of any length with all that goop on my face."

"You have something to get ready for? What would that be? Have you told me this before and I just spaced on it?"

"No. I forgot to tell you about it last night. But why don't you talk first? You're the one going crazy here."

"Actually, it just feels good to have a distraction while I wait for the clock to tick—there's not that much to tell. So go ahead and give me the details."

"I have a date with a guy from the office. Not a real date though. I just agreed to go out with him because I was so flattered that he even asked."

"So this is someone other than Bradley? Why haven't I heard about him before?"

"Probably because of all these changes I've been going through. Just last Monday I thought he was the perfect match for me. Ruthless in business, not afraid of putting people under the knife. We just clicked so well on a professional level and then …"

"And then?"

"Tuesday happened. All I've been able to do since that day in the crosswalk is focus on how to keep this hidden. And I've been going through all these emotions lately. You know how I usually am. Pretty much fireproof. But this has knocked me flat—especially these past two days. You've seen what I look like. At least, what I looked like a few days ago. Then Bradley started coming over and I don't know … I've been going through so much turmoil. But whenever he's around, everything feels more … bearable …"

"And yet you have a date with this other guy. What's his name?"

"Sean. It felt so good to be seen as attractive that I just said yes. To top it all off, my eyes have been opened to the truth of his character. He's really just a superficial, self-centered pretty boy with no values and cut-throat ambition. Which was me five days ago. So here I am getting ready for this date when I don't even want to go."

"Then cancel it."

"I know. I should. But I feel like if I go, I'll feel better about this situation I'm in."

"And how would that work out? 'Hi Sean, thanks for asking me out, but I really look like an old lady and I'm hoping you'll find me attractive anyway?'"

Ann sighed, "I just feel like I want to go. Maybe to prove something to myself."

"I don't know what this so-called date could prove, but go ahead and go. From your description of him, I'm hoping he doesn't chew you up and spit you out."

"Well it's not like I'm going to let him see me. I'll have to cover it all up somehow."

"Sounds like a thrilling bit of stress. Suit yourself, but you know I'm casting my vote for Bradley and I think this date is just a waste of your time."

"Probably is. But the truth is, I'm not suited for anyone right now. You know I'm not. I have been getting feelings for Bradley, but he couldn't be with me in this condition. No one could. I don't even want to think about all that."

"Have you seen that old lady since the last time I talked to you?"

"No. I thought I saw her from the train yesterday, but couldn't be sure. I'm trying to hold on to some hope, but it's getting harder and harder to do that."

"Sorry Ann, but I'm getting the feeling we should get off the phone. We both have to put ourselves together before stepping out. I'll keep praying for you. And I'll especially storm the gates about your being able to meet up with that old woman."

"Thank you. Call or text the minute you get the news about the job."

"Will do. Take care of yourself and I'll talk with you soon."

"Okay, bye."

Ann hung up and checked the time. 10:15. Was she really going to be able to pull this off in forty-five minutes? And what if he decided to be early?

She sat on the edge of the bed and looked down at her hands. Today was the first day she'd taken a serious look at them. Her skin tended to be dry, so she always kept hand lotion around. Everywhere. In fact, Cassie frequently ribbed her about being obsessive over it. So because she was constantly applying lotion, she hadn't noticed that her hands had been aging too. And today they were looking so bad that she'd have to cover them along with everything else.

Okay … think …

The great challenge wasn't going to be how to cover all this up. It was how to explain the cover-up.

She could say she'd broken out in a rash that covered her entire body. That way, she could get away with covering her face with a scarf and wearing a pair of latex cleaning gloves on her hands.

Simple. Now it would be easy to get ready in a short period of time. All she had to do was get dressed and throw on the scarf and gloves. By the time Sean came to the door, she was armed and ready.

The first words out of his mouth were, "Wow—what's up with you? You look like a mummy from *Night of the Living Dead*."

Ann told him the whole story and he asked when she was planning to get in to see a doctor about all this.

"I'm going to get in as soon as possible—hopefully Monday or Tuesday."

"Good luck with that. I mean—it's Saturday. And you haven't even made an appointment yet?"

"Well, sometimes people cancel. It's worth a try. I'll leave a voicemail at my doctor's office over the weekend so I'll be first on the list should someone decide to cancel."

"Unless someone is on the waiting list ahead of you. Why don't you just go to a doc-in-the-box?"

"I don't want to go to a same-day clinic because I don't trust the staff as much. They usually use nurse practitioners on the weekends and I want a full-fledged doctor."

"What do you say we continue this conversation as we walk to the garage? I have reservations."

"Okay. Where is this place anyway?"

"Out in the middle of nowhere. It's in a revamped farmhouse that sits on fifteen acres of land. The owners grow all their own herbs and produce and they raise chickens and cattle too. So the beef is all grass-fed and the chickens are free-range. They even make their own cheese."

As they were getting into the car, Ann asked if these owners ever slept.

"Oh, they have plenty of help. Foodies and culinary students from all over flock to this place to work side by side with this chef. The place is actually world-renowned. I'm surprised you haven't heard of it."

"Well, you know, I don't get out much."

As they pulled out of the garage, Sean suggested it was time for a change. "That's a tragedy for one so fine as you. We definitely need to work on that. All we have to do is get you all fixed up. Then, the sky's the limit, I'll take you everywhere. We'll wine and dine our lives away and spend every penny we make at the magazine."

His words stung. She wouldn't be suitable for this glamorous lifestyle with Sean unless she first got "all fixed up." What if she couldn't get all fixed up? What if she wasn't able to connect with this old woman? Would she die of old age before the year was out? She needed to change the subject.

"So, did you get a chance to talk to Marvin yesterday?"

"Ooh. Sore subject. I didn't want to crack this bottle open until we got to the restaurant. But since you brought it up, of course I talked to Marvin. Right after you left. He was pretty disappointed that you wouldn't let me help out more with Green Jeans. Then he said something about how we'd have to catch them on the next round." He fidgeted as he prepared to deliver the next piece of news. "Then he said he wanted me in his office Monday morning at seven o'clock sharp."

"Why so early?"

"Not sure." He squirmed in his seat, as though the conversation was hitting an unwanted nerve. "He just muttered something about the office ..."

One thing Ann knew for certain: Marvin never muttered. Obviously, Sean didn't want to delve any more deeply into the subject. So she let it go.

Sean decided it was time to put the top down. "We're almost on that country road I was telling you about, so it's time for a little sunshine and fresh air."

Once he put the top down, Ann began to freeze. She tried not to say anything about it, but Sean could tell she was cold.

"Are you actually cold? It's sixty-one degrees outside."

"Well it isn't sixty-one degrees in this car. The wind is making it colder."

"I have a blanket in the trunk. Do you want me to pull over and get it out for you?"

"That would actually be great. Thank you."

As Sean found a spot to pull over, he mentioned it was time to rev things up. He explained that this was the greatest part of the drive. He was able to wind out the engine to his heart's content and there were hardly any cops out here.

Ann had never been into fast cars. She'd always thought the concept was a bit juvenile. All the guys in the high school hallway would talk about their fast cars while the girls swooned and giggled. She would always keep her distance and find a quiet place to study.

By now, Sean was ready to go and Ann was wrapped in her blanket, dreading the rest of the drive. "Okay harem girl, let's go."

First I'm a character from Night of the Living Dead, and now I'm a harem girl? Thanks Sean.

It seemed like every other word out of Sean's mouth was a jab. If he wasn't jabbing at her, it was something, or someone else. How could she have been so blind to this side of him? She never knew how cold and belittling he could be. All she'd known of him was his office persona, where he'd proven himself worthy of taking up residence in the shark tank right beside her. Since she'd started working at the magazine, no one else had ever merited such a coveted position. Well—there was Nancy—but she was in a league of her own ...

As the car went faster, the wind picked up. Ann had to keep one hand on top of her wig and the other on the scarf that was covering her face, for fear of having them blow off.

"Can you slow down a little?"

"What? Slow down? Are you kidding me? This is half the reason we're coming all the way out here. It's supposed to be one of the highlights."

"Well I'm still cold and..."

"And what?" He twisted his voice and mocked her with a grimace on his face. "Is it going to mess up the pretty little girl's hair?"

He pushed the wrong button. Ann's reflective state was immediately replaced by a blinding rage. The red that flashed in her eyes couldn't be detected due to her glasses, but the seething volcano of anger took mere seconds to fully erupt.

"Stop the car."

"What? Stop the car? What is it *now*, princess?"

Ann gritted her teeth. She stabbed him with her eyes as well as she could from behind the glasses and repeated herself. "I mean it, Sean Mobley. Pull over to the side of the road and stop this car. Now. If you don't, I'm going to grab the steering wheel and steer the car *for* you. And don't think I won't."

Sean found a place to pull over. Once he came to a complete stop, Ann was out of the car and standing over him on the driver's side before he could put the parking brake on.

"Sean Mobley, the way you're treating me is despicable. It's atrocious and inexcusable and I won't put up with it for one more second. I don't even know what possessed me to agree to this date. I'm going to get back inside your little toy car and you are going to turn it around and take me back home. Now. Got it?"

"What? You can't take a joke? I was only having fun with you."

"Uh—that wasn't my idea of fun, Sean."

"Well then, what *is* your idea of fun? Anything? You're not acting anything like the devil-may-care woman I knew at the beginning of the week. I've never seen this side of you. Could it be all this medical stuff or is this the real you? Because if it is, I'm wondering how you could have managed to hide this stranger all this time. You've always been a shark at the office, someone I respected and admired."

Ann suddenly felt weary of the term "shark." It was a label Marvin had applied after she landed her first big account. She'd always been proud of this attribute, as though it had made her invincible. But at this point, she was finished with the term.

She sighed. "I guess it does have something to do with all this medical stuff." She could think of nothing else to say and neither could he. He started the car, turned it around, and they spent the rest of the drive in silence.

Once they reached Ann's building, they both knew it wouldn't be necessary for him to park in the garage and walk her to her door. He pulled the car up to the curb to drop her off.

As she reached for the door handle, Ann had only a few words to end this adventure.

"Thanks for showing me the real you."

"Likewise."

He sealed their mutual sentiments by speeding away from the curb as if he was one of those boys from the high school hallway. *Good riddance* was all that came to Ann's mind as she watched him drive away.

Now that she was by herself again, a mixed bag of emotions jumbled together like a lump in the pit of her gut. Rather than trying to sort them out, she reached for her phone on the way up to the condo. Perhaps Sara had sent her a message.

But she couldn't find her phone. She checked all her pockets and dug through her purse, but couldn't find it anywhere. She wondered if she'd left it inside the condo.

Great. So now my mind's going too?

Once inside, the first place she checked was the bedroom. Sure enough, it was right there on the dresser. Again she felt dismayed by her absentmindedness. It reminded her of the thought she had earlier regarding whether or not she'd live to see the end of the year. Or even next fall for that matter.

When she checked her phone, she saw three messages. One from Sara, one from Cassie and one from Bradley. She decided to check Sara's first.

"Got it," was all it said. This lifted Ann halfway out of her dark hole, so she called her sister immediately.

"Hey Ann, can I call you back? We're still hashing out details and I'm going to want to have a long conversation with you—including all about how your date went. So give me a few, okay?"

This caused Ann to slip back down the hole again, because she really needed to vent about this "date." But what could she do? Her sister was in the middle of an important meeting. She decided to call Cassie next, saving Bradley for last. She had a feeling he might very well be the sunshine that could penetrate all the way into her dark hole and draw her back out again.

Cassie sounded out of breath when she answered the phone. "Hello, Ann?"

"Yep it's me. Why are you so out of breath?

"Oh. I've been running around in the backyard. Since the girls have all clustered together, Simon has deemed me his very own personal playmate. So first, we had to dig for worms, then he wanted to play soccer. It doesn't take much for me to get winded. Unlike you, I barely get any exercise beyond chasing after Simon. You're probably wondering why I called."

"Yeah. I just got back from a drive with Sean and didn't get your message until just now. I hope it wasn't urgent."

She immediately kicked herself for sharing that. With Cassie, of all people. Too late now—she couldn't retract her words. She braced herself for whatever Cassie might have to say about it.

"Sean, huh? How did that go? I can't believe you followed through with this little excursion. I've never known what it is you see in that snake."

"Well, to tell you the truth, I'd never been fully exposed to the snaky side of him until today."

"Really? What caused the scales to fall from your blind eyes? Frankly, I'm delighted."

Ann told her about how rude he'd been and how she'd insisted they cut things short. She told Cassie about Sean's juvenile departure, how he squealed his tires while speeding away from the curb.

"Sean is all about Sean, Ann, even where you're concerned. Don't flatter yourself by thinking his attraction to you has been genuine. From what I can see, he's just wanted to get close to you so he could learn all your tricks, move in on Marvin and take Nancy's office away from you as soon as possible."

Ann felt embarrassed about how blind she'd been. "How have I missed all this?"

"To be brutally honest, your self-centered cocoon is made of the same material as Sean's. Since I've known you, you've never been able to see anyone but yourself, and how you treat others has never been a consideration. Not as long as you've been making your way to the top in Marvin's eyes. Sean has appealed to you because the two of you are so much alike."

Yeah. Fellow sharks. How enchanting.

"Well, thank you for the enlightenment Cassie, I knew I could count on you."

Cassie's bluntness had never been hidden from Ann before, so she wasn't surprised by Cassie's negative responses. What did surprise her was how good it felt to connect with Cassie right now. She'd been devastated by her date with Sean and let down that she couldn't talk to her sister about it right away. Cassie was proving to be an encouraging substitute.

"Thanks for letting me vent. But I know you didn't call me to ask about my date with Sean."

"No I didn't. I wanted to give you the Valerie report, and was hoping to get details about the conference call."

"Well between the two, I'd rather hear about Valerie first. How's she doing?"

"She's doing great. She's really clicking with the girls and Simon just loves her. She's excited about going to church with us in the morning and can't wait to share her special popcorn with everyone for the movie tonight. So I wanted to double-check and make sure it was okay to have her again tomorrow night."

"Yeah. Of course. As long as it's all right with my sister."

"We already called her. She said yes, but I wanted to know how you felt about it. After all, you've had company all week. It might not be that appealing to you to be alone two nights in a row, now that you've had a taste of what's it's like to have people around."

Ann felt embarrassed again. This conversation was making her keenly aware of how okay she'd been over the years *without* the presence of others around. It seemed the rest of the human race thrived on having a lot of social interaction. Why was she so different?

"No, Cassie. I'm fine. Really. I'm used to being by myself all the time. Don't worry about me."

"Okay then, topic number two. How did the conference call go yesterday? I gathered it didn't go very well by your brief responses, then Marv let you off for the rest of the day. What happened?"

Since Ann didn't want to hash through every minute detail of the phone call, and secretly hoped it would disappear from her memory altogether, her response was short. "It bombed."

Cassie could not settle for such a simple answer. "So what happened? Why did it bomb?"

"Because they only committed to a two-page spread. I was supposed to convince them to give us four pages. Marvin intimated that this never would have happened had I utilized Sean more. Now he's the blind one ..." Ann didn't want to admit that it was her rudeness with Murphy Lawman that caused most of the trouble. Nor did she want to tell Cassie the truth about what she now knew about Green Jeans.

"Well, we all know that Sean's input wouldn't have mattered that much. And as you said, now Marvin's the blind one. But that's been Sean's mission all along. Move in on Marvin and take over your spot."

Ann felt like she might be experiencing an unknown side of Cassie. Could it be possible that Cassie was feeling sympathetic toward her situation? This wouldn't be like the Cassie she knew.

"Well, now you know the whole scoop. I'm sure the news has made your day."

"Not really. You know very well that I stand with the entire office against Green Jeans. In my opinion, it's all downhill for *Top Rung* now. I'm sure the magazine will lose some of its faithful followers as a result of this alliance. Remember the National Knitting League?"

Ann did and it gave her another twinge of embarrassment.

"Now that's the Cassie I know and love. Thank you for sharing. I'm going to have to get off. I have two more phone calls to make."

She was feeling so alone after her date that she truly didn't want to end the call. For a split second, she even considered how it might feel to share her predicament with Cassie. It might be nice for someone in the office to know what she was going through. But she didn't want to hear anymore reminders about what a fool she'd been regarding Green Jeans, so thought it best to end the conversation.

Cassie broke right into her thoughts. "You have two more phone calls to make? Well aren't you popular? It's fine to get off now anyway, I only wanted to know about the conference call because I don't want to be distracted by curiosity on Monday. It's going to be Nancy's day and I want to be focused on making her day special."

"That's right. The office party. Did you buy some cookies for me?"

"No, Ann, I didn't. Given all Nancy's done for you, I figure you should put in a little effort on your own. Anyone can throw money around. But when it comes to Nancy, you're not just anyone. So dig deep. I'm putting your ten dollar bill toward tonight's pizza."

Ann's momentary warmth toward Cassie instantly dissolved. "Well thanks for nothing my friend. Call if you need to. I really need to go now."

After hanging up, Ann figured the best thing to do at this point would be to get outside and walk. She needed to check on Charlotte and it might be nice to run into Lisa at the park again. Then she remembered what Cassie had said about digging deep and coming up with a contribution to Nancy's party all on her own.

Ha. I'll show her ...

Rather than leave immediately for an outing, Ann decided it was time to break into the back of her hall closet where all her childhood memories were stored. Her mother's chocolate chip cookie recipe was hiding somewhere back there. She pulled out a box that contained a handful of framed photos. She found her old pair of snowshoes. *Why didn't I ever get rid of these?* She moved her violin out of the way and her heart skipped a beat when she saw what was behind it, underneath an old jacket that had fallen off its hanger.

There, sitting on the floor in the corner of the closet, was the black kettle. The one her mom had used for creating so many fond memories from their old house in Colorado. The one she'd brought over from Ireland because she wanted to hold onto her own past of being raised in that beloved country. She used to share that it was the only remnant of her upbringing that mattered enough to pack up and haul all the way to the states. That, some loose pictures, and a dilapidated cookbook.

Ann pulled the kettle out and lifted the lid. The old cookbook and pictures were right there inside it. How many warm meals had her mother prepared in this kettle? She remembered her mother's special Irish stew, corned beef and cabbage, and the potatoes she'd boiled for shepherd's pie. And how many nights had she and Sara sat in the living room, waiting for the popcorn to pop in that old kettle? They never knew what to expect when it came to their mother's popcorn. She used to flavor it with all sorts of things. One time she even poured chocolate sauce all over it. That was a disaster. Everyone agreed it made the popcorn too soggy.

Ann was curious about the old cookbook. For some reason, she'd forgotten all about it. She pulled it out carefully and began turning pages. As she flipped through, she noticed several of the pages were torn from the binding, so she tried to be gentle. One page broke loose and fell into the lid that was flipped over on the hallway floor. Ann had to smile. Of course it was the cookie recipe.

She decided since she was on a mission, she'd refrain from looking at all the pictures just now. That might take a little more time than she wanted to spend at the moment. Instead, she packed everything but the recipe back into the closet and went to the kitchen to make a list of what she'd need to make the cookies.

She couldn't believe she was actually going through with this. Of the two sisters, only Sara had taken up an interest in cooking and baking. This being the case, she wondered how she was the one who ended up with the black kettle and the cookbook ... so many things she couldn't remember about that dark time ...

Rather than allowing herself to dwell on that topic, Ann smirked when she thought of how satisfying it would be to show up Monday with a batch of her mother's mouth-watering chocolate chip cookies. Oh how she'd revel in Cassie's shock and disbelief.

Her spirits had lifted so much at the thought that she decided to leave her phone home on purpose as she set out for her shopping trip and walk. She didn't want anyone to interfere with this elated feeling. She might even try to make it to yoga later.

First stop was the drugstore. Cecile was at the counter with a customer, so Ann figured Charlotte hadn't come back to work yet. She made herself comfortable in the chair while she waited for Cecile.

As soon as Cecile tied up the transaction at the register, she walked over to Ann. "So how are those hips of yours feeling? We got a new shipment of canes yesterday after you left. One of them has mother-of-pearl in the handle. You should take a look."

Ann struggled to respond without revealing her full-scale irritation. Would this woman ever quit? "No thank you, Cecile. I'm doing better today. I just wanted to come by for an update on Charlotte and her mother."

"Oh, Charlotte's mom is a lot better. In fact, Charlotte's just going to spend today with her, then she'll be coming into work tomorrow following early service."

"Early service? I thought you said her mom was doing better."

Cecile laughed. "I don't mean that sort of service. I mean, Sunday church service. Usually, Charlotte runs the store on Saturday so she can attend service on Sunday morning. But today she wants to stay with her mom, so I told her I'd work for her, then open the store in the morning. I'll just catch the eleven o'clock service once she gets here."

Church service. Of course. Was there anyone in Ann's immediate sphere of human beings that *wasn't* a Christian? Yes. Peggy. Peggy was a confirmed atheist. No wonder they got along so well.

Ann quickly got up from the chair. "Okay then Cecile, it was nice seeing you again. I'll probably be back by tomorrow. If you hear from Charlotte, tell her I said hello."

"Okay. Wait. What's your name again?"

Ann answered her from the door as she was walking out. "It's Ann." She didn't hear whatever words Cecile closed the conversation with as she left the store.

Clouds had rolled in since she left the condo. The weather forecast had mentioned something about cloudiness and wind, but the sunshine was supposed to return tomorrow. She felt chilled by the sudden drop in temperature and decided to end this trip at the grocery store, rather than swinging by the park first.

A lot of other people seemed to have the same idea. The store was packed. She found a stack of hand baskets, picked one up and made her way up and down the aisles. Too bad Valerie wasn't here to help this time. She barely knew this store. By the time she finally got in line, she was ready to be done. Her hips had begun to hurt and she was feeling exhausted, even though she'd slept in. She probably wouldn't be going to yoga after all.

As she was rejoicing over being just two people back from checkout, she realized she hadn't picked up the brown sugar. How could she have missed that with the shopping list right there in her hand? No matter. She'd have to give up her coveted position in line and start all over again.

She had to squeeze past everyone who was standing behind her in line and as she did, she noticed how aggravated they all seemed to be. She couldn't blame them. For some reason, she couldn't get her hand basket up high enough to clear everyone's shopping carts as she backed out of line; she kept bumping into everyone as she went. One man even rolled his eyes at her and sighed as she bumped his shoulder while trying to get past.

Finally, she made it back to the baking aisle. She grabbed a box of brown sugar and made her way back to the front of the store. On the way, she noticed a display of reading glasses on the end of the aisle. She decided to buy a pair. Not that she wanted to give in, but it was getting to be more and more of a hassle to try and read with her tiny magnifying glass. Of course, she wouldn't use them at the office. But she could have them on hand and pull them out whenever she was at home or out running errands. She found a pair that enabled her to read her list with ease and got back in line.

The line was even longer this time around. She could barely get comfortable as she waited. She kept shifting her weight from one leg to the other while trying to find a position that didn't cause more pain to her hips and lower back. She wondered if it was making matters worse that she had this basket hanging off of one arm. Her heavy bag wasn't helping—it pulled on her shoulder like a child not wanting to leave the playground just yet.

When she finally reached the register, she looked back at all the people in line and wondered again what had brought them all out at the same time.

The cashier gave her the total and she reached for her debit card. In honor of keeping the line moving, she already had her wallet out so she could grab her card quickly. Only it wasn't there. Frantically, she searched every pocket of her wallet. No card.

Panic built inside her. Not only had she always put her card in the same spot, but beads of sweat began to dampen her forehead as she sensed the exasperation of those behind her in line. No one had to tell her about how not to hold up a line. She was always on top of that one. Until now. When she couldn't find her card.

She looked over and sheepishly said "I'm sorry" to all the piercing eyes behind her in line. She asked the cashier if she minded her taking the glasses all the way out of their packaging so she could look in her purse.

Now the cashier was rolling *her* eyes. "Yeah. I guess." Her voice was laced with sarcasm and impatience as she made eye contact with the other customers in line.

Ann put the glasses on and tried to look all through her bag, but still couldn't see very well. *Oh yeah,* she thought, *my phone has a flashlight in it.*

But she didn't have her phone. She'd left it behind in the condo.

Then the comments started coming.

"Hey old lady, did you forget to take your memory pills this morning?"

"Yeah. Why don't you just void it out, *then* go find your money in your purse?"

"While you're at it, why don't you check out a new prescription for those glasses?"

"Yeah. Just be sure to go to the geriatric lane."

At this, everyone started laughing.

As she continued digging, she couldn't figure out how it was her age was showing. She still had her wig on. And she'd put on her dark glasses before leaving the condo. But not her scarf. And then she looked down at her hands. Her ungloved, spotted and wrinkled hands. Dead giveaway. Geriatric lane indeed.

Then she remembered the last time she used the card. She caught the L to get home yesterday. She wanted to get on the train quickly, so she'd shoved her card into one of the outside pockets of her handbag. Which one though? She felt flames engulf her cheeks as she checked all the pockets. Once she found her card and paid the cashier, the entire line of customers broke into applause. She grabbed her grocery bag and practically ran from the store.

In her haste, she didn't see the small, cloaked figure standing next to the grocery carts on the opposite side of the checkout counter. She missed the lines of compassion that etched themselves into the forehead of the old woman who stood knowingly by.

She'd been too humiliated to take in her surroundings as she'd dashed for the door.

Too disconcerted to catch sight of the single tear that quietly slipped down the old woman's cheek.

She could barely breathe as she made her way home. The flood of tears that had threatened to burst through her wall earlier in the week made its presence known again. So much stronger. So much more insistent. She felt as though she couldn't hold it back. She pressed her entire will against it until it felt as though the wall would crumble anyway, due to the effort she was exerting.

She tried redirecting her attention. What had those people said? Did one of them say something about the geriatric lane? Aren't those the words she'd spoken to the woman in the crosswalk? She thought so. Then she remembered how she'd treated the old lady at the store the day she and Valerie had gone shopping. Then she recalled everything else she'd said to the woman in the crosswalk.

And the flood returned.

By now she'd reached the condo, so there would be some instant distractions waiting for her as soon as she stepped through the door. Like checking the phone.

She struggled to unlock the front door. Her hands were shaking and she dropped the keys twice before finally getting the right one in her hand. Then it was a matter of inserting the key into the lock, and she dropped the keys again. She'd never been so shook before.

Utter defeat crept like a shadow across her soul. She barely knew what to do with herself once she finally got inside the door.

That's right. I have to put these groceries away.

She put the groceries away and found the phone. Sara and Bradley had both called and left messages.

First she called Sara. Sara was all excited about how everything played out at lunchtime, and the meeting that followed. She was so chipper that Ann didn't want to share anything about what she'd just gone through. In fact, she couldn't. She was numb by now. And when Sara finally asked how the date went, Ann fell silent. All she could say was, "Can I call you back tomorrow? Something happened."

Sara said something about hoping everything was all right, but Ann didn't hear her specific words. She just mumbled a "goodbye," a "sorry," a "talk to you later," and hung up.

It was almost 4:30 and she realized she hadn't eaten since breakfast. She just now noticed how famished she was feeling. Perhaps some of this numbness had to do with low blood sugar. She didn't know what she'd say to Bradley, but decided now was as good a time as any to call him.

He answered the phone in his typical, upbeat Bradley fashion and asked how her "thing" went today.

She barely had a response for him. She was so withdrawn that he may as well have been talking to her through a tin can. She was barely present in the conversation and wondered why she'd even called him in the first place.

He noticed something was off and asked if everything was all right.

Her voice was thin and void of emotion. "No. Everything is not all right. Not at all."

Bradley's heart stirred within his chest as her ghostly words hit him. This was not his Ann Finlayson. This was someone else. Someone who needed help.

"Have you had dinner yet?"

"No. I haven't even had lunch yet."

"Then I'll be right over. I'm bringing Chinese."

She hung up the phone and laid down on the couch.

Bradley knocked lightly on the door. Ann remembered that she'd left her scarf and gloves in the bedroom earlier. Her wig was still on and her glasses were on the coffee table. By the time she answered the door, she was fully suited for the occasion.

When she opened the door, Bradley asked if he was at the right place and if not, might the girl who answered the door happen to know what had become of Ann Finlayson?

Normally, Ann would have laughed at Bradley's lightheartedness. But this heaviness that gripped her spared no room for joviality.

She could smell the Chinese food and although she was hungry, she had no interest in it. She told him to put it on the kitchen table for now, then she sat down on the living room couch.

He sat down beside her and felt at a loss for words. Normally, he was the talker. But he was so perplexed by her appearance and her strange demeanor that he wasn't sure what to say. Finally, curiosity got the better of him.

"So—what's up with the gloves?"

She sat silent for the longest time. She had no idea of what she might say. Or do. She didn't want to tell him the rash story. She was so tired of having to hide this from everyone. She was sunk so low from the weight of everything that all she could do was look at the floor and contemplate. How much of a relief would it be to just tell him? Better yet, just show him? What had she to lose anyway?

The floodgates were still just as pressurized as they'd been all the way home from the grocery store. What happened in the store had been the final straw. If the pressure wasn't released, she wouldn't last another five minutes here with Bradley. So she made a decision.

First, she removed her gloves. Then, she took off her scarf. When she got to the glasses, Bradley was already dumfounded by her hands, throat and face. When she got to the wig, he let out a gasp. "What … happened … to … you?"

The floodgates swung wide open and every shred of emotion that had been bottled up all week came rushing out with a force that could not be contained. Ann buried her head in Bradley's chest and released every tear that had been denied and discarded every fig leaf of secrecy that she'd used to cover up. Her soul was bared and the torrent of emotions that swept over the jagged rocks that lay inside her plunged headlong into Bradley's compassionate heart. He held her through every tear and every gulp of breath. He smoothed her hair and asked no questions as she laid against him with her overwhelming need.

He waited patiently, knowing words would follow soon enough. He'd sit on this couch all night long if he had to. Ann was still now, except for a few intermittent moments of catching her breath and wiping fresh tears on Bradley's shirt.

When she finally did speak, she stayed right where she was and clung to Bradley's arm. He still held her head against his chest with his right hand and although her words were muffled by his shirt, he was able to hear her.

"Do you remember when I told you about that old lady in the crosswalk last Tuesday? Well, ever since then I began having symptoms, or should I say signs? I instantly began aging. I went through early menopause. I'd dye my hair in the morning and by lunchtime it would be gray again. I haven't been able to read without a magnifying glass.

"Now you know why I've been making up all these stories about migraines and light sensitivity. I just bought the wig on Thursday because I knew you'd be showing up early yesterday morning. I didn't even notice how bad my hands looked until this morning. So on my date with Sean, I had to wear a pair of latex gloves to cover them up. I told him I'd broken out in a rash all over my body ..."

A massive wave of incredulity crashed into Bradley and forced him to stop Ann midsentence. He pulled her away from his chest and spewed, "What? Sean was your thing? Your eleven o'clock thing was Sean? Are you kidding me?"

Such a radical subject change. Ann didn't know whether to laugh or ask Bradley whether or not he'd heard anything else she'd said, or for that matter, if he'd fully taken in her new look. She had just bared her soul and the reality of her appearance to him and all he seemed to care about was the fact that she'd gone out with Sean.

"Yes Bradley. I went out with Sean. But can we get back to this old lady thing? I mean, don't you think this new look of mine is a little more off than the fact that I went out with Sean?"

"No. I mean yes. But then again, no. What on earth could ever have tempted you to hook up with the likes of Sean? He's nothing but a conniving, underhanded ..."

"Snake."

"Yes. And he has absolutely no morals and all he's ever wanted to do is use you ..."

"To get to Marvin."

"Yes—wait—so if you know all this, why did you agree to go out with him?"

"Because, while I've been so devastated about this aging thing, it felt good to have someone attracted to me. I'm not attracted to him in any way, I just caved in to flattery. What I'm not getting here is, I just took off my wig, glasses and scarf and all you want to talk about is Sean?" She waved her hand in front of his face. "Hello. Your eyes are open. Haven't you noticed I look like a seventy-year-old woman?"

"Well, yeah. But you're still Ann. You're still my favorite office sidekick and have recently been upgraded to my favorite hang-gliding, rock-climbing violinist. Other than your white hair and wrinkles, about the only thing that's different about you is the fact that you soaked my shirt with tears and you're usually Miss Cool and In Control. But, back to the aging thing. You think it has something to do with the old lady in the crosswalk?"

"I know it does. It wasn't even an hour after the confrontation that I discovered I couldn't read anything up close. Then I was up all that night with hot flashes. When I woke up Wednesday morning, my hair was covered with gray. I had to stop by the drugstore on the way to work so I could buy something to cover the gray with."

"And that's why you were late that morning."

"That's why I've been late every morning. It's also why I've been taking such long lunches. I had to buy a bunch of new clothes because I gained weight overnight on top of everything else. I've been so sick and tired of having to cover up and lie about all this. It's been so stressful."

Bradley's initial shock began to wear off as he considered what Ann must be going through. "I bet." He took a good, long look at her and struggled with what he might say next. What words of comfort could he offer? He looked toward his lap and shook his head. "Wow. I find all this so hard to believe. I don't really believe in curses or magic, yet here you are. This must be agonizing for you."

"It has been. But I can't begin to tell you how good it feels to have finally told you. The only other person who knows about it is my sister. And Charlotte. But she doesn't count because she's never met the real me."

"Who's Charlotte?"

"She's the lady who runs the drugstore around the corner from work. She's been my lifesaver. She's helped me every day since all this started. She picked out my hair dye and loaded me up with all this facial goop. She even got me a deal on this lovely wig."

Ann plucked the wig from the coffee table and twirled it around in the air.

Bradley took it from her hand and held it up to get a closer look. "Yes. Very nice." He put the wig back on the table. "But I have to tell you, for a seventy-something your real hair is still quite gorgeous." He smiled and drew a piece of it away from her face.

Ann's heart quickened at this gesture. She knew he couldn't possibly be attracted to her now, but what he just did with her hair made her feel like a shy and hopeful high school girl. She deflected the feeling by mentioning how hungry she was.

"I'm about to die of starvation. Can we break out that Chinese?"

"I never thought I'd hear you sound so enthusiastic about a load of high-fat carbs and sodium."

As they brought the cartons, plates and chopsticks into the living room, Ann explained, "At the rate I'm aging, why not pull out some dietary stops?"

Bradley dished up and grabbed some chopsticks. "Have you ever thought about trying to find the old woman who did this to you so she could undo the curse?"

"Of course I have. I've seen her a few times, but she always escapes me. Lately I've just been trying to resign myself to the inevitable. Which is, I'm on my way out. And now that you've seen me, you *know* I won't be able to keep working. I'm going to have to quit the magazine. Possibly this week."

Bradley was pensive. "Yeah. I can see that." Then he let out a big sigh. "I'd miss you though, Fin." He put down his plate and found her eyes. "I really would."

Ann was so moved. He called her Fin. He was treating her as though none of this had happened, as if he was unfazed by her appearance.

She shook her head inwardly as she realized this man sitting beside her could have become her one and only. He could have been the one she would have opened up to and shared the rest of her life with. It made her want to cry all over again.

Bradley noticed her mood shift and asked if she was all right. She told him she was just shook from it all and having a difficult time sorting out the realities. He decided to broach a new topic.

"So ... about that bad day at the office ..."

"Oh yeah, that." She told him about blowing the conference call and Marvin's radical reaction. She mentioned Marvin's disgust over the fact that she hadn't utilized Sean more. Then she told him what Marvin said about the positional shifting that might result.

"Really? He hung all that over your head? That makes him a bigger weasel than Sean. What's wrong with these people? You'd think they'd never laid eyes on a Green Jeans ad."

Now that the floodgates had swung open, Ann didn't want to hold anything back. She confessed to Bradley that she'd never laid eyes on a Green Jeans ad until yesterday following the conference call.

"And what did you think?"

"I think everyone was spot on in their opinions and I had no business supporting something I didn't research beforehand. I'm black and blue from beating myself up about it."

"No need to do that. Marvin cornered you with it and gave you no time for research. He enlisted Sean to placate all those in opposition, and to help pull the wool over your eyes. Sean is smooth, I'll give him that. But before I forget, what happened with Valerie the other day? I never did get a report on why she was in the nurse's office."

Again, Ann felt like baring all.

"You remember how she was acting on Thursday? How she seemed angry about the fact that you weren't coming over?"

"Yes."

"Well, she was so full of anger because she didn't want to be alone with me." Her eyes welled up with tears again. "She had to come home early because some bullies had cornered her in the school bathroom."

Bradley just listened and waited for her to continue, so she went on.

"She didn't want to be alone with me because there were times during the week when I was mean to her. Really mean. In fact, the morning I ran into the lady in the crosswalk, I'd spoken very harshly to Valerie on the way to school." She paused for a moment as her heart sunk with the weight of her next confession. "I even called her a name."

Bradley winced and looked at the floor.

Ann paused again as she strove to collect her emotions and continue. Fresh tears beat against her bottom lashes and her chin began to tremble. She looked down at her knees as she emptied the last bit of trash from her conscience. "Here she was getting bullied at school all week long and she didn't have anyone to talk to about it." She lowered her voice to a near whisper. "She didn't have anywhere to turn because her own aunt hadn't provided a safe haven for her." She lifted her eyes and made eye contact with Bradley. "You've been the closest thing she's had to *that* all week long."

As she broke into a new set of sobs, Bradley held her again, then offered his shirt sleeve to her.

At this she lifted her head and smiled weakly. "Thank you for offering your shirt, but I think I've soaked you enough tonight."

She left to get some tissue from the bathroom as Bradley sat quietly, waiting for her to return and continue. Ann kept saying she wasn't good with kids, but Bradley assumed she'd been putting her personal issues aside since Valerie was a family member. He grieved over his beloved Valerie. What monumental sorrows she'd had to bear.

When Ann returned from the bathroom and sat back down on the couch, it appeared as though she was out of words. Bradley picked up the conversation.

"I don't know what to say. All this time I figured the two of you were getting along fine. No wonder she was clinging to me so tightly last Thursday. I was so disturbed by it, all I could do was pray all the way back to the office."

Ann was instantly derailed from her former track. "What? You too?"

Bradley had no idea what she was talking about. "What do you mean by that?"

Ann asked the question, but it was void of the usual acid. "I mean. Are you a Christian?"

"Yes I am. Is that so shocking?"

Ann suddenly felt the urge to be alone. So many thoughts and faces began swarming around her that the room felt thick.

"No. I've just been surrounded lately. You know, I fully believe that had I not been so hard on Valerie the morning of the crosswalk encounter, all this crazy aging stuff might never have occurred. I was so upset by my exchange with her that I was distracted from driving. It didn't help that I was running late. By the time I got to that intersection and nearly hit that old woman, I was already so worked up. I just lost it all over her too."

Bradley rose to his feet and paced a few times. Then he stopped and caught Ann's eyes.

"You know what, Ann Finlayson? You need a break from all this. We need to go on a real date. Tomorrow. We'll go to the Skydeck, then to dinner. I'll pick you up at three. And you can bag the costume. No wig, no glasses, no scarves and no gloves. Whadd'ya say Annie?" He stopped and smiled. "It could very well prove to be your best day ever. You know you want to say yes."

Once again, Ann's heart melted. Not just because he'd called her Annie again, but after all she'd just told him—including the truth about what a monster she'd been in all respects—he tells her he wants to go on a date. She was dumbstruck as she rose to her feet and said something about what a long day it had been. As she walked Bradley to the door, an image of the Grinch's heart growing three times its normal size and bursting through its feeble frame popped into her head. She had to stifle a snicker.

As they reached the front door, she didn't hide her smile as she answered Bradley's question. "Yes Bradley Newman, I will go to the Skydeck with you, then to dinner. Thank you for being here for me."

He oozed all the Bradley charm he could muster as he tipped his imaginary hat and cocked his head. "It's the least I could do for my damsel in distress. See you at three." With that, he walked out the door and Ann watched him walk all the way to the elevator.

She realized it was a good thing she'd told Sara she couldn't talk until tomorrow. She needed time to digest everything that had just happened. Relief wasn't a word that even came close to how she was feeling. Sheer elation might be a better description. How was it humanly possible that anyone could have treated her the way Bradley just had in light of what she'd just shared? Had it been Sean, he would have run to the door the minute she'd taken her gloves off. And it wasn't just Bradley's treatment of her that had her floating. She

151

finally got to share what was going on with someone other than Sara. Better yet, a co-worker.

A thousand planes had just flown from the deck of her aircraft carrier, and the heavy sacks of flour she'd carried on her shoulders all week went with them.

The iron shackles that had been locked around her ankles were broken.

She felt like the World Series had been won and the Blue Angels were soaring overhead.

He even said we could go on this date without my hiding anything!

She wasn't exactly praying, but as she got ready for bed, and before she turned off the lamp in her bedroom, all she could think of was one thing.

Thank God for Bradley Newman.

Chapter 10

Ann woke up feeling like a new woman. Despite the fact that she'd just suffered through another ragged night, she felt renewed. Even hopeful.

Bradley's acceptance of her in this new state had meant the world to her. She felt energized as she began to map out how to spend the hours before pickup time at three. She thought she might get outside and look for the old woman today to try and have the curse reversed. Again, with Bradley's support helping to hold up both of her arms, she felt hopeful. While sitting on the edge of the bed, she observed how pleasant it was to face the day without despair casting its gruesome shadow across the door of her heart.

As she drafted her day, she thought it best to put calling Sara on top of the priority list. She'd left her sister in the dust last night and didn't want her to keep worrying. But as she rose to get her phone, she realized it was only seven o'clock Denver time. Since she didn't want to risk waking Sara up, she decided to wait an hour or two.

On her way to get her robe from the closet, she stopped dead in her tracks. An involuntary groan escaped her throat as she reached for the first thing she could find to steady herself. She put one hand on the dresser as she tried to regroup and breathe. The pain in her hips this morning was unbearable and her left knee had completely locked up. She propped herself up on the dresser while trying to mildly bend and flex her knee to work out the kink.

Every muscle in her body ached. She wondered if she'd found a compromising position while tossing and turning all night because she could barely move her neck. She continued to stand next to the dresser, stretching all the sore muscle groups to the point where she felt she could walk to the closet.

Once it felt safe to move, she went to the closet and put her robe on, then headed for the bathroom. She grabbed a water on the way and went straight to the medicine cabinet. After rummaging around, she found the ibuprofen. Normally one would do the trick, but today she took two. She would definitely be swinging by the drugstore now. Either Charlotte or Cecile could probably recommend a good joint supplement.

While standing at the sink, she couldn't help but look in the mirror. Although Bradley's heart had been gracious, she realized she wouldn't be able to go through the day without fighting her reflection a little. She slapped on some more Egyptian mud and went to the kitchen to make coffee.

Her mind replayed moments from yesterday as she waited for the coffee to brew. She thought of how rudely Sean had treated her. She cringed as she inwardly admitted that he'd been no worse toward her than she'd been toward Valerie all week. Then it struck her that the tables had been turned again while she was in the grocery store. All those people freely vocalizing their annoyance with her.

Last Saturday, she'd shown the same level of intolerance toward the old woman who took too long at the register. She recalled her impatience as she'd cut across the man in line ahead of her to throw a dollar on the counter. How could she have been so unfeeling toward others?

For some reason, her self-disclosure to Bradley last night served to sharpen her sensitivity. It was as if giving full vent to her emotions while releasing all that pent up guilt and shame had cleansed her. Somehow, it had given her permission to feel vulnerable.

A peace that verged on ethereal settled over her as she poured her coffee. Once she sat back down, she remembered her second order of business on the list was to bake cookies for Nancy's retirement party. She even felt excited about the prospect. Before she'd finished half a cup, she became consumed—all she could think about was where she might have put the recipe. She remembered digging it out of the closet yesterday and using it to make a shopping list, but where did she put it?

"Oh there you are." The recipe was on the kitchen table under the salt and pepper shakers. She thought it funny that of all the things she'd chosen to take out of the boxes containing her share of her parents' belongings, it was the salt and pepper shakers. Everything else had remained in the back of her hall closet all these years.

She took a good long look at these old ceramic testaments to her former life.

They were a pair of bakers. Each wore a white baker's hat and a red apron. The salt shaker, who was the female representative of the pair, held a rolling pin at her side. The man of the seasoning house held a wad of pizza dough in his hands that he was about to toss into the air. Both wore extraordinarily jolly expressions, complete with red, puffy cheeks and twinkling eyes. Growing up, they reminded Ann of her parents. Her mother and father had always been so happy together. Although they weren't a pair of bakers, they frequently wore the same jolly expressions, right up to the twinkling eyes. Their joy ran so deep, as did their love—both for each other and for their highly cherished daughters.

As Ann continued to study the two bakers, she was filled with enthusiasm toward making these cookies. They were always the favorite. Whenever her mom made them, she had to make extra so they could have lots of raw cookie dough in between batches. Then the girls would have a mug of milk ready in order to sample at least one cookie per batch. Her mother always made the cookies on a whim. It might be before dinner, it might be after. But every time she got the urge, the family was drawn together with a sense of delight and closeness that filled Ann's heart even now.

She just couldn't wait to make these cookies.

She didn't even bother with the second cup of coffee she usually had. In a rush, she pushed away from the table and nearly ran to the bathroom. She wanted to wash the mud off and moisturize quickly so the great cookie extravaganza would be well underway before she got on the phone to Sara. She noticed that the ibuprofen had helped. She wasn't anywhere near as stiff and sore as she was when she first woke up.

She hummed while completing the skin care regimen. Suddenly, she longed for the presence of Bradley, and even Valerie, as she prepared for the day. She would have enjoyed sharing this joyful feeling with them.

Once she was fully gooped, made-up and dressed, she went to the kitchen and dug out everything she'd need to make the cookies. She got out the cookie sheets, measuring spoons and cups, and all the ingredients she'd purchased yesterday. One thing that wasn't in her kitchen cupboards was the bowl. The special blue and white, hand-cast ceramic bowl that her mother always used for the cookie dough.

Back to the closet. Past all the pictures, the kettle and the violin. There it was. She wasted no time digging it out and carrying it to the kitchen.

Now she was all ready to go. Oven preheating, ingredients out and all the measuring cups and spoons on the counter. She began putting everything together. First the dry ingredients, then the butter, sugar and eggs in another bowl. Then the phone rang.

Ann was discomposed by all the activity when she picked up the phone. "Hey Sara. I meant to call you an hour ago, but was afraid of waking you up."

"Seriously? I've been up since six, worried sick about you. I was afraid of waking *you* up. You sounded so distraught yesterday. And distant. All I could do was pray. So what in the world is going on? And why do you sound so out of breath?"

Due to the encounter with Bradley last night, and her newly refreshed interest in the art of making cookies, Ann had to strain her brain to recall where her mindset was when she called her sister last night.

"Oh that's right," she remembered, "I'd just gotten back from the store and was devastated by what had happened there. And I still needed to tell you about what happened on with my date with Sean. I'll tell you later why I'm out of breath."

"Yeah. So what *did* happen on your date?"

Ann told Sara about how rude Sean had been. Then she painted a picture of the scene from the grocery store—about how she'd held up the line because she couldn't find her debit card. She told Sara about how impatient the people in line had become—enough to throw out a host of rude comments while laughing at her.

"So that's why I called you. I was devastated by how those people treated me."

Sara's heart was crushed. "Oh honey, that's so awful. And it all started because you couldn't find your debit card?"

"Yeah, but there was a lot more to it. The whole experience caused me to feel a bit of panic. I always put my debit card in the same spot and when I couldn't find it, I became flustered. Even confused. I think it has to do with this aging thing. I'm really worried that it's affecting my mind now. I've always been the queen of keeping a line moving. I always have everything out and ready so by the time I get to the register, I won't hold up the people behind me. It just felt awful. You should have heard some of the comments."

Sara fell silent as she considered her sister's misery and hopelessness. Then she let out a long sigh. "The timing on this new job is so poor. I feel like I need to be with you to help you through this. I just can't imagine …"

In the face of Sara's compassion, all Ann could do was revel in the way things had taken a turn for the better once she got home. Bradley's visit had kicked the blanket of discouragement from her shoulders and completely brightened her outlook.

"Well, it has been truly horrible, and yesterday was the worst so far—but then a few other things happened that have been total game-changers."

"Like what?"

"Like how Bradley came over last night after I talked to you and how I told him everything. I even pulled off my wig and everything else so he could see what I was dealing with."

"Wow, really? What did he say? What did he do?"

"Oddly enough, he acted like it was no big deal. I totally broke down when I told him. He held me while I cried. Then he asked me to go out tonight and told me I could bag all the cover-up. No wig, no glasses, nothing I've been hiding under all week. He made it clear that I needed to go out in public as I was, and silently let me know he'd be right there beside me with no thought of this aging thing."

Sara felt relieved. Obviously, Bradley was some sort of saint. She was elated about this news. Not only did Ann now have someone in her corner that was close to home, but she was on a better emotional plane than she'd been all week. Now Sara wouldn't have to worry about her as much.

"So Bradley saves the day again. You really need to find this old woman. You and Bradley need to be together."

"Don't I know it? He's even called me Annie a few times. No one but Dad ever called me that. I wish you could have been a fly on the wall last night. You wouldn't have believed him. I can't even describe to you how wonderful he was."

"Yeah, but it sure does stink. You finally find the man of your dreams and you're too old for him. This just can't continue. I'm going to beg the Lord harder than ever that you'll be able to run into this old lady. I'm going to have to buy some kneepads."

"Please do. But now that I've told you everything that's been happening in my world, let's talk about the next few days. Do they still want you to stay until Monday? Valerie told me you gave her permission to stay at Cassie's another night."

"Yes, they still want me to stay. I'm hoping to catch an early flight Tuesday morning and catch the train to your office. I was also hoping you could drive the car to work that morning and bring Valerie and all her stuff with you. That way she and I could drive straight home, tie things up with the movers and get on the road. Do you think your boss would mind?"

"Probably. But none of his votes count anymore. I no longer share his vision for the magazine. And, if I don't run into that old woman, I'm going to have to quit the magazine anyway."

She didn't want to discuss her fear of coming to the end of her life soon, so she changed the subject. "Hey—speaking of Tuesday—do you think it might be possible to squeeze in a quick hospital visit?"

She told Sara about Charles' wish to see Valerie again. Then she mentioned how much it would mean to Lisa if they were able to make this visit happen. She explained how Lisa had been holding on by a thread with no family in town to support her through this. She told Sara that Lisa's husband was deployed and couldn't get to the states just yet because of all the red tape.

Sara was all in. "Of course we can do that. I'm not going to start work until a week from Monday, so we can leave a little later on Tuesday. Valerie's referred to Charles several times. She wants to see him too. She worries about him all the time—she's such a little mama."

"Yeah, I guess she is. Meanwhile, I have to go. I have to get back to that 'out-of-breath' thing."

Sara remembered asking about that at the beginning of the conversation. "And what would that be?"

"I'm making cookies for an office party tomorrow."

"Really now. Are you making Mom's chocolate chip cookies?"

"Yep. I dug the recipe out yesterday."

"Yum. I bet if you put a few in a sandwich bag, they'll still be good by Tuesday."

"I think I could manage that. But I really do have to go now. I have a few other things to accomplish by the time Bradley gets here at three."

"Okay. Call and tell me how everything goes."

"Okay. Talk to you later."

It didn't take long for Ann to make the cookies since she already had everything assembled. It did take a moment, however, for her to get the hang of things. She lightly burned the first batch, but not so badly that she'd have to throw them out. The rest of them came out perfect. To keep with tradition, she had to sample one from each batch.

Just as good as Mom's. Sara won't believe it. Come to think of it, neither will Cassie.

She was so pleased with herself she decided to put one in a baggie for Charlotte.

After all the cookies had cooled enough to store in airtight containers, she was off.

The weather was favorable enough for a nice walk and a trip to the park. The sun was playing peek-a-boo and it was colder today than it had been all week, but Ann wore a light jacket and her wig helped keep her warm.

She was feeling fairly used to it by now. Lydia had showed her how to pin it down in certain spots so it wouldn't shift too easily. The worst part of it was, it made her head itch. But she put up with it because she couldn't stomach the thought of going out in public with her head of white hair. The rest of the world didn't know she was only thirty-two, but she didn't care. She still felt humiliated by it, even if Bradley *did* tell her how gorgeous it was.

It took a while to get to the park because her hips were hurting again. Once she got there, the sun came out full force and it felt a little warmer. So before she sat down on her bench by the fountain, she took her jacket off. A little while longer and she took her scarf off as well. Sitting in the direct sunlight was making her head itch like crazy, so she even took her wig off. She'd brought her large handbag, so it fit easily inside.

It felt so good to feel the sun on her head. It made her long desperately for a life where she wouldn't have to hide all this. At that, she reminded herself to keep one eye out for the old woman. She'd give anything to have this curse reversed so she and Bradley could be together.

But if she did run into the old woman and become young again, she didn't know whether or not she'd want to stay at the magazine. She'd been going through so many changes that being an advertising mogul at a prestigious magazine was no longer appealing. Especially not with *Top Rung.* She was now in total agreement with Nancy that the magazine's morals had dipped too far below the bar. She found herself not wanting a thing to do with the company she'd called home for the last seven years.

She tried to think outside the box as she considered what other career might be attractive to her. Apart from the magazine, all she'd ever done was work a few summer jobs in Colorado in addition to her two-year position as a guide with the Colorado Mountaineers. Granted, the jobs were interesting enough. After all, how many people could add rock-climbing guide to their resume?

She smiled as she recalled that time of her life. Who needed friends when one had the Rocky Mountains of Colorado in their backyard? She'd never been as happy as when she was outside scaling mountains or hiking next to raging rivers. And she got paid to do it. Her hang-gliding stint didn't last too long. She loved it but it worried her mother to death, so she decided to call it quits.

Her mom had wanted her to call every time she left to go hang-gliding, because she wanted to pray for her daughter's safety before every excursion. Ann fondly remembered coming to the decision to stick solely to hiking, rock-climbing and the safer winter sports. It wasn't so difficult, considering all her mom had done for her growing up. Where her father had provided all the wit, whimsy and wonder for the family, her mother was the primary fusser.

How she'd fuss over the girls' appearance. She'd take them both clothes shopping every year and make sure their hair was always pristine and tidy. No one could braid hair like their mother. She and Sara used to think they could win a contest for the most hair accessories. They had ribbons, bows and clips in every color of the rainbow. And the girls' appearance wasn't all their mother fussed over.

At the first sign of a cold, she'd take their temperature. When they were sick, she'd sit on the bed and stroke their hair until they fell asleep. She'd read to them, sing them all sorts of songs, bake for them, cook for them and help out in their classrooms as much as possible. And she wasn't only good at cooking, she seemed to enjoy it. This was a concept Ann could never grasp.

She remembered how her mother had worked so many nights on a dress she made for one of Ann's school dances. A few times, she stayed up until two in the morning. Doug had invited Ann, and her mother had to make sure her princess was the belle of the ball. She even sewed a hairpiece for Ann. She painstakingly hand-stitched tiny seed pearls into a ribbon that she wove into Ann's thick, braided hair. Somehow, she'd been able to stash enough cash to buy Ann some special makeup and nail polish. By the time Doug had come to the door, Ann looked like she was ready for the red carpet.

But that was a night Ann would much rather forget. It was the night Alicia first started flirting with Doug. His head was turned and he never looked back.

As Ann continued to soak up the sun, she thought of how both her parents had been unsurpassed in how well they loved their little family. No emotion was ever brushed aside or minimized. No dream was too big or ridiculous. Hugs and laughter were shared more frequently than meals. And her mother had sacrificed so much. She could have been the concertmaster for any orchestra she chose, but she laid it all aside so she could be there for her girls. As Ann recalled, her mom had been toying with the idea of joining an orchestra once Ann graduated from college.

But that idea was cut short. Something else Ann didn't want to think about.

As she watched the faces in the fountain, she smiled as she wondered how her mind had shifted from a possible career change to a private showing of *Growing Up with the Finlayson's*. Not long after she turned her attention toward the fountain, she saw a woman pushing a child in a wheelchair. For a moment, it looked like it could be Charles and Lisa. But they were too far away for her to be sure. Then, just as Lisa recognized Ann and began waving, Ann remembered that her wig was still in her handbag. She quickly put it back on, hoping Lisa might not have noticed from that distance. She reassembled the rest of her cover as well.

As quickly as she could, Lisa pushed the wheelchair over to where Ann was sitting. From a few yards away she called out, "Ann. I wasn't sure it was you at first. From so far away, it looked like you had something white on your head. But I thought I recognized your face, and you were sitting in your usual spot. Then I remembered you like to wear scarves, so I decided to wave and get your attention, just in case."

Ann felt relieved that Lisa thought her white hair was a scarf. "Well, I'm glad you did. I wasn't sure it was you either."

As the two talked, Charles sat quietly in the wheelchair and added nothing to the conversation. He wore a thick blanket that covered his lap and legs, and he stared toward the fountain. Ann wanted to ask how he was doing, but not while he was sitting right there. Lisa broke the ice for her.

"He's really tired today. He hasn't spoken much since he got up. About the only thing he did say was that he wanted to go to the park. I explained that I'd have to push him in a wheelchair and he said he didn't mind. So here we are. I don't think we're going to stay long though."

Ann thought about how hard this must be for Lisa. She'd be completely lost in a situation like this, but Lisa was handling it all like an old pro, despite how overwhelmed she felt. She thought of how easy it was to relate to Lisa. The two of them barely had anything in common, yet they'd been able to connect in ways she'd never connected with anyone but Sara before last

Tuesday's encounter. Because of her comfort level with Lisa, she wondered if she could go out on a limb with her.

It had felt so good to let the cat out of the bag as she had with Bradley that Ann toyed with the idea of sharing with Lisa. Both Lisa and Bradley had an easy-going, compassionate nature. And with Sara moving out of town soon, plus the likelihood that Ann would soon have to quit the magazine, it might be good to have a true friend in her corner. Although she considered Charlotte to be a friend of sorts, she was so much older than Ann that they could truly only relate in a few areas. Charlotte felt more like an adopted mother than anything else. As Ann and Lisa continued to sit silently while churning their own thoughts, the desire to tell Lisa the truth sat like an immovable boulder in the middle of Ann's chest.

Oh what could it hurt anyway? We only met a week ago ...

Just as Ann resolved to say something to Lisa, Lisa began to get up, mumbling something about needing to get Charles back. But Ann worried that if she allowed the moment to pass, she might not get up this level of courage again.

She remained seated, and touched Lisa's arm. "Lisa, can I talk to you about something before you go?"

Lisa sat back down. She thought it must be important—there was an urgency in Ann's voice. "Sure. I'm usually the one doing all the talking. I'd be happy to give you a turn."

Then, as she had with Bradley, Ann let her appearance speak for itself as she removed her wig, glasses and scarf.

Lisa was shocked speechless, as Ann knew she would be, so this time she did all the talking. She told Lisa the story of what had been happening to her as a result of the crosswalk encounter. She explained that the first time they met in the park, when Valerie was there, she hadn't yet run into the old woman, so that was her true appearance.

"Wow. So it's only been a week and you look like this?"

"Actually, it hasn't even been a full week yet."

"Now I remember that day when both Charles and I noticed how different you looked. Charles spoke up about it, but I just told myself I must be some sort of crazy." Lisa looked straight ahead and silently shook her head. "I'm sorry Ann, I don't know what to say. I can't wrap my mind around this. So it wasn't a white scarf I saw on your head from across the park. It's so ... impossible. I've never heard of such a thing."

Ann assured her it was all right, she didn't expect any other response. She'd only wanted to come out of the closet because she was tired of hiding. It was Charles who finally relieved the awkwardness of the moment.

His voice was croaky from exhaustion and it seemed to take some effort for him to speak at all. He looked up at Ann from his wheelchair and squinted from the sun hitting his eyes. "You look a lot like my grandma. Only I don't have a grandma anymore. Are you anyone's grandma?"

Apparently, he was so out of it that her identity hadn't registered with him.

"No, Charles Latham the third, I'm not anyone's grandma."

"You can just call me Charles. Can I sit in your lap?"

Ann wasn't sure of how to handle this. She turned her desperate eyes to Lisa for help. Lisa gave her a half-smile and shrugged her shoulders as if to say, "Why not?" She was just as surprised as Ann was at this request.

So Ann said, "Sure Charles, you can sit in my lap."

It was a team effort getting him out of the chair and onto Ann's lap. Lisa took the blanket that was wrapped around him. Then Charles leaned forward while Ann pulled him up. As she did, she noticed even her arm strength was beginning to fail. Once he was up, Lisa wrapped the blanket around him and he nestled into Ann's chest.

He settled in for a moment, then spoke so softly that he could barely be heard by either Ann or Lisa. "You could be my grandma. If you want, you could be my grandma at the park. Would that be okay? Could you be my grandma at the park?"

Once again, Ann was at a loss and didn't know what to say. She turned to Lisa again and decided not to say anything. Tears were streaming down Lisa's face. All Ann could think of to do was grasp Lisa's hand and hold it.

Charles shifted in her lap and folded in more tightly, with his arm around Ann's waist. She pulled him closer and marveled at all the emotions she was feeling. This was the first time she'd ever cradled a child. A warmth she couldn't have manufactured by any other means spread through her. There wasn't a hot tub or hot yoga session in all of Chicago that could simulate this feeling. She relished the moment, but at the same time her heart ached for Lisa. As she looked at the frail young woman beside her, tears began forming in her own eyes.

As she considered Lisa's situation and how well she bore up under it all, her attention moved to one end of the fountain. She watched the changing faces for several minutes, then something happened that couldn't be real. She had to have imagined it. There, in the fountain, a new face appeared. It was the old woman. She was looking down on the three silent figures and smiling. Only this smile wasn't a defiant smirk. It held all the tenderness in the world. Then, just before her face was replaced by a new one, the woman looked Ann right in the eyes and nodded. Her smile grew broader and appeared to be brimming with approval and joy. And did Ann also detect a hint of pride? As she tried to sort this out, the image disappeared.

Ann wasn't as shocked by this as she was perplexed. By now she was used to strange occurrences, like being cursed by a stranger in a crosswalk, aging overnight or seeing someone she knew in the park fountain. What puzzled her was, why was the woman's face full of kindness? And why, after trying to chase her down for so many days, did she show up today? And what was that smile about? Ann swore to herself again that she detected a measure of pride in that smile.

She didn't have any more time to think about it because Lisa rose to her feet again, announcing it was time to go. After seeing the woman's face in the fountain, Ann had to agree.

They both got Charles back into the wheelchair and wrapped into his blanket. He'd fallen asleep in Ann's lap, so he was still groggy as he sat through all the goodbyes. The two women hugged tightly and Lisa told Ann how sorry she was that Ann was going through this. She told Ann she'd pray for her and Ann didn't bat an eye. She started thinking the only people in her life who weren't Christians must be the ones she exercised with at the yoga club and Tae Kwon Do.

Just before they parted, Charles looked up at Ann and asked, "Do you know Valerie?"

So he truly didn't recognize her. Because his question reminded her of this coming Tuesday, she didn't ponder how to answer. Instead she turned her attention to Lisa.

"That's right Lisa, I was going to send you a text. I talked to my sister this morning and she said we could swing by the hospital on Tuesday. We should get there sometime between eleven and twelve if everything works out with my sister's flight."

Lisa was all smiles. "Oh, that would be great! Charles will be so thrilled to see Valerie."

Charles added to the conversation. "So you do know Valerie?"

Ann turned to Charles and said, "Yes I do," while Lisa mouthed the words, "I'm sorry."

Ann told Lisa she'd send a text regarding Tuesday and Lisa, embarrassed by the fact that Charles didn't recognize Ann, suddenly appeared to be in a great hurry to leave. She said something about Charles being disoriented and how they really needed to go, as she tucked his blanket more tightly around him. Ann and Lisa hugged one more time and went their separate ways.

By now the ibuprofen had worn off completely—the walk to the drugstore was grueling. But the necessity to move slowly due to pain forced Ann's mind to slow down as well. All it could do was focus on the image of the old woman in the fountain. There had to be a reason she showed up like that today. Be it real or imagined, it couldn't have been a coincidence. And if she was willing to make an appearance in Ann's life from out of nowhere, why had she been so elusive all week? Why had she never stopped the times when Ann had spotted her? It just didn't make sense. Nevertheless, something told Ann that this was not going to be the day she physically caught up with the woman. Ann wondered if the strange apparition, if that's what it was, was meant to serve as some sort of message.

She was almost to the drugstore now and her hips were hurting more than they ever had before. Each step was painstaking and it felt like her knee was going to lock up again. Thank goodness Charlotte had that chair by the register. Whether Charlotte was there or not, the chair was now the main target of Ann's focus. She couldn't get to it fast enough.

When she finally reached the door, she was delighted to find Charlotte standing behind the counter. She called out in spite of herself. "Charlotte!"

Charlotte beamed as she came out from behind the counter. She swept Ann up in an embrace that threatened to snap Ann's back. "Ann! How good to see you. I've been wondering about you. How have you been? I see the wig is working out nicely. How have all the skincare products been working out for you? Would you like to try another?"

In the face of all these questions, Ann continued to have only one response on her mind. "Sorry Charlotte, but I can't answer a single one of those questions until I get a chance to sit down. My hips are killing me." As she was speaking, she eased herself into the chair.

"That's right, Cecile told me about that. She said you refused to buy a cane because you were going to start physical therapy. So have you started yet?"

"No Charlotte, not yet. But I want to know about you. How's your mom doing?"

"Oh she's doing a lot better. She's a fighter, that one. She's still having symptoms, but she's forcing herself to get up and move around every day. She says it helps keep things from settling into the system. She reminds me of you Ann—fighting like a trooper." Then, like music to Ann's ears, Charlotte let out her signature laugh. Something about that laugh always told Ann's soul that all was well with the world and everything was going to be okay.

Charlotte milled about the drugstore and straightened shelves as she continued telling Ann about all she'd been through the last few days. About how scared she was when her rock solid mother requested to be taken to the hospital because of pain in her chest. About how good everyone from church had been during the experience.

"They made me meals and sat with me in the hospital room. They prayed with my mother and me in shifts. One would leave when the next one came.

Even my pastor and his wife came by. I love my church. It's tiny, but what a great group." She chuckled again. "Would you like some tea?"

It was so good to be here with Charlotte. For all this warmth, Ann may as well have been sitting on Charlotte's living room sofa on a sunny day with the windows wide open.

"Yes Charlotte, I would love some tea."

"Okay. It'll just take a minute, but I'm sorry to say I only have one kind left. It's some sort of green tea with pomegranate and raspberry. Would that be all right?"

Ann smiled and giggled inwardly. Even Charlotte's apology was a comfort to her heart.

"Absolutely, Charlotte. I appreciate whatever you have."

Ann sunk into the chair and closed her eyes for a moment. How good-natured Charlotte was. Ann began to wish she could be half as kindly and hospitable. She mourned again over the terrible person she'd been over the last few years. But as she heard footsteps coming toward her, she felt revived again.

"Here you go. I picked out the red mug with the gold flowers. It's one of my favorites. My mom gave it to me for Valentine's Day one year. It was loaded with chocolate and I practically ate it all in one sitting." As she punctuated this story with another chuckle, Ann noticed that she had put everything on a tray with a selection of sugar, a spoon, a couple of creamers and a glass of water. "I brought you a couple of ibuprofen too. Thought it might help with the hip pain."

"Thank you Charlotte." Ann gratefully took the gel tabs and wrestled with something else she'd been thinking of. "Charlotte, do you know how Cecile told you she offered me a cane but I didn't want it at the time?"

"Yeah. She thought you were nuts."

"Well, I've been hurting so badly I wouldn't mind looking at one today."

"All right, Ann. I think it would be a good idea. But let's wait until you finish your tea and the ibuprofen has a chance to work."

Just then a young couple popped in to ask where the baby monitors were. Charlotte seemed so thrilled to help the couple with this task that Ann didn't even try to hide her smile.

Charlotte shot off a round of questions and comments that the couple could barely keep track of.

"Do you know what it is? When are you due? Is the nursery all set up? We have a group of people in our church who help young couples track down gently used baby stuff. If you have an interest, I could give you the number. How about names? Do you have any picked out? I once knew a couple who didn't name their baby until five days after it was born."

Her cheerful benevolence won them over instantly and when all was said and done, they did write down the number Charlotte had offered. They even said they were new to the area and wouldn't mind checking out her church.

As the exchange continued, Ann began feeling the clock. She wanted to give herself plenty of time to have lunch and freshen up before Bradley came at three. So after the couple left, she asked Charlotte about the cane again.

"Oh that's right, I almost forgot." She went down an aisle as she continued. "Weren't they a darling couple? Preparing for a new baby to come into the world is such a special time." When she came back, she held out a cane with a shimmering handle. "Cecile thinks you should have this one."

"She does, does she? And why is she so sold on this one?"

"She likes mother-of-pearl so she thought you would too."

Ann thought it so funny that Cecile was bent on selling her on her own personal taste. She laughed, "Then mother-of-pearl it is."

"Wait. Stand up first and try it out. You'll want it to feel comfortable."

Ann stood and did a loop around one of the aisles. As she did, she noticed two things: the ibuprofen had kicked in, and the cane helped immeasurably. She returned to the counter and fished for her debit card. "I'll take it."

"That's good, Ann. I'll have to tell Cecile. You know, our church is full of good people. Both Cecile and Lydia go there. If you'd like to come sometime, just let me know."

"I'll think about it. When do you go?"

"I usually go on Sundays. The only reason I'm here today is because Cecile worked for me yesterday. She normally goes to the Saturday night service. And Lydia goes to the Sunday morning service with me. So if you ever want to go, let me know."

"Okay, I will. I almost forgot I also need a good joint supplement. Can you recommend one?"

Charlotte went and grabbed something from a shelf and returned to the register. Ann paid and got ready to leave. As she was putting her card and receipt into her bag, Charlotte stopped her with some parting words. She put her hand on Ann's arm and gently reminded Ann to keep her posted about the physical therapy. Then she repeated how good it was to see Ann again and hugged her one more time.

As usual, Ann was touched to the core. She'd separated herself from any kind of intimacy for so long that she didn't even know how thirsty she was for connectedness. Not until this crosswalk encounter entered her life like a train wreck and turned her world upside down.

Before last Tuesday, she didn't need anyone. She was quite content to live as a hermit with nothing but superficial relationships that had to be indulged due to unavoidable proximity to fellow human beings. They were in the office and at the gym. Other than the necessary exchanges that must occur in these environments, she was fine by herself.

She thanked Charlotte again and lied about the possibility of coming to church, then she left.

Between the ibuprofen and the cane, the walk home wasn't too taxing. Ann hated resorting to the cane, but it really did help.

Once she walked through the front door of the condo, she noticed how sleepy she was. The day's events, plus all the walking and ibuprofen, tired her to the point of wanting to take a nap. She'd overestimated the time she needed to get ready for her date with Bradley, so it would be possible. But when she looked at her sink full of baking dishes she couldn't stand the thought of lying down without cleaning the kitchen first.

There weren't many dishes to do, but Ann made a production of it anyway. She filled the washtub with warm, soapy water and took her time.

She remembered helping her mom do dishes in their humble Colorado kitchen. Both she and Sara would be on board to help. Mom would wash, Ann would rinse, Sara would dry and put things away. Mom would make a game of it and throw soap bubbles at the girls and they would get her back. In this moment, Ann realized she would give anything to revisit even five minutes of those happy days.

There were golden moments like that when Ann and Sara got along beautifully, and other times when they fought like cats and dogs. But just before Sara had made the decision to move to Chicago to go to college, their relationship had taken a turn. Sara was three years older than Ann, and when she turned seventeen, the two began to enter into a friendship that could never be shaken. Rather than getting into silly fights and arguments, they began talking to and confiding in each other.

The timing was perfect for Ann. It had only been a year since her only friend had moved away and left her feeling like a lost puppy. That was the year she spent nearly every waking hour playing her violin in her bedroom and creating some of her own compositions. Her grades had begun to slip as she struggled to make time for studying and homework. Her parents prayed silently for her behind the scenes and tried their best to be there for her, but it was Sara who ended up helping the most.

She began looking for moments when she and her sister could talk about things. Ann remembered one time when Sara knocked on her bedroom door and asked her flat out how she was doing. She boldly confronted Ann about how she'd been hiding in her bedroom and neglecting her school work. Although she already knew the answer, she came right out and asked if it had anything to do with Ann's friend having moved away. It was then that Ann finally poured her heart out over the pain of her loss.

Sure, she and her friend could talk on the phone once in a while, but that didn't help Ann with the awkwardness she felt at school every day. It didn't provide her with a lunch buddy. It didn't supply her with a friend who insisted they sit next to each other in class. And although a year had passed, she still hadn't bonded with anyone else at school.

It was true that now she and her classmates were in junior high, some of the comments had stopped—they no longer called her the violin geek—but she noticed how clusters of girls would giggle in the hallway, then look in her direction. She noticed how they'd suddenly stop talking when she walked past. She puzzled and puzzled over why they treated her this way, but could never figure out a reason. Perhaps it was because she wasn't as beautiful as they were or because she was so quiet. Her parents had finally purchased contact lenses for her to replace the thick glasses she'd worn in elementary school, but she still wore braces. Maybe that was it.

As she told her sister all this, Sara could not contain her tears. After Ann finished telling her everything, Sara wrapped her arms around her sister and broke into a fit of sobs that racked her body.

She clutched Ann with all her might and asked, "Why didn't you say anything? Why have you never told us about how you were being treated at school?" She continued to hold her sister while repeating the words, "I'm sorry, I'm so sorry," over and over again.

As Ann stood at her kitchen sink remembering all this, tears slipped softly down her own cheeks. She didn't even try to stop them. She rinsed and dried the last dish, then wiped her hands. Then she recalled how lost she felt when Sara moved away.

Ann was only fifteen. They'd barely moved onto this new plane in their relationship when Sara made the decision to attend college in Chicago. Ann still hadn't made any new friends at school and Sara wasn't even there when Ann and Doug started dating.

But at least Ann still had her parents.

The reminiscing stopped there.

Once she finished doing the dishes, she decided to take a nap after all. Bradley had said he'd call before coming over so she put the phone on the table next to the couch.

The phone rang an hour later. Ann picked up and croaked a hello while forcing herself into a sitting position.

"Hello my great adventurer. Are you all ready to embark on this journey of a lifetime?"

Ann laughed, "Oh, is that what this is? I had no idea."

Bradley returned the laughter. "It is now that I know your dirty little secret."

"And what secret would that be?"

Bradley quieted his voice as if trying to keep this between him and Ann alone. "The daredevil girl that used to indwell you has given up residence for someone who's afraid of heights. We must find this girl. We must retrieve her and bring her back. I believe she was last seen on the Skydeck Ledge."

Laughter rolled from Ann's core as she hung up. She couldn't wipe the smile off her face as she got ready to go. She didn't have much to do. She planned on wearing what she already had on, with the addition of a warmer jacket. Vanity wouldn't allow her to go without the wig, but she did bag all the rest.

When Bradley came to the door he expressed dismay over her decision. "I thought you were going au naturel."

"Sorry Bradley. I just couldn't do it. Per our agreement, however, I am ditching the gloves, glasses and scarf. Shall we cancel, or are you going to say yes to the wig?"

Bradley looked at the floor and sighed. Then he lifted his eyes and smiled. "Okay—you win."

Ann giggled and said, "Good thing." Then she went to the kitchen and grabbed her cane. When she walked out of the kitchen and held it up to Bradley, she laughed. "Does this little beauty make up for it? I could bring it along and make this old lady thing really official."

Bradley became more serious. "Have you been in pain? I didn't know."

Ann told him about how badly her hips hurt from time to time. She also told him about how her knee had locked up this morning. She mentioned her trip to the drugstore last Friday and how Cecile had tried to convince her to buy the cane. Then she shared her visit with Charlotte today and how she finally relented because the pain had become so great.

Bradley smiled, "Then by all means, bring the little tag-along." He reached out and touched the side of Ann's face with his compassionate eyes locked on hers. "I'm sorry you've been hurting."

Unhinged by his touch, Ann fumbled as she told him it was okay, she was getting used to it. She recovered enough to mention she hadn't made it to yoga since all this started—she was sure that would help.

Before Bradley had known about Ann's hip pain, the plan had been to walk.

"Ann, would you rather I drive? We'll be walking to the Tower, then to the restaurant. Are you up for all that? I know you have the tag-along, but I don't want to set you up for extra pain."

"No—I really think I'll be fine. This is going to sound crazy, but I think movement helps. The pain gets even worse when I sit a lot."

Bradley recalled, "I did once hear a physical therapist say that motion is lotion." Then he bowed his legs and tipped an invisible hat. "So all right there, little lady—get your groove on. We ain't got all day."

Ann giggled at Bradley's cowboy accent as they walked out the door.

Since Bradley had already purchased tickets they didn't have to stand in that line, but there was a substantial crowd of people waiting to get up to the Ledge.

Ann marveled about the fact that she'd worked in this building for seven years and never experienced the reality of having the Skydeck Ledge in her backyard.

"Wow—all these people. Is it always this busy?"

Bradley reminded her that it was the weekend. "But also, tourist season is upon us. Things always get crazy during the spring and summer months."

Ann saw people cluster around a variety of computer screens and exhibits and asked Bradley what that was all about.

Bradley told her the exhibits and interactive touch screen activities were loaded with a mass of Chicago's history. "But you don't need to look at those." He tapped the side of his head and said, "I have all of Chicago's history right up here."

Ann was filled with curiosity.

"Have you been here so many times you have it all memorized?"

Bradley smiled and raised his eyebrows. "Nope. History buff. I minored in history at the university. In fact, I've always wanted to write a historical novel."

"You're kidding. Now it's my turn to be impressed by one of your secrets. So—oh self-proclaimed master of Chicago history—prove yourself. Share some fabulous facts about Chicago that I don't already know."

"All right. Since you asked. Did you ever hear of the great Chicago fire?"

"Everyone's heard about the fire, Bradley. Come on now—you have to do better than that."

"Okay, I will. The fire burned from Sunday, October 8 to Tuesday, October 10 in the year 1871."

"Hmm. Very good. Now toss me another."

"Okay. In reference to the renaming of the Sears Tower …"

Ann put her hand up to her mouth. "Ho hum. Yawn, stretch. You'll have to dig deep to impress me with any knowledge regarding *that*."

Bradley wore a smug expression as he continued. "Sears Roebuck and Company sold and moved out of the building in 1988, but the Sears Tower name remained the same. A global insurance group from London called Willis Group Holdings had been leasing space in the building for a while. In 2009, the company obtained the building's naming rights. The Willis Group Holdings company considers the Tower to be their Midwest home. Would you like to know more about the Tower or should I stop here?"

Ann was feeling intrigued by all this information, so she told Bradley to continue.

He gladly took the podium again. "Before the Tower was built, the World Trade Center was the tallest building in the world. The Sears Tower took the title and reigned supreme from 1973-1998. Then, the Petronas Twin Towers in Malaysia took over. They held the position from 1998-2004."

"Tell me about the building that stole the title from Malaysia and I'll let you off the history hook."

"Okay. The Taipei 101 took over in 2004 and held the title for six years. After that, it was the Burj Khalifa ..."

Ann put her hand up. "Enough enough—I told you I only wanted to know about the one after Malaysia." She laughed and told him he just won the Pulitzer Prize *and* the award for History Buff of the Year. "Besides—I hate to burst your bubble—but history was always my least favorite subject. Too much having to memorize a bunch of dry facts and dates. During lectures, most of my teachers would just list fact after fact and date after date. It always put me to sleep."

"Which is precisely why I'd like to write historical fiction. History is fascinating and if I could make it come alive to people by couching it in fiction, I would feel as though I'd touched the moon."

"Wow, this is really a thing for you. Have you started anything yet?"

"No. It's hard to find the time. Between volunteering, and tinkering with my brother's old station wagon on the weekends, I haven't felt I could squeeze it in. Then there's that work thing. At times Marv's buried me with so many side projects I barely have room to breathe. But I won't give up my weekend activities for anything."

"Wait a minute—back up. 'That work thing'? I thought you loved your job at the magazine."

Bradley paused to formulate a response. He'd never been forced to verbalize his thoughts on this topic before. Normally, he just went through the demands of each day, savoring the fact that the weekends were always there waiting to take him away from all this. Prior to this moment, he'd never analyzed what it was about working at the magazine that caused him to feel so lukewarm about the job.

Finally, he was able to pinpoint the truth.

"I do love my job at the magazine. And I don't. My favorite part about the job at this point is helping others achieve their goals. It was great to help Noel edit his article the other day. But what I truly desire is to work on my own writing projects. I'd much rather get paid for getting myself out there than for helping promote the works of a company I'm barely attached to. Especially one that would endorse the likes of Green Jeans."

"Yeah that. I guess we're all on the same page about it now. Well, everyone but Sean. But I want to hear more about this volunteering thing. What do you do?"

"Come, come now. We must save something for dinner conversation. It's your turn. What brought you to Chicago?"

"Let's see, where do I start? You already know my family lived in Colorado. When I was about fifteen, Sara decided to go through a nursing program here. I was just about to become a sophomore in high school when she left. For the next two years I took as many advanced courses as I could, not knowing whether or not I wanted to go to college, but wanting to be prepared just in case. At my high school they also had a forestry program so I went through that as well. I worked so hard in high school that I could have graduated early. But I wanted to walk with my class."

"Forestry huh? That fits."

Ann smiled as she recalled the next segment of her life. "I guess it did at the time. I was always into the outdoors. Between all my outdoor experience and the forestry program I completed, getting a job with the State Parks and Recreation Department was a piece of cake. I helped maintain trails and campgrounds, did cabin checks and restocked firewood where needed. I also volunteered for a non-profit called the Colorado Mountaineers where I led tour groups and guided hikes in the summer, and cross-country skiing and snowshoeing trips in the winter. It was a blissful time until my dad lost his job."

Bradley winced. "Ouch. That always hurts."

"Yes it does. And just about the time it happened, Sara was telling him about all the opportunities that were available for him in Chicago."

"So that's when you moved."

"No. That's when they moved. I was so torn. I was already so lonely. It was really hard for me when Sara moved, and things got even worse once I graduated from high school. Everyone else had their grand plans, knowing exactly what they wanted to do, but I just floundered. When my parents decided to move I wasn't sure of what to do. The side of me that suffered from loneliness was dying to go with them, but I didn't feel like leaving Colorado. Leaving the mountains for life in the big city felt like a root canal. I decided I couldn't leave, so I moved in with my aunt."

"Is she still around? Did she move here too?"

"No, she ended up moving to Philadelphia, but that wasn't until years later. While living with her I decided to take classes at the local community college in order to broaden my options. By then I'd quit working for the state in order to work solely for the Mountaineers. But after a while, although it was a thrill for me to lead expeditions, I realized that line of work wasn't something I'd want to do for the rest of my life.

"While I was on one of these expeditions, I met a guy who'd just completed his degree in business and marketing. He said it was a good degree for people like me who didn't know what they wanted to be when they grew up. In addition to that, I'd just composed a brochure for the Mountaineers and found I had a flair for it. I had a natural instinct for targeting what would appeal to the public and attract business. Following the release of the brochure, business increased by forty percent."

"Ah—so the shark in you was born in the belly of a mountaineering brochure."

"It certainly was," she laughed. "Only back then I wasn't so sharkish. Shortly after that, I found a business and marketing program in Chicago and the rest is history."

The line had been moving along steadily while Ann and Bradley were talking. Soon after Ann finished, it was their turn to go to the Ledge.

Ann began to feel shaky about this adventure. Not even she could figure out why a person who used to thrive on heights would now be terrified of them. She'd always been such a thrill-seeker. Now she clutched Bradley's arm as though something was sure to hurl her off the 103rd floor of the Sears Tower before she even got close to the Ledge.

Bradley sensed her apprehension. "Ann—we don't have to go through with this if you don't want to."

"No—I want to. I want to get over this. I used to love heights. I can't figure out why it's scaring me so much, but I want to do this."

"Okay then. But I'll hold onto you if you need me to. Just let me know."

"Okay Bradley. Thank you."

They moved to a viewing spot that was unoccupied. Bradley took Ann by the hand and led her onto the Skydeck Ledge. Just as they stepped onto the glass, Ann gasped. "Bradley, please hold me. Sorry, but I need to take you up on that."

Bradley reassured her with a soft ray of sunshine in his voice. "It's all right, I have you."

He stood behind her with his arms wrapped around her. As he held her, he noticed how fragile she felt. Not like the executive-devouring, messenger carnivore he knew from the office. She felt small, delicate and vulnerable, and once again he allowed his mind to drift toward all that could be, if only. If only Ann hadn't been zapped by that crazy old lady. If only she could be thirty-two again. If only she could find the old woman and have this curse reversed.

As he stood behind her, he couldn't feel or see any signs of aging. This captivating thirty-two-year-old he held in his arms had found a room in his heart he didn't even know existed. She'd breezed in like a bird returning from its winter pilgrimage. Somehow she'd managed to find that room, set up house and open all the windows to let out the stuffiness. Had it not been for Ann Finlayson, he never even would have known about that room. But now, as his heart became full with this new occupant, he realized he never wanted her to move out.

Now that Ann was feeling safe and secure in Bradley's arms, she began to enjoy the view. She'd been feeling the same warmth toward him as he had toward her, but she wanted to push those feelings away. She thought it pointless to give reign to such emotions while the reality of true togetherness was like gripping sand.

"So, Mister Bradley, you've been up here before. Why don't you point out some of the sights? I found Millennium Park and O'Hare Airport, what else am I looking at?"

Bradley was happy to comply. He showed her where Wrigley Field was, and the Lincoln Park Zoo. He pointed out Navy Pier and named all the buildings. Then she was able to spot a few more places on her own.

The distraction was good for both of them.

After a while, Ann mentioned how hungry she was getting.

Bradley pulled out his phone. "Hmm—what time is it anyway? I thought Thai food might be safe for your dietary needs. I found this great little hole in the wall restaurant that's very popular, yet not so busy that the wait exceeds an hour on a Saturday. But since this is Sunday, we might have less of a wait. What do you say Fin? Are you up for Thai food?"

"I'm up for just about anything. And when it comes to dietary needs, you are speaking to a woman who had chocolate chip cookies for breakfast this morning."

"Chocolate chip cookies? Is that what I smelled when I came to the door? I thought I smelled something, but had to remind myself whose condo I was visiting. You normally wouldn't even *eat* cookies, let alone bake them."

Ann put her hands on her hips and leaned forward with a smile. She put on a southern accent and said, "Well you'd be surprised what old age can do for you." Then she laughed and added, "Or was it the command slash challenge I got from Cassie yesterday?"

"Whatever the reason, you'd better save me a few. What was Cassie's challenge?"

"She told me I needed to make something to bring to Nancy's retirement party tomorrow. I'd given her money to buy some cookies at the store and she decided to use it to buy pizza for the kids. She said after all Nancy's done for me, the least I could do is make something. Which is probably true, but I also believe she doesn't think I'm capable. And therein lay the challenge. I just *had* to prove her wrong."

"Hmm. I'm curious now. I'd better sample one when I get you back home."

Just then, Ann realized she never did give Charlotte the cookie she'd put in her bag.

"Just your luck. I happen to have one right here."

"This is music to my ears. Would you like half? I know how hungry you are."

Ann told him no thanks, she wanted to save her appetite for some real food. Then she mentioned her hips were hurting. She winced when she took a step and confessed, "I hate to admit defeat, but I think I might need to use the tag-along."

"No matter. Whatever it takes to make this your best day ever."

His smile was contagious. Feeling shy as she returned it, she looked to the floor and told him it certainly had been so far.

On their way to the restaurant, Ann drank in the sights while Bradley munched on his chocolate chip appetizer. It wasn't often she ventured out in the evening hours. When she did, it was usually to go to Tae Kwon Do. Other than that, her evening activities had been trained on work catchup and housework. She preferred getting out and about during daylight hours. But here, with Bradley's company, she enjoyed seeing things all lit up and bustling with activity.

When they got to the restaurant, they were told the wait would only be fifteen minutes. The restaurant was lively and packed. Once seated, Ann was glad to get a corner table where they might actually be able to hear each other speak.

It didn't take long for them to decide what to order, but it did take a while for the server to come to the table.

Ann told Bradley it was his turn.

"My turn for what?"

"Your turn to talk about your family and what brought you here to Chicago."

"Oh that. Well the how I got here part is easy enough. I was born here. My dad was a history professor at the university and my mom ran a daycare. We lived in the suburbs, but my parents both agreed it was crucial for my brother and me to get out of the city and experience rural life. So every summer they'd send us to my grandpa's farm. He raised cattle and all sorts of other animals. Not all for financial gain—my grandma was an animal lover." He laughed as he fondly recalled, "She even insisted on a few llamas. She never did anything with them, she just enjoyed having them around.

"They sold eggs from their chickens and some fruit and vegetables at the local market in the spring and summer. But their main source of income came from the grass-fed beef. That's where Brett and I came in. We'd get up early and help with all the immediate chores like mucking stalls and feeding the chickens, then we'd ride out with Grandpa to water the cattle and repair fences. But of course, the chores weren't the best part of living in the country during the summer months."

Bradley told Ann about how his grandpa used to take him and his brother fishing. He also reminisced about getting to drive the tractor and riding in his grandpa's old pickup truck. "All that time spent outdoors during the summer served to fill me with a great disdain for the big city. Like you, I grew up with a raging preference for the wide open countryside."

Ann asked the obvious question. "Then why have you stayed?"

"Like anyone else carving out a life in downtown Chicago, I had to make some real money. I wasn't born with the farmer gene. I've never wanted to be a teacher. About the only thing I've ever wanted to do was write. And thanks to my degree and some great connections I made in college, I've been able to do just that." As the dinner plates arrived, Bradley let out a long sigh. "The sad part is, I've never been able to do the sort of writing I truly want to do. I've just been paying the bills."

Ann reminded him that he was supposed to tell her about his volunteering on the weekends.

Bradley looked at the table and let out a long, "Hmm." He took a moment to gather his thoughts and prepared to answer while tapping his fingers on the table. "This will be a far bigger task than it was to tell you about my life as a kid. There's a huge background story that must be told. Are your ears prepped for all that listening?"

Ann smiled. "Of course they are. I'm the one who brought it up."

"Okay. Let me try to consolidate. When I was in college I met the love of my life. But apparently, I wasn't hers. She took me for a ride for a few years. After she dumped me, I went on a fast tumble down an icy hill. I began drinking heavily. Very heavily. My brother decided this would be the right time to offload the church lecture on me again. He'd been trying to get me to follow in his Christian footsteps for years before that, but I wanted nothing to do with it. Of the two of us, I'd always been the troublemaker."

Ann was shocked. "What? You? Mr. All American?"

"Yes me. And the worst was yet to come. A few years later, my brother died. I really spun out then. Even though we were at odds in our religious views, we were always close. In fact, after my parents moved to the Blue Mountains, Brett became my anchor. After he died, all the lights in my life went out completely and I was going through all the motions in the dark. Two choices laid before me at that point. I could either kill myself with alcohol or somehow find a way back to a life that had some sort of meaning.

"I'd been helping my sister-in-law with estate issues and trying to be there for my niece when I decided to go to church with them one Sunday. I think the pastor wrote the message just for me. I remember feeling like he and I were the only two people in the building. He spoke of how another name for the Holy Spirit was The Comforter. He talked about our need for comfort and how, as in 2 Corinthians, we should pass it along once we've received it ourselves. And then it hit me. That's what I'd wanted after my girlfriend dumped me. I wanted comfort. And all the alcohol in the world could not satisfy that need. And I needed it that day in church, when I was suffering so much over my brother's death. So when the pastor gave an altar call at the end of service, I couldn't get up there fast enough.

"After that, I continued going to church every Sunday. I started going to a men's Bible study on Tuesday nights. Eventually, I helped develop an after school program for at risk youth, and started a men's mentoring and discipleship ministry. The guys and I decided to take the after school program one step further and offer a place for kids to hang out on Saturdays too. Then we started getting kids to church on Sundays as well.

"So that's what I do on the weekends. I work with the youth and young men who come to the church for help with life issues. Sometimes I shoot hoops with a group of them in a court down the street from the church."

As Bradley struck one familiar chord after another, Ann couldn't help but drift a little into her own thoughts. So many parallels to her own life. Right down to the religious sibling. Hadn't she shut down after Doug dumped her? That was when she began throwing herself into exercise with a vengeance. She began working out every spare moment while developing a strict dietary regimen. She used to think Doug might take her back if only she were more slender. More vibrant. More something. But his only excuse was that they were too different.

And Sara had moved to Chicago.

Then there was the accident.

Bradley couldn't help but notice Ann had vacated the conversation, so he ended his discourse to ask where she went.

"Well, you got me thinking. It's funny how death and loss affect everyone so differently. My parents' premature death is what planted the final, immovable wedge between me and the God thing. Yet my sister Sara will tell you that's how she got her 'h'."

"What do you mean by that?"

"You know the story of Sarah and Abraham and how Sarah didn't have an 'h' in her name until God gave her one?"

"Yeah, but in my Bible, her name was Sarai."

"Beside the point. My mom knew that, but decided on just plain Sara instead. Sarai was such an ancient name and she thought Sara with no 'h' would be much simpler. Anyway, my mom always said that her greatest desire was for her girls to come to the decision to follow Christ of their own accord, not just because she and Dad were devout Christians. So she named her firstborn after Sarah in the Bible and told my sister she'd know when God gave her the 'h'. So when they died, Sara went full force into the church thing. She wanted to reconnect with those Christian roots in order to find some sort of comfort."

"And did she?"

"Yeah—I guess. She's always trying to convert me. She constantly tells me about how she's praying for me. But I still can't get past the fact that this great big God who can calm storms, walk on water *and* divide it in half would also allow two incredible, God-fearing people to die in a car crash."

Ann's eyes misted. "It was reckless driving." Her voice had thinned to a whisper. "The driver who caused it walked away with barely a scratch."

Bradley reached for her hand. He said a silent prayer, asking God to help him with this segment of the conversation. So many people rejected God for this same reason. They just couldn't accept that a loving God would allow such atrocities in their own life and in the world around them. So he drew from his own experience as he carefully responded.

"For a long time, I struggled with the same issue. My brother was a pillar for his family—and that included me—and he was well-respected in the community. Why would God take his life, but leave me, the loser, to go on living? But over time, as I began to dig deeply into the Word of God, I came to see His sovereignty. I began to see that He, as God, does have the right to give life and to take it away." He paused for a moment to fish for a good example. "When those terrorists flew the planes into the Twin Towers on 9/11, God was not holding them at gunpoint. He didn't say, 'Okay boys, we're going in.' Did He allow it? Yes. He created mankind with free will, hoping we might choose Him of our own accord. He didn't want robots, programmed to love Him. Did He grieve over loss of life in that tragedy? Oh yes. I'm sure He raised the water level of the oceans by several feet with His tears."

Bradley paused another moment to compose his thoughts.

"So when we ask why God would allow such horrible things as premature death by motorcycle and car accidents, all I can tell you is, I think I may have always had a propensity for addictive behavior. It took my brother's death to reveal it. And, had he not died, I wouldn't have gone to church that Sunday. I wouldn't have experienced the joy of working with at-risk youth. I wouldn't have known the selflessness it took to help my sister-in-law with all the paperwork, house stuff, her moving back to Florida …" He looked into Ann's eyes and smiled. "I wouldn't have landed a job at *Top Rung* and I never would have met you."

"So you're saying that God was planning the accident so you'd become a better person?"

"No. Not at all. I'm saying accidents just happen. God is not to blame for them. Some guy didn't see my brother's motorcycle turning a corner and he hit him. It was purely an accident. What I am saying is, God loves His kids. And He knows how to raise good things from the ashes of tragedy."

He thought about sharing some scripture references, but decided not to. The story of Joseph would have been a perfect illustration, as well as the verse in Romans where Paul refers to God working all things together for our good, but he didn't want Ann to feel Bible-thumped. At least not at this stage of their exchange. It struck him that it might be better to share his own experience.

"So on an even more personal note, all I can tell you is this: The God I've come to know brought me comfort when I needed it. He was there for me in a deeply personal way. No one else could have reached that far inside me in order to address my pain."

Then he went on to explain the gospel and how we all fall short of God's glory. He told Ann that God sees her feelings of guilt and shame over her treatment of Valerie and He loves her anyway. He told her that God is love and He forgives her for her behavior. He explained that God's only desire for Ann would be that she might come to know Him and experience all the joy, peace and abundant life He has to offer.

"And now I'm sounding like my brother. Wow." He chuckled at himself as he waved one hand in the air as if he were calling the server back to the table. "Podium please."

They both laughed over this, then Ann excused herself to use the restroom. Not only did she need it for functional purposes, but it was good to escape all the heaviness of the conversation they'd just shared.

Only she couldn't.

She remembered seeing her parents in the hospital after the car accident. They were so out of proportion from the impact that they were barely recognizable. She'd only graduated from college the week before. She remembered her dad giving her the pen and telling her she was going to do great things with it.

Following the accident she inwardly collapsed. She built a barricade around her heart that became a fortress. She vowed to stay in her own cocoon and cleave only to her immediate life, which included finding a job. She would maintain her tiny, toned frame through strict dieting and exercise in order to look the part of high-power marketing executive as she worked on her resume and beat the pavement. She decided to make herself known to the world as Ann, rather than Anna, because it sounded more sophisticated. The only person she had to rely on now was herself. So she decided to craft the best version of herself that she could possibly think of. And from now on, she would keep all people an arm's length away, including Sara. People always died or left anyway. Why get attached?

With these gloomy thoughts swirling around her, she returned to the table.

Bradley had ordered dessert. He said, "I thought we needed a subject change and this felt like the best way to do it."

Ann's mood lightened instantly as she agreed with him. She even decided to share a few bites when she remembered something he'd said earlier.

"In all your talk about the God thing, you mentioned something about your meeting me because of your brother's death. So what's so great about me? The post-crosswalk me is a saggy mess and the pre-crosswalk me has been a ruthless, hard-nosed shark. You must expound."

Bradley looked at the ceiling and sighed. "Okay, you asked. Since I started at the magazine I've had a hunch there might be more to you than met the eye. And ears ..." He locked eyes with her and smiled. "And nerves."

Ann reached across the table and said, "Hey. Watch it buddy," as she lightly slapped his shoulder. Then she reminded him of her black belt in Tae Kwon Do.

Bradley laughed. "I already told you. You asked, so I'm giving you the answer. Where was I? Oh yeah—the nerves part. You may not have noticed this yourself, but since you ran into that grandma lady, you've softened. I'm beginning to believe that crosswalk encounter may have been a divine appointment. And, as I've been coming to know the real Ann Finlayson, I've secretly longed for encounter number two, where she changes you back."

His eyes glinted with impish lights as he smiled and added, "Then again, maybe she could make me as old as you are."

Ann rolled her eyes and told him he wouldn't like it. "No—this aging thing is highly overrated. All glitz and glam with nothing to show for it but aching hips and a sea of gray hair."

"Yeah, but just think—we could leave the rat race. We could sell everything and move to the Blue Mountains of North Carolina."

"The Blue Mountains? That's right. You said your parents moved there."

"Yeah. When they retired they bought a piece of property there. The property came with a house they planned to live in and they built a cabin in case my brother's family or I might want to visit." Bradley's expression grew pensive. "Come to think of it, since my dad died a year ago, my mom could probably use the help. Although she's surrounded by a great community of people who care about her, I still worry about her."

Ann giggled and said, "You're almost sounding serious."

"Maybe I am. Just think. I could write my historical novels and you … you could … I don't know—ever consider teaching violin lessons?"

"Oh Bradley—you are too funny. Would you really want a thing to do with all that lies beneath these fancy clothes?"

"Well, I'd be saggy too."

They both laughed and Bradley mentioned how fun it would be to walk out of *Top Rung* and into the sunset years with everyone watching them go. "I can hear them now. 'Wow. Those two old folks that just left the building looked an awful lot like Ann and Bradley.' And something else just dawned on me …"

"Oh yeah? What would that be?"

A boyish grin filled Bradley's entire face. "I could tinker. Isn't that what you're supposed to do when you retire? I mean, I tinker now with my brother's old station wagon, but my dad built a workshop. I could … make stuff."

Ann giggled and flashed him her skeptical look. "Oh—so you know how to make stuff?"

"No. But I could learn."

"Yeah, right."

"Okay, I am getting a little out there, but I do believe what's happened to you might be straight from the hand of God."

Ann feigned frustration, shook her head and smiled. "Are we going there with the God thing again?"

"Why yes we are. If you must know, I've been praying for you for a long time."

"You've been praying for me?"

"Yes. I told you I always thought there was more to you than met the eye …"

Ann interrupted teasingly. "And ears. And nerves."

Bradley laughed. "Yeah—don't forget about those."

"So what were you praying for?"

"That God would soften your heart. That He would reveal to you how harshly you treated others and that you might come to know His lovingkindness. He did a work in me. I knew He could do a work in you as well. He turned me into a giver whereas before, I'd always been a taker. I knew it wasn't impossible for Him to take a gruff person like you and help you understand the meaning of kindness."

Ann half-muttered, half-sighed, "What's desirable in a man is his kindness."

"What? How do you know that verse?"

"I know it because both Valerie and Cassie have said it to me. That is, they've lectured me on it."

"Well, they were right to do so. And even you have to admit this experience has given you a new set of eyes."

"Yeah. The wrinkly, crinkly kind." She laughed and asked, "But why did you pray? Why didn't you just come and call me out on all my wicked behavior? Why didn't you preach to me like Cassie, Valerie and Sara?"

"Because God is a gentleman. He doesn't force Himself on anyone. I figured the best thing I could do was surround you with prayer and shower you with God's kindness."

"You should share some of this vast wisdom with Cassie. But you know what? I'm getting tired. Let's call it a night."

Bradley walked Ann to her front door and said goodnight while tenderly stroking her cheek. He told her he was still praying for her, then he kissed her lightly on the forehead.

Ann thanked him for a great best day ever and slipped into the condo. She tried to figure out what to do first. She was supposed to call Sara, but didn't feel like it right at the moment. So she went into the kitchen and put her bag and keys on the table.

Then her eyes landed on the salt and pepper shakers.

Out of nowhere, an unannounced pool of pain and anguish rose to her throat. With her eyes still fixed on the salt and pepper shakers, she cupped her hand over her mouth and sat down at the table. After all these years, she could no longer hold these emotions at bay. While images of her parents, both dead and alive, swarmed through her head, she felt powerless over the waves of grief that clutched her throat. She opened the gates and allowed the neglected tears to flow.

Once she gave them permission to escape, they wouldn't stop. A half hour passed and she didn't even get up to grab a tissue. She just kept wiping her face and nose with her hands while suffering through relentless waves of pain. More came, but they began to subside. She continued sitting and taking short breaths until she couldn't stand the mess anymore.

As she got up to grab a napkin from the kitchen drawer, she felt overwhelmed with a sense of calm. A few more tears streamed down her cheeks as she embraced the peace.

She returned to the kitchen table and sat there for the longest time, just missing her parents. She missed her mother's laugh and her dad's witty one-liners. She missed the cold nights on the couch, wrapped in blankets with popcorn and movies. She missed the warm strength of her father as he helped her navigate through so many difficult moments. And so many good ones. Most of all, she wished she could hear her mom play the violin just one more time.

Her mind replayed the conversation she'd just had at dinner with Bradley.

She thought of what he said about how she'd treated Valerie. About how God still loved her even though she'd been so cruel. Then she recalled how she'd treated the courier, as well as Cassie's attempt at making the guy feel better after her rough treatment of him.

While thinking of Cassie, she considered the insensitivity she'd displayed through all of Craig's cancer treatments. She'd never once asked how Cassie was doing or how the treatments were going. She'd just barked orders and expected Cassie to perform at optimum level—as though nothing was going on in her life that was out of the ordinary.

Conviction led her to the living room couch and suggested she do something she'd never done before.

Get on her knees before the throne of her almighty Father.

Although she felt awkward, she complied. First, she thanked God for the eye-opening evening with Bradley. Then she apologized to Him for how despicably she'd treated so many people for so many years. She mentioned each one of them by name or incident as a fresh set of tears accompanied her sorrow. She recounted what she'd done to each and every one of them, right down to the elderly lady at the grocery store. She ended with Valerie.

Although she felt sheepish about the rest of the prayer she intended to pray, she forced herself to continue. Pride attempted to pull her up from the floor, but she pushed it away.

At the restaurant, Bradley shared what he had prayed after he got home from church that one Sunday. He'd told God he wasn't satisfied with merely saying the repeat-after-me prayer he recited during the altar call. He wanted to make it personal. So he got down on his knees and said his own version of the salvation prayer.

Despite the pride that continued to taunt her, Ann spoke the words that Bradley had shared, and added a few of her own. She was careful to speak the name that had turned her stomach during so many conversations with Sara. She told God that she understood what Jesus had accomplished for her at the cross, and that she was ready for Him to move into her heart and become her Savior.

Then pride packed up and left.

She stayed on the floor until her knees began to hurt. When she got up, she decided now would be a good time to call Sara.

But Sara beat her to it.

She got to the phone by the second ring. "Hey Sara—how's it going?"

"Well, you already know all of my news. I have to ask what's happening with you. How did your date go?"

Ann paused as her voice strained with tears. She couldn't help but let them come out as she answered her sister. "To tell you the truth, I have more pressing news."

Sara heard the tears and worried something terrible had happened. "Ann. What's wrong? Are you all right?"

Ann spoke so softly that Sara had to strain to hear. "Sara? I think I just got my 'h'."

Sara shrieked. "What? How? You've got to be kidding me! Are you saying what I think you're saying?"

Ann sniffed and her voice cracked as she answered, "Yes I am."

Now Sara had tears to talk through. "And I was just expecting to hear about your date. This is so monumental. Really—how did this happen?"

Ann told Sara about her conversation with Bradley at the dinner table. She told her about how she and Bradley had shared some similar life experiences, and about how poorly Bradley had handled some of his heartbreaks. She shared everything. About the girlfriend he had and lost. About his drinking to numb the pain. About the motorcycle accident that killed his brother. And about how he didn't want to continue drowning emotional pain with alcohol, so he went to church.

"As he was talking, I became aware of how I've responded to pain and heartache these past few years. I never shed a tear over Mom and Dad's death. Until tonight."

"What? Sorry to keep saying this, but you've got to be kidding. I cried for days and weeks and months. I still get tears from time to time. How did you manage *that*? I don't mean to sound harsh, it's just that they meant so much to you. Remember how Dad used to reach out to you when you were having troubles at school? I remember feeling jealous over all the little dates he took you on. But Mom set me straight by reminding me that it was Dad's way of helping you get your mind off things. And you and Mom? Where would I start? Not just with your learning to play the violin as well as she could, but … she did so much. For both of us."

Now Sara battled tears again over her parents' memory. "I don't mean all this to sound accusatory, I just can't understand how you could not have cried all this time."

"Well, because of tonight I realized I'd hurt so much I didn't want to feel anymore. My best friend moved away. Then you moved. Then Doug happened. Then when Mom and Dad died, I shut down entirely. Somewhere along the line, I made a decision to stop feeling. And to stop needing people. I decided to throw myself into becoming the new Anna Finlayson. You know—the one without the 'a'? And … I don't know … somehow I was able to bury it all in work and exercise."

Sara took in a deep breath and exhaled loudly. "Okay. I guess that would explain a thing or two. So how are you doing now?"

"I'll answer that when I'm not so tired. I don't think I can string anymore words together tonight, so let's hook up tomorrow. I need to go to bed."

"Works for me. I have to get up pretty early. So goodnight." Her voice softened as she added, "And congratulations on your new life."

Ann smiled and said, "Thanks." Then she hung up and settled in for the night. She had a hunch she was going to sleep like a baby.

Chapter 11

Ann woke before the alarm went off. Her hunch was correct—she did sleep like a baby. Throughout the night, she'd only woken up once.

When her feet hit the floor, she noticed she wasn't quite as stiff as she was yesterday. She figured it had something to do with the extra sleep. But after all the pain she'd suffered yesterday, she decided to take an ibuprofen just in case. And since she had time for exercise, she skipped the elliptical in honor of doing some yoga stretches instead.

She couldn't believe the difference in how she felt after that. She smiled as she recalled thinking how fun it might be to teach a yoga class for seniors, starting with Charlotte and the girls. That, however, was back when she was sure she'd be able to have the curse reversed—it was merely a funny picture in her mind. But now, she wasn't sure this curse would ever be broken. And the reality of learning to live life as a senior wasn't something she truly had the stomach for. All she wanted was to be with Bradley ...

As these thoughts began pulling her into a tunnel of depression, Ann fought them. She told herself this was going to be a fantastic day. She would celebrate with Nancy at the office. She would wow everyone with her fabulous cookies. And Valerie would be home tonight.

One of the chief reasons she looked forward to that was because she wanted to apologize to Valerie. She wanted to confess all the wrongs she'd committed and set things right. And not because Sara was coming home tomorrow, but because it was the right thing to do. It always had been and she knew it. As the need to apologize had kept badgering her all week, she realized she'd been pushing it back with pride. But now, that pride was gone.

With a fresh attitude, she finished getting ready for work. As she looked at her face and hands, she realized she'd have to keep the migraine and rash story going. Her hands bothered her the most—she didn't have to look in the mirror to see them. They were always there, in front of her eyes, whittling away at any vestige of hope that remained within her.

So she'd have to wear the gloves. And all the rest. But since Sean bought the rash story, she figured she could sell it to everyone else at the office. After all—her highly polished, executive appearance may have left the building, but the marketing major who could sell anything to anyone, was still intact.

On her way to the office, Ann made a spontaneous stop at the flower shop. She bought a spring bouquet and perused the shelf that was stocked with decorative gift boxes. She already knew the cookies were going to be an office sensation, but dressing them up in one of these boxes might make an even bigger splash. She bought one and transferred the cookies right there in the store. She sighed with satisfaction as she admired the final presentation. On her way to the elevator, she commented right out loud, "Oh yes. This is going to be splendiferous."

With this lightness filling her heart, she entered the office with a smile on her face.

As usual, Cassie couldn't let Ann get to her desk without her typical comments and news flashes. "Well, well," she half-smirked. "What's this? A smile? *And* flowers? Did you actually buy Nancy flowers?"

Ann was about to respond, but Cassie wouldn't let her. "By the way, before you get all settled behind your desk, Marv wants to see you. But you might want to ditch the glasses and gloves—he was in one of his serious moods. What's up with the Jackie Kennedy look anyway? And why is your face all covered? You trying to create a new self-image?"

"No. These headaches just won't go away and I'm still sensitive to light. And I broke out with a rash over the weekend. It's all over my hands and face."

"Wow. You better get to the doctor. Do you want me to look one up for you?"

Ann answered on her way to her desk. "No thanks, I can find one."

Since Ann wasn't normally a granter of blessings, she felt awkward responding to another of Cassie's questions. After all, Cassie didn't know about the new Ann.

After a long pause she said, "The flowers are for you."

Now they were both out of character. For once in Ann's office life, Cassie was speechless. It was her turn to falter in terms of a response.

"But why? I'm not the one with the party."

Ann wished she could take her sunglasses off and make eye contact.

"Because, Cassie. I've been doing a lot of thinking lately. It's been bothering me that I haven't been more of a support to you regarding Craig's health. And you do so much for me around here. I don't think I've ever said 'thank you.' So I'm saying it now."

Flabbergasted beyond words, Cassie took the bouquet and muttered something about finding a vase. She left her desk and went down the hall.

Ann situated the cookies and took a deep breath before going to see Marvin. She had a bad feeling about this. On the way to his office, she had to explain her appearance to everyone she passed by. She longed to just announce it over the intercom and be done with it.

Once she reached Marvin's office, it took one look at him for her suspicions to be confirmed—he was wearing his bad news, stone face. The one he always wore before firing someone or letting a staff member know their article would have to be cut. But before he could deliver whatever news it was, he too had to ask about Ann's appearance. She explained and he told her to sit down.

Never a good thing.

"What I'm about to say will probably come as no surprise. I told you not to blow the Green Jeans call. I told you to partner with Sean in order to guarantee success. One you did do; one you did not. So as of today, Sean is taking over your position. He will be moving into Nancy's office tomorrow morning. You will be working directly under him. And for crying out loud, why don't you get yourself to the doctor?"

Ann wished she could reply with a witty comeback, but she was fresh out. She just said she understood and yes, she would get to the doctor.

She was grateful Sean wouldn't be able to take over Nancy's office until tomorrow. It gave her a chance to step inside Nancy's office and connect with all the emotions that were running through her. Was she surprised? No. Did this news sting? Like crazy. Was she willing to work under Sean? No way. Standing face to face with her immediate, yet unsorted future, she noticed a familiar sound.

Nancy's fountain was still sitting on the table. Why hadn't she taken it with her? Was it included in the artwork she was offering Ann? If so, Ann would love to take it home with her. The quiet, gurgling sounds of the fountain had already begun working to settle her nerves. How she would love to mingle this constant, calming murmur with the pictures she'd chosen for the condo. She closed her eyes and listened. As she did, she envisioned which picture would hang where. She knew just the table she'd use for the fountain.

Then her eyes flew open with the thought that 11:30 could not come soon enough. She became so anxious to talk to Nancy at the party that she could barely stand it.

At this she made her way back to her desk, fielding questions about her appearance all the way there. Which was why she was so happy to see Bradley standing beside her desk. He was the only person in the office who needed no explanation for her appearance.

He'd been talking to Cassie when Ann returned. They both stopped talking when she got there.

Bradley flashed one of his broadest grins. "Hey you—we were just talking about you. Sort of. We've been hashing out a plan for getting Valerie home. Either I could pick her up after work or Cassie could go grab her sometime during the party and she could spend the rest of her day here at the office. She was disappointed to have missed you Friday."

This idea didn't sit well with Ann. "Oh, I don't think that would be a good idea. Marvin doesn't like kids at work and I'd feel obligated to entertain her. Why don't you go ahead and pick her up after work? It would mean more time for her and the kids anyway."

"For which they'd all be elated," Cassie added. "Valerie has made such a nice addition to our family that I'm afraid we want to keep her. I know you wouldn't mind our confiscating Valerie, but it's your sister I worry about. I've talked to her at great length a few times recently and she's just as terrific as her daughter is." Then she shifted into Caustic Cassie mode. "I find it impossible to believe the two of you are sisters."

Ann smiled and nodded. *You still don't know about the new me.*

She thought perhaps Cassie should be the second one to know. After telling Sara last night, she wanted Bradley to be next. But she didn't uncharacteristically bring Bradley flowers ...

Cassie solved the dilemma for her. "Incidentally, Marvin wants you and me to set up for Nancy's party today. We have to brew extra coffee and make a bowl of punch on top of decorating the break room. Everyone has been putting their potluck donations in there and we have to bring it some semblance of order. By the way, did you bring something?

Ann was most pleased to answer. "Why, yes I did. Remember how I teased you about making chocolate chip cookies?"

"Yeah—but of course you were being facetious."

Ann proudly picked up her gift box and held it in the air. "Well I'm not now."

Bradley was still standing by, so he had to share his enthusiasm. "And they are amazing!"

Cassie looked perplexed. "What? You've had one?"

Ann answered for him. "Let's go down to the break room and I'll tell you all about it."

When they first got to the break room, Cassie filled Ann's ears with all the events of the weekend. She shared with Ann how well all the kids got along, and about everything they did as a group. "And Valerie is so great with kids. Usually, the two older girls don't want Simon to hang out with them because he is, after all, only six. But Valerie found a way to incorporate him in all their activities and he didn't feel left out at all."

"But when I talked to you on the phone, you said the girls were sticking together so you had to be Simon's personal playmate."

"Oh, that's right. Well, right after I hung up from talking to you I went back to the backyard and they were all playing together. Simon had asked

Valerie to come and look at his worm collection and Valerie complied. Before long, they were all digging for worms. Then they broke into a round of soccer and I went back inside. It was like that for the rest of the weekend. All I had to do was keep the snacks and drinks coming. I don't know what they're up to today, but I'm grateful Val was able to stay another day. So what about you? How did you fill the hours after your fateful date with Sean?"

"Funny, all that comes to mind is, I filled them with Bradley."

"Bradley? Do tell."

Ann chronicled some of her weekend moments for Cassie while they busied their hands dressing up the break room. She highlighted a few of the moments she spent without Bradley, like digging through her closet to find the cookie recipe. She told her about her encounter with Lisa at the park, and about how Lisa was also experiencing hardship due to cancer.

At this point, Cassie broke in. "Sounds like someone I'd like to meet."

"Now that you mention it, I think she could be. She's been through so much. And her husband's deployed. She really has no one around to lean on but the hospital staff."

Cassie was quick to correct her. "And you."

Cassie's words stung. It may have sounded to her like Ann was there for a complete stranger she met at the park, but never showed an ounce of compassion toward Cassie's situation with Craig. She decided now might be a good time to move into deeper waters.

"Yeah, we've shared a few chance encounters at the park. But I wouldn't want you to think we've been bonding over this on a regular basis. I wouldn't want you to feel like I cared more for someone I just met a week ago than I care for you."

"Yeah. About that. Since when did you start caring about anyone at all? And what gives with the flowers? This is not you. Did someone zap you with a laser beam? Did you drink some magic potion?"

Here goes nothing.

"You could say that. In fact, you can blame the flowers on a little bit of magic, plus all the time I spent with Bradley over the weekend."

Cassie stopped moving dishes around and looked intently at Ann. "Okay. You have my attention. What do you mean by 'a little bit of magic'?"

Ann took off one of her gloves.

Cassie's eyes widened and she audibly sucked in air. "Tell me what's going on."

Ann told her about the day she ran into the woman in the crosswalk. She told Cassie this was the reason for all the extra clothes and dark glasses. She explained that all those mornings of coming in late had to do with trips to the drugstore for help with covering the gray hair and wrinkles.

"So that gray hair on the back of your head the other day wasn't caused by peroxide?"

"No. In fact, I've been wearing a wig the past few days. My hair is completely white now."

"Well, don't just stand there, pull it off and let me see."

Ann shook her head. "I don't want to risk it here. Maybe sometime we could find a safe place for me to show you, but it's too crazy around here today."

"This is beyond bizarre. So many things are making sense now ..." While Cassie was speaking, her eyes were on the break room table. They'd both stopped working by now. "But look at what time it is. We need to hustle. And you still have to get to the Bradley part."

Ann told Cassie about revealing to Bradley what had been going on. She told her about some of the experiences she'd had, including what had happened at the grocery store. "So Bradley offered to come over because he asked how I was doing and I said not well. I'd been so tired of having to hide this all week long that it was a relief to tell him. He was so sweet about it."

"That would be Bradley. So then what happened?"

"All I can tell you is, between last Saturday and the date we went on yesterday, we've had several heartfelt conversations. And I don't know ... I guess you could say God did a work in my heart."

Cassie had to stop working again. "What? Are you serious?"

Ann felt uncomfortable about this disclosure. It made her feel stripped and vulnerable and she didn't want Cassie to gush. "Yes Cassie. But please don't make a big deal of it. After being so hard-nosed about it for so long, it feels weird to admit to certain people that this has taken place."

"By 'certain people' do you mean me?"

"Yeah, I guess I do. I've been harsher toward you than anyone else when it comes to this topic." Ann didn't want to add, "Everyone but Valerie," so she changed the subject.

"Where do we keep all the paper products and plastic utensils? I'll start digging those out."

They were almost finished when someone poked their head in the door to announce Nancy had arrived. At this piece of news, Ann felt her stomach flutter. She was so anxious to talk with Nancy. All she wanted to do was grab her and whisk her down to her office where they could have some privacy. But she did have to share—it wasn't like she was the only person in the office with whom Nancy had bonded.

She forced herself to calm down and wait for an opportune moment.

The party had been underway for nearly an hour. Ann noticed that most people brought gifts. She felt terrible because she hadn't even thought of that. So great was her triumph over the cookies, and her desire to break down some walls with Cassie, it hadn't dawned on her to purchase a gift for Nancy.

Oh well. What I want to tell her might be just as good as a wrapped present.

She and Sean avoided each other. She was grateful no one noticed. While biding her time waiting to steal Nancy away, she mingled with some of the staff members she hadn't spoken with before. She'd never been comfortable with this sort of gathering, so she put into practice the art of asking questions.

As she listened to a few stories, she began to kick herself for all the years she'd spent isolating herself from these people. After a few discussions she began to notice how everyone had their share of heartaches and victories. The magazine staff had always been loaded with Bradleys and Charlottes, she'd just never taken the time to invest in anyone but herself.

Ann chewed on this for a moment, then went to refill her punch cup. Just as she was reaching for the dipper, Nancy tapped her on the shoulder.

"Hey you. I've been saving myself for a moment when you and me could be a bit selfish and have a private conversation. I think I've touched base with everyone in the room by now. Why don't we go down to my office and have a chat."

Ann was elated. "Music to my ears. Since you got here, all I've wanted to do is bag everyone else and totally monopolize your time."

They reached the office and Nancy closed the door. "So. A little bird told me the call with Green Jeans didn't go very well. They also told me that Sean is now going to take over my office instead of you. Bad news. How are you taking it?"

Ann didn't know where to start. "I don't completely know. I've barely had time to absorb it. But Marv did warn me something like this might happen." She smiled at her next thought. "Frankly, all it's done so far is convince me I should take that fountain of yours home with me. After all, I wouldn't want Sean to have it."

Nancy laughed and said, "It's yours."

Ann confessed to Nancy about never having seen a Green Jeans ad before last Friday. They had a brief exchange about Ann's appearance. Then Ann shared the biggest reason for why she wanted to have Nancy all to herself for a few moments.

"You remember the last part of our conversation Friday?"

"You mean the part where I said I'd pray for you?"

"Yeah that part. Well last night, God answered your prayer."

Nancy grabbed Ann's shoulders and nearly shouted, "This is wonderful news! What in the world cracked your nut? After you bit my head off last Friday, I practically gave up on you."

"Yeah—sorry about that. It's never been my favorite topic. But I went out to dinner with Bradley last night and he shared his story with me. We talked about a lot of things. For some reason, that stirred the pot."

Nancy smiled and put her hand on Ann's shoulder. "Well again, I'm thrilled. I wish we could stay here longer. I have so much to share with you now that you've told me this news. But we must be getting back."

"You're right. But first I have to tell you how much I love the pictures you gave me. I haven't hung them yet, but they remind me so much of home. I can't take a decent picture to save my life. That photographer is outstanding! And so is the calligrapher. Do you know the artist personally or did you just happen upon the artwork on the walls of some gallery?"

Nancy giggled, "Aw shucks, Ann, thanks."

"You mean you're the one who took those pictures?"

"And I did the calligraphy. It's always been a hobby."

"Wow—you should set up a website and make it more than just a hobby. You could show your work at an art gallery."

"Funny you should say all that. I just finished putting together a website and hope to contact a few galleries soon. These were the options I was telling you I wanted to explore. Much more appealing than staying here, trying to survive Marvin's detestable ideas."

"They are that. We better get going before they send out a search party."

"Yes, we must. Don't forget the fountain."

By the time they returned to the break room, most people had already cleared out. Cassie was cleaning up and Bradley and Marvin stood talking in the corner.

Cassie looked up and said, "I was wondering about you two. Nancy, all your cards and gifts are over there on the counter."

Ann felt bad all over again about not getting anything for Nancy, and she told her so.

Nancy grabbed one of Ann's gloved hands and said, "Not to worry. You gave me the greatest gift of all just now. And, I hear you're responsible for making those fabulous chocolate chip cookies. I never knew you had it in you."

"I don't really. You can blame it on my stubbornness. Do you want to take them home with you?"

Nancy pinched her sides and said, "No, no, my dear. This abundant waistline does not need any contributions from you. I'd be tempted to hide them from my husband and eat them all myself, so I will definitely pass."

Bradley walked up to the two of them. "If you'd like, I can take those off your hands."

Ann hesitated. "You can, but it just dawned on me that Valerie might like to try a few. So you can take the rest when you drop her off."

"Sounds like a plan." He turned to Nancy. "It's good to see you Nancy, but alas, I must take leave. Duty beckons."

Nancy looked at the pile of gifts and cards and sighed, "And I need to start hauling stuff out to my car. So Ann, keep in touch. And Cassie, you're the best. Thank you for all your labors." She hugged them both, but said goodbye to Marvin from across the room. He didn't seem to notice her lack of affection. She gathered up an armload and set out on trip number one.

Marvin called Ann over to where he was standing. He told her he wanted her to start putting together all her client information so Sean could make a seamless transition into her position.

She told him sorry, she had a doctor appointment and wouldn't be in for the rest of the day. Then she picked up the fountain and went to her desk.

After grabbing her bag, she popped her head in the break room and said goodbye to Cassie. She had no words for Marvin.

Ann didn't have a plan as she stepped into the condo. She put the fountain on the coffee table and plopped herself on the sofa. Everything felt so empty. She felt empty. What was she going to do with her life? She was finished with the magazine. How could she remain there and work under Sean of all people? How could she remain there anyway? Physically, she was nearing seventy. And if she were to remain in this state, how could she get a job? Who would want to hire a seventy-year-old woman and what would she do anyway? Bag groceries?

Her first thought was to change clothes and beat the pavement. Perhaps today could be the day she'd be able to make contact with the old woman. She consigned herself to this agenda and stood up to go to the bedroom. Then she sat back down.

How futile would this be? Setting out to find someone in downtown Chicago she'd only spotted by chance here and there over the past week? And every time she'd caught a glimpse of the woman, she'd been too far away to catch her. Or, the woman's face was in a fountain while the rest of her was who knows where. Always elusive. Always unattainable. No. This would not be a good idea.

Ann figured that whatever she decided to do with the next few hours would be better in comfy clothes. So she got up and went to the bedroom to change.

She tried not to look at herself in the mirror as she changed, but couldn't help herself. Everything was sagging now. Since all this started, she hadn't been able to exercise or even get to her yoga class. She couldn't stand the sight of herself and knew there must be a way to tighten things up a bit through exercise, despite her new age. She'd have to talk to Peggy about her thoughts on the matter. Peggy was back in town now, but Ann would have to put that meeting on hold for a few more days.

Valerie was still here.

Ann's only thoughts of her lately had been attached to guilt and shame. But here, in the quiet of her bedroom, she paused to more seriously consider her niece. She thought of this little trooper who constantly claimed she was nothing but a wimp. What kind of wimp would suffer so greatly and so silently through all that bullying at school, yet still be able to stand up to the likes of Ann when the heat was turned up?

And Valerie had her own reasons for her silence about being bullied. Some of them had to do with her own personal interests. She knew her mom might not get the job, so saying something might jeopardize her future at the school. Mean kids don't appreciate tattlers. But Valerie was also tending to the needs of her mother.

She knew her situation at school was big enough for her mom to throw away the possibility of this dream job by coming home immediately, in which case she'd remain stuck in a rut of struggling and stress. What kind of wimp would be so protective of another's dreams? And through this entire miserable experience, that of surviving the bullies at school and the bigger one at home, Valerie had put on a most refreshing attitude. Always lighthearted. So easily brought to laughter. Willing to dance at a moment's notice and so deeply moved by music …

Girl after my own heart, really.

What everyone else had seen all along, Ann had completely missed.

Valerie was also compassionate—look at how she unified Cassie's kids by including Simon in their play because he felt left out. And always so concerned about Charles Latham the Third. Always worried about her mom. Always a good sport about their financial situation. This little niece of hers was truly a delight. And she was no wimp.

Now Ann knew what to do with the rest of this day. She would use the next few hours preparing to celebrate her niece. Valerie was leaving tomorrow, so Ann would have to make it really special. She resolved to put on her chef's hat and prepare a nice dinner. She would insist Bradley join them for Valerie's last night in town. But first, she would expel the sterility that had taken up residence in the condo, and turn it into a home.

She dug through one of her kitchen drawers and found a hammer and some nails. Her dad had always told her to keep such things around, so she dedicated one drawer to some screwdrivers, hammers and measuring tape. She'd never used them before, but if she could scale the face of a mountain, she could certainly pound a nail into a wall.

She recalled the configuration she'd formulated in Nancy's office, then got to work. She hung three of Nancy's pictures, saving her favorite one for the most prominent location in the room. On the wall between the kitchen and the hallway, right above the table where she was going to place the fountain.

That came next. She took the fountain from the coffee table and brought it to the small table that sat under the picture. She plugged it into an outlet that was conveniently located right under the table, and turned it on. Heaven entered her ears as the fountain gurgled joyously. And it was perfect to have it placed under the picture with the water pouring over the river rocks. Such beautiful music.

Music.

She went straight to the hall closet. She took out her violin, then searched for its stand. While she looked, her mother's words rang clearly in her mind: "Always leave your instrument out of its case. You'll play it more."

She found the stand and pulled out the box with the pictures in it. Now that she'd readmitted her parents into her heart, she decided it was time to extract some family photos from the closet. She found three pictures that would fit on the table by the fountain. One of Sara and her when they were little, one of her parents, and a family photo someone had taken of them on a camping trip.

Last but not least, she pulled out the black kettle. This would be the day she attempted to make stovetop popcorn, just like her mom used to do. But how would she flavor it? She didn't have any seasoning salt like her mom used. All she had was sea salt. Well, with that, some coconut oil and parmesan cheese, it would certainly be a hit.

As she was placing her violin in its stand in a corner of the living room, the phone rang. It was Bradley.

"Hey—long time no talk. I barely saw you at the office today, then you disappeared. Where'd you go?"

Ann was warmed by his voice. "Sorry. I meant to send you a text to tell you I left early, but I got busy with a few projects."

"Oh. So Marv just let you go early? He was sharing with me all he wanted you to accomplish today. I'm surprised he let you go."

"He had no choice. I told him I had a doctor appointment."

"Needed some alone time, eh? Of course I heard the bad news. He wants to have a staff meeting first thing Wednesday morning to make an official announcement."

Ann cringed at the thought. She answered, "Well maybe I'll have to skip out on that too. You know this news is more than just bad. It's intolerable. I refuse to work under Sean."

"Can't say as I blame you. So what are you going to do?"

"Funny—that's precisely what I was thinking about when I first got home from the office. What about my future? What about my next job? If I don't run into the old woman again, who would want to hire me? Yaddee-yaddee-yadda … But then I tossed it all aside and decided to celebrate Valerie instead."

Bradley was overjoyed. "That's a great idea! But why the sudden transformation? Valerie's been nothing but a burden to you all this time and now you want to celebrate her? What happened?"

"You happened. Everything we talked about last night hit home and framed several issues for me that had been long-buried. In a tomb. Several feet underground. In a different country."

"Wow. That radical huh?"

"Yes. Absolutely. And as a result, I broke down when I got home. I told Sara I got my 'h', but I'll tell you I went to church and made it to the altar."

"Oh wow—really? That's great!"

"I couldn't say anything this morning because life at the office was all about Sean and Nancy. Sorry I didn't tell you in person."

"Oh, that's all right. It would have been impossible to talk at the office. But I need to get to the real reason I called."

Ann asked, "And what would that be?"

"That would be, Valerie sent me a text. She wanted to come home a little early so she could start getting ready for tomorrow. Marv let me off so we're on our way."

Ann was instantly unraveled. "But you can't come home now. I'm not ready. I thought I had a couple more hours."

"We don't have to come straight there if you don't want us too, but Valerie does want to get things together. What are we interrupting anyway?"

Ann sighed, "Well, if you must know, I was hoping to make us all a nice dinner. And I haven't been able to get to the store yet."

As always, Bradley came up with the perfect solution. "I have an even better idea. Why don't Valerie and I go shopping on our way there and we can all three fix dinner together?"

Bradley couldn't see Ann smiling and nodding her head. "Why Mister Bradley, that is most certainly a better idea."

"Okay then—see you in a bit."

"Yeah—see you."

Ann hung up and wondered what to do with all this spare time. She looked at the walls and admired all the artwork Nancy had given her. She smiled as her eyes rested on the table with the fountain and pictures. Such a shame she'd left everything in the closet all these years—she'd never even felt at home in her own place. Her heart filled with joy as she considered what a difference a few personal touches could make. She looked around the rest of the room and found her violin.

When she used to play at home as a child, it was usually because she was suffering from loneliness. She would shut herself up in her bedroom and play all the more somber pieces she knew by heart, as well as compose some of her own serious melodies. It was only when she played with her mother that she'd engage in more uplifting selections. This was where she learned Celtic tunes and country fiddle songs.

With anticipation of the upcoming evening, and the air of celebration that was settling in around her, she felt an overwhelming desire to play. So she took the violin out of its stand and considered what she was most in the mood for. She recalled some of her mother's favorite songs and played those first. Then she shifted to some of the more sonorous tunes that had brought her comfort as a child. She felt like she was becoming reacquainted with the Anna Kathleen Finlayson she'd left behind so long ago. And it felt good.

After playing for half an hour, she put the violin back and thought of Valerie. Sometime tonight she would have to apologize. But merely stringing the words "I'm sorry" together would not be enough. She hoped to list each offense she'd committed and apologize for them one by one. She wanted to make sure Valerie registered the true depth of her sorrow. This would have to take some time and she hoped the evening would allow it.

But before she could think any more about it, the front door heralded Bradley and Valerie's arrival.

Bradley's first words were, "Honey, we're home." He laughed as he set Valerie's overnight bags on the floor. Valerie carried two grocery bags which she set on the kitchen counter, then she ran to use the bathroom.

Ann used the moment to slip Bradley her first-ever prayer request.

"Toss up a quick prayer please. I need to apologize to Valerie before she leaves and it's going to take some time."

"All right, I will. Are you sure you want me here tonight? Perhaps the two of you should spend Val's last night alone."

Ann insisted, "Not on your life! After all you've meant to her? You need to be here just as much as I do, if not more. Besides, I may need your help in the kitchen."

Bradley laughed, "True that."

They both went to the kitchen and started sorting the groceries when Valerie joined them.

Ann felt several emotions at once. With all her guilt and shame exposed and washed away, she felt relieved to see Valerie. So much so, that she wanted to scoop Valerie up in her arms and tell her how glad she was to see her. But that would be awkward—Valerie didn't know of her recent transformation. She scrambled for an appropriate greeting.

She walked over and lightly placed her hands on Valerie's shoulders. Then she smiled into Valerie's eyes and said, "It's good to see you."

Valerie was puzzled by this—her aunt had never been glad to see her before. But she was even more puzzled by Ann's appearance. She backed up and asked Ann why she was dressed that way.

Ann had become so accustomed to her costume by now, she was barely aware of it. She told the headache and rash story one more time and Valerie asked her a few more questions. Like, "Where'd you get all the pictures and why haven't you ever put them up before? Why's the violin out? Is that fountain new or was it in your closet this whole time?"

Ann answered her questions one at a time, then suggested they all get busy in the kitchen. Bradley was already chopping vegetables by now, so he assigned tasks to the girls. In no time at all, they prepared a feast. Bradley had composed a Thai dish that wouldn't be too spicy for Valerie. And even though Ann was now given to eating cookies for breakfast, he was careful to come up with a gluten-free concoction.

Dinner conversation consisted mainly of Valerie's tales from the weekend. Ann told them she was going to attempt to make stovetop popcorn for the movie and Bradley just kept everyone laughing with his random comments. Time slipped by as they enjoyed one another's company.

Valerie asked if she could be excused to do some packing while Bradley and Ann cleaned the kitchen. Sara called and chewed up some phone time. As the clock marched forward, Ann began to wonder whether or not they'd have time for popcorn and a movie, let alone her talk with Valerie. She mentioned this to Bradley as they finished the dishes.

Bradley reminded her that hang time could be just as significant as a deep, verbal exchange. "You haven't seen Valerie for several days and from what you've described, you've barely bonded this whole time. I propose we all get cozy and watch the movie. You could make the popcorn right now while Valerie finishes putting her things together. There'll be time enough for you to apologize to her. Our God is gracious and His timing is perfect. Let's just make this Valerie's best, last night ever. Besides, you want to score some aunty points? Wow us with your stovetop popcorn. I, for one, can't wait to try it."

Ann laughed and agreed that it might be better to keep things light for now. Valerie probably needed to let down a bit after being away for a few days. And Ann could make up for the last time they watched *Tangled.* Or rather, Valerie did. Ann just sat there with her computer in her lap, ignoring the movie for the most part.

It pained her to think of who she was a little more than a week ago. How great would it be to redeem herself? So, with an air of triumph she announced, "Then it's settled."

She pulled out the kettle and everything else she'd need. She told Bradley it was all about timing, and put him to work. Valerie came in to watch the production and said something to the tune of, "Wow Auntie—I never knew you could do all this."

Ann replied, "I can't, really. That is, I've never tried before. This is merely a trial run that must succeed." She waited for the oil to heat up as she continued. "I used to watch my mom do it all the time and I think I remember all the steps. Okay, the oil's heated. Here goes nothing."

She burned the first batch and had to throw it away. Valerie and Bradley couldn't stop laughing while everyone scrambled to clear the smoke. Ann turned the fan on, Bradley waved a towel under the smoke detector and Valerie fanned the front door. They'd also cracked all the windows and opened the deck door, so it didn't take too long.

After things settled down, Bradley said, "Well, so much for that idea. Let's get the movie going."

But Ann was determined.

"No, no, no—I will not accept defeat. I'm going for round two. You guys just clear the kitchen and go set up the movie."

Bradley saluted. "Yes ma'am."

He and Valerie left the danger zone, giggling up a storm. They joked about having pillows on hand to stuff in their faces while waiting for the second batch. Bradley shouted as much into the kitchen. Then he saw Ann put the kettle on the stove again and said, "Fire in the hole," as he and Valerie stuck their heads in a couple of pillows."

"Very funny," Ann shouted back. She realized all she had to do was turn the heat down, so batch number two was popped to perfection. As she poured the popcorn into a big bowl, she asked, "Are you two lazy bones just going to sit there or are you going to come out here and help me?"

Valerie and Bradley answered the call and came to the kitchen. Bradley was in charge of melting more coconut oil, while Valerie helped determine how much salt to use. Ann mixed in the cheese and they all admired the final masterpiece. Ann punctuated the moment with a final, "Ha—and you thought I couldn't do it."

Bradley said, "I must confess, I had my doubts. But that right there's a work of art. Now let's go watch the movie, shall we?"

They started the movie and in no time at all, Valerie fell asleep. After devouring two bowls of popcorn, she'd laid her head on Bradley's shoulder and gone down for the count. Ann tapped Bradley's arm and put her finger over her lips while nodding at Valerie. He'd been so engrossed in the movie that he hadn't noticed. He looked at Ann and nodded back.

They situated Valerie on the couch with a pillow and some blankets and turned the movie off. Then they lightly stepped to the front door and spoke as quietly as possible.

Ann was the first to speak. She expressed discouragement over not getting the chance to talk to Valerie. "But you were right. The movie and popcorn proved to be the best idea." She laughed as she said, "Especially the popcorn, right?" As she said this, she jabbed him with her elbow.

He responded, "Why yes—especially the popcorn. Then again, I really liked that horse. I want to watch that whole movie sometime."

"Oh yeah—the horse was great. But the thing with the frying pan was cracking me up too. I'm with you—we'll have to watch the entire movie sometime." Then she sighed and looked at the floor. "But I so desperately wanted to talk to Valerie tonight. Tomorrow morning's going to be so hectic, then she's going to leave ..."

Bradley lifted her chin and reassured her. "God will make a way. Tonight was a night for bonding and memories." He put on his impish grin and added, "And what a bunch of memories, huh? I thought we were going to have to call the fire squad."

"Ha-ha. We *were* the fire squad."

Bradley stroked her cheek. "That we were." Then he became more serious. "Annie, I just don't know what to do about us. I mean, here you are, this older version of yourself, and I can't imagine life without you. I feel like I've found my one true heart, but things could never work as they are."

Ann's initial response was grave. "I know Brad. I feel the same way." Then she lightened things up as she gleamed and captured his eyes. "Maybe we could escape to the Blue Mountains after all. Whadd'ya say? Are you up for it?"

"Oh I could be. In a heartbeat. But there is still this slight age difference ... And you called me Brad just now. You've never called me that before."

"I'm getting tired and it just slipped out. Funny about names. Only my dad has ever called me Annie. And my real name's Anna. I just went with Ann when I started looking for work because I thought it sounded more professional."

"And no one ever called me Bradley until I got to the magazine. It's always been Brad to my family and everyone at church."

They left it at that and called it a night. After saying their goodbyes, Ann got ready for bed as quickly as she could. When she finally got under the covers, she felt like she would pass out immediately. But before she did, she prayed a very short prayer.

"Dear God, please work a miracle so Bradley and I can be together. And please make time for me to talk to Valerie. And thank you for tonight …" She dropped off before she could finish her sentence.

Chapter 12

Ann was disoriented when the alarm went off. She lay on her back trying to remember what Tuesday was all about. She pondered aloud as she struggled to wake up.

"Tuesday ... Tuesday ... something's scheduled for today, but what is it?"

She sat straight up in her bed when her memory kicked in. "That's right—Sara's going to come to the office and pick Valerie up."

She threw her robe on and raced to the kitchen to make coffee while pouring over the day's events in her mind. She was driving Sara's car to work. Valerie was supposed to bring all her stuff. Sara would be at the office around ten. Then they were supposed to go to the hospital to visit Charles. Which prompted Ann to look at her phone.

Sure enough, there was a message from Lisa. "Still on for tomorrow?" She must have sent the text while the movie was on. Ann hadn't wanted to be interrupted so she'd put the phone in her bedroom. She sent a quick reply, then started getting ready.

She felt panicked over what seemed like so much to do. She assembled herself quickly in order to wake Valerie.

Valerie seemed just as drowsy as Ann when she sat up and rubbed her eyes. She asked what all the hurry was about and Ann explained that today was the day she was going home.

Valerie said, "I still don't see what all the fuss is about. All I have to do is pack my things into the car. I don't even have to make my bed. Did I fall asleep during the movie?"

Ann considered Valerie's words as she answered, "Yes you did. And I guess you're right. I probably didn't need to wake you up yet. Do you want to go back to sleep for a while?"

"No, it's all right. I'll just take my time getting ready to go. My mom told me we get to go visit Charles in the hospital, so I'll fix my hair and put on my best clothes."

While Valerie assembled herself, Ann poured a cup of coffee and carried it with her into the bedroom. She mulled over what might be causing all this internal anxiety as she sat on the edge of her bed. There really wasn't anything to rush about, so why was she feeling so frantic? She recalled the times her sister spoke of all the little things she prayed about. Ann used to think Sara was crazy for asking God to show her where she put her keys, or for help deciding what to make for dinner when she was so tired after work she couldn't think. She told Ann that she even prayed for God to find her a parking space whenever she drove into the city. Ann used to make fun of her, but Sara always assured her that God was in the little things as well as the big ones.

So Ann decided to pray.

She asked God why she was feeling so rushed and anxious. She told Him, "It doesn't make sense. It's not like I have to drive Valerie to school. I don't want to feel this way while I'm trying to fight traffic, so will You please show me what's going on so I can calm down before getting in the car?"

His answer was swift and simple: *It has to do with the office.*

Ann thought about this. *But what about the office? Oh yeah … everything.*

Today was the day Sean would be moving into Nancy's office. Ann hadn't said anything to Marvin about bringing Valerie to work with her—he had no kids of his own and was adamantly opposed to people allowing children to enter the doors of his temple. Then there was the part about leaving early to go to the hospital. And finding an excuse to stay away for the rest of the day. And having to communicate with Sean. At all. The list went on. It was all about the office all right. But also, Valerie was leaving and Ann still hadn't apologized. There wouldn't be time this morning and Valerie had to leave right after the hospital visit. On top of all that, Ann had to admit she was sad that her sister and niece were moving so far away.

Enough already. Spinning your wheels isn't going to get you anywhere.

Ann got up and finished getting ready. On the topic of not being able to talk to Valerie, she forced herself to believe what Bradley said about God making the time. As far as what awaited her at the office, she'd just have to roll with the punches.

Fortunately, traffic wasn't all that bad—Ann and Valerie made it to the Tower in no time. They were able to stop and get Valerie a bagel on the way to the office. She'd recently proclaimed that bagels were now her favorite food, thanks to Bradley.

When they entered the office, Valerie squealed when she saw Cassie. She immediately ran over to her and hugged her tightly around her shoulders. Cassie told her to let her get up out of her chair so she could greet her properly. She stood and returned the hug while exclaiming what a delightful surprise this was.

Ann said, "Speaking of surprises, Marv doesn't know anything about it either. Could you please hang onto Valerie while I go tell him?"

"'Could you please?' How polite of you. And yes, I will gladly hang onto Valerie."

Ann thanked her and dashed down the hall to Marvin's office. His door was closed, which usually meant he was having a conference with someone. Figuring it had to be Sean, she braced herself for the worst. She lingered at the door contemplating whether or not she should just knock and get it over with. Just as she decided to go for it, the door opened.

It was Bradley filling the doorframe, not Sean. Ann breathed deep sighs of relief and said, "So glad it's you. Is anyone else in there besides Marvin?"

Marvin's voice boomed from behind his desk. "No Fin. No one else is in here at the moment. Come on in and thanks for sparing me from having to track you down."

Ann mouthed the words "see you" to Bradley as she slunk into Marvin's office.

Marvin wasted no time. "Glad to see you're on time today. You'll need some of that to take care of the project I gave you yesterday. Sean's already working on some contacts, but he needs all of yours ASAP, along with every scrap of client information you can dig up. So get started and don't so much as raise your head until you've finished. We've already lost a day."

"About that Marvin …"

"Oh no—what now Finlayson? Another doctor appointment?"

Ann straightened her back and delivered her news with as much confidence as she could manufacture. "Well, as a matter of fact I do. Later. The medication they gave me to try yesterday has caused a reaction. Meanwhile, my sister is coming to the office at ten to pick up my niece, then we have to go to the hospital to visit a sick friend. So I can work on contact info until ten and tie it up after the hospital visit. It shouldn't take very long—you know how organized I am."

Marvin's face grew red with anger as he cut Ann off. "Organized? What about respectful? This is your boss you're talking to. What ever happened to asking permission to do things outside of my direct orders? I told you yesterday to compile all that information and you're telling me you have to leave the office early? Again? And something tells me your niece must be here because your sister is coming here to pick her up, right? Why wasn't this cleared with me first? You know I don't allow kids inside this office unless they come with a client."

"I know Marv, but this is her last day in town. After today, everything will be back to normal." She'd been shaken by the intensity of his anger, but hoped to have hidden it well enough for him to back down.

Her theatrics paid off. Marvin exhaled loudly and rolled his eyes while looking down at his desk. "All right, Fin. But get as much done as you can by ten. And you'd better be cordial to Sean. I noticed the two of you weren't talking yesterday."

So someone did notice …

"Yeah Marv, got it." With that, she got up and returned to her desk.

Cassie told her that Bradley had set Valerie up in the break room with his laptop and some headphones. "He also got her some paper in case she felt like drawing or writing. She should be fine for a couple of hours."

Ann looked at the clock. "I wish it was a couple. It's already 8:30 and I'm supposed to compile all my client information for Sean by ten when my sister gets here."

Cassie was puzzled. "So why do you have to get it all done by ten? Can't you work on it after Sara gets here?"

"No, because we're all going to go visit Charles in the hospital. He wanted to see Valerie one more time, and Lisa could use a visit herself."

"And Marvin's okay with this?"

"He wasn't, but somehow I convinced him. I'm hoping to knock most of it out right now, then finish after the hospital visit. I'd like to be able to cut out at one."

"Another half day? It's amazing you still have a job. You know absenteeism is Marvin's pet peeve. How are you getting away with all this?"

Ann couldn't help but smile. "Remember? I have a medical condition. I can get away with another fake doctor appointment. And my sister's getting Valerie today, so my life's about to stabilize and settle back into normal. See? I have plenty of watertight excuses."

"It sounds like your main goal in life is to be anywhere but here."

"At the present time, it is." Ann walked over to Cassie's desk, looked around the room and lowered her voice. "How do I make this as brief as possible?" She looked down at Cassie's desk to gather her thoughts before continuing. "I don't know if this curse on me will ever be lifted, so I feel like my days are numbered. Not just here at the magazine either. If my age keeps progressing, I might not even be alive six months from now. I'm going to have to quit and figure out what to do. Apart from all that, I wouldn't be able to stay and work under Sean anyway. I might make an announcement at the meeting tomorrow."

The weight of what Ann just shared sunk slowly into Cassie's heart. But once it fully landed and made itself comfortable in the middle of her chest, she was filled with anguish. She asked Ann to lower her glasses.

Ann was enraged. "Why? So you can see how bad my face really looks? After everything I just shared you suddenly want to satisfy your curiosity?"

Tears rimmed Cassie's eyes as she peered directly into Ann's face. "No, Ann. It's because I want to look you in the eye as I say what's on my heart to say."

"Oh. Sorry."

Ann lowered her glasses. Despite the fact that Cassie mentally knew what to expect, nothing could have prepared her for the image she saw before her. Ann looked as old as her grandmother. She tried to hide her shock as she locked eyes with Ann. "I have to tell you how sorry I am for what you're going through. I'm just so sorry. I wish there was something I could do to help you, but I feel like all I can do is pray. I can't imagine how you must be feeling, so I can't show you any true empathy. But I do know emotional pain and I can be with you in that boat. I'm going to ask the Lord to grant you another encounter with that old woman and to slow down the aging process. I'm going to pray incessantly." Fresh tears fought to escape her eyes as she took Ann's gloved hand and presented a tender, compassionate smile. "Thirty-two is far too young for anyone to die of old age."

She fought the battle with her emotions by changing the subject. "So. You have less than two hours to compile all this information. Why don't I help you?"

Ann felt temporarily immobilized by Cassie's words. She too struggled with tears that wanted to take her to a bathroom stall for the next half hour and allow them to run their course. But she pulled herself together and told Cassie she might be able to help put client files together.

The two of them worked together for the next hour and nearly reached the end of the list.

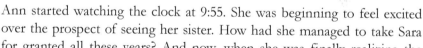

Ann started watching the clock at 9:55. She was beginning to feel excited over the prospect of seeing her sister. How had she managed to take Sara for granted all these years? And now, when she was finally realizing the importance of family, her sister was leaving. The last remnant of immediate family Ann had at her disposal was moving back to their home state. Ann longed to go with them. But she still had Bradley to figure out. And how she was going to eke out a new existence for her ailing, seventy-something self.

The opening of the office door crashed her thoughts and caused her heart to pound with anticipation. The moment she caught a glimpse of a strawberry blonde head, she was at the door.

Tears streamed down both of their faces as Sara and Ann tightly clung to each other. For the longest time, neither of them spoke. Then Sara pushed back a little, took hold of Ann's shoulders and said, "Oh Anna, it's so good to see you. I've been so worried about you—I can't tell you how much." Then she giggled, "And don't you dare chastise me for using your little girl name. I'm about to leave this state and I can call you Anna if I want to. I'm going to miss you so much, my little sister."

Cassie watched from a respectful distance, but she was chomping at the bit to run over and put her arms around Sara. The two of them had bonded so well over the weekend that now Cassie was feeling sad regarding Sara's departure.

As if Cassie's concerns had been transmitted through the air waves, Sara turned her head and made eye contact with her. "And you must be Cassie."

Cassie came to the door and squeezed Sara's hands before hugging her and saying how good it was to meet her in person.

In the midst of all this rousing joy, Sara half expected to see Valerie come bounding around the corner. But the rest of the office seemed oblivious to this cheerful reunion—no one left their cubicle to come see what was going on. Valerie was tucked away in the break room so she had no idea her mother had returned from her long trip.

Sara asked where she was and Ann led her to the break room.

When Valerie caught sight of her mom, she nearly knocked her chair over while trying to run to the break room door. And this greeting was not a quiet one. Valerie called out to her mother so loudly that Bradley wondered what all the ruckus was about. Although he pretty much already knew, he came to the door to see for himself. He too, wanted to meet Ann's sister.

The four of them were so hyped by the moment that they were all talking at the same time. Bradley had to formally meet Sara, Sara wanted to know how things had been going for Valerie at school, Valerie wanted to know what the new house was like, and Ann was trying to remind them all that Lisa was anxious for their hospital visit.

Marvin was the one who broke up the commotion. He burst through the door like a freight train and told everyone they needed to pipe down or get out of the office. Now.

So Bradley went back to his desk. On his way out the door, he whispered "we need to talk" in Ann's ear.

Ann, Valerie and Sara cleared the breakroom of all papers, books, and Bradley's computer, then hiked down to the parking garage. Along the way, Sara mentioned how surly Marvin was. "Is he always like that? I couldn't take ten minutes of that man if he were my boss."

Due to the fact that Ann had put herself on the fast track from the moment she was hired, she hadn't taken much notice. At the time, she and Marvin were cut from the same cloth and all she cared about was advancing her career. But now that her eyes were opened, she looked at him from a different perspective.

"I guess he always was like that, I just never took notice. You know how I've been since I got this job. I've been on a single-minded conquest where I've been blind to everything around me. All I saw was that shiny success trophy off in the distance and I was going to reach it no matter what. I never told you this before, but the office staff has always referred to me as 'the shark.'"

"Well, that doesn't surprise me."

Once they reached the car and started loading, Sara took a brief moment to touch Ann's arm and tell her she wished they had more time. "I really feel like I need to have a sit down, face to face with you, but it's impossible right now. Perhaps I could help you with a plane ticket once we get settled. The timing on my getting this job and moving to Colorado just feels so wrong."

Ann thought of Valerie. "But in truth, the timing is perfect. Believe me. And we will have that visit as soon as I figure out my immediate future. I only wish I could take off all this gear and show you what I look like before you leave. Lisa and Charles have both seen me, but of course, Valerie hasn't. And today would not be the day to show her." She climbed into the passenger seat and said, "But right now needs to be about Lisa and Charles, so let's make it count for them."

"Agreed. Did you bring the hospital address? I need to plug it into the GPS."

By the time they reached the hospital, it was nearly 11:30. It took them no time at all to locate oncology. There was a special wing dedicated to pediatric cases. Ann had typed the room number in her phone, but Valerie was the one who found it.

"Look guys, it's right here. Room 107B."

In an effort to present her new self to Valerie, Ann paid her a compliment. "What a sharp cookie you are. We didn't even need my phone."

Valerie smiled politely and walked into the room.

Charles was asleep and it appeared as though Lisa had been nodding off as well. Ann lightly tapped Lisa's shoulder to let her know they were there. Lisa had become so accustomed to all the nurses and doctors coming and going that she didn't even jump at Ann's touch.

Her eyes opened slowly as she attempted to orient herself. "Hey guys. So glad you could make it. I'm sorry, I must have fallen asleep—we had a long night last night." She focused on Valerie first. "Oh Valerie, I'm so glad you could be here. Charles has never stopped talking about you. So many times he's asked me to take him to the park so we could run into you again." At this point, she smiled at Ann. "But so far, we've only run into your aunt."

Sara was instantly enchanted by Lisa's sensitive demeanor. She wasted no time in reaching for Lisa's hand and introducing herself."

Lisa replied, "Of course you're Valerie's mother. Just look at that beautiful hair. Dead ringer." At this, she smiled weakly and apologized again for being so lethargic.

Ann responded to her apology by stating that they could just go ahead and go, unless Lisa might be up for a cup of coffee.

"Would I ever," Lisa responded. "If you don't mind, perhaps you guys could leave Valerie here and go get a cup while I stay and wake Charles."

Ann said, "No problem Lisa. We'll be right back."

As Ann and Sara made their way to the cafeteria, Sara commented on Lisa's character. "She seems lovely, like someone I'd like to get to know better. And you say she's been facing all this alone?"

"Yeah, just until the army releases her husband to come home. She truly does show a lot of backbone and strength, although she'll tell you otherwise. I knew you two would get along, just as I knew how well you'd click with Cassie."

Sara grew pensive and her response was quiet. "Yeah, well it's amazing what God can do with a mother who finds herself being the sole supporter of her household. Be it financial, emotional, or both, the Lord is able to strengthen us for the needs of our children."

Ann breathed out a heavy sigh. "I guess that's where we part the ways. I've never had kids of my own so I barely know what you're talking about."

Sara allowed herself to dwell just one more moment on all the hardship Lisa was going through, then she recommended they find a women's restroom. "I'm with you on wanting to see what you look like in person. Those tiny pictures you sent from your phone could not have begun to do justice to reality."

They found a bathroom not far from the cafeteria.

Ann mentioned they should be quick since Lisa was dying for a cup of coffee. Fortunately, no one else was in the bathroom. Ann removed her gloves first, then her scarf, glasses and wig.

Sara gasped at the sight. She grabbed Ann's hands and looked at the floor. "I don't know what to say, Ann. Do you mind if I just pray with you?"

"Okay but remember, we have to get back to Lisa."

"I know, I'll be brief." The two closed their eyes as Sara began. She was at a bit of a loss for words, so she asked God for help. "Oh Lord, please help me with this prayer. I don't exactly know how to lift this up, but I know You can help me." She paused and started again. "My heart aches for my sister and You alone know the plans You have for her life. This predicament of hers comes as no surprise to You, so please be with us now as we come before Your throne of grace. Lord, we know You are sovereign. We know that our times are in Your hands and we know that nothing is impossible for You. So Lord, we beg You to enter into this situation with Your mighty hand and outstretched arm and bring about a solution. To our hearts and minds, the greatest solution would be for You to change Ann back to her former state. But You are God, Lord, and we know that sometimes You don't give us the answer we desire." Her voice trembled with the words that followed. She continued with a quiet sob lodged in her throat. "So if You decide to leave Ann as she is, for whatever reason, we ask that You would at least raise Your hand against the aging process and spare Ann's life. I wish we had more time with this prayer. But you know our hearts and the time crunch we're experiencing, so we place ourselves in Your capable hands and humbly await Your answer. We ask all this in the holy name of Jesus, amen."

By the time they got back to the room, Charles was sitting up in his bed and he and Valerie were giggling wildly over something. Lisa's smile couldn't have been bigger as she watched the two of them. She thanked Ann and Sara for the coffee and told them it was a relief to have them here. "I don't think you could ever know what this visit is doing for both of us. And to make it even better, we got a call from my husband last night. He'll be home in three days."

Both Sara and Ann surrounded Lisa with hugs and exclamations of how wonderful this news was. Then a nurse came in and told them they had to clear the room in order for the doctor to come in and do an examination.

Lisa stood up and hugged both of them while Valerie said her goodbyes to Charles. She promised to write him a few letters and assured him she'd be checking in through texting as well. She hugged both Charles and Lisa a final time and she, Ann and Sara prepared to leave the room. But Valerie stopped at the door, then ran back to the bed. "I promise Charles. I'm going to check up on you. Pinky swear." They locked pinkies and said goodbye one more time.

Ann walked Sara and Valerie to the car and told them she didn't mind walking back to the office.

"Are you sure?" Sara asked. "It wouldn't be any trouble at all for us to drop you off."

"No, really, it's all right. Besides—I don't even want to go back to the office. I might just take my time and enjoy some breathing space."

When they reached the car, Sara took Ann by the shoulders and apologized for being in a hurry.

Ann said, "No need to apologize. You gotta do what you gotta do."

"I know—but first I had to rush through that prayer and now I have to rush through this goodbye. The movers are waiting for us and we have to get on the road. Take care and keep me posted, and I do mean daily. I hate leaving you like this. Give Bradley and Cassie hugs from both of us. And I don't think I got a chance to tell you—the man's a saint *and* he's gorgeous. I will not stop praying, believe me."

"I know you won't. And thank you for that. I think I'm going to resign tomorrow, so pray for that too."

She turned to Valerie and caught her up in an enormous hug. She didn't care if Valerie was stunned by the uncharacteristic display of affection. She'd have to explain later. Somehow. She stepped back and held Valerie's chin as she struggled for words. She still had to apologize, but now was not the time. She said something about getting off on the wrong foot, and please excuse her for blowing it at times. She reiterated how foreign it was for her to have kids around and promised to do better next time.

Since Ann had wisely opted not to pour it on too thick, Valerie was only mildly stunned. She couldn't remember ever being hugged by her aunt before. She politely said it was okay and "thank you for letting me stay" and "thank you for getting us to see Charles" and a host of other words that helped cut through the awkwardness of the moment. Being clueless to Ann's recent heart change, she still felt resentful toward her aunt. In fact, at this point she didn't care if she never saw Auntie Ann again in her whole life. But she put a good face on it. Dutifully, she hugged her aunt back and said goodbye.

Ann sighed as she watched them drive away. She dreaded returning to the office and she was shook over Valerie's departure. The poor kid didn't know anything about how Ann was feeling, about how sorry she truly was. She decided to swing by the drugstore on the way back to the office.

Both Charlotte and Cecile were there when Ann stepped into the store. Charlotte was overjoyed to see Ann, whereas Cecile mainly wanted to know about the cane.

Charlotte ran to the door to give Ann a hug while asking a million questions. "Have the joint supplements been helping? Have you gone to physical therapy yet? Why are you wearing those gloves?"

Charlotte's tendency to ask so many questions in a row filled Ann with delight and she couldn't help but laugh as she responded. "The joint supplements are helping, but I think getting back into yoga will help more. I'm going to try that rather than physical therapy. I'm wearing the gloves because I have a rash on my hands. The cane has been especially helpful, but again, I think yoga will do more for me than anything else."

At this point, Cecile piped in. "So where's the cane now? Charlotte told me you liked the mother-of-pearl handle."

Ann smiled fondly over Cecile's thing with the cane. "Yes Cecile. I like the mother-of-pearl. I didn't think I'd need the cane today since I didn't plan on doing that much walking. So how have you two been? I just came by to say 'hello' on my way back to the office."

The three of them chatted for about fifteen minutes, then Ann said she had to get back to work. After saying their goodbyes, Ann felt glad to have made this visit. It was the perfect interlude in the midst of such an emotional day.

So was the walk back to the office. The closer she got to the Sears Tower, the more she felt at peace regarding her decision to quit the magazine. She had no plan for what to do next, but figured it would become clear as she put one foot in front of the other. By the time she reached the office, she felt refreshed and ready to tackle the final touches on those client files.

Cassie greeted her with a sandwich in her hand. "Hey, guess what? I was able to finish the files for you. You can look them over to make sure I got it all right, but I think they're ready to submit to Sean. Who isn't here at the moment. So you could probably zip through the pile and get out of here before he returns from lunch."

"Oh Cassie—you're amazing!" Ann ran over to Cassie and expressed her gratitude by wrapping her arms around her, nearly knocking the sandwich out of Cassie's hand.

Cassie regained her footing and said, "Woah girl, you almost knocked me down. This new you still has me stunned—bear with me as I adjust." Then she stepped back and smiled at Ann. "I know how badly you want to get out of here so I worked through lunch to get it all done. Now hurry up and get this stack on Sean's desk before he gets back. Ugh. I can't even stand to say, 'Sean's desk.'"

She grabbed Ann's shoulders and pointed her toward the stack of files. "Go on—get out of here!"

Ann thanked her again and grabbed the pile. Cassie was right, this was an excellent idea. She hurried down the hall to Nancy's office—she would never call it Sean's—and placed the pile on his desk. She didn't bother to look them over. If anything was missing, he'd have to dig it out himself.

Ann rushed back to her desk to grab her purse and get out the door. Cassie's parting words were few:

"I'm still praying for you."

What to do now? Ann couldn't stand the thought of being anywhere near the office, but she had no idea of how she was going to spend all this extra time.

She went to the condo and sat down to send Bradley a text. He'd mentioned earlier that they needed to talk, so she asked him what that was all about.

He informed her they'd either need to talk in person or on the phone, so he'd get back to her later. For now, he was working with Sean and Marvin.

Ann sent a reply, then looked around the condo. It felt so homey now. Again, she puzzled over how she'd ever been able to stand it before she decorated. When she looked in the kitchen, she noticed she hadn't put the black kettle away, so she got up and took it down the hall. As she tried to put it back where it had been inside the closet, her hand brushed against a box she hadn't opened yet.

The box was small and vaguely familiar. *More pictures?*

As she lifted the lid and parted the tissue on top, she realized she'd stumbled across one of her greatest treasures. When her father was still living in Norway, he'd taken a tole painting class in high school. Two of the pieces he'd created were inside the box: a bowl and a plate. Ann had always loved these and told him she wanted to keep them when she grew up. How could she have forgotten about them?

She spent the next few minutes trying to decide where to put them. She found counter space in the kitchen and vowed to find something that would serve to display them better. Especially the plate. She'd forgotten how artistic her dad was. As she admired the detail, she felt freshly endeared to him. He could dance. He could sing. And he could create a work of art worthy of its own, complimentary plate stand.

She sat at the kitchen table and her thoughts drifted to Valerie. How could she have let her get away without an apology? She didn't want to apologize on the phone, yet the matter was urgent. Even if she were to fly to Colorado, she wouldn't feel right about visiting before they'd had a chance to unpack and settle in.

She grinned as a new idea entered her mind.

The phone rang, bursting through clouds of confusion and fogginess as Ann struggled to sit up. She must have fallen asleep on the couch.

It was Bradley.

"Hey there stranger. You keep disappearing from the office without my knowing."

"I know. Sorry about that. I just had to get out of there before Sean came back from lunch. I can't stand to be there anymore with everything that's been going on."

"Which brings me to the reason for this phone call. Do you want me to spill the beans on the phone or should I just come over?"

Ann looked at the clock. That was a long nap. "Wow. I fell asleep and had no idea how late it was when you called. Why don't you go ahead and come over. I don't have anything else going on."

"Okay, I'll be right there. Do you want me to stop at the store for anything?"

"No—just hurry up and get here. I'm anxious to hear your news."

"As well you should be. I'll see you in a second."

Ann hung up and a knock came to the door. She looked out the peephole and saw Bradley standing there with a bouquet of flowers.

She cracked the door with a giggle and said, "Password please."

Bradley chuckled. "Marvin. And Sean."

Ann opened the door wide and asked, "Oh no—what now?"

He walked in and told her he'd answer her after getting the flowers in a vase.

Ann didn't have any vases, so they put the flowers in a pitcher that accommodated the bouquet beautifully.

Bradley moved to the couch.

Ann insisted, "Out with it. What's going on?"

"Well, you must have noticed all these little talks Marvin and I have been having lately. He's let me know that he now wants me to function as Sean's right hand man. And without coming out and saying it, he's indicated that I'd be replacing you."

Ann sat silent for the longest time, allowing Bradley's words to soak in. Finally, she responded. "So what was he planning to do with me? Where would I fit into this plan?"

"He didn't say and I didn't ask. There are so many things I want to tell you at once. For one thing, I wouldn't want to work under Sean any more than you. I feel like delivering the same news you hope to deliver at tomorrow's meeting. I want to submit my resignation and leave the magazine. I can't stand the thought of being there one more day. This may sound crazy, but I'm tempted to call my mom and tell her we're coming to live in that cabin as soon as we settle our affairs here."

He smiled and looked into Ann's eyes.

"But there are two small problems with that. I'm an old-fashioned guy who would have to be married before cohabiting with a woman. And of course, there's the age difference." He paused before altering his course. "I don't know about you, but financially I'm set. I have a house and a car to sell, and a big fat savings account. When my dad passed, I received a chunk of inheritance money that just sits in the bank and grows. And my sister-in-law was so grateful for my help with selling her house after my brother died, she gave me half the proceeds. So you see? I'm set."

Ann shook her head and looked at the table. "Bradley—you can't be serious. Are you? You can't spend the rest of your life with a seventy-year-old woman. This is crazy talk."

"I know it's crazy talk, but I can't think of any other solutions. As Jonathan was with David, I feel knit to your soul."

"Bradley, I don't even know who those guys are."

Bradley winked at her. "That's all right, you will." Then he buried his face in his hands and lamented, "Oh you're right. This could never work as things are now." He looked up with desperation in his eyes. "What are we going to do?"

Ann grinned and replied, "We're going to eat some dinner."

Bradley returned the smile. "Good plan."

Over dinner, they talked about anything but the future. They enjoyed each other's company, did the dishes and settled back on the couch to share the last chocolate chip cookie. Ann turned on the stereo and they sat in silence. She rested her head on Bradley's shoulder and nearly fell asleep again.

They sat there until Bradley kissed Ann on the forehead and said he should go. Ann agreed it was getting late, and walked him to the door.

At the door Bradley hugged her tight, then held her shoulders while holding her eyes in his. He looked miserably torn as he professed, "I love you Anna Kathleen Finlayson. It's as simple as that, and as complicated. I'd give anything to be with you." He looked away and blinked tears from his eyes. Then he turned his head toward her again and whispered, "I couldn't get away without telling you that."

Ann wanted to cry. All she could say in response was, "I love you too Bradley Newman."

After closing the door, Ann got ready for bed. She didn't have the heart to call Sara. She didn't even have a prayer.

All she could do was crawl under the covers and soak her pillow with tears.

Chapter 13

When the alarm went off, Ann noticed the sound of birds singing to greet the day. Too bad she didn't feel like that. Quite the opposite in fact. Not only was today the day she was going to quit *Top Rung*, but she had a fresh set of emotions to deal with.

Like how to handle the pain in her heart caused by the exchange with Bradley last night.

She decided to call Sara as soon as she was able, then got up and made coffee. Since she got up on time this morning, she also decided to throw in a few yoga stretches. It felt so good that she continued for another twenty minutes. The stretches relieved her aches and pains so much that she would have jumped on the elliptical had there been more time.

But she had to call Sara. And she needed to sit down to do it.

She hoped Sara was already up when she called. Normally, she would have waited another half hour at least, but she couldn't wait.

Sara picked up right away. "Hey sis, what's happening? It's pretty early."

"I know, but I had to take a chance. In fact, this is worth waking you up over, but it sounds like you were already up."

"Yeah. We spent the night in St. Louis and have to finish the drive today so I had to wake up early. What's going on?"

Ann paused a moment. "Last night Bradley told me he loves me. He wishes he could marry me and move to the Blue Mountains."

Sara felt slugged in the gut. "Oh no, Ann. I mean, it's wonderful that he came out and told you how he's feeling, but—I don't suppose you've seen that old woman since we left?"

"No. But with everything that's been happening at the office, I'd practically want her to turn Bradley into the older version of himself rather than make me thirty-two again. Marvin has lost his mind. I'm going to quit the magazine today and step out of the rat race. I don't know what I'd do as a seventy-year-old lady, but I'm sure I could come up with something. Perhaps an online business where I troubleshoot for people's marketing needs or something."

"Oh my sister, that's nuts. Not the part about starting a business, but would you really want Bradley to be the same age you are now? That would be a terrible thing to do to someone."

"I know Sara. It's not like I'm ever going to see that lady again anyway. Just dreaming ... So I guess I'll let you go. I just wanted to tell you what Bradley said last night."

"You know I'd be rejoicing if it weren't for the circumstances. Congratulations on landing Mr. Right and I'm going to keep praying. I haven't given up yet."

"Well thank you for that because I have. How's Valerie doing?"

"She's great. I've shown her pictures of the new house, including the front and back yards. She's really excited about the new house, but even more so over all the surrounding property. She's already landscaping and orchestrating the gardens. From Chicago to St. Louis, all she's done is write her ideas down in a notebook. She's barely come up for conversation. She certainly does have a green thumb."

Ann smiled as she pictured Valerie's reaction to Lurie Garden.

"Yes she does."

Ann reached the office with ten minutes to spare, so she went searching for Bradley. She found him in the break room.

"Hey, Mister Bradley."

"Good morning sunshine. It's been a while since you got here early."

"I know. I wanted to grab you before the meeting. Do you want to meet at the park for lunch today? It's a pretty big bomb I'm about to drop. I'm going to leave right after, so I want to hook up with you regarding the aftermath."

"Yes indeed—I'd be happy to meet for lunch. But you can chill your jets. Marvin decided it would be better to start the meeting at nine rather than eight. He said 'in case of stragglers.'"

Ann laughed. "By that, he probably meant me."

"Ha—probably. But at least now you have time to clean out your desk."

"You know me—not one to keep extraneous stuff around. About the only thing I need to take with me is my Mont Blanc pen. But come to think of it, for memory's sake, I'd also like to take the special pen holder you gave me. And the cup you put the pens in."

Bradley grinned. "Just your luck. I still have the screwdriver I used to install the pen holder. And I have the time to get it off your wall."

Ann thanked him and returned to her desk. She wanted to touch base with Cassie before the meeting and inform her she was solid on her decision to quit the magazine.

Cassie was saddened by the news, but not surprised. "Okay, first Nancy, then you? I wonder how long Bradley's going to last. Apart from Nancy, you guys are the only ones who've kept me hanging in there all this time. I might be tempted to look for another job myself."

"Frankly Cassie, I think you should. With Sean and Marvin at the helm, things are only going to get worse around here."

Cassie sighed, "Don't I know it?"

Bradley entered the scene waving his screwdriver in the air. He sang, "Here I come to save the day."

Ann noticed he was on pitch and wondered how well he could really sing.

He wrestled slightly with the pen holder while trying to take it off the wall, then handed it to Ann. "Here you go, my lady. Now I must return to my grueling tasks." He bowed and returned to his desk.

Ann was at a loss as to how to pass the time. Because she'd never warmed to the idea of social media, she couldn't pull her phone out to browse Facebook or Twitter. She'd have to use her magnifying glass anyway, which meant flipping through a magazine was also a no. She decided to run down to the gift shop.

With a song in her heart and a spring in her step, Ann entered the elevator knowing exactly what she was going to look for. She'd never been inside the shop before, but had a hunch the object of her desire could be found inside.

And it was. There were several shelves dedicated to picture frames and plate stands of all sizes and colors. She settled on a black stand and made the purchase.

Outside the shop sat a bench that seemed to beckon her with a private invitation. She answered the call. While sitting with her treasure in her lap, she spent the next few minutes people-watching. As she watched the parade of faces, she wondered about some of the lives behind them.

One woman wore an expression of stress and tension that caused her to frown. Ann wondered if she knew it. She wondered because she knew how often she'd probably worn the exact same look over the last seven years. Then she saw an elderly man pass by, holding the hand of a very young boy. This made her think of Charles. She wondered how he was doing and felt happy they'd made the decision to visit him. She'd have to call Lisa later. Then her mind drifted to the elderly man who was walking with the boy.

Two weeks ago, this scene would have gone completely unnoticed by her. But today, she was touched by the man's tenderness toward the child, and it struck her that he might be the boy's grandfather.

She thought of her parents and how they'd never make it to this phase of life—the phase where they could provide extra doses of love and security in the lives of their grandchildren.

Then another thought came to mind—one that crept in from an unknown land and banged loudly on her vanity door—the older generation seemed to possess a tremendous amount of value and had much to offer the world around them.

Where did that come from?

From the time she was little, Ann knew she never wanted to grow old. She couldn't stand the look of older people and they always seemed so slow. She never wanted to look like that and she never wanted to be robbed of the energy it took to climb trees and run through mountain meadows. She remembered hearing stories of all the aches and pains older people could get. And some of them seemed cranky. Like the old man at the drugstore she and her dad used to visit. The one who sold them candy on their dates. Across the span of their numerous visits, he never smiled. Not once.

Then her mind turned to Charlotte, Cecile and Lydia. They all had a patience that transcended the world around them. Charlotte always took time with her customers, tending to each and every one as though they were a precious relative. All three of them were warm and kind.

Ann removed one of her gloves and looked at her hand. Having resigned herself to this age, she hoped God would give her the opportunity to show that same caliber of warmth and kindness to others. She hoped He would allow her at least a few more years of life so she could atone for the ones she'd lost to self-centeredness and pride.

She looked at her phone to check the time. Definitely time to go.

Ann's stomach dropped to her feet as she entered the conference room. Knowing what she was about to do and actually doing it, were suddenly feeling like two very different things.

Good thing Cassie saved her a seat.

Marvin opened the meeting with a host of announcements regarding deadlines for the next issue and how everyone needed to stay on track. Then he expressed his dismay over what had happened with Green Jeans.

"Since last Friday's conference call, I've learned that they've decided to drop us altogether after the May issue. But Sean here is about to step in and make sure that doesn't happen."

He kept the announcement regarding Sean low-key. He didn't have Sean rise from his seat for a round of applause. Instead, Sean remained seated while Marvin magnified the value of what Green Jeans could do for the magazine.

"We've been stalled in the same position for quite some time and we need to take a step up. Sean and I both feel that landing Green Jeans could give this magazine a major facelift and launch us into the number one slot. We want to become the most popular publication in today's market. I feel that Sean Mobley is the one who would be best suited to fill Nancy's shoes. Both Nancy and Ann have brought the magazine the success it now enjoys, but Sean will be the one who fulfills the vision of our becoming number one."

At that point, Sean did stand. No one clapped. Some struggled to paste fake smiles onto their faces, while others glued their eyes to the table.

Not even Marvin knew how to handle this awkward moment. Sean just stood there, not knowing whether to speak or sit back down. He had no clue that the entire office was against this decision.

It was Ann who broke through the awkwardness. She stood and said, "Thank you Marvin, Sean." At this, Sean sat back down. "Thank you for this meeting and providing us the opportunity to hear your opinions regarding the future of this magazine." Then she looked at all the faces sitting around the table. She wished she could take her glasses off as she continued. "Most of you don't know this, but I'd like to share something with all of you. Until last Friday, I'd never looked at a Green Jeans ad. And now that I've seen one, I stand with all of you against the hope of our ever landing an account with them. Consequently, today is my last day with *Top Rung Magazine*. It's been wonderful working with all of you but," she looked directly at Marvin, "I quit."

Her escape plan was already in place. She left the room, walked to her desk and grabbed her bag before anyone could say anything. She didn't even care about the aftermath. She would've liked to have said goodbye to several of her co-workers, but it wouldn't have served her well to stick around. She would have had to confront Sean and Marvin, and everyone would have wanted to hear more details and express their feelings over the news of her departure.

No. This was a much better plan.

Ann reached the condo and went to the bedroom to change. The scarf, the glasses, the wig, the gloves, all went flying to the top of the bed. She looked at the pile she just made, then took a good, long look at herself in the bedroom mirror. A feeling that took her completely off guard fluttered across her heart and caused her to smile.

She felt thankful.

As she continued standing in front of the mirror, she considered who she was just over a week ago, and who she was now. Her vanity didn't appreciate the method that was used to get her to where she was today, but she couldn't have felt more pleased over her internal transformation.

The old Ann was brittle and cared for no one but herself. The old Ann hurt people. The old Ann even went so far as to all but discard her own sister. The old Ann deeply wounded a child in need. And, she supported a company that used provocatively suggestive imagery in their advertising. And truth be told, she had no friends.

The new Ann was soft, pliable and vulnerable. She cared for the interest of others. She could be deeply touched by the lives around her, whereas the old Ann couldn't care less. And, although she couldn't be with him, the new Ann had met the love of her life.

Again, she thought of how little she cared for the image that faced her now, yet felt thankful to God for cracking her hard, insensitive shell.

"Thank you God, for allowing this to happen to me. You know I don't like the way I look, but it certainly worked to get my attention. I don't know what I'm going to do now, but You do. And since there's nothing I can do to change my physical state, I place myself in Your hands. Amen."

In that moment she vowed never to cover up again.

After deciding what to wear to the park, she grabbed the bag from the gift shop and went to the kitchen. She pulled out the plate stand, set it on the counter and placed her father's plate inside it.

"Perfect." She smiled with satisfaction and headed for the door.

The streets were crowded today, so it took a moment for her to spot a familiar figure across the street.

Ann could not believe her eyes as they landed on the individual who had eluded her all these days.

The woman who had become the bane of her existence.

The one who had uprooted her from all she'd ever been, and immersed her into this new life.

And she was about to enter the same crosswalk as Ann.

The walk light came on and Ann wasted no time. Marching rabidly into the crosswalk, her steps were driven by one flaming intent. It only took a few strides for her to reach the hooded figure she'd been trying to capture for so many days.

So aggressive was her advance that a look of fear fell upon the woman's face and she strove to dodge sideways in order to avoid an encounter. But it was too late. Ann had her by the shoulders and held her while the rest of the pedestrians milled past them. What happened next was something the old woman would have least expected.

She was caught up in a death grip of an embrace.

Ann held her tightly and buried her head in the woman's shoulder while releasing an ocean of deep, gut-wrenching sobs. They stood locked in that position until the traffic light turned green. As aggravated honks began to blare, Ann gently took the woman's elbow and escorted her to the sidewalk.

She began filling the woman's ears with words that could barely be deciphered above the surrounding din. Her animated gestures were so exaggerated that a few heads turned, hoping to catch a piece of the dialogue.

When she'd completed her initial outpouring, Ann cupped her hand to the woman's ear and whispered something that stilled the moment between them. The downtown rush disappeared completely as the old woman strained to hear what Ann had to say.

Then, for the first time since Ann first spotted the old woman she nearly hit with Sara's car, the woman lifted her hood from her head. With her glorious gray crown of hair and wrinkled face fully exposed, she gifted Ann with a smile that could light up the town in a blackout. The dance in her twinkling gray eyes belied her age as she nodded her head like a teenager that had never slipped away.

As they parted, both were beaming from ear to ear. The old woman remained on the corner while Ann briskly strode toward the park.

The woman watched Ann disappear into the throng, then turned and stretched her arms out above her head with her palms facing upward. She bent her head back and faced the sky. Then she uttered a stream of words in her ancient dialect—the one Ann heard her using on the day of their first encounter. By the look and sound of her, one would think she was calling forth a great storm. But when she finished, nothing out of the ordinary appeared to have occurred. Anyone who heard her babble just assumed she was crazy and kept moving. Grinning with satisfaction, she crossed the street when the light turned green.

From the way Ann's heart was fluttering, one would think she was a six-year-old on her way to the pet store to pick out a puppy.

She anxiously paced in front of The Bean, where she and Bradley had agreed to meet. Her mind was racing as she considered how the next few moments would play out. The knots in her stomach tightened with impatience, so she tried to think of something else.

The Bean was flooded with tourists today, all scrambling to take pictures in front of it. They came in pairs and clusters, all with their cameras and phones ready for the perfect shot. One couple approached Ann and asked if she could take a picture for them.

They were an older couple, possibly in their seventies. Ann thought they looked adorable together as she pondered what it might have been like to see her parents reach their silver years. She grieved at the thought of not being able to know them at this stage. She imagined that they would have aged well and remained active. Her mother would probably still be holding the first chair position in some orchestra and her father would have found a creative way to serve the community.

Her thoughts fled as the couple showed her how to focus the camera. She took a couple of pictures, then the couple came over to review them with her. They had her pick out a favorite, then left to complete their park adventures.

Ann was still facing the huge metallic structure after the couple left. She looked up and found her reflection, then her heart dropped out of her chest.

She caught a glimpse of another reflection that was slowly ambling toward her. Even though the figure was far away, Ann recognized the yellow shirt Bradley had worn to the office today.

She could only take short breaths as she anticipated this encounter. As she watched him approach, she considered the man who had captured her heart. Here was the man who touched places inside her that no one else had ever detected. Here was the man who always saw right through her obsessive, health-crazed exterior, deep into the beautiful woman who dwelt several layers below the surface. And the love of her life was now only a few feet away.

She turned and reached out for the hands of her perfect match as the gap closed between them. She smiled into his deep blue eyes as he clasped her hands and told her how stunning she looked in the sunlight.

She told him he didn't look so bad himself. Then he located their reflection in The Bean.

All he said was, "So you found her."

He studied the lines in his face and reached up to touch his thick mass of silver hair. Then he turned to Ann and cupped her face in his hands. He gently kissed her forehead and Ann took a step back to get a better look at him.

From the top of his silver head to the age spots on his hands, she thought he couldn't be more perfect. Not only did he appear to bear his new age well, but to Ann, he was positively striking.

Anyone in Ann's immediate circle would have called her crazy for having made this decision. But Ann and Bradley saw the world spread widely before them, holding nothing but possibilities. They both considered it a fresh start to a vast, new adventure they couldn't wait to touch, taste, see and hear. And like the woman in Proverbs 31, Ann smiled at the future.

After all, the Blue Mountains of North Carolina were calling.

Chapter 14

A few days after Sara and Valerie arrived in their new home, Valerie received a letter from Aunt Ann. She couldn't think of a thing her aunt might have to say to her in a letter, but she was curious. And since she was in dire need of a break from unpacking, she opened it immediately. It read:

Dear Valerie:

I hope this letter finds you well. It's never easy to unpack and organize an entire house, so I hope you and your mom aren't too overwhelmed. I bet you're curious about why I've written this letter. I have so many reasons for writing you and so many things to say, I barely know where to start. So please bear with me as I try to muddle through. You might want to take a seat. I have a feeling this is going to be a long one.

While you were staying here with me, you frequently berated yourself and voiced the desire to be braver and stronger than you feel like you are. You kept comparing me to Katniss Everdeen and wished you could be made of similar mettle. You referred to yourself as nothing but a whisper. You said one of your greatest talents is that you're good at gardening and what's so great about having a green thumb? You essentially accused yourself of being a wimp and you claimed that being able to dance was no big deal. So how do I break all this down?

I say it's more important to be able to make the world beautiful for others than it is to be able to conquer it. Greatness doesn't always look like Katniss Everdeen. Look at Adam and Eve. They're a pretty famous couple. And due to the fact that they were the first two human beings to occupy this planet, not to mention the fact that God fashioned them with His own two hands, they practically wrote the book on greatness. And they were master gardeners!

Give yourself some credit. Gardeners beautify the world around them and not everyone is good at it. I told you I kill plants just by looking at them. But you planted irises that grew to be four feet tall! Just look at all the beauty that can fit into one clump of dirt! And consider all the joy that can be produced by a single rose or a patch of daisies. One small pot of flowers can brighten someone's day for weeks! You have the ability to create endless joy in the hearts of those around you. You can lift spirits, comfort grieving souls and infuse moments with colorful celebration with your gift. So that's what's so great about having a green thumb.

Now I'll tell you what's so great about being a whisper. A whisper is what we hear in a summer breeze. It's what we see in a spray of forget-me-nots on a country road. It's a bird in flight and it can encourage a little boy in a hospital who's fighting cancer. Never apologize for possessing this trait. Never cut it off. Nurture it and protect it, because if you cast it off in honor of being accepted and popular, you will become hard and crusty. God's garden is comprised of all varieties of flowers. Some people are like grandiose rhododendrons, whereas others are more like the tiny flowers you liked at Lurie Garden. All have merit. All bring joy. None is greater than the other and God loves them all equally. So never be ashamed of being "nothing but a whisper."

And finally, you call yourself a wimp. You wish you could be a warrior. You wish you could fight. Well let me tell you something—you stood up to me when I was in the wrong and there was nothing wimpy about it! A wimp doesn't put up with bullying in order to protect her mother's dream of landing a good job. A wimp doesn't suffer silently, yet still manage to delight everyone around her with her light-hearted nature. A wimp can't even paint a smile on her own face, let alone the face of others while wading through deep and difficult waters. You even proved you could dance, despite the fact that you were living with the biggest bully of them all!

Which brings me to the most important reason for this letter. How do I even begin to apologize to you? I guess I should start by telling you that God has answered your prayers—I gave my heart to Him a few days ago. So that might help explain how I'm even able to write this letter in the first place. You and I both know I couldn't have written it a week ago.

I'm so sorry Valerie. I'm sorry for all the times I showed you irritation, like the time we had to go back to the store because you forgot to put some items on the list. I'm sorry I called you a name. I'm sorry I bit your head off when you were so loaded with questions on the way home from Tae Kwon Do. I'm sorry I was so mean to you that you couldn't stand the thought of being alone with me. And I'm so sorry I didn't make you feel safe enough to talk about what was going on at school.

And, since I'm on the apology train, I must also mention that I'm sorry I didn't enjoy you more. Frankly, I didn't even know how, especially when you first got here. I'm sorry I didn't get to know you better. I'm sorry we didn't get to share more musical moments. I'm sorry

I never prayed with you. And I hope I don't have to say that I'm sorry for having lost you forever.

Please forgive me Valerie. It pains me beyond words to think of how poorly I treated you. Please accept my apology and believe me when I say I'm not the same person I was a week or so ago. Just ask your mom. She'll tell you all about it.

Meanwhile, try to have fun unpacking. You get to start over in a brand new place and create a home that will serve as a haven from the outside world. So make it a good one. And God bless you, my niece.

Love, Auntie Ann

While reading the letter, Valerie had walked over to sit on an unpacked box. She was so shocked by the words she'd just read, that she sat on the box until it became uncomfortable. She got up and moved to the sofa and read the letter again. Then she read it a third time. She sat there so long that her mom had to come find her.

Sara saw her sitting on the sofa and asked, "Whatcha got there?"

Valerie told her it was a letter from Auntie Ann. "Auntie told me to ask you about what happened to her to change her from being a mean person to a nice one." Valerie chose her words carefully. She didn't want her mother to fret over all the ill treatment she'd suffered while staying with her aunt. She decided to leave out any details of how mean her aunt had been and continued by stating, "She said in her letter that she asked Jesus to live in her heart and that you'd tell me all about it."

So Sara sat down and told Valerie everything—even about the crosswalk experience and Ann's sudden aging nightmare. Ann had already given her sister a heads up about the letter. And she told Sara to share everything with Valerie. After all, if they were to share any kind of relationship in the future, Valerie would have to know the truth regarding her aunt's new physical state.

Valerie found it all difficult to believe, but it also explained a lot of things. "So that's why she kept dressing funny and wearing gloves and stuff. She even wore sunglasses inside the condo."

"Yes, that's why. And now that you've taken a nice long break, let's get back to work."

About a week later, a second letter came:

Dear Valerie:

I had to send you a P.S. to the first letter. I called Mrs. Campion a few days ago and she told me what disciplinary action the school was going to take against your tormentors. I thought you might like to hear the game plan:

First of all, each of the five kids must research the topic of bullying and how it effects the victims. Then, they have to compose a two-page report on the subject. After that, the school is going to host an all-school assembly in their honor where each of them will stand in front of the whole school and confess what they did to you. Their confessions will have to include all the details. Following their confessions, they will have to read their reports in front of the entire school. On top of all that, they will each have to perform ten hours of community service over the summer and have it all completed and documented before school starts again in the fall.

Ah—sweet vengeance—how does it feel?

Love, Auntie Ann

Valerie inwardly responded to her aunt's question in typical, Valerie fashion: She felt sorry for them. She hated the thought that they'd have to embarrass themselves in front of the school. And instead of gloating with victory, she prayed for them.

The one thing that did please her was the fact that they had to research the topic of bullying. It would be good for them to learn of its damaging effects and she hoped they'd feel genuinely sorry for what they did to her. She decided to pray about that too. She figured if God could perform such a major work in her aunt, He most certainly could change the hearts of those kids.

After folding the letter and putting it in a special box with the other one, Valerie vowed never to share the letters with her mother.

Epilogue

It didn't take Ann and Bradley long to seal their lives in Chicago. Both of them lived in locations that were considered prime real estate, so their homes sold quickly. Bradley changed his mind about selling his brother's station wagon though. He'd been working on it so long that he'd become attached.

Before setting off for their new lives in North Carolina, they'd arranged a charming, but small wedding ceremony. It was held in a tiny chapel in the heart of the city. Cassie, Nancy, Charlotte, Lydia and Cecile were in attendance, as well as Lisa. Sara and Valerie couldn't make it due to Sara's new job, but they agreed to come visit the newlyweds in their new home.

Bradley's mother passed away a year after Ann and Bradley moved into the cabin, leaving the larger house on the property up for whatever the newlyweds chose to do. It turned out they felt so cozy in their small cabin that they decided to turn the big house into a bed and breakfast. Although the two of them prepared breakfast for their guests every morning, Bradley was the head chef. He quickly became known for his French toast bake and savory frittatas.

By this time, Ann had been giving private violin lessons both in their home, and in the community center in town. She'd also begun teaching yoga there shortly after moving in. Her class grew to be so large that she had to find a second time slot in order to accommodate those who'd put their names on a waiting list. Her classes were filled with people of all different sizes, shapes and ages. Her youngest student was nine.

While Ann was engaged in her teaching activities, Bradley was hard at work drafting his first historical novel. He also developed a youth program in town, similar to the one he headed in Chicago.

Ann and Bradley quickly won the hearts of those in their community. During the winter months, they'd host popcorn and movie nights and they frequently had the locals over for music and sing-alongs in front of the B & B's colossal fireplace. As it turned out, Bradley possessed another hidden talent that swept Ann even further off her feet:

He could play the piano. And the sitting room with the fireplace came complete with a baby grand.

In the summer months, they'd have campfires and marshmallow roasts and everyone was welcome, from local residents to any of their guests who cared to join them. Bradley was always willing to take carloads of people fishing, so the station wagon ended up getting plenty of use.

Their home was always open to any who might want to stop by for a visit. Sara and Valerie came as often as they could. Charlotte even made it out to see them once.

Bradley set his first book in medieval times. It sold like hotcakes and it didn't take long for him to crank out several more.

Ann and Bradley's love never ceased to continue growing over the years to come. Their bliss was so apparent that sometimes people came to them seeking marital advice. Eventually, they set up a ministry in their church where people could come see them on a regular basis following service.

They enjoyed so many years together that they outlived some of their closest friends. They seemed to have stopped aging on the very day Bradley met Ann at The Bean. The aging process didn't start up again until about forty years later.

When they turned seventy.

Charles Latham the Third healed completely. He became the proud, protective big brother of two little sisters. His favorite thing to do was visit kids in hospitals.

When he was in high school, he played a major role in leading the soccer team to a state championship. That was when he decided to become a high school teacher and soccer coach.

Cassie's husband lost his battle with cancer. Ann was right there to help her through her grief. Not long after the funeral, Cassie came and spent some time with Ann and Bradley in their mountain home. She came alone while Craig's mother stayed with the kids.

While she was there, she filled Ann and Bradley in on everything that happened at the magazine after they left.

Following the meeting and Ann and Bradley's departure, most of the staff immediately went job hunting. Within two months, only three employees remained that had been there when Ann left. Sean was one of them.

Even Cassie got a new job. She was hired at a hospital to be a ward clerk on the day shift. It turned out it was the same hospital where Charles had been getting treated. So Cassie and Lisa met and it took no time at all for them to become good friends.

Cassie eventually remarried and the magazine eventually folded.

Valerie's reign as only child ended after she and Sara had been in Colorado for about two years. Not long after Sara started her new job, she met a doctor who took an immediate interest in her. They dated nonstop for a mere six months before realizing they should just commit and get married. Valerie was granted the privilege of naming her new little brother. She decided to call him Charles.

Several years later, Valerie got a job at a florist shop where she quickly learned the tricks of the trade. The owners were near retirement when she took the job and they agreed to sell her the shop when they finally did decide to retire.

Once Valerie was able to take over, business exploded. Fortunately, there was room to expand. The shop sat on two acres of property where the owners had been able to grow most of their own flowers. Valerie ended up adding on to the shop and having a small gazebo built in the back amongst the flowers. She then turned her giant backyard into a wedding wonderland and could barely keep up with all the bookings. So great was her success that she was able to hire two more employees and a second wedding planner.

At one of the many ceremonies she'd organized, she met the man who became her husband. He was a physical therapist with a highly successful practice that she met at the reception. When he learned she was the one responsible for the exquisite venue and wedding ceremony, he became intrigued. What sealed the deal was when Valerie agreed to break one of her cardinal rules, which had to do with keeping a professional distance from the wedding attendees. It was all right to mingle, but only at the discretion of the guests themselves and never beyond the level of mere pleasantries. In other words, don't tear up the dance floor.

But he asked. And she said yes. And that was that.

Following the birth of their first child, Valerie felt it would be safe to cut some of her hours at the shop and pursue another passion that had been brewing inside her. She wanted to make a difference in the lives of children who might be lacking the tools and resources to be successful in life, as well as in school. She developed an after school program where kids could come and get help with homework or just hang out if they wanted to. She never forgot Mrs. Campion's kindness and how great a help she was to her own working parent.

Eventually, the program outgrew the small space she'd created in her home and she moved it to the local church. The program became so popular that she was eventually able to rally volunteers to provide various sports activities. She even landed a Tae Kwon Do instructor.

She also developed a class designed to educate the kids in all aspects of bullying. She wanted to make it clear that if anyone was experiencing any kind of bullying, they needed to tell someone. She also wanted to emphasize the corrosive nature of bullying in case any kids in the class had ever harassed someone or were considering it. As a result of her efforts, some of the kids confided in her about having been targeted at school. One of them even came to her to express guilt over having antagonized someone on the playground.

The parents of the children who were benefitting from Valerie's expertise urged her to compile all the information and introduce it to the schools in the area. So Valerie introduced her anti-bullying campaign to the entire school district and they implemented it immediately.

In the midst of these ambitious aspirations, Valerie always made ample space for her family and of course, her flowers.

And as often as they could, she and her family made excursions to the Blue Mountains to spend time with Auntie Ann and Uncle Bradley.

About the Author

Judy Greene was born and raised in Seattle, Washington. She obtained her BA in English Literature from the University of Washington. She is an avid songwriter and passionate musician with a strong background in musical and theatrical performance. Two of her plays, *It's Just So* and *The Velveteen Rabbit*, have been performed by a local children's theatre. She and her daughter presently reside in Puyallup, Washington.

Printed in the United States
By Bookmasters